#1 *New York Times* Bestselling Author

SHERRYL WOODS

Dream Mender

 HARLEQUIN® BESTSELLERS

Recycling programs
for this product may
not exist in your area.

ISBN-13: 978-0-373-60598-9

DREAM MENDER
Copyright © 2010 by Harlequin Books S.A.

The publisher acknowledges the copyright holders
of the individual works as follows:

DREAM MENDER
Copyright © 1992 by Sherryl Woods

STAY...
Copyright © 1998 by Allison Lee Johnson

Printed in U.S.A.

CONTENTS

For Karon Gorham, with thanks for her insights
and technical expertise and for
sensitive burn-unit experts everywhere

DREAM MENDER

New York Times Bestselling Author

Sherryl Woods

SHERRYL WOODS

With her roots firmly planted in the South, #1 *New York Times* bestselling author Sherryl Woods has written many of her more than 100 books in that distinctive setting, whether her home state of Virginia, her adopted state, Florida, or her much adored South Carolina. She's also especially partial to small towns, wherever they may be. *Dream Mender* is a rare foray into a West Coast setting, but Woods's distinctive heartfelt emotions are still very much at the core of the story.

A member of Novelists Inc., Sherryl divides her time between her childhood summer home overlooking the Potomac River in Colonial Beach, Virginia, and her oceanfront home, with its lighthouse view, in Key Biscayne, Florida. "Wherever I am, if there's no water in sight, I get a little antsy," she says. Sherryl loves to hear from readers. You can visit her on her website at www.SherrylWoods.com or contact her directly at Sherryl703@gmail.com.

Chapter One

Frank Chambers prowled the narrow hospital room, feeling like a foul-tempered bear awakening from hibernation with a thorn in its paw. He stared at his own bandaged hands and muttered an oath that would have curled his mother's hair and earned him a sharp rap across his already-injured knuckles. He wanted to smash something, but settled for violently kicking a chair halfway across the hospital room. It skidded into the pale blue wall with a satisfying crash, but did nothing to improve his overall mood. His mother, a wise woman with little sympathy for self-pity, would have said it would have served him right if he'd broken his toe.

The door opened a cautious crack and yet another nurse peered in, an expression of alarm on her face. "You okay?"

"Just dandy," he growled.

When he didn't throw anything, she visibly gathered her courage and stepped inside, marching over to his bed and folding her arms across her chest, assuming a stern posture clearly meant to intimidate. Considering her tiny size, it wouldn't have been an effective stance even if he hadn't been feeling surly.

"You ought to be in bed," she announced. She pulled back the sheet and gestured in the right direction just to make her point.

He glared at her and ignored the invitation. "I ought to be at home. I'm not sick."

"That's not what your chart says."

"I don't give a—"

She never even took a breath at the interruption. She just kept on going, talking over his swearing. "Less than twenty-four hours ago you were in a serious fire. When they brought you in, you were suffering from smoke inhalation. Your blood gases still don't look all that good. You have second-degree burns on both hands. You need rest and therapy."

It was not the first time he had heard the same detailed recitation of his medical condition. "I need to go home," he repeated stubbornly. He tried another fierce scowl to emphasize the point. Grown men had cowered at that scowl. He was certain of its effectiveness.

Clearly unintimidated, the nurse rolled her eyes and left. He doubted she'd gone to get his release papers. None of the others had, either. Hell, his own mother hadn't sided with him when he'd insisted he didn't need to be admitted in the first place. He'd been whisked up to his room and hooked up to oxygen so fast it had left his head spinning. He'd tried bribing each of his brothers to spring him, but they'd ignored his pleas. Not even his softhearted baby sister had taken pity on him. She'd patted his arm and suggested to the afternoon-shift nurse that they tie him down if they had to.

"Et tu, Brute," he'd muttered as Karyn had winked at him

over her shoulder. Then she'd linked arms with her new husband and sashayed off to dinner.

The attitude of the whole Chambers clan rankled. That good-natured defiance was the thanks he got for all those years when he'd put his own life on hold to help his mother raise his five brothers and his sister. When his father had died, he'd reluctantly stepped into the role of parenting and discovered that it fit, even at seventeen. Maturity and responsibility had been thrust on him, but he'd somehow liked being needed, liked being the backbone of a large and loving family. In a curious sort of way he'd even suffered through the empty-nest trauma, watching as his siblings had matured and struck off on their own.

Karyn's recent marriage to race-car driver Brad Willis might have been the first wedding in the tight-knit family, but it was hardly the first sign he'd had that it was time to get on with his own life. He'd been told to butt out so often in recent years he'd had no choice but to start focusing on himself instead of his siblings. He'd been doing just that—most of the time, anyway—until yesterday afternoon. Now, suddenly, at forty he was discovering what it was like to have the tables turned on him, to have to depend on others for his most basic needs. And, he didn't like it, not one bit. What man would? No wonder his brothers chafed at all his well-intended meddling. Now they were giving it back to him in spades.

Left alone with his unpleasant thoughts through the long night, Frank tried to face facts. He told himself he could live with the pain the doctors were warning him to expect as the nerves in his hands healed. Hell, he could even live with the long-term scars. He'd seen burn scars, and while they weren't pretty, his big, work-roughened hands hadn't been much to write home about anyway. What *was* killing him, though, what was creating this gut-wrenching fury, was the absolute, utter helplessness of it all.

He couldn't do the simplest things for himself with these layers of gauze wrapped around his fingers, turning them into fat, clumsy, useless appendages. Forget holding a fork. Forget turning on the shower or washing himself. Forget pushing a button on the damned TV remote or holding a book. He couldn't even go to the bathroom on his own. Nothing, ever, had left him feeling quite so humiliated. They might as well have lopped the damned things off at the wrist.

And all because of a stupid accident. One careless instant, a still-smoldering cigarette butt tossed into a trash barrel by one of his unthinking co-workers, and the next thing he'd known the entire woodworking shop had been in flames. He'd grabbed for a fire extinguisher, but the metal had already been a blistering red-hot temperature. He'd done the best he could, but with all the flammable material around, it had been like battling a towering inferno with a garden hose. He'd managed to get a few things out of the workroom before the blaze and smoke had gotten out of control, eventually destroying everything. He'd gone back in one last time to rescue one of his co-workers who'd panicked and found himself trapped in a workroom with no exit except through the fire. Only when he was outside, gulping oxygen and coughing his head off had he noticed the blistered, raw layers of skin on his hands. The adrenaline high had given way to shocked horror as paramedics rushed him to the hospital. His co-worker had been treated for smoke inhalation at the scene.

The injuries could have been worse, they'd told Frank in the emergency room. Third-degree burns, with the possibility of damaging tendons and bone, could have been devastating for a man who worked with his hands. His career, most likely, would have been over. He would have lost the woodworking skills that had turned his imaginative, finely crafted cabinetry into an art that was making its way into some of the finest homes in San Francisco. With second-degree injuries, he had a chance.

The recovery, though, would be slow, tedious and painful. Frank had never been out sick a day in his life. Now it appeared he was headed for a long vacation, courtesy of workmen's comp. The concept didn't sit well. Worse was the faint, terrifying possibility that he might never again be able to do the delicate, intricate carving that made his work unique and gave him such a sense of accomplishment.

By morning, after hours of focusing on the "what ifs," panic had bubbled up deep inside him. He dragged air into his injured lungs. Each breath hurt and did nothing to calm him, nothing to wipe away the bleak images of a future without the work that he loved.

Determined to get out of the hospital, even if he had to escape on his own, he used his foot to lever open the closet door. The task was easier than he'd expected, and his confidence soared. Hope crashed just as quickly with the realization that the only clothing hanging in the closet was his robe. His sooty shirt and jeans were no doubt ditched in some trash receptacle. He'd never get past the nurses' station, much less out of this place, wearing just an indecent hospital gown and a robe that still had a price tag hanging from the sleeve.

On the nightstand beside the bed the phone rang. Grateful for the interruption, Frank lunged for it, knocking it to the floor with his inept hands. Another stream of profanity turned the air blue. How the hell was he supposed to answer a phone with fingers that stuck straight out like prongs on a damned pitchfork?

"Nurse!" he bellowed, rather than bothering with the call button. "Nurse!"

He glared at the door, waiting for it to open, fuming because he couldn't even manage that simple task. This time, however, rather than inching open bit by cautious bit, the door was suddenly flung wide. Instead of a nurse, therapist Jennifer Michaels stepped into the room with all the confidence of a woman whose head hadn't yet been bitten off by the fuming, foul-tempered patient in Room 407.

Frank recognized her at once. He had still been dopey from medication when she'd poked her head into the room the previous afternoon, but he hadn't forgotten that perky, wide smile and that mop of shining Little Orphan Annie curls. Nor had he forgotten the cheerful promise that she would be back in the morning to begin his therapy.

"What do you want?" he asked, regarding her suspiciously.

Ignoring his challenging tone, she stepped briskly into the room, took in the situation at a glance and, with one graceful move, retrieved the phone from under the bed. "I was at the nurses' station when we heard your dulcet tones echoing down the hall," she told him.

"And you drew the short straw?"

"And I was on my way to see you anyway. How'd the phone land under the bed?" she inquired, as if it weren't obvious.

He stared at her incredulously, then glanced pointedly at his bandaged hands.

If he'd expected pity or understanding, he didn't get either. She shrugged and hung up the receiver. "I suppose some people would consider that an excuse."

Frank glared at her just as the phone started to ring again. He stared at it, cursing it for the helplessness it stirred in him again. He took all of his frustration out on the therapist. "Get out!"

As skinny as she was, he was surprised his bellow alone hadn't blown her from the room. She didn't budge, every puny inch of her radiating mule-headed stubbornness. A tiny little bit of respect found its way into his perception of Ms. Jenny Michaels.

"I thought you wanted someone to answer the phone," she said, all sweet innocence over a core of what was clearly solid steel.

"I'll manage."

"How?" she said, voicing his own disgruntled thought.

"What the hell difference does it make to you?"

"I'll consider it the first step in your therapy."

She waited. He glowered, his muscles tensing with each damnable ring of the phone. Finally, thankfully, it stopped.

"It's probably just as well," she said. "It is time for your therapy. I usually like to start with something less complicated."

"Push-ups perhaps," he suggested sarcastically.

"Maybe tomorrow," she said without missing a beat. "In the meantime, why don't I just show you how to start exercising those fingers? You can repeat the exercises every hour, about ten minutes at a time."

"I'm not interested in therapy. I just want to be left alone."

Ignoring that, she ordered, "Sit," and waved him toward the bed.

"Forget it," he said, bracing himself for a fight. He'd been itching for one all morning. Everyone else had sensed that and run for their lives. Jennifer Michaels wasn't scaring so easily.

"Okay, stand," she replied, not batting an eye at his surliness. "Hold out your hand. I'll show you what I want you to do."

He backed up until he was out of reach. "What about me? What about what I want?" he thundered. "Don't you get it, lady? I'm not doing any 'exercises.'"

"You'd prefer to have your hands heal the way they are now?"

Her voice never even wavered. Frank decided in that instant that his initial impression had been right on target: Jennifer Michaels was one tough little cookie. He took another look and saw the spark of determination in her eyes. He tried again to get through that thick, do-gooder skull of hers.

"Listen, sweetheart," he said with deliberate condescension. "I know you have a job to do. I know you probably think you can accomplish miracles, but I'm not interested. The only thing I want out of life right this second is to be left alone, followed in very short order by my discharge papers."

She winced once during the tirade, but recovered quickly. After that her expression remained absolutely calm. Not stoic. Not smug. *Calm.* It infuriated him. The only people he'd ever seen that serene before had been drugged out or chanting. Around San Francisco it was possible to see plenty of both.

"I could leave you here to stew," she said as if honestly considering the possibility. "Of course, it would make me a lousy therapist if I let you get away with your bullying tactics."

"I'll write you an excuse you can put in your personnel file. The patient was uncooperative and unresponsive. That ought to cover it, don't you think?"

She nodded agreeably. "It's certainly accurate enough. Unfortunately you won't be able to hold the pen unless you do the exercises."

"Dammit, don't you ever give up?" he said, advancing until he was towering over her. She swallowed hard, but stood her ground as he continued to rant. "I'll type it. I ought to be able to hunt and peck, even with my fingers like this." He waved them under her nose for emphasis.

She leveled her green eyes at him and tried to stare him down. When he didn't back off she shrugged. "Suit yourself."

She headed for the door and suddenly, perversely, Frank felt uncertain. At least she was company. And as long as they were hurling insults, he wouldn't be alone with his own lousy thoughts. "You're leaving?"

"That is what you said you wanted. I have patients who are interested in getting better. I don't have time to waste on one who's feeling sorry for himself. Think about it and we'll talk again."

She pinned him with an unflinching green-eyed gaze until he couldn't stand it anymore. He turned away. A sigh shuddered through him as he heard the door shut softly behind her.

Well, Chambers, you definitely made a horse's ass out of yourself that time, he told himself. Not that Jennifer Michaels couldn't take it. There had been that unmistakable glint of steely determination in her eyes and an absolute lack of sympathy in her voice. At almost any other moment in his life that combination might have impressed him. He admired spunk and dedication. He was not in the habit of dishing out garbage the way he had just now, but on the occasions when his temper got the best of him, he appreciated knowing that the target had the audacity to throw it right back in his face. Jennifer Michaels had audacity to spare.

In her case, the unexpectedness of that tart, unyielding response had caught him off guard. He doubted she'd learned that particular bedside technique in therapist school. But he had to admit it was mildly effective. He felt guilty for a full five minutes before reminding himself that, like it or not, he was the patient here. Nobody was exactly coddling him.

Not that he wanted them to, he amended quickly. The papers might be calling him a hero for rescuing his co-worker, and his family might think he was behaving like a pain in the butt, but either label irked. He didn't feel particularly heroic. Nor was he ready to don a hair shirt just because his attitude sucked. He figured he had a right. With his hands burned and his livelihood in jeopardy, it was little wonder that his stomach was knotted in fear. If he wanted to sulk, then, by God, he was going to sulk, and no pint-size therapist with freckles, saucer eyes and bright red curls was going to cheer him up or lay a guilt trip on him.

But to his amazement, the memory of her sunny disposition and sweet smile began to taunt him. It couldn't be easy dealing with angry patients, some of them injured a whole lot worse than he was. How did she do it day after day? How much of the abuse did she take before lashing back? How much would she withstand before truly giving up? Somewhere deep inside he knew that she hadn't given up on him after this one brief skirmish. She'd only staged a tactical retreat, leaving him with a whole lot to think about.

Frank spent the rest of the day intermittently pacing, staring at the door, waiting. Every time it opened, his muscles tensed and his breathing seemed to go still. Each time, when it was just a nurse or a doctor, disappointment warred with relief.

Finally, exhausted and aware that, like it or not, he wasn't going anywhere today, he crawled back into bed. He was stretched out on his back, counting the tiny pinpoint holes in the water-stained ceiling tiles, when the door opened yet again. This time he didn't even bother turning his head.

"Hey, big brother," Tim said from the foot of the bed. "How come you're not out chasing nurses up and down the corridors? There are some fine-looking women around here."

"I hadn't noticed."

His youngest brother stepped closer, a worried expression on his face. He placed a hand against Frank's forehead. "Nope. You're not dead. Must be the smoke. It's addled your senses."

"My senses are just fine." He paused. "Except maybe for touch."

Tim chuckled. "That's better. A little humor is good for healing. I'll go tell Ma it's safe to come in now."

"She's here?"

"They all are. They're just waiting for me to wave the white flag."

Frank groaned. "All of them?"

"Everyone. You're the one who taught us to travel in packs in times of crisis. We're here to cheer you up. Feed you your dinner. Help with a shower. Of course, if it were me, I'd invite one of those gorgeous nurses to give me a sponge bath."

Frank's lips twitched with a rueful smile. "I'm sure you would."

"I know you're much too saintly to think in such terms. I'm a mere mortal, however, and I don't believe in wasting opportunities that come my way. If life hands you lemons, make—"

"I know. Make lemonade. If you ask me, too damned many opportunities have come your way," Frank grumbled, treading on familiar, comfortable turf. "You're like a bee in a field of wildflowers. It's a wonder you don't collapse from overexertion."

"Do you realize how many women get on a bus every single day?" his brother countered. "You want me to make an informed choice, don't you?"

"I knew I should have insisted that you work your way through law school by cutting lawns for little old ladies instead of driving a MUNI bus."

Tim stared at him thoughtfully. "I wonder if I could get them to bandage your mouth shut for a couple of weeks."

Frank sighed. "You and most of the staff around here."

"Yeah, that's what your therapist said."

Immediately interested, he searched Tim's face for some indication of his reaction to the conversation. "You talked to Jennifer Michaels?" he prodded.

"Listened is more like it. That woman can talk a mile a minute. She had plenty to say, too. I'd say you got under her skin, Brother. What did you do? Try to steal a kiss? Ma's out there trying to calm her down and convince her that at heart you're a good-natured beast worthy of saving."

"She's just frustrated because I won't do her damned exercises."

"I wouldn't mind doing a little exercising with her. She's a fox."

The observation, coming from an admitted connoisseur of the fair sex, irritated the daylights out of Frank for some reason. "Stay away from her, Timmy."

A slow, crooked grin spread across his brother's face. "I knew it. You're not dead after all. Just choosy. Actually, I think you've made an excellent choice."

"I didn't make any damned choice."

Tim went on as if he'd never uttered the denial. "Redheads are passionate. Did you know that? Fiery tempers and all that."

Frank thought about the therapist's absolute calm. "I think our Ms. Michaels may be the exception that proves the rule. She's unflappable."

"Are we talking about the same woman? Not five minutes ago she told Ma if you didn't get your butt out of this bed and down to therapy in the morning, she was going to haul you down there herself. I think she has plans for you."

The first faint stirrings of excitement sent Frank's blood rushing. "I'd like to see her try to drag me out of here," he said, a hint of menace in his tone. The truth of the matter, he suddenly realized, was that he really would like to see her do just that. If nothing else, going another round with Ms. Miracle Worker would relieve the boredom. Maybe if he tried her patience long enough, he'd witness a sampling of that fiery temper Tim claimed to have seen.

Before he could spend too much time analyzing just why that prospect appealed to him, the rest of the family crowded into the room and filled it with cheerful, good-natured teasing and boisterous arguments. Once he'd finished the tedious task of eating tasteless chicken and cold mashed potatoes with the

help of his nagging sister, Frank leaned back against the pillow
and let the welcome, familiar sounds lull him to sleep.

Tonight, instead of the horrible, frightening roar of a raging fire,
he dreamed of a fiery redhead turning passionate in his embrace.

Jennifer Michaels could feel the tension spreading across the
back of her neck and shoulders as Frank Chambers's chart
came up for review at interdisciplinary rounds. The doctors and
nurses on the burn unit had their say. Then it was her turn. It
was a short report. In a perfectly bland voice she recited his
status and his refusal to accept therapy. At least she thought she
was keeping her tone neutral. Apparently she was more transparent than she'd realized.

"You sound as if that's something new," Carolanne said when
rounds had ended and the others had left the therapy room.
"Almost every patient balks at first, either because of the pain,
because they're depressed or because they refuse to accept the
seriousness of the injuries and the importance of the therapy."

Jenny sighed. She'd delivered the same lecture herself
dozens of times. "I know. My brain tells me it's not my responsibility if the patient won't begin treatment, but inside it never
feels right. It feels like failure."

"Must be that Catholic boarding school upbringing again.
You haven't developed a full-fledged case of guilt in months
now. You were overdue."

"Maybe."

The other therapist watched her closely. "Or maybe something specific about Frank Chambers gets to you."

Jenny thought of the anger in his voice, the strength in his
shoulders, the coiled intensity she had sensed just beneath the
surface. Then she thought of his eyes and the wounded,
bemused look in them that he fought so hard to hide. He was

getting to her all right. Like no patient—or no man—had in a very long time.

"I'm right, aren't I?" Carolanne persisted. "Want me to see him tomorrow? I can take over the case."

Jenny hesitated. That would be the smart thing to do, run while she had the chance. Then she thought of the lost, sorrowful expression in those compelling blue eyes.

Because she understood that sadness and fear far better than he or even Carolanne could imagine, she slowly shook her head. "No," she said finally. "Thanks, but I'll see him."

How could she possibly abandon a man who so clearly needed her—even if he couldn't admit it yet?

Chapter Two

"When am I getting out?" Frank demanded as his doctor bent over his bandages first thing in the morning. Nathan Wilding was one of the top burn specialists in the nation. In his fifties, he was compulsively dedicated, returning to the hospital at a moment's notice at the slightest sign of change in any of his patients. Occasionally gruff, and always demanding, he insisted on excellence from his staff. Because he accepted no less from himself, his staff respected him, and his patients elevated him to godlike stature. He'd been featured in almost as many San Francisco newspaper stories as any 49ers quarterback, and treated with much the same reverence. Frank considered himself lucky to be the patient of a true expert, but that didn't mean he wanted to hang around this place any longer than necessary.

"When I say so," Wilding mumbled distractedly as he carefully snipped away another layer of gauze. When the nasty wounds were fully exposed, he nodded approvingly. Personally

Frank thought they looked like hell. He stared with a sort of repulsed fascination.

"Am I going to be able to work again?" he asked, furious because his voice sounded choked with fear.

"Too soon to say," Wilding replied. "Have you been doing your therapy?"

Frank evaded the doctor's penetrating gaze. He sensed the doctor already knew the answer. "Not exactly."

"I see," he said slowly, allowing the silence to go on and on until Frank met his eyes. Then he added, "I thought you wanted to get full use of your hands back."

"I do."

"Then stop giving Ms. Michaels so much grief and get to work. She's one of the best. She can help you, but only if you'll work with her."

"And if I don't?"

"Then I can't promise you'll have any significant recovery of dexterity." He pulled up a chair and sat down. "Let me spell it out for you, Mr. Chambers. Your injuries are severe, but not irreversible. Maybe even without therapy, given time, you'd be able to hold a glass again or grasp a fork, if the handle is wide enough."

He waited for that to sink in. Certain that he had Frank's full attention, he went on, "It is my understanding, however, that you are a craftsman. In fact, my wife bought one of your cabinets for our den. The workmanship is extraordinary in this day of fake wood and assembly-line furniture production. The detail is exquisite. If you ever hope to do that sort of delicate carving again, there's not a minute to waste. You'll do Ms. Michaels's exercises and follow her instructions without argument. She's a damned fine therapist. Cares about her patients. She doesn't deserve any more of your abuse."

Frank could feel an embarrassed flush creep up his neck. "She complained that I behaved like a jerk, right?"

"She didn't tell me a thing."

"Then she wrote it in the chart."

"The chart mentioned that you were uncooperative and unresponsive." Amusement suddenly danced in the doctor's eyes, chasing away the stern demeanor. "It also mentioned that you told her to write that."

As the doctor rewrapped each finger in solution-soaked gauze, he said, "Listen, I know you're frustrated and angry. It's understandable. I'd hate like hell being in your position. A doctor's not much use without his hands, either. But the fact of the matter is that you're the only thing standing in the way of your own recovery. If you think it's bad now, just wait a couple more days until the pain starts full force. You're going to hate the bunch of us, when that happens. There's not one of us you won't think is trying to torture you. You're going to be downright nasty. You'd better hope you've made a few friends around here by then. We can walk you through it. We can remind you that the pain will pass. And Ms. Michaels can see to it that you don't let the pain make you give up and decide to find a new career that doesn't demand so much of your hands."

"In other words, it's time to stop feeling sorry for myself and get to work."

"That's about it."

The last time Frank had had a straight, no-nonsense lecture like that he'd been a teenager similarly hell-bent on self-destruction. Angry over his father's death, terrified of the sudden, overwhelming responsibilities, he'd gone a little wild. He'd been creeping into the house after three in the morning, staggering drunk, when his mother had stepped out of the shadows and smacked him square on the jaw. For a little woman, she had packed a hell of a wallop.

Having convinced him just who was in charge, she had marched him into the kitchen and poured enough coffee to float a cruise ship. While he'd longed for the oblivion of sleep, she'd told him in no uncertain terms that it was time to shape up and act like a man. He'd sat at that table, miserable, unable to meet her eyes, filled with regret for the additional pain he'd inflicted on her.

And then she had hugged him and reminded him that the only things that counted in life were family and love and support in times of trouble. She'd taught him by example just what that meant. She was the most giving soul he'd ever met. Some instinct told him that deep down Jennifer Michaels might be just like her.

If he'd learned the meaning of love and responsibility from his mother, Frank had learned the meaning of strength and character from his father. Until the day he'd died of cancer, his body racked with pain, the old man had been a fighter. Reflecting on his own behavior of the past couple of days, Frank felt a faint stirring of shame. He resolved to change his tune, to cooperate with that pesky little therapist when she finally showed up again.

"She'll have no more problems with me," Frank assured the doctor. "I'll be a model patient."

Unfortunately that spirit of cooperation died the minute she walked into the room pushing a wheelchair, her expression grimly determined. He didn't even have time to reflect on how pretty she looked in the bright emerald green dress that matched her eyes. He was too busy girding himself for another totally unexpected battle.

"What's that for?" He waved his hand at the offensive contraption.

"Time for therapy," she announced cheerfully, edging the

chair to the side of the bed. "Hop in, Mr. Chambers. We're going for a ride."

"Are you nuts? I'm not riding in that with some puny little wisp of a thing pushing me through the halls. My legs are just fine."

She backed the chair up a foot or so to give him room. "Let's see you move it, then. The therapy room is down the hall. I'll give you five minutes to get there." She spun on her heel and headed for the door, taking the wheelchair with her.

"Something tells me I'm not the one with the attitude problem today," he observed, still not budging from the bed, arms folded across his chest.

Jenny abandoned the wheelchair, moving so fast her rubber-soled shoes made little squeaking sounds on the linoleum. Hands on hips, she loomed over him, sparks dancing in her eyes. The soft moss shade of yesterday was suddenly all emerald fire.

"Buster, this attitude is no problem at all. If I have to bust your butt to convince you to do what you should, then that's the road I'll take. Personally I prefer to spend my time being pleasant and helpful, but I'm not above a little street fighting if that's what it takes to accomplish the job. Got it?"

Frank found himself grinning at her idea of playing down and dirty. In any sort of real street fighting, she'd be out of her league in twenty seconds. He gave her high marks for trying, though. And after what he'd put her through the previous day, he decided he owed her a round. He'd let her emerge from this particular battle unscathed.

"I'll go peacefully," he said compliantly.

She blinked in surprise, and then something that might have been relief replaced the fight in her eyes.

"Good," she said, a wonderful smile spreading across her face. That smile alone was worth the surrender. It warmed him deep inside, where he hadn't even realized he'd been feeling cold and alone.

"I had no idea how I was going to haul you into that chair if you didn't cooperate," she confided.

"Sweetheart, you should never admit a thing like that," he warned while awkwardly pulling on his robe. "Tomorrow I just might get it into my head to stand you up for this therapy date, and now I know I can get away with it."

"Who are you kidding?" she sassed right back. "You knew that anyway. You're nearly a foot taller than I am and seventy pounds heavier."

"So you admit to being all bluster."

"Not exactly." She gestured toward the door. "I have a very tall, very strong orderly waiting just outside in case my technique failed. He lifts twice your weight just for kicks."

"Which confirms that you weren't quite as sure of yourself as you wanted me to believe."

"Let's just say that I'm aware of the importance of both first impressions and contingency plans," she said as she escorted him to the door.

Outside the room she turned the wheelchair over to the orderly, who was indeed more than equal to persuading a man of Frank's size to do as he was told. "Thanks, Otis. We won't be needing this after all."

The huge black man grinned. "Never thought you would, Ms. Michaels. You're batting fifty-eight for sixty by my count. It's not even sporting fun to bet against you anymore."

"Nice record," Frank observed wryly as they walked down the hall. "I had no idea therapists kept scorecards. I'd have put up less of a fight if I'd known I was about to ruin your reputation."

"Otis is a born gambler. I'm trying to persuade him that the track is not the best place to squander his paycheck."

"So now he takes bets against you?"

"I'm hoping eventually he'll get bored enough to quit that, too. I think he's getting close." She peered up at Frank, her expression hopeful. "What do you think?"

What Frank thought, as he lost himself in those huge green eyes, was that he was facing trouble a whole lot more dangerous than the condition of his hands. His voice gentled to a near whisper. "Ms. Michaels, I think a man would be a fool to ever bet against you."

Her gaze locked with his until finally, swallowing hard, she blinked and looked away. "Jenny," she said, just as softly. "You can call me Jenny."

Frank nodded, aware that they were suddenly communicating in ways that went beyond mere words. "Jenny," he repeated for no reason other than the chance to hear her name roll off his tongue. The name was simple and uncomplicated, not at all like the woman it belonged to. He had a hunch he'd done a whole lot of miscalculating in the past couple of days. It might be fascinating to discover just how far off the mark he had been. "And I'm Frank."

"Frank."

They'd stopped outside a closed door marked Therapy and might have stood right where they were, awareness suddenly throbbing between them, if Otis hadn't strolled past, whistling, giving Jenny a conspiratorial wink. Suddenly she was all business again, opening the door, pointing to a chair. "Have a seat. I'll be right with you."

Frank stepped into a room filled with ordinary, everyday items from jars to toothbrushes, from scissors to jumbo-size crayons. He wasn't sure what he'd expected, but it certainly wasn't this dime-store collection of household paraphernalia. He hooked his foot under the rung of an ordinary straight-back chair and pulled it away from a Formica-topped table so he could sit. He eyed the assortment of equipment skeptically. He suspected his insurance was going to pay big bucks for this therapy, and for what? So he could play with a toothbrush? His spirit of cooperation took another nosedive.

"What's all this?" he asked derisively the minute Jenny joined him.

"Advanced therapy," she retorted. "If you're lucky and work hard, you'll get to it in a week or two."

He regarded her incredulously. "It's going to take two weeks before I can brush my teeth? I thought you were supposed to be good."

"I am good. You're the patient," she reminded him. "Two weeks. Could be longer. The bandages won't even be off for three weeks. Think you can handle it sooner?"

There was no mistaking the challenge. "Give me the brush," he said.

"Get it yourself."

He reached across the table and tried to pick it up. He managed it with both hands, by sliding it to the edge of the table and clamping it between his hands as it fell off. At least his quick, ball-playing reflexes hadn't suffered any.

"Now what?" Jenny said, all bright-eyed curiosity. The woman was just waiting for a failure. Frank was equally determined not to fail. He was going to set a few recovery records of his own.

He pressed harder to keep the brush from slipping and tried to maneuver it toward his mouth. "Do you have to watch every move I make?" he grumbled, sweat forming across his brow with the taxing effort.

"Yep."

Irritated by his inability to manipulate the brush and by her fascinated observation of the failure, he threw it down. "Forget it."

"Maybe we ought to work up to that," Jenny suggested mildly. There wasn't the slightest hint of gloating in her tone.

He scowled back at her, but her gaze remained unwaveringly calm. "Okay, fine," he bit out finally. "You call the shots. Where do we start?"

She sat down next to him, inching her chair so close he could smell the sweet spring scent of her perfume. "We'll start with flexing your fingers. I'll do the work this first time, okay? It's called passive motion."

Momentarily resigned, he shrugged. "Whatever you say."

With surprising gentleness, she took his hand in hers. At once Frank cursed his fate all over again. He couldn't even feel the unexpected caress. His imagination went wild though. He wondered if her skin was as soft as it looked, if the texture felt like rose petals. He was so fascinated with his fantasizing, in fact, that he barely noticed what she was doing, until she said, "Now you try it."

"Mmm?" he murmured.

She regarded him indignantly. "Frank, weren't you paying a bit of attention?"

"My mind wandered."

If she was aware of exactly where his wayward thoughts had strayed, she showed no evidence of it, not even the faintest blush of embarrassment. She picked up his other hand.

"Try to pay attention this time," she said as she slowly flexed each finger back and forth. The range of movement was minuscule. Frank couldn't believe how little she expected or how inept he was at accomplishing it. He *needed* her to move his fingers for him—and he hated that weakness.

"That's it?" he scoffed when she stopped. "That's your idea of therapy? You dragged me all the way down here for that?"

"You could have done it in your room, but we tried that

routine yesterday and you didn't seem to like it. It occurred to me you might take it more seriously if I brought you down here. Just remember there's an old saying that you have to walk before you can run."

"It usually applies just to babies."

Jenny rested her hand on his forearm and regarded him intently. Compassion and understanding filled her eyes. "In this instance it might be wise if you think of your hands as being every bit as untutored as a newborn's," she told him. "The instincts are there, but the control is shaky. Right now we're just trying to assure that the joints don't stiffen up as you heal and that the skin maintains some elasticity."

Frank wasn't interested in baby steps. He wanted desperately to make strides. "All I need is to get these bandages off and I'll be just fine."

"You will be if you do the exercises religiously, ten minutes an hour. Got it?"

"I've got it."

"Want me to walk you back to your room or send for Otis?"

"Hardly. My legs aren't the problem."

"I'll be in later to check on you."

Her tone was all business and her gaze was directed at his chart as she scribbled in a notation. Frank found it thoroughly irritating that he'd apparently been summarily dismissed now that she'd gotten her way. He was just about to tell her in grumpy detail what she could do with her ridiculous therapy, when the door opened and another patient was wheeled in by the formidable Otis.

The young girl was swathed in bandages over fifty percent of her body. Only one side of her face peeked through the gauze and only one arm remained unbandaged. Even so, she struggled for a smile at the sight of Jenny. Frank felt his heart wrench at the pitiful effort.

"Hey, Pam, how's it going?" Jenny asked, her own smile warm, her gaze unflinching.

"Pretty good. I just beat Otis at poker. He has to go out and bring me a hamburger and fries for lunch."

Otis leaned down, his expression chagrined. "I thought that was going to be our little secret."

Jenny chuckled. "That will teach you, big guy. There are no secrets between therapist and patient. As long as you're buying, you can bring me a hamburger, too."

"Women! The two of you are going to put me in the poor-house," the orderly grumbled, but he was grinning as he left.

Frank watched the byplay between Jenny and the teenager for a few more minutes, irritated by their camaraderie, the easy laughter. He could feel the pull of the warmth between them and envied it. Feeling lonelier than he ever had in his life, he finally slipped out the door and went back to his room.

Late into the night, long after he probably should have been asleep, he struggled to move his fingers just a fraction of an inch. He wasn't sure whether he was trying to prove something to himself...or to Jenny.

Chapter Three

Jenny had met some tough, self-defeating patients in her time, and Frank Chambers ranked right up there with the worst of them. Right now he was suffering more from wounded pride than he was from his physical injuries. A man like Frank, used to doing for others, according to his family, would hate being dependent, even temporarily. And she could tell that he was going to fight with her every step of the way, try to hide his unfamiliar weakness. She had to make him see that it took real strength to admit the need for help.

She'd once heard a burn therapist from Miami say that a patient who was a winner in life before his injury would be a winner afterward. Despite his initial surliness, she could tell that Frank Chambers was a winner. She just had to remind him of that. She had to get him past his anger and fears and on to more practical things that could speed his recovery. Sooner or later his intelligence would kick in, and he'd realize that his attitude was only hurting.

Fortunately Jenny was by nature a fighter. She'd fought her own personal demons in this very hospital, and she'd learned from the humbling experience. Sometimes that enabled her to reach patients other therapists wanted to abandon as lost causes. Knowing how easy it was to slip into despair strengthened both her compassion and her determination to keep that self-defeating slide from happening.

Yesterday, by threatening to force Frank into a wheelchair, by hinting he was worse off than he was and allowing him the victory of proving her wrong, she had won the first round. Yet it was a shaky, inconclusive victory. Today was likely to be more difficult. He was going to be expecting miracles, and if he hadn't improved overnight, he'd consider the therapy a failure and her an unwelcome intruder.

She considered sending the massive, intimidating Otis after him, but decided it would be the cowardly way out. She did take along the wheelchair though, just in case Frank needed a little extra persuasion.

Jenny breezed into the room just in time to see his breakfast tray hit the floor. She grabbed an unopened carton of milk in midair and guessed the rest. He'd gotten frustrated over his inability to cope with the milk and the utensils.

"Hey, I've heard hospital food is lousy, but that's no reason to dump it onto the floor," she said, keeping her expression neutral as he made his way from the bed to the window.

"I wouldn't know," he muttered, his rigid back to her as he stared outside. His black hair was becomingly tousled from sleep and his inability to tame it with a comb. She was touched by the sexy disarray and poked her hands in her pockets to avoid the temptation to brush an errant strand from his forehead. The shadow of dark stubble on his cheeks was equally tempting, adding to a masculine appeal she was finding it increasingly difficult to ignore.

"You could have asked for help," she said mildly.

"Dammit, woman, I am not a baby. I don't need to be fed."

"You may not be a baby, but at the moment you're acting like one. You've been burned, not incapacitated for life. There's nothing wrong with accepting a little help until you can manage on your own."

He whirled on her. "And when in hell will that be? I've been doing your damned exercises."

"Since yesterday," she reminded him.

He ignored her reasonable response, clearly determined to sulk. "Nothing's changed. I still can't even open a damned carton of milk."

She regarded him with undisguised curiosity. "Do you actually like lukewarm milk?"

"No," he admitted. "I hate the stuff."

"Then what's the big deal?"

He scowled, but she could see a faint flicker of amusement in his eyes before he carefully banked it and returned to his study of the foggy day outside. "It's the principle."

"Pretty stupid principle, if you ask me."

"Who asked you?"

"Call me generous. I like to share my opinions."

"Share them somewhere else where they're appreciated. I'm sure there are a dozen places on this corridor alone where Saint Jennifer's views would be welcomed."

The barb struck home. It wasn't the first time she'd been accused of being a Pollyanna, of nagging where she wasn't wanted. It came with the job. Even so, she had to swallow the urge to lash back. Forcing a breezy note into her voice, she said, "You probably wouldn't be nearly this cranky if you'd had your breakfast. Come on. If you don't squeal on me, I'll treat you to a couple of doughnuts and a cup of coffee in the therapy room. I guarantee there won't be anything you have to open. And the doughnuts are fresh. I stopped at the bakery on the way in."

He turned finally and regarded her warily. "Are you trying to bribe me into coming back to therapy?"

"I'm trying to improve your temper for the benefit of the entire staff on this floor. Now come along."

Blue eyes, which had been bleak with exhaustion and defeat, sparked briefly with sheer devilment. "Do I have a choice?" he inquired, his voice suddenly filled with a lazy challenge.

"You do, but just so you know, the wheelchair's right outside."

"And Otis?"

"He's within shouting distance, but I didn't think I'd need him today." Her gaze held a challenge of its own. She could practically see the emotions warring inside him as he considered his options. She pressed a little harder. "So, are you coming or not? I have jelly doughnuts. Or chocolate. There's even one that's apple-filled."

Temptation won out over stubbornness. She could see it in the suddenly resigned set of his shoulders. Apparently she'd hit on a weakness with those doughnuts.

"You are a bully," he accused, but he followed her from the room.

"Takes one to know one. What's it going to be jelly, chocolate or apple?"

"Jelly, of course. You could probably see my mouth watering the minute you mentioned them."

"I did sense I had your attention."

"Why do you do this?" he asked as they walked down the hall.

"Buy doughnuts?"

The evasion earned a look of disgust. "You know what I meant."

"They pay me to do it."

"So you've said. I'm more interested in why someone would choose a profession that requires them to put up with nasty-tempered patients like me."

"Maybe I'm a masochist."

"I don't think so. What's the truth, Jenny Michaels?"

There was a genuine curiosity in his eyes that demanded an honest response. "Sometimes," she said softly, "sometimes I can make a difference."

He nodded at once with obvious understanding. "Quite a high, huh?"

She grinned at the way he mirrored her thoughts. "Quite a high."

He glanced sideways at her. "I'd guess the lows are pretty bad, though."

Jenny sobered at once, thinking of the patients who struggled and lost against insurmountable odds. "Bad enough."

Inside the sunshine-bright therapy room, she put two jelly doughnuts on a plate and poured a cup of coffee for Frank as he nudged a chair up to the table with some deft footwork. She sat beside him and encouraged him to talk about himself. As he did, almost without him realizing, she broke off bits of the doughnuts and fed them to him. More than once her fingers skimmed his lips, sending a jolt of electricity clear through her. He seemed entirely unaware of it, thank goodness.

"So you worked odd jobs from the time you were a kid and helped your mother raise all of those handsome characters I've met," she said.

"You think they're handsome?" he asked, watching her suspiciously. "All of them?"

She nodded, playing on the surprising hint of vulnerability

she detected. "One of them is a real charmer, too. What's his name? Tim?"

"He's a little young for you, isn't he?" he inquired, his gaze narrowed, his expression sour.

Jenny chuckled at his obviously suspicious response to her teasing. "Who are you looking out for? Him or me?" She decided not to mention the third alternative, Frank himself.

"You. Tim learned to take care of his own social life long ago. It's very active."

"And yours?"

He suddenly looked uncomfortable. "Not so active, at least not lately."

"Why not? You're the best-looking one in the bunch," she said. She wasn't above using flattery to get her way, but in his case it wasn't necessary. Frank Chambers had a quiet strength and serenity about him when he wasn't raging at the universe. He seemed like the kind of man a woman could depend on. And everything she'd heard about him from his adoring family confirmed that. Plus, his slightly crooked nose, the firm, stubborn line of his jaw and the astonishingly blue eyes gave his face a rugged appeal. She'd always preferred that type to the polished professionals in their designer shirts, designer watches and phony smiles. In Frank's case the internal strength and diamond-in-the-rough exterior added up to a potent and very masculine combination.

"I'm astonished no woman has snapped you up," she said with honesty, wondering as she did so why she felt so glad that he was free and unencumbered. She never got involved with her patients. Lately, in fact, she never got involved with any man. Keeping her tone light and bantering, she added, "You're obviously domesticated. You probably even do dishes."

He shook his head adamantly. "Oh, no. Not if I can help it. That's probably the single greatest advantage I can think of having so many younger brothers and a baby sister. When I was younger, my turn to do dishes only came about once a week. If I was really on my toes, I'd land a job mowing lawns whenever it was my turn, or bribe one of the others to take it. Karyn earned more doing dishes for me than she ever did baby-sitting."

Suddenly his gaze fell on the empty plate and coffee cup. His expression became perplexed. "How'd you do that?"

She grinned at him. "It's all a matter of technique."

"That kind of sleight of hand belongs on stage."

"Hey, for all you know, I ate it all myself."

"Not a chance."

"How come?"

Before she realized what he intended, he scooted his chair closer, reached over and brushed the tip of one bandaged finger across her lips. The gauze tickled, but there was nothing humorous about the emotional impact. Jenny felt the sizzle of that touch somewhere deep inside. "No jelly," he said softly. "No powdered sugar." He looked suddenly regretful. "I almost wish there were."

"Why?" she said in a voice that trembled as she lost herself to the intensity of his gaze.

"So I could see if it tastes even sweeter on you."

Jenny's pulse skittered wildly. She swallowed hard and dragged her gaze away. Countering the rush of unexpected feelings, she was suddenly all business.

"Talk about distractions," she murmured, partly to herself. The sizzling tension shattered like fragile glass as she injected an energetic note into her voice. "All this talk has kept you from your therapy. Let's get to work. Do something a little more challenging. Try squeezing this washcloth."

She handed him a cloth that had been folded into a thick rectangular wad. With infinite patience, she closed his hand around it. It would be days before he could complete the closure, days before the tips of his fingers could comfortably touch his own palm.

Frank, obviously, didn't understand the difficulty. He shot her a look of pure disgust. "Any two-year-old can do that," he said, obviously ignoring the difficulty of yesterday's even less taxing assignment.

"Then it should be a breeze for you."

She deliberately turned her back on him, sat at her desk and attacked her paperwork. When his cursing turned the air blue, she smiled, but she didn't give an inch.

"You're doing this just to break my spirit," he muttered finally.

Jenny glanced up and saw the furrows in his brow as he struggled with the simple task. "Mr. Chambers…"

"Frank, dammit!"

"Frank," she said quietly, countering irritation with determined calm. "A rodeo bronc rider couldn't break your spirit. What I'm going for here is a little spirit of cooperation."

"Right," he muttered between gritted teeth. But when the time came for him to return to his room, she had almost as much trouble getting him to leave as she'd had getting him there in the first place.

Something astonishing had happened to Frank in that therapy room, while doing those ridiculous yet nearly impossible exercises. He'd decided to fight. Not in some half-baked way, either, but with everything in him. Maybe it was because the prospect of doing anything else didn't sit well with a man used to being firmly in control of his own life. Maybe the smoke had finally cleared from his brain so he could see things straight again.

Or maybe it was just that one flash of insight he'd had, when he'd realized that he'd do almost anything to earn Jenny's approval, to win one of her warm and tender smiles. He'd searched a long time to find a woman who was part hellion and part angel. And something told him he'd finally found her.

He was back in his room, still squeezing the devil out of that washcloth, when his mother turned up. He smiled at her entrance. She was sixty-two now and her once-raven hair had turned gray, but nothing had daunted her spirit. She came in with all the bustle of the briskest nurse on the floor.

"You've eaten your lunch?" she said, fussing around him.

"Hours ago," he said, resigned to the straightening of the sheets, the rearrangement of the flowers crowded on top of the room's small dresser, the quick check of the trash can to assure that the housekeeping staff was on its toes.

"Brushed your teeth?" She straightened up the things on his nightstand. Flicking away some invisible speck of lint.

He endured the bustling activity as long as he could, then said, "Ma, settle down."

Not used to being still, she spent about ten seconds in the chair by the bed before she was up again, fiddling with the blinds until they let in the pale light of the sun as it burned off the last of the day's fog. "You still giving that therapist trouble?"

"No."

She nodded. "Good." She shot him a pointed look. "She seems like a nice girl."

"She is."

"Pretty, too."

The description was far too bland to describe Jenny, but he nodded anyway. "Yes. What's your point?"

Shrewd blue eyes danced with amusement. "If you can't figure that one out, boy, there's no hope for you."

Frank nearly groaned aloud. If his mother got it into her head to play matchmaker, neither he nor Jenny would have another moment's peace. "Stay out of it, Ma."

The remark was met with startled innocence. "Out of what? I was just making an observation."

"Your *observation* is duly noted."

"Is she married?"

"Ma!"

"Okay, okay, you do what you want. You're not like your brothers. They're always looking. Saturday night doesn't pass, they're not out with this one or that one. There are times I think I did you a terrible disservice by giving you so much responsibility. Maybe you think you've already finished raising your family. I just thought maybe you needed reminding that Karyn and your brothers aren't the same as having a wife and kids of your own."

"Believe me, I'm aware of that."

"Are you really? You didn't exactly rush into marrying Megan. Kept her dangling long enough."

At the mention of his ex-fiancée's name, Frank felt a familiar tightness in his chest. "I don't want to talk about Megan."

"That's the trouble. You never did. You kept it all bottled up inside. Five years you dated that woman and then, poof, it was over. You never did say what happened, not even which one of you broke it off."

"And I don't intend to say so now. Megan is history."

"Then let's get back to the present. When are you seeing this Jenny again?"

"Ma!" The muttered warning gave way to a chuckle. "You're incorrigible."

She bent over and planted a kiss on his cheek. "There, then, that's much better. It's good to see you laughing again, Son. I've been worried about you. You've been entirely too glum these past few days."

"I'll survive."

"I know that. Even when you were a little boy, you were a survivor. Of all my kids, you were the one who never shed a tear. Your father used to say you'd been born with a stiff upper lip."

"Not so stiff," he countered. "Half the time, it was split from losing control of my bike on the hills and slamming into some wall or car."

They were laughing at the memories when Jenny came by. Frank saw her hesitate in the doorway. "You can come in."

"I'm so used to hearing shouts from this room, I wasn't quite sure what to make of this new cheerful sound. Thought for sure I had to be in the wrong place."

Frank caught the beaming smile of welcome on his mother's face, the speculative gleam in her eyes.

"Come on in, child. We were just talking over old times," his mother said.

"I could come back later," Jenny offered.

"No, indeed," his mother said. "You sit right over here." She shoved the room's only chair even closer to the side of the bed. "I think maybe I'll go get myself a cup of coffee."

Jenny backed away a step. "Really, it's not necessary. Maybe if you stick around, he won't grumble quite so much about the therapy."

"Don't you believe it. He enjoys shocking me with his language. He knows he's gotten too big for me to wash his mouth out with soap."

"Ma, you never once washed my mouth out with soap," Frank protested, enjoying the expression of amusement on Jenny's face.

"Only because you didn't use any of those foul words until you knew you outweighed me."

Frank turned to Jenny. "Don't believe her 'poor, pitiful me' act. She wouldn't hesitate to take on any one of us no matter our size or our age."

"That's the truth," Kevin said coming through the door just then. "She may be tiny, but she has us all cowed."

"Says you," Tim scoffed, entering right on his brother's heels. "I'm not scared of Ma."

Mrs. Chambers drew herself up to her full height, which was about as intimidating as a sparrow's. "Well, you ought to be, young man," she said sternly. "Where were you last night?"

Tim immediately blushed furiously. Avoiding Jenny's laughter-filled eyes, he said meekly, "I had a date."

"What kind of date lasts until three a.m.?"

"Whoa," Frank said, enjoying seeing Tim squirm. "Now you're going to catch it, baby brother. You know what Ma's like when she doesn't get her beauty rest."

Tim gave a dramatic shrug. He slid his arm around Jenny's waist. "Since I'm already in hot water, what are you doing tonight?"

"She's going home," Frank said, suddenly no longer amused.

Jenny's gaze shot to him, and her lips formed a mutinous frown. "Oh, really? Who made you the keeper of my social calendar?"

Frank's eyes narrowed. His voice dropped. "Do you want to go out with him?"

"Oh, for heaven's sake," she said with a shake of her head that set her curls bounding indignantly. "Whether I do or I don't is not something I intend to discuss in front of a roomful of people."

"We could go outside," Tim said at once, his eyes bright with mischief.

"You do and I'll be right behind you," Frank countered.

His gaze locked with his brother's. In that instant of masculine challenge, a clear message was sent and received. Tim draped an arm around his mother's shoulders. "Come on, Ma, I guess it's you and me, after all. Kevin, you, too."

"But we just got here," Kevin grumbled.

"Now," Tim said with the kind of firm diplomacy that would have made him the perfect State Department emissary. Of course, the family liked to tease him that by the time he finished law school, he'd probably be too old to board a plane, anyway.

Blessed silence descended the minute they were gone. Jenny began inching backward toward the door.

"Sometimes, they're a little overwhelming," Frank said. "But they mean well."

"I can see that."

"Did you come by for a reason?"

"I just wanted to check and see how things were going with your therapy before I took off for the night. They should be in soon with your dinner tray."

"Do you follow all your patients this closely?"

There was no mistaking the hint of pink that tinted her cheeks. "As a matter of fact, I do."

"Then why does it bother you that I asked the question?"

"Who says it bothers me? Look, if you're okay, I'll be on my way."

"I'd be a lot better if you'd stick around."

"And do what?"

"Talk to me."

"Your family could do that. Why'd you chase them out?"

"I didn't chase. They left. Besides, they talk to me all the time. I've heard all their stories. I'd like to hear yours."

Jenny sighed, but she stopped inching toward the door. "My stories aren't all that fascinating."

"They would be to me."

She stared at him, her brow knit by a puzzled frown. "Why?"

"Does there have to be a specific reason?"

"There usually is," she said with a distinct trace of cynicism.

"I'm not exactly likely to put any moves on you," he said, holding up his bandaged hands.

The remark earned him a genuine chuckle. "True."

"Then there's nothing to be afraid of, is there?" Frank wasn't sure why he was pushing or why she was so afraid. He only knew it was important to his soul in some elemental way to keep her from leaving. When she finally sat, even though she kept the chair a careful distance away, he breathed a sigh of relief.

"So, Jenny Michaels, exactly what makes you tick?"

Chapter Four

Frank scowled at the ringing phone. How the devil was any man with five interfering brothers and one doting sister supposed to get to know a woman? he wondered as the phone rang for the third time in the hour since he'd encouraged Jenny to tell him all about herself. It was not the first time in his adult life that he'd been faced with the dilemma. Which was probably why it had taken him five years to figure out that Megan was the wrong woman for him and another two months to let her down gently. She'd fit in so well with the entire family, he hadn't noticed until too late that she didn't suit him. He had no intention of making the same mistake again.

"Karyn," he told his sister after listening to five minutes of household-repair questions, "I love you dearly, but why are you asking me how to fix the sink, when you have a perfectly good husband? Is Brad out?"

He glanced over and caught Jenny's amused expression.

Rather than seeming frustrated by the nonstop interruptions, she appeared relieved. In fact, she seemed to enjoy them. She tucked the receiver between his chin and his shoulder each time and eavesdropped blatantly.

"No, but my husband races sports cars and sells ritzy sedans," Karyn retorted. "What makes you think he knows anything about sinks? Talk about sexist remarks."

"Any man who can tear a carburetor apart and put it back together again in five minutes flat ought to be able to open a trap under the sink and clean out whatever's stopping up the drain. For that matter, you ought to be able to do it yourself."

Karyn sighed heavily. "With six brothers in the house, who needed to learn?"

"Now who's being sexist?"

"Never mind. I'll call the plumber."

"Are you sure the sink's actually clogged?" he inquired suspiciously.

"Well, of course it is. Why else would I call?"

"Maybe you just don't want me to feel useless while I'm lying here in my hospital bed."

"Frank Chambers, I am standing here in an inch of water and you're accusing me of lying?"

"It wouldn't be the first time, Toots. I love you for trying, though. See you tomorrow."

He heard her indignant huff as he signaled to Jenny to put the phone back in its cradle. "I swear to you I didn't ask you to stay just so you could answer the phone."

"It's okay. I love seeing you with your family. How many are there again? When they're all here, it seems like dozens."

"Five brothers. One sister. One brother-in-law. All trouble."

She studied him thoughtfully, her green eyes intent. "Something tells me you don't really mind," she said after a thorough examination that nearly left him breathless, despite its innocence. Never before had he been with a woman who had the uncanny ability to see inside his soul.

"Am I that transparent?"

Apparently she detected the nervousness in his voice, because she laughed and reassured him. "No, it's actually something you said the other day. You understood what I meant about making a difference, about being needed."

"You get the same fix from your patients."

"Absolutely."

"No brothers or sisters?"

"Nope. I'm an only child. My parents live back East. I don't see them that often."

Frank couldn't imagine what it was like for her being separated from the only family she had. For all his grumbling, he rarely went more than a day without dropping in to see his mother or one of the other members of the tight-knit Chambers clan. They all checked in daily by phone, just to touch base, exchange news or seek advice. To his occasional regret, the latter was growing increasingly rare.

"Don't you miss your parents?" he asked Jenny.

"Yes, but we were never as close as your family is. We love each other, and they're great people, but they raised me to be independent. When the time came, they nudged me out of the nest just like a mother bird does. None of us has ever looked back. Holidays generally give us enough time to catch up."

The phone rang again. Frank glowered at it. "Tell 'em I've gone to Tahiti," he suggested.

"You wish," Jenny countered, answering it and then putting the receiver next to his ear.

"Well, well," Jared said. "Look who's answering your phone at seven o'clock at night. Does she get overtime for that?"

Frank scanned Jenny's face to see if she'd overheard the teasing comment with its sly innuendo. She seemed awfully intent suddenly on settling just so in the chair by his bed. She smoothed her dress over her knees, crossed her legs, smoothed her dress again.

"She's not a nurse, and cut the jokes," he muttered to his irreverent brother. "Did you call for a reason?"

"I take it I'm interrupting something," he said with delight. "Did you share a cozy dinner of Jell-O? Maybe some fruit cocktail?"

"You always were the perceptive one. Why aren't you hanging up?"

"You've got me mixed up with Tim." Jared went blithely on, refusing to take the hint. "Want to talk about what color you'd like me to paint your house? I thought I'd take a couple of days off work and work on it. We've been talking about it for a while now. I was thinking something cheery, maybe bright yellow."

The thought horrified Frank sufficiently to draw his attention away from the fascinating way Jenny's dress clung to her curves. He knew that Jared was perfectly capable of slapping on the most outrageous shade of paint he could find. The walls in his own apartment were the color of tangerines. The year before his bedroom had been neon green until his girlfriend rebelled. Frank did not want Jared near his house with a paintbrush unless he was on hand to watch every move and to inspect the bucket of paint.

"You paint my house yellow and it will seriously impair any plans you might have for a future family life," he warned as emphatically and discreetly as he could. Jenny's eyes danced with merriment.

"Okay, no yellow," Jared said agreeably. "How about mauve? Maybe with green trim."

Frank groaned. "And have the place look like a damned bouquet of violets? You've got to be kidding. Do we have to discuss this now?"

"Absolutely not. We don't have to discuss it at all. I can choose."

"Good God, no! How about white? Simple, straightforward, normal."

"Boring," Jared retorted succinctly.

Frank glanced at Jenny. "What's your favorite color?"

"Blue," she said without hesitation. "Why?"

"The lady says blue. Bring the paint chips by tomorrow and we'll decide on the shade. Now go away."

Jared chuckled. "Your seduction technique has taken a fascinating turn, big brother. I wonder how Ma'd feel if she knew you were painting your house to impress a woman. She'd probably start ordering wedding invitations. Should I pass on this startling development?"

"Go to hell."

"Night, pal."

This time Jenny was slow to hang up the phone. Her expression was a mix of curiosity and astonishment. "You're going to paint your house blue on a whim?"

"Actually Jared's going to paint it."

"You know what I mean."

"It needs to be painted. Blue's as good a color as any," he said, determinedly making light of his decision to pick a color that might please her. He wasn't entirely sure himself why he'd done it. "With white trim. What do you think?"

"I think you're nuts."

"Don't say that to Dr. Wilding. He'll find some shrink and send him in for a consult."

The night nurse poked her head in just then. "You want anything to help you sleep tonight?"

Frank shook his head. "Nope," he said, glancing straight at Jenny. "Something tells me I'm going to have very pleasant dreams."

He held her gaze until he could see the slow rise of heat that turned her cheeks a becoming shade of pink. For some reason he enjoyed the thought that he could fluster the usually unflappable therapist.

"Maybe I'd better get out of here and let you rest," she said, clearly nervous at the intimate turn the conversation had taken.

Instinctively he reached for her hand, then realized he couldn't grasp it in his gauze-covered mitts. He drew his hand back, but held her in place with the sheer force of his will. "Don't go, please. It gets too damned lonely around here."

She shook her head. "I can't stay."

"You have plans?"

"No, not exactly."

She looked so miserable, he finally relented. "I'm sorry. It was selfish of me to ask. You probably can't wait to shake this place at the end of the day."

"It's not that. It's just that this…"

"This?"

"Being here with you, it's not such a good idea. I should never have stayed."

"Will it make the other patients jealous?" he teased.

Suddenly she looked angry. "Don't act as if you don't know what I mean," she said, marching toward the door. He could read the conflicting emotions warring on her face as she cast one last helpless look at him and left.

"Sweet dreams," he murmured.

Frank's dreams, however, were anything but sweet. He awoke in the early hours of the morning to the slow return of sensation in his hands. At first there were just tiny pinpricks of feeling. In no time, though, his hands felt as if someone had stripped off the skin and dipped them in acid. The excruciating pain blocked out everything else.

In agony he fumbled for the call bell and tried to press it. The effort cost him all his reserves of energy, and he wasn't even sure he'd succeeded in rousing anyone at the nurses' station. As he waited, he sank back against the pillow and tried to fix a picture of Jenny in his mind. Her image brought him some small measure of comfort as he fought to hypnotize himself against the pain.

He couldn't say that Dr. Wilding hadn't warned him. He'd always held the mistaken notion that healing meant an end to pain. In the case of burns, however, he was just discovering that the healing of the nerve endings brought with it a nearly unbearable torture.

The door opened and one of the night nurses peeked in. "You okay?"

"I've had better nights," he said, his teeth gritted together.

Her relaxed, middle-of-the-night composure was instantly transformed into alert briskness. "Pain," she said at once. "I'll be right back. There's an order in your chart."

The five minutes it took her to get the medication and bring it back were the longest of Frank's life. Even the shot, with its promise of relief, brought no immediate change. Nor did the nurse's soothing words. He tried to remember all those spills from his bike that he'd survived so stoically, but none had affected him like this. Nothing had ever hurt like this.

The door whispered open, but with his eyes clamped shut he couldn't tell if someone had come in, or if the nurse had simply left. Suddenly the scent of spring flowers seemed to fill the room. Jenny!

He opened his eyes. "What are you doing here at this hour?

It must be three or four in the morning." He winced as his hands throbbed.

Still wearing the same bright silk dress she'd had on earlier, she came closer. With cool, soothing fingers, she caressed his brow. "It won't be long now before the shot kicks in. Think about something quiet and peaceful."

Her voice was low, hypnotic, but he fought the effect. He had to tell her…something. His aching hands kept interfering. He fought the pain as he tried to capture the elusive thought.

"You knew, didn't you?" he said finally.

"Knew what?"

"That the pain might start tonight. That's why you stayed."

She didn't bother denying it, just pressed a finger to his lips. "Quiet. Close your eyes."

Frank didn't want to close his eyes. He wanted to keep staring at the woman who cared so much that she'd spent the night at the hospital on the off chance she might be needed. Despite his efforts, though, the medication began to take hold and he found himself fading out. He fought for one last glimpse of Jenny, who'd drawn the chair close beside him and was gently rubbing his arm. Maybe his own weary eyes were playing tricks on him, but it seemed for just an instant that he could see tears shimmering on her lashes.

He reached out to her, found her hand and touched her gently. "Thank you."

At last he was able to relax into the pain, rather than fight it. Finally, thankfully, the pain dimmed and he fell asleep. This time his dreams were sweet indeed.

Every therapy session over the next couple of days was torture for the both of them. It made the fire and those first days of exercise seem like child's play. Though Frank was in agony, he was stubborn. His therapy sessions were scheduled right after the dressing changes when the medication was in full force, and he was determined not to miss one. Jenny was equally unrelenting. She pushed, and pushed some more. He had to admire her spunk, even as he sometimes cursed her dedication and his own weakness.

He couldn't have pinpointed the precise moment when his feelings for Jenny began to change into something more than respect, when her magnificent, gentle spirit invaded his soul and made him whole again. Maybe it was when she was giving him hell. Maybe it was when she touched his bandaged hands with a gentleness that took his breath away. Maybe it was when he caught the glitter of tears in her eyes, when his pain was just this side of unbearable and neither of them backed away from it. Maybe it was simply when she sat by his bed and talked him through the endless nights. He didn't know quite what to make of the new feelings, but they were there and growing hour by hour.

"Go home," he said after the third night, when she'd stayed with him yet again. "You look lousy."

"Flattery will win me over every time." Her tone was light, but there was no mistaking the exhaustion in her eyes, the pallor of her skin. Even her bouncy red curls seemed limp.

"I'm not interested in flattering you. I'm interested in seeing you get some sleep. You can't stay awake with me and then turn around and work all day."

"I'm okay. I get home for an hour or so in the morning to take a shower and change. Then I sneak in naps in the staff lounge."

"Well, that certainly eases my mind," he said dryly. "Jenny, go home. If you don't, I'll skip therapy, my hands will heal like this and you'll be to blame."

"Oh, no, you don't," she countered. "I'm not falling into that trap. I didn't burn you and I'm not responsible for your recovery. My only obligation is to show you the way to get your strength and dexterity back. What you do with that information is up to you."

"Tell me, does this treatment you're obliged to provide include being mean and nasty?"

"When it's called for."

He grinned. "You think you're pretty tough, don't you?"

"Tough enough."

"Oh, Jenny, I hope you never figure out what a marshmallow you really are."

"A marshmallow?" she said indignantly. "You're not in here wallowing in self-pity anymore, are you?"

"No."

"And who badgered you out of it?"

"You did," he said dutifully. "But, lady, you don't know the meaning of badgering until you've seen what I'm capable of. Go home."

Her chin rose a stubborn notch. "And if I don't?"

"I have the name and number of the director of physical therapy right here." He patted the pocket of the pajamas he'd had Jared bring him when he could stand the flapping, indecent hospital gown no longer.

Those impudent, saucer eyes of hers widened. "You wouldn't dare," she said.

He folded his arms across his chest and grinned. "Just try me."

"That's blackmail."

"I prefer to think of it as tough love."

At the mention of love, Jenny went absolutely still. Her previous serene eyes were filled with a riot of emotions. "You're breaking that vow."

"What vow? I don't remember any vow. You must be hallucinating. Due to lack of sleep, no doubt."

"In this very room. Two nights ago. You were muttering in your sleep."

"Ahh," he said knowingly. "So, now I'm the one who was asleep. You can't hold me accountable for what I said then."

She glared at him. "You woke up and said…something."

"And what did you say to this incredible declaration of… something?"

"I told you that all patients feel that way."

His gaze narrowed. "*All patients?* I am not just any old patient, Jennifer Michaels."

She sighed heavily. "I didn't mean it that way. Why are you doing this? You swore you'd drop this crazy idea that you…" She hesitated, stumbling over the obvious word. "That you like me."

Frank did not recall a single word of the conversation she was describing, but that didn't mean it hadn't happened. The words seemed to reflect all too clearly the thoughts that had been on his mind a lot the past few days.

"*Like?*" he repeated. "Now there's a word without much oomph. No, Jenny Michaels, I can't say I *like* you." His low, suggestive tone left no doubt as to an alternative word choice.

"I'm leaving," she said at once.

His grin broadened. "Now I know the trick," he said smugly. "Mention love and you run like a scared rabbit."

"Nobody in this room mentioned love," she retorted. "And no one will, if they have a bit of sense."

"Yes, ma'am," Frank said as she stalked from the room.

But it was pretty damned hard not to fall in love with a woman with that much sheer audacity. He'd just have to keep his feelings to himself until it suited him—and her—to make them perfectly clear. While he was still in the hospital was not the time, but soon, though. *Very soon.*

Chapter Five

"Hey, Otis! You got a break coming up?" Frank called out as the orderly passed his room pushing Pam to her therapy session. Otis paused, and the teenager gave Frank one of those wobbly smiles that came close to breaking his heart. He winked at her.

"In thirty minutes, why?" Otis said.

"I've got a deck of cards. Care to try a little five-card stud?"

Otis's eyes lighted up. "Stakes?"

"Matchsticks. Aspirin. Nickle-dime. Whatever."

A little of the gambling enthusiasm waned. "Better than nothing, I guess. Where'd you get the cards?"

"My sister. I told her I wanted to play gin rummy."

"Ah, a devious man after my own heart."

Frank shook his head. "No, a man who is bored to tears. Do you know how outrageous daytime television is? I'm not sure I could watch one more talk show deal with men who like to wear ladies' panties or women who've been tortured by drug-addicted kids. It's giving me a very peculiar and very depressing view of society. I will even stoop to luring you into a poker game to escape watching another one of those illuminating discussions. God will no doubt punish me for my sins and for my shortsightedness about society's ills."

"I don't know about God, man, but Jenny's gonna have your hide." Otis chuckled. "Mine, too. I'll be back in a flash."

"Wait a sec," Pam said, a glint of mischief in her eyes. "I want to play, too."

Frank and Otis exchanged a look. "I don't know," Frank said. "Leading Otis down the road to perdition is one thing, but you're just a kid."

"A kid on her way to therapy," she reminded them pointedly, her dark brown eyes very serious.

"Meaning what?" Frank countered, trying to contain a grin at her blatant blackmail tactics.

"Meaning she'll blab her head off if we don't say yes," Otis grumbled. "She and Jenny are thick as thieves." He peered down at her. "You know, Pam-e-la, I just might decide to park you in a linen closet and forget where I've left you."

"You wouldn't dare," she said knowingly. "If Doc Wilding found out, he'd make you pay him back that ten you borrowed to bet on the Giants' opening-day game. A game they lost, in case you've forgotten."

"For a skinny kid who's confined to a bed, you sure know a lot," Otis grumbled.

"Enough," she said proudly. "This place has more gossip than *General Hospital*."

"Okay, say we let you play," Frank said, studying the teenager. "You any good?"

"I can hold my own," she said with what was probably sheer

bravado. Even wrapped in gauze bandages, she managed a jaunty demeanor.

"You know a straight from a full house?"

"I know the full house wins. Four of a kind and straight flush beat that."

Frank grinned and relented, which he'd known he was going to do from the moment she'd asked. Nobody could refuse a kid like Pam, who was trying so hard to be brave and upbeat. "Be in my room in thirty minutes."

Pam beamed. "You bet. Otis, don't you dare forget to pick me up in the therapy room."

The orderly shook his head. "No, ma'am. Wouldn't dream of it." He looked at Frank. "Something tells me the kid here is gonna mop the floor with the two of us."

"I'm not worried," Frank said. Not about Pam, anyway. However, he was just the teensiest bit concerned about what Jenny was going to have to say if she ever found out about the card game.

There was approximately ten dollars in change piled in front of Pam when he found out exactly how Jenny would react. His own neat stacks of nickels and dimes had been dwindling almost as rapidly as Otis's. It didn't matter since Jenny sent the entire supply of change flying with one sweep of her arm. The coins rained down like sleet, tinkling on the linoleum and rolling every which way.

"You two should be ashamed of yourselves," she said, glaring from Frank to Otis and back again, her hands on her hips.

"What about her?" Otis grumbled, turning an indignant look on Pam.

"I was winning!" the teenager protested accusingly to Jenny. "Why'd you do that? I almost had enough to buy a new magazine and a box of candy from the gray ladies this afternoon."

Jenny looked defeated and miserable. She sank down on the side of the bed. "I don't believe this. You've corrupted her."

"Corrupted her?" Frank said. "I'd like to know how. The girl has the instincts of a Las Vegas house dealer. She's a shark."

Pam looked pleased. Jenny didn't.

"And that makes it right?" Jenny snapped. "Couldn't you have played just for fun?"

"This was fun," Frank countered reasonably.

"But you lost how much?"

"A couple of bucks, less than I would have spent to go to a movie, and I can't even get to a movie."

"What about you?" she said to Otis.

"About the same."

"And added to what you've lost this week, how much does that make it?"

Frank interrupted before Otis could respond. "Look, it's my fault, okay? I was bored. I suggested the game. A little cash made it more interesting. That doesn't mean we're all candidates for Gambler's Anonymous."

"Maybe not you and Pam," she said pointedly.

Otis rose slowly to his feet. He glowered down at her. With his size, it would have made Frank think twice about arguing with him. It didn't daunt Jenny in the slightest.

"Don't you try to intimidate me, Otis Johnson," she said. "I thought you wanted to buy a new car, find a nicer apartment. How do you expect to do that if you keep losing your shirt on these crazy bets. Dammit, Otis, you promised."

It seemed a lot of people were making promises to Jenny that they weren't keeping. Frank almost felt sorry for her, but he wasn't sure what all the fuss was about. Making a few bets was no big deal.

"Ain't nothing crazy about betting on a flush, king-high," Otis grumbled.

"Did you win?"

"The kid had a full house. What can I say?"

Jenny sighed. "I don't get it. Where's the fun in throwing away your money like that?"

"Stick around and I'll show you," Frank offered.

"I'm not betting one dime in a card game."

"You won't have to," he promised. He exchanged a look with Otis who apparently guessed his intentions. The orderly suddenly glanced at his watch.

"Break's over," the orderly said hurriedly. "Come on, Pam, I'll give you a push back to your room. Leave those coins on the floor. I'll pick 'em up later."

"And bring me my share," Pam warned.

"Don't worry, kid. You'll get what's coming to you," he promised.

When they'd gone, Frank waved Jenny toward a chair. "Take a seat." He nodded toward the cards. "You'll have to shuffle and deal. Just sit the cards in this contraption Otis rigged up."

She scowled at him. "This is ridiculous."

"You wanted to see why we think poker's so much fun. I'm going to show you. Deal. Five cards."

He watched the way Jenny handled the cards and suddenly the temperature in the room seemed to soar about ten steamy degrees. He imagined those strong, supple hands working their magic on him. The effect on his body was immediate and downright uncomfortable. If Jenny had any idea of what the stakes were now, she'd have run for her life. Instead she shuffled intently.

"You might consider locking the door," he said blithely.

She shot him a startled look. "Why?"

"The game I had in mind isn't meant for observers."

Her gaze narrowed suspiciously. "I thought we were playing poker."

"We are. Strip poker."

The cards hit the table with a smack. Her eyes flashed dangerously. "Oh no you don't, Frank Chambers. Are you out of your mind?"

"What's the matter?" he inquired innocently. "Chicken? You have to admit it would be a whole lot more fascinating than nickles and dimes."

"In your dreams."

He nodded cheerfully. "That's as good a place as any to start."

She bundled up the deck of cards and stalked to the door. "If I catch you trying to lead Otis and Pam astray again, I'll…" She seemed suddenly at a loss for words.

"What?" he taunted, grinning.

"I don't know, but you won't like it."

His smile widened. "Bet I will."

"You are impossible."

"You wouldn't want to bet on that, would you?"

Jenny groaned. "I think maybe I liked you better when you were surly and unresponsive."

"That's just because you don't trust yourself around me now."

"Oh, no," she said. "That's where you're wrong. In fact, that's one bet I'd take you up on."

"Liar," he taunted, but he said it to her back just before the door slammed behind her.

Okay, so she lied. Jenny wasn't quite sure what to make of this mellower Frank Chambers or her own response to him. Though his initial anger had impeded his progress at times, at least it was an emotion she understood. Now, suddenly, his personality had undergone a complete turnaround. He was joking with the staff, playing cards with Otis, no longer badgering the doctors for his release. He was hardly meek, but he was cooperative. She should have been grateful. Instead she was scared to death. He spent so much time in the therapy room these days, he could have taken over with the other patients. Whenever he was there, she had trouble concentrating. Her gaze kept shifting to him, and each time it did, her pulse raced.

As a patient in trouble, Frank had been someone in need of caring, in need of her help. Now she could no longer ignore the warm-as-honey, deep-inside response she felt to the sexy, generous man. The transition endangered her objectivity. Far worse, in the long run she feared it endangered her heart.

She was sitting in the therapy room stirring cream into her coffee when Carolanne came in and sank down in the chair across from her.

"What a day," the other therapist declared wearily. "It's days like this that make me wish I sold little cones of frozen yogurt for a living. No stress. No life-or-death crisis. No temper tantrums."

"Obviously you've never been around a three-year-old whose cone just upended on the ground."

"It couldn't possibly be any worse than this," she said fervently, then turned her full attention on Jenny. "Come to think of it, you don't look so perky yourself. Even your curls have lost their bounce. What's the story, or need I ask? What's the gorgeous Frank Chambers done now?"

"He invited me to play strip poker."

Carolanne's eyes danced with amusement. "Well, well, that is progress. Talk about incentives to get those hands working again. You've obviously inspired him. You should be proud."

"Proud? The man terrifies me."

"Because you're responding to him, right? So what's the big deal? It's about time you let yourself fall in love again."

"Who said anything about falling in love? All I mentioned was a sneaky attempt to get my clothes off."

"A man like that would not strip you naked in a hospital room unless his intentions were very serious."

Jenny groaned and put her head down on her arms. "This isn't happening."

"What isn't happening?"

"Frank Chambers is not interested in me and I am definitely not interested in him."

Carolanne nodded slowly. "Okay. I think I get it. Nothing's happening between the two of you, so there's no reason for you to go crazy, right?"

"Right."

"Then why have you added cream to a cup of cold water?"

Jenny glanced down and saw the murky white liquid in the coffee cup. "Oh, dear Lord."

"*He* might give you an answer," Carolanne said. "But there's someone a lot closer who could really clear things up."

"Who?"

"Frank Chambers."

"He can't clear anything up. He's the problem."

"Why?"

"If I knew that, there wouldn't be a problem."

Carolanne looked more bewildered than ever. "One of us in this room is going to be in need of psychiatric counseling very shortly, and something tells me it's going to be me unless you start talking plain English."

Jenny drew in a deep breath. "All patients tend to form a bond with their therapist, true?"

"Yes."

"So what Frank thinks he feels for me is no more than a passing infatuation, right? Maybe mixed in with some gratitude?"

"That's not the look I saw in his eyes, but I'll go along with you for the sake of this conversation."

Jenny shot her a disgruntled look. "I should be used to that kind of reaction. It's never bothered me before."

Carolanne's expression suddenly brightened with under-standing. "But it does this time, because you're falling for him."

"I am not!" Jenny's blurted denial echoed in the therapy room.

Her friend sighed. "If you say so, though why you're fighting it is beyond me. At least half a dozen nurses on the unit are taking bets on which one can win the man's heart, and he hasn't asked any of them to play strip poker. I'm going home to my simple, uncomplicated cat."

Jenny mustered a faint smile. "There is nothing uncompli-cated about Minx. She's as neurotic as the rest of us."

"Speak for yourself," Carolanne said, getting her purse from her locker. She paused at the door. "Call if you need me, okay?"

"Sure. Thanks for listening."

When the other therapist had gone, Jenny tried to concen-trate on some of the supervisory paperwork entailed in the job, the paperwork she couldn't seem to get done when Frank was in the room. She couldn't work up any enthusiasm for it now, either. An hour later, tired of fighting the inevitable, she headed back down the hall to Room 407.

Outside Frank's door, she could hear the deep rumble of con-versation, the frequent bursts of laughter. Opening the door a crack, she peered inside and saw that he was once again sur-rounded by family. One of the men, a little shorter and stockier than Frank but unmistakably a Chambers, was holding up a handful of paint chips. It had to be Jared, she thought, grinning at the sight of all those shades of blue.

Just as she was about to let the door drift closed, Frank looked up, his gaze locking with hers. That jolt of awareness that came each time their eyes met shot through her. Her knees nearly buckled with the shock of it.

"Hey," he called softly. "Come on in. You're the one who got me into this. You have to choose."

Half a dozen pairs of fascinated eyes immediately turned to her. Jenny tried to ignore the not-so-subtle exchange of glances—from Jared to Frank to Tim to Karyn and yet more of the Chambers brothers she had yet to meet. The family resemblance was obvious, though.

As if they'd sensed her discomfort, every one of the brothers began to talk at once, spurred by Karyn's blatant attempt to distract them with what was clearly a familiar family argument. In the midst of the chaotic babble, Jenny's gaze sought Frank's again. The look in his eyes drew her closer. "Sit here," he said, sliding over on the bed until there was room on the edge.

Seated next to him, hip to hip, her pulse skittered wildly. He held out the dozen or so paint chips. "What do you think?"

The shades ranged from vivid royal blue to palest turquoise, from chalky Wedgewood to deepest azure. The one that drew her, though, was the clear blue tint that matched Frank's eyes.

"This one," she said at once, suddenly oblivious to the crowd of fascinated onlookers. She was surprised when a heated debate erupted over the choice.

"Why that one?" Tim demanded.

"I'll bet I know," Karyn said, meeting Jenny's gaze with a look of instinctive feminine understanding.

Jenny found herself grinning despite the risk of embarrassment. "I'll bet you do, too."

"Why?" came the masculine chorus.

"Never mind," Karyn said briskly, giving Jenny's hand a warm squeeze. "Let's get out of Frank's hair, you guys. I think he's due for another therapy session."

"At this hour?" Jared said, then blinked rapidly at a forceful nudge from his sister. "Oh, yeah. Just like the other night. Let's go, guys."

"Pretty intuitive bunch," Frank said when they'd swarmed out. "Is that what you had in mind, a little therapy?"

Jenny shook her head. "I'm not sure what I had in mind."

"Maybe an apology?"

Her defenses slammed into place. "From me? I haven't done anything to apologize for."

"No, but I have. I guess I didn't realize that you were really worried about Otis's gambling. I've been thinking about your reaction ever since you left here this afternoon. I'm sorry if I did anything to make it worse."

She shook her head, weariness settling in. "I shouldn't blame you. I can't run his life for him. All I can do is encourage him to get help if it gets out of hand. I have a hunch he makes it sound a whole lot worse than it is just to bug me."

"Has he ever borrowed money from you?"

"A few dollars before payday, but he's always paid it back. Other people around here have given him loans, too." She stood up and began to pace. "He's not a deadbeat, though. I don't think he's really in debt to anybody. If it were just a form of entertainment like going to the movies, I wouldn't worry so, but he seems a little compulsive about it."

"And I took advantage of that just to keep from being bored. It won't happen again."

"Thanks."

His gaze fastened on her. "So if you didn't stop by to drag an apology out of me, why did you come?"

"Must be your charming company." She tossed the words out casually, but she sensed that her nervous pacing of the room betrayed her. Frank seemed to see right through her.

"Want to tell me what's really on your mind?" he said quietly. He moved to where she stood by the window.

She wondered what he'd do if she simply blurted out that he was affecting her deeply in a way that made her long for things she'd nearly forgotten: love, family, companionship, romance. Not that she was likely to make that kind of an admission and damage their professional rapport.

"Maybe this?" he suggested, leaning close to brush his lips across hers.

The kiss was no more than the whisper of butterfly wings, but it rocked her. When his arms clumsily drew her closer, she stiffened, then relaxed into the wonderful sensation. His lips covered hers again and this time there was nothing sweet or innocent about the touch. It was all heat and hunger and claiming. If the first had been a gentle spring rain, this was all lightning and thunder. Just when she felt as if the world might be spinning off its axis, buffeted by the powerful force of that kiss, he pulled back.

"Of course, I could be wrong," he said in a voice that was meant to be light, but seemed somehow choked. The blue of his eyes was shades darker than the color she'd matched only moments before.

Jenny couldn't seem to catch her breath or to form a single sensible thought. She was still caught up in the taste and feel of that potent kiss.

"We could always play poker," he teased, when she remained silent.

She finally found her voice and even managed a little feigned indignation. "Forget it. I hid the cards."

"If you really want to stick around, we could watch TV."

That struck her as innocuous enough. "Okay."

Frank moved back to the bed and hit the remote control to turn it on. "There's room next to me, if you'd care to snuggle up."

That kiss made her cautious. She grinned and pulled up the chair. "Don't press your luck."

"Too bad there's no popcorn. What's a movie date without popcorn?"

The cozy image was too appealing to ignore. "I could go get some from the vending machine and put it in the microwave."

"Do you want some, too?"

She thought about it and nodded. "Yes, as a matter of fact. I'm starved."

It wasn't until she'd come back with the popcorn and the sodas that she realized exactly how devious Frank's suggestion really was. The only way he could eat the buttery kernels was if she sat next to him on the bed and fed them to him.

"You're a sneak," she accused as she perched uneasily by his side. "And don't turn that innocent look on me. You're about as innocent as Don Juan."

"You didn't have to share the popcorn," he argued.

"Sure. I could have stayed in the chair, munched away and watched you pout."

"You wouldn't have done that."

"You think you know me pretty well, don't you?"

"Well enough."

"And?"

"I think you've finally decided to stop fighting me."

Jenny sighed and gave herself up to the unfamiliar feeling of contentment that was stealing over her, to the memory of that intense kiss. "Just for tonight."

For once, Frank didn't argue with her. "That's a start, sweetheart. That's a start."

Chapter Six

Frank felt as if he'd been sucker-punched. After days of progress, after days of focusing more intently on Jenny then on his own situation, he suddenly slammed into reality. The bandages were off for good, the skin healed over sufficiently to avoid the danger of infection. He stared at his badly scarred hands as if they belonged to someone else.

Sure, he'd glimpsed them during other dressing changes, but somehow he'd been expecting an improvement, some miracle that would cause the scars to vanish overnight. Now Dr. Wilding was telling him matter-of-factly that wouldn't happen, that the redness would fade eventually, but the scarring was permanent. He tried to imagine spending the rest of his life with this kind of disfigurement. He'd thought it wouldn't bother him. Now his stomach churned at the prospect.

"Not bad," the doctor murmured in satisfaction. "You're lucky, young man. It could have been worse."

Lucky? What was lucky about having hands that ought to be covered with gloves around the clock? He tried to remind himself of the way they'd looked before, of the nicks and cuts, the calluses that had made his work-roughened hands anything but picture perfect. Even that had been a hell of an improvement on this.

Frank finally tore his gaze away from the fresh scars and dared to meet Jenny's eyes. His whole body tensed as he waited for some faint sign of repulsion.

She was frowning, her lower lip caught between her teeth, but he'd come to realize over the past few days that she did that often, whenever she was worried or deep in thought. Slowly her lips curved into a familiar reassuring smile. It reached all the way to her incredible eyes, but Frank wasn't convinced. Doubts very nearly overwhelmed him. What woman would ever want hands like this touching her? He tried to imagine the tight red skin against the perfect pale silk of Jenny's breasts, the curve of her hip, but his imagination failed him.

The anger of those first awful days, the doubts he'd had before about his professional future, were nothing compared to the agonizing emptiness that now stole into his soul. He would never know the sweetness of an intimate moment like that, never to allow himself to sully her perfect beauty with his ugliness.

There was a bitter irony to discovering a woman he could love, only to realize that a relationship between them could never happen. Gentle, tenderhearted Jenny was filled with compassion, not just for him but for the entire world. He'd seen it in the way she cared for her other patients, in the way she worried about Otis. It was sweet temptation to let himself bask in that warmth, to accept her pity and call it love.

He couldn't do it. Filled with a raging anger at the injustice, he vowed he wouldn't. He steeled himself against all the longings that had been building for the past days. It would take every bit of his strength not to act on the desire that teased his senses whenever she was near. That one deep, drugging kiss they had shared the night before would never be repeated, not if he could help it. The minute those discharge papers were signed, he'd walk out of this hospital and out of her life.

As the last days of his hospital stay passed, Jenny knew exactly what was going through Frank's mind. She'd seen it all before. She recognized that gut-deep uncertainty that had him shouting at everyone within range again. The reaction might be typical, but in Frank it was magnified a thousand times because of the kind of man he was. Used to creating flawless beauty, he was being forced to come to grips with imperfection. It might be superficial and unimportant in her eyes or anyone else's, but to his artistic view that first this-is-it view of his burn-scarred hands must have seemed devastating.

After that one instant of raw anguish she'd read in his eyes when the bandages had come off for good, he'd shut himself off from her—maybe even from himself. For the past three days he had come into the therapy room on schedule, but he'd barely spoken. Today was more of the same.

He sat now, his back rigid, doing his exercises with ferocious intensity, oblivious to the beads of sweat forming on his brow, ignoring the tension that was evident in the powerful muscles across his shoulders. When she could stand it no longer, she pulled out the chair next to his and sat. Her heart aching for him, with one hand she reached over and stilled his.

"Enough," she said.

The quiet order brought his head up, his combative gaze clashing with hers. She sensed he was about to argue, but then his gaze slid away. He slowly and deliberately withdrew his hands and hid them beneath the table, his emotional and physical retreat complete.

"No," she insisted and held out her hand. "Please don't ever hide from me. Don't hide from anyone."

As she waited, she could hear each tick of the clock as its big hands clicked off the passing minutes. Finally, an eternity later, Frank put his hands back on the table. Jenny took the right one in hers and gently stroked the marred skin. The muscles in his forearm jerked, then stilled. His jaw clenched, but this time he didn't draw away from her. Nor did he look at her.

"Such wonderful, powerful hands," she murmured. "I've been to see your work, you know. I've never seen anything so beautiful."

"That's over now," he said, his expression bleak.

"You know better than that," she said impatiently. "You've had a temporary setback because of the fire, that's all. You'll work again. You're improving every day. Can't you see that?"

He shrugged with clearly feigned indifference. "Maybe. Maybe not."

She studied him, the way he avoided looking at her, the way he glanced at his hands—and hers—then at the floor, his dismay evident. "You're worried about how the scars look, aren't you?" When he started to shake his head in denial, she stopped him. "No. Don't even try to deny that little bit of vanity. It's perfectly natural."

He regarded her with angry astonishment. "You think this is about something as trivial as my vanity?"

"Isn't it? We're the sum of all our parts, you know, not any one. Yet we have a way of focusing totally on what we perceive as our flaws."

She watched him closely, trying to gauge his reaction. His eyes were shuttered. "Have you ever noticed that?" she prodded. "We're the first to mention an imperfection in ourselves, to draw attention to it, joke about it, just to let everyone know we're aware of it, just to get in the first critical remark. You've heard women joke about their thighs or men kid about their baldness. They want the world to know it doesn't matter to them, when what they're really proving is that it does matter terribly…to them."

Frank listened attentively, but his expression remained skeptical. Not even her touch seemed to reassure him. She tried again to coax him out of his self-pity.

"If you let the scars become important to you, then they'll be important to everyone you know. Accept them, Frank. Accept them, just the way you do the color of your eyes and the beat of your heart. They're a part of a man who's very special."

As she spoke she could feel her throat clog with emotions she rarely allowed herself. Her words had a too familiar ring, dredging up old hurts, old emotions she had thought long buried. A tear clung to her lashes, then spilled down her cheek. When the dampness fell onto Frank's hand, he lifted a startled gaze to meet hers. Whatever he was feeling, though, he covered it, as usual, with anger.

"What the hell do you know about it?" he demanded roughly. "Is this lesson number ten on the road to recovery? It's all so pat. You're good, Jenny. I'll give you that. You almost had me believing you. The tears did it. Did you major in therapy and minor in acting?"

This time she was the one jerking away. This time she was the one who could feel the fury building up like the winds of a hurricane. "Damn you!"

"Someone beat you to it. I've already been damned. I look at these hands and all I see is the ugliness, all I feel is the pain. How can you even bear to touch them?"

"What you feel is self-pity, you arrogant, self-centered jerk!"

For the first time in her career, Jenny allowed her fury to

overrule her professional demeanor. It felt wonderful. She couldn't have banked the anger now if her entire career had depended on it. Emotions that had little to do with Frank and much to do with her own tattered pride came pouring out.

"Do you think you're the only person ever to be badly scarred? Do you?" she demanded. "There are a dozen patients in the unit right now who are worse off than you. Some will have hideous facial scars that no amount of surgery will fix. Some will be lucky to survive at all."

He waved a hand dismissively. "I'm not talking about them. I know that compared to them I'm damned fortunate. I look at Pam and it makes me sick to think what she'll go through. Right now, though, I'm talking about you. Where do you get off telling me or any one of the others how to feel, how to live our lives and accept ourselves? I'm sick of the platitudes, sick of the condescension."

She stared at him in astonishment. "Condescension? You think that's what this is all about? Damn you, Frank Chambers hasn't it ever occurred to you that I could know exactly how you feel? *Exactly!* Maybe my scars aren't visible, but they're there."

He opened his mouth, but she cut him off, her outrage unmistakable. "You listen to me for once," she insisted. She sucked in a deep breath, then said more quietly, "When they cut off my breast to rid me of cancer, they left me with an ugly gash across my chest. Oh, the surgeon was good enough. He prettied it up with neat stitches, but there's no mistaking that kind of wound. You try telling me, telling any woman that losing a breast doesn't matter. Try telling us we're still whole. We won't believe you. Every swimsuit ad, every television commercial, says otherwise. We know what feminine beauty is all about."

She was barely aware of Frank's sudden indrawn breath, the tenderness that instantly replaced cold fury in his eyes.

"Don't you get it?" she asked him. "We can only learn to live again when we can say it to ourselves, when somewhere deep inside we do believe that we're whole and attractive despite the scars. So, don't you act like some macho jerk because your hands aren't pretty. You'll live, dammit, and in the end that's the only thing that matters."

"I'm sorry," Frank whispered, his voice ragged. He was shaken to the very depths of his being by Jenny's astonishing tirade and even more unexpected revelation. When she turned away, when she would have run, he grabbed her, oblivious to his own pain, tormented by hers and the inadvertent way he'd added to it.

"Don't you know how beautiful you are?" he said, holding her. He raised his fingers to her cheek, hesitated, then forced himself to caress the silken curve of her jaw, knowing as he did so that from this moment on he would be lost. There would be no turning back now from the love he felt for her, from his need to protect and cherish her. He wouldn't be able to make the noble sacrifice of walking away, not when she was filled with so much pain, so many doubts of her own. "Don't you know how proud any man would be to be with you?"

A deep sigh shuddered through her, but still she wouldn't look at him. Her gaze was fixed firmly on the floor as if there were something in the pattern of the tiles more fascinating than anything he could possibly say.

"Jenny, I'm sorry. I'm sorry for being such a fool."

She sighed heavily and her arms slid around his waist. She pressed her cheek, damp with tears, against his chest. "You don't get condemned to hell for being a fool," she muttered finally.

"Maybe not by God," he agreed. "How about by you?"

She lifted her head then, very slowly. More tears had welled in her eyes and were spilling down her cheeks. "I've never condemned you for hurting, Frank. I've just wanted to make it stop. I've just wanted you to know that I understood what you're going through. It's not easy picking up the pieces and going on when life slams you with a setback like you've had, but you have to do it. Sooner or later, you have to let go of the anger and do whatever needs to be done."

"And have you done that?" he asked, certain that she hadn't been nearly as good at taking the advice as she was at dishing it out. "Have you let go of the anger?"

"Most of the time. Maybe it's easier for me, because I can hide the scar. I don't have to deal with it, not out loud."

He studied her closely and sensed that there was so much she wasn't saying, so much she might not even be admitting to herself. "But out loud isn't the hard part, is it?"

She gave him a wobbly smile. Like Pam's brave attempts, it shattered his heart.

"No," she admitted. "It's what happens deep inside in the middle of the night. That's when there's no stopping the doubts, no holding back the terror."

As Frank held her, he prayed she could feel the compassion surround her, strengthen her if only she'd let it. For some reason, though, he could tell she was holding back, refusing to take what he was offering.

"Have you been with a man since the surgery?" he asked out of the blue, guessing suddenly at the real reason for her torment. Some fool had fed her doubts, had failed to offer the reassuring touch that she had just offered him. His voice was gentle, but from her instantaneous transformation, he saw that the question ripped through her defenses and opened old wounds. Jenny reacted to the raw pain with instantly renewed fury.

"How dare you ask me that? Have you forgotten what our relationship is? It's professional. I'm a therapist. You're my patient. No more. That doesn't entitle you to pry into my personal life."

"You opened the door. From the first day you walked into my room, we've both known there was something more between us, something we couldn't walk away from if we tried."

"No," she denied too quickly. She raised her hands as if to ward off any further painful intrusions. "You're wrong."

Backing away from him, from the emotions, she said, "I have to go. Dr. Wilding intends to discharge you in the morning. I'll try to come by before you leave."

But she didn't come by. Frank waited, watching the door all morning. When he could stand it no longer, he left his room and walked down the hall to the therapy room. Otis was standing just outside the door.

"Hear you're going home today," the orderly said. "How am I supposed to win any money with you gone?"

"I'm afraid my gambling days are over."

"So she got you, too?" he asked with a chuckle. "That woman thinks she can save the whole wide world. She's got a good heart." Eyes the color of melted chocolate watched Frank's reaction. "You ain't mistaking that for something else, are you?"

Frank shook his head. What he felt for Jenny was no mistake. What she felt for him was just as powerful. He had to convince her of that. He had to apologize, though, for the way he'd intruded so crudely into her personal life last night, asking questions that he hadn't led up to first with flowers and sweet words to prove how much he cared. He had to show her that there was no need for secrets between them. He had to know if some foolish man had shattered her fragile self-esteem with a careless remark, a flicker of revulsion at the sight of her scars.

He would spend the rest of his life making that up to her, proving that she was all woman, both inside and out.

"Is she in there now? I need to see her."

"She's with a patient." He didn't move an inch, his body blocking the door.

Frank's gaze narrowed. "Otis, did she say something to you about me?"

The orderly's expression remained perfectly bland, but there was no mistaking the streak of protectiveness in his stance. "Is there something to say?" he countered.

Frank sighed. "No. Nothing. Tell her I'll be in my room another hour or so. Kevin's picking me up on his lunch hour."

Jenny had recognized what was happening with Frank even before last night. Hell, she and Carolanne had even talked about it. She'd had patients think they were in love with her before. She'd blithely ignored their protestations, knowing that as soon as the link of therapy was broken, they would resume their old lives. They had. And once Frank left today, he would be no different.

Except in her heart. Something about the wonderful, foul-tempered beast had gotten to her. He had so much love to give. He was a living monument to the theory that the more love you gave, the more you had to give. She'd never met a man who had more people relying on him and who thrived on it so.

For nearly two weeks now she'd been on the fringes of all that love and loyalty, and she'd felt like a kid with her nose pressed to the window of a toy store. But as much as she'd come to care for Frank, as recklessly as she'd indulged in her fantasies about sharing the warmth of his family, a life for the two of them simply wasn't in the cards. Once he'd coped with his own scars, she wouldn't burden him with hers.

She hadn't planned to tell him as much as she had about the

breast cancer. It wasn't something she hid from her friends, but it certainly wasn't relevant to their patient-therapist relationship. At least it never had been with any other patient. If they'd thought her compassion deeper than most of the staff's, they'd never seemed to wonder why. With Frank, though, a lot of things about that professional relationship were shifting like sands at the whim of an angry tide.

She was standing just inside the door of the therapy room when she thought she heard his voice. She could hear Otis's mellow tones countering Frank's. Her heart climbed up to her throat and seemed to lodge there. When it was finally silent again in the hallway, she peeked out.

"He's gone," Otis said dryly, "though why you'd want to be avoiding him is beyond me. I ain't seen a man so far gone over a woman in a long time."

"I think the psychological term is transference."

"Funny, I thought it was lust."

She glowered at him. "You can leave now, Otis."

"I've done my part, so you don't need to listen to what I have to say? I don't think so," he said, backing her into the room, his big hands shooing her toward a chair. "You sit for just a minute, miss, and let me tell you what I see here."

"Otis!" she warned.

"Don't you go all prim and proper on me. You and me, we've always understood each other, from the day I wheeled you down the hall to surgery and back again. You held this hand of mine and spilled your guts, so I guess I've got a pretty good idea what's on your mind now."

"Otis, I really don't want to talk about this," Jenny said.

"That's okay by me. You can just listen. That's a fine man who just left here. Any man who's got the love of a family the way he does has done something special to deserve it. You'd do well to hang on to him. If you don't, that's up to you. The way I've got it figured, though, you owe him."

She opened her mouth to argue, but he kept right on lecturing. "You're the one who single handedly gave him the will to fight. You abandon him now, he just might give up, and we both know he's a long way from being recovered. Now you can send Carolanne or one of the others over there to help him settle in at home, and you can assign one of them to work with him when he comes in as an outpatient, but that's the coward's way out. Maybe I'm wrong, but I don't think you're a coward."

He waited a beat, his gaze expectant. Jenny could feel her cheeks turn pink. Satisfied with her embarrassed reaction, Otis nodded. "I guess I've said my piece. You think about it." He turned on his heel and walked out, leaving her with more to think about than he could possibly imagine.

"But I *am* a coward," she whispered to his retreating back. She wasn't just running from Frank. She wasn't simply afraid of loving.

She was terrified she wouldn't be around long enough to make it last.

In her heart, she knew Otis was right. She couldn't abandon Frank now. If it took every ounce of courage she possessed, she would see this through to the end.

Chapter Seven

Frank stood in the doorway of his private woodworking shop at home, unable to tear his gaze away from two intricately carved, skillfully crafted cabinets in unfinished cherry and oak. He rarely did his cabinetry at home, but these had been special orders and he'd spent his spare time rushing to complete them. His dedication had saved them from the fire. He wondered, though, if they would ever be finished, if the twining flowers along the edges would ever reach as high as he'd intended.

His gaze moved on to the smaller, partially carved blocks of wood that sat amid the fragrant shavings on top of his worktable. Smooth, polished pieces, ready for a summer gallery showing, lined a shelf along one wall. Each one was a triumph of his artistic imagination over nature. It wasn't until he'd studied the grain of the wood that he decided what shape it would take. It was as if each square or rectangular block spoke to his mind's eye. Stepping inside, he slowly approached the complete figures, his heart aching at the prospect of never again being able to create such beauty.

He'd heard it said that the first step in any difficult task was always the hardest, and this one had been pure hell. It had taken him days just to work up the courage to come this far. He'd insisted that Kevin shut the door to the back room the day he'd come home from the hospital. He'd skirted the room ever since, not even glancing at the closed door when he could avoid it. He'd spent the days going for walks. Long, exhausting walks. Nights, he'd lain in bed and thought of Jenny and a future that seemed even emptier without her. It was still impossible for him to accept that she hadn't come, that she'd meant it when she'd said there could be nothing between them. And he thought of the painful revelation that, to her way of thinking, might have made it impossible for her to come. He drifted to sleep eventually filled with terrible questions.

When he'd awakened late this morning, he'd known he could no longer put off the inevitable. He had to know just how bleak the future was, just how crippling his injury had been. Once he knew that, maybe he'd know what to do about Jenny as well, whether he dared to pursue her, whether he'd have the strength to help her face her own demons.

Now that he was inside the room with happier memories crowding in, risking it seemed like a lousy idea. Maybe it would be better not to know just how terribly inept his fingers had become. Maybe he should just accept that fate had intervened and set his life on a different course. But what course? What the hell would he do with the rest of his life if not this?

For years, beginning at the age of seventeen, he had taken safe, low-paying, unskilled jobs to help out at home. Only when his extra income was no longer needed had he dared to begin the uncertain career that had beckoned to him from the first time he'd held a stick of wood and been taught whittling by his Tennessee-born father. From the first day of his apprenticeship to a master craftsman, he'd been filled with a soul-deep sense of accomplishment. What if all that was truly over? How would he handle it? Could he go back to those other less challenging, less satisfying jobs?

Finally, when he could bear it no more, he reached for one of the unfinished pieces. Gritting his teeth against the pain, aware of the tautness of his skin as it stretched almost beyond endurance, he closed his hand around the chunky block. With an artist's tender touch, he rubbed his still raw fingertips over the wood, stroking it as if it were alive, caressing the rounded shape of a blue jay's belly as it emerged from the uneven surface.

There were those who said that it was possible to distinguish each fragile feather on figures he'd carved. On this piece he had yet to complete the basic carving, much less start the delicate detail. Fingers trembling, he reached for his knife. Slowly, painfully, he closed his hand around it, defying Jenny's warning not to rush his attempts to hold smaller objects, not to allow his expectations to soar too high. With grim determination, he touched knife to wood, only to have the sharp instrument slide from his feeble grasp.

With a muttered oath, he picked it up and tried again, ignoring the agony, ignoring the sting of perspiration that beaded across his brow and trickled into his eyes, ignoring the sick churning of fear in his belly. Again, the knife clattered to the floor.

With each faulty effort, with each demoralizing defeat, his determination wavered, but he tried again...and again. Sweat ran down his back. His arms and shoulders ached from the effort of trying to master no more than a firm hold on what had once seemed a natural extension of his body.

It was on his tenth try or his thirtieth—he had lost track—when he heard the whisper of sound. He turned to find Jenny standing in the doorway, her face streaked with sympathetic tears. The leaden mass that had formed in his chest grew heavier still at the sight of her brokenhearted expression.

"How'd you get in?" he asked dully, his shoulders slumping.

"I knocked. I guess you didn't hear me. I tried the door and it was open." With her distraught gaze fixed on his hands, she said, "You shouldn't be doing this. It's too soon."

"I had to try. I had to know the worst."

Something that looked like guilt flickered in her eyes. "I should have been here," she said, almost to herself. Her gaze rose, then met his. "You're my patient. I should have come the first day you missed your outpatient appointment."

"Why didn't you?" he asked accusingly.

"It just seemed so complicated. I kept thinking you would come back to the hospital. Today, when you missed the second appointment, I knew there was no choice. I had to come."

The weight of her guilt got to him. "Don't go blaming yourself," he said, feeling a twinge of guilt himself. Had he known that staying away would bring her to him? Maybe so. Maybe the real blame was his. He said only, "I knew the risk I was taking by not continuing the therapy. I figured a few days off couldn't matter all that much."

"A few days?" she questioned. "Or were you really giving up?"

He shook his head. "Not until today."

Tears welled again in her eyes, but she blinked them away. "I won't let you do that, Frank."

Those tears were going to be his undoing. "Don't cry," he pleaded, his own voice ragged with emotion as he found himself offering comfort to a woman whose slightest smile had come to mean comfort to him. He yearned to take her in his arms, to touch her as he had no right to touch her, to show her what she'd come to mean to him.

She started to speak again, then shook her head.

"What the hell," he said with pure bravado, hoping to win a smile, an end to the unbearable tension throbbing between them. "I can always hold the handle of a saw. Maybe I can build houses."

"You will carve again," she vowed. "I promise."

Grateful beyond belief that she had come at last, Frank was still in no mood for promises that might never be kept. In a gesture of pure defiance, he swept his arm across the worktable, sending wood and tools flying. "No, dammit! Don't lie to me, Jenny. Never lie to me. Let me adjust. Let me get on with my life."

A familiar mutinous expression settled on her lips, firmed her jaw. She swiped away the tears. "What kind of a life will it be, if you can't do what you love?" she demanded. "You can't stop trying."

"I can," he said, just as stubbornly. "And I will."

She sucked in a breath and stood straighter, every inch filled with that magnificent indignation that could have daunted kings or generals. He was no match at all when she declared, "I won't let you."

Frank's laugh was mirthless, just the same. "Jenny, there's not a blessed thing you can do about it," he mocked.

As if he'd thrown down a gauntlet in some medieval challenge, she marched into the room. "Watch me," she said, picking up the first tool she came to and slapping the handle into his hand. "Squeeze it, damn you."

Raw pain seared his flesh, but by instinct his fingers curved around the instrument, the skin stretched taut, the nerve endings on fire.

"Tighter," she demanded, her body pressed against him in a way that had him thinking of things far softer than oak, far more compelling than carving. The force of the desire spiraling through him shook him to the very core of his being.

Their gazes clashed, hers filled with furious determination, his own filled with God knew what revelation. When the knife threatened to slide from his grasp again, she folded her own hand around his, adding enough pressure to secure it. Every muscle in Frank's body tensed at this new and very difficult strain, but he refused to let go, refused to acknowledge the agony of the effort. Jenny was clearly willing to goad him into trying, and he was too stubborn and too proud not to accept the challenge. Nor could he bear the thought of her moving away. God help him, he wouldn't deny himself the sweet, sweet pleasure of her nearness.

"You know the drill," she said finally, her voice oddly breathless. "Ten minutes an hour."

"Who's going to be around to make me?"

"I am."

"Your job as my therapist ended when I walked out of the hospital."

Green eyes sparked with emerald fire. "Like hell. A condition of your discharge was that you continue therapy as an outpatient. If I hadn't come today, Dr. Wilding would have sent me over to find out where the hell you've been."

Despite himself, Frank's lips twitched with amusement. A whisper of relief sighed through him, and he felt himself begin to relax. "Think you're pretty tough, don't you?"

That earned a dimpled smile that faded quickly into a clearly feigned scowl. "You bet," she declared.

"And if I don't cooperate?"

"You don't want to know what kind of tortures I can invent for an uncooperative patient."

He chuckled, fully aware of the kind of tortures she could

impose without even trying. His body ached from them. "Is that so?" he taunted. His gaze fastened on the lush curve of her lips.

"Care to test me?" she taunted right back.

"Lady, I intend to give you a run for your money." He winked as he said it, suddenly feeling better, more hopeful, even if hope was folly. "By the way, what do I get if I cooperate?"

"You get to work again."

"I had something a little more intimate in mind."

"I'll just bet you did," she retorted. As if suddenly aware of the way her body had molded itself to him, she backed away, a step only, but it was too far for him. Frank wanted to curse at the sudden deprivation.

"You finish that blue jay and then maybe we'll talk," she said.

"Talking is the last thing on my mind," he said bluntly so there could be no doubts about his intentions.

A blush crept into her cheeks, but her eyes were stormy. Hands on slender hips, she said, "Mister, if your hands heal half as well as your libido, you'll be in great shape in no time."

At the sound of a deep-throated chuckle, they both whirled around to see Tim lurking in the doorway. Amusement danced in his eyes. "Hey, Bro, what's this about a libido? I thought I had the reputation in the family for chasing skirts."

Disgruntled by the untimely interruption, Frank said, "Listen, *Bro,* you're interrupting my therapy."

"Oh, is that what this is? Where can I sign up?" He winked at Jenny, and the brazen little hussy winked back. Frank wanted to throttle them both as the charged atmosphere disintegrated. Another few seconds of sparring, another half dozen words of challenge and Jenny would have been in his arms, maybe even in his lonely king-size bed just down the hall. A betting man— Otis—could have made book on it.

"If you don't get out of here in the next ten seconds, your broken arm will qualify you," Frank said grumpily.

Jenny shook her head. "Okay, enough, you two. I'm out of here. Play nice."

Tim's eyes widened at the teasing admonition. "You sound just like Ma."

"Is it any wonder, when you sound like a couple of five-year-olds?" She turned her very best, most intimidating therapist-to-patient glare on Frank. "And you, ten minutes every hour. Got it?"

"Have you ever thought of a career in the military?" he inquired.

"Why, when I have guys like you to order around already? Be at the clinic tomorrow. Bring your tools with you. We might as well work with the things that are relevant to you."

"Why not have the sessions here?"

There was no arguing the logic of the suggestion, but Jenny's instantly terrified expression spoke volumes. She wasn't about to spend an hour a day with him in his home, where they both knew that therapy would take second place to mounting desire.

"Policy," she said tightly, her tone daring him to contradict her.

Much as he wanted to, suddenly Frank didn't have the stamina for it. The previous hour had stolen the last of his reserves of energy.

"I'll be there," he said.

When she nodded, secure again in the victory, he added, "But don't think you're one bit safer there, Jenny."

Patches of pink colored her cheeks for the second time in minutes. Avoiding Tim's laughing gaze and Frank's challenge, she scooted to safety.

Only when she had sashayed out of the room, the determined picture of feigned self-confidence, did Frank collapse onto his workbench. He was exhausted with the strain of coming into this room, of confronting his frailty all over again. The swing of his emotions from hope to defeat and back again had taken its toll.

Tim's expression immediately turned worried. "You okay?"

"Just a little tired."

"From the therapy, or from the stress of keeping your hands off the therapist?"

Frank grinned ruefully. "The only interest the therapist has in my hands is their increasing manual dexterity."

"Sounds promising."

"Very funny."

Tim's expression sobered. "What about you? You're really attracted to her, aren't you?"

"What's not to like? She's beautiful. She's bright. She's caring. She's gentle. She's sexy. And all she feels for me is pity." He said the last as a diversion, praying it wasn't entirely true, unwilling to admit it might be.

"I don't think so."

"You didn't see the look on her face when she walked in here an hour ago."

"Did it ever occur to you that maybe it was compassion, not pity? Jenny strikes me as a woman who feels things deeply. Maybe what she was feeling was the ache inside you. Anyone who knows you can see what kind of hell you're going through."

Frank prayed that Tim was right, that his own instincts about Jenny's susceptibility to him were equally on target. He regarded his brother curiously. "You know something, little brother? I think maybe I've been selling you short all these years. Under all that flirtatious, chauvinistic attitude beats the heart of a true romantic. I predict that once you truly fall for a woman, it's going to be a crash heard round the entire Bay area."

"God, I hope not. We have enough quakes as it is."

* * *

Jenny discovered that just because Frank was on her turf, just because he'd agreed to continue the therapy at the hospital's outpatient clinic, it didn't stop the lingering looks. Every time their fingers brushed, her whole body came alive. It was the most amazing reaction. She would have sworn that his were the damaged nerves, yet she felt as if it were her own that were healing. Contact meant only to guide took on a deeper meaning. She began to long for those casual, innocent touches, needing them for the good they did her, rather than the comfort and guidance they gave him. It had been years since she'd allowed herself to hunger for that kind of physical closeness.

She was careful, though, to make sure that there were always other patients around. When the scheduling failed her, she begged Carolanne to stay in the therapy room to finish paperwork.

"What are you afraid of?" Carolanne demanded. "Frank Chambers is getting too close, isn't he? He's tearing down that wall of reserve, brick by brick."

"That's about it."

"What's so terrible about that?"

"Yeah," an all-too-familiar voice echoed. "What's so terrible about that? I'm a nice guy."

With a fiery blush creeping up her neck, she turned to meet Frank's laughing eyes. Carolanne made a beeline for the door. "Traitor," Jenny muttered as her so-called friend left.

When Carolanne had gone, she bustled around the therapy room, giving orders, avoiding Frank's gaze, ignoring the thudding of her heart, the quick flare of heat deep inside.

"What'd you do last night?" he inquired casually as he dutifully began his exercises.

She blinked up from the paperwork she was pretending to

read and stared at him. He didn't usually ask personal questions. "What?"

"I asked what you did last night."

"Why?"

He grinned. "What's the problem? That's a fairly typical question among friends. Fits right in there with 'Hi, how are you?' So, what did you do?"

She had to search her brain to recall what had filled the lonely hours until sleep had claimed her. "I read a paper on the importance of infection control in burn therapy."

"Sounds dull," he said, but he looked smug for some reason that eluded her.

"Actually it was fascinating." She launched into a desperate detailing of every word she could remember. She was only sorry the paper had been so short. More of the medical jargon might have dampened the unmistakable gleam she saw in his eyes.

"Still sounds dull," he said when she'd finished. "How come you didn't have a date?"

"Why the sudden interest in my social life?"

"I've always been interested in your social life. I've just never asked about it before."

"Why now?"

"Just scouting out the competition."

"There is no competition. You're not even in the running." The rapid clip of her pulse called her a liar.

So did the skeptical look in Frank's eyes. A lesser man would have been insulted. He apparently twisted the words to suit himself. "We'll see," he countered mildly.

Flustered, and determined not to let him see it, she moved to stand squarely in front of him and demanded, "Why are you doing this?"

"Doing what?"

"Trying to turn this into something personal. I can't continue working with you, if you insist on doing that. I'll have to turn you over to Carolanne."

"Hmm," he muttered thoughtfully. "That raises an interesting point."

"Which is?"

"If you're no longer my therapist, then you'd be free to go out with me. Am I interpreting this correctly?"

Jenny felt as if she were falling off the top of a very tall building with no net below. The sensation was heady but terrifying. "No. Absolutely not. That is not what I was saying at all," she sputtered with enough indignation to draw an unrepentant grin.

"You know what they say about ladies who protest too much."

Jenny might have slapped that smug expression right off his face, if she hadn't had just enough sense left to realize how he'd interpret that. "That's no protest, buddy," she said quietly. "That's a fact. You and I are patient and therapist or we are nothing. Is that clear enough for you?"

He smiled happily, which was not the reaction she'd been going for at all. "Very clear," he said cheerfully.

Why, if he was being so agreeable, did she have the feeling that she'd just lost a dangerous final round?

Chapter Eight

"I could really use some help from you in the kitchen," Frank mentioned casually to Jenny at the end of his third outpatient therapy session. "If you're not too busy, that is."

Jenny's instantly suspicious gaze shot to his. It was astonishing how deeply she distrusted his motives. Rightfully so, in this instance, he conceded ruefully.

"Meaning?" she said.

"I keep dropping those little microwave containers. Half the time my dinner ends up on the floor."

He made it sound as pitiful as possible, as if he were very likely to starve to death without assistance. The time had come to take drastic measures if he was going to get Jenny to begin trusting him outside the safety of the therapy room. For the time being, he wasn't going to worry about how trust might suffer when she discovered his sneaky, underhanded tactics.

"Couldn't your mother or Karyn help you out?" she suggested, a definite note of desperation in her voice. "Maybe your brothers could take turns."

Actually they had been doing exactly that, but Frank was not about to admit that to her. He didn't need their company. He needed hers. He needed the incredible lightness that his soul experienced when he was surrounded by her tenderness and optimism. He needed to give back to her some of the strength she'd shared with him. Most of all he needed the hot, urgent stirring of his blood that just being in the same room with her brought.

"Ma's been really good about bringing things over for dinner," he admitted. "It's getting them on the stove and then the table that's the problem. I don't want to tell her that, though. She'd just worry more than she already does. As for Karyn, she's left town with Brad while he preps for the Indy 500. She's a lousy cook anyway."

"That still leaves five brothers."

Fortunately Frank had anticipated all of her arguments and prepared. "Tim's working nights and he has his law classes all day. Jared's just started helping a neighbor paint his house. The others do what they can, but I want to be independent. I'm not used to having other people wait on me. If you could help me out a little, maybe fix up some gadgets so I could handle things better, I'd be able to make do on my own. A few more weeks and I should be past the worst of this, right?"

Suspicion darkened her eyes again. He could tell she was torn between that and the very real possibility that he hadn't had a decent dinner in days. "I'll come by tonight," she said finally. "About six?"

"Whatever's good for you. Consider it a treatment. Put it on my bill."

She scowled at him. "Don't be ridiculous."

"No, really. I want this to be strictly professional. I don't want to take advantage of you. I know how you feel about me not stepping over that line."

He sounded so noble, he couldn't imagine her not believing him. Even so, there was a long silence while she obviously continued to weigh his apparent sincerity against her doubts. "You can share the dinner with me. That'll be payment enough," she said finally, though she was clearly unnerved by the prospect of sitting across from him at a dinner table. She was staring at the wall when she made the offer.

"That'd be great," he said with a shade too much enthusiasm. He quickly banked it, when her gaze shot back to him. "I mean, if you have the time."

"I do," she said curtly. "Shall I pick up the groceries, or do you already have something you'd like me to fix?"

"Surprise me," he said, his gaze locking on hers. He lowered his voice to a seductive pitch. "I really love surprises."

"Frank," she began, her voice filled with renewed doubts.

"Yes?"

She sighed. "Never mind. I'll be there at six with the groceries."

"Reach in my pocket and grab my wallet," he suggested. "There should be enough in there for what you'll need from the store."

She looked every bit as panicky as if he'd blatantly suggested they make love in the linen closet down the hall. "This is my treat," she said hurriedly, taking a quick, revealing step back.

"No. I insist. How can it be your treat, if dinner is supposed to be my way of paying you back for cooking it?" He fixed his most innocent gaze on her. "My wallet's in the back pocket." He helpfully turned his backside to her.

Jenny complied with the enthusiasm of someone told they could have a million bucks as long as they didn't mind a few electrical shocks during the snatching of it. Only a seasoned pickpocket had the knack for removing a man's wallet without intimate contact. But for all her gifted hand gestures in therapy, Jenny was no pickpocket, and the photo-crammed wallet was a snug fit.

His breath caught in his throat as her hand slid nervously into his back pocket. Clumsiness turned the move into a lingering caress. Heat roared through him. Every nerve in his body throbbed in awareness. Even after Jenny had the wallet and was extracting a twenty-dollar bill, Frank trembled. If she was equally shaken, she hid it well, leaving him to wonder just who'd been the victor in this devious war of nerves.

Only when she glanced up and he saw the riot of emotions in her eyes did he declare the victory for himself. She shoved the wallet back in his pocket with so much force, he was surprised the denim didn't rip.

"I'll see you at six," she said and raced from the room.

Laughing, Frank went down the hall in search of Pam. Aware of the monotony of a long hospital stay, he'd been dropping by after his therapy sessions. He found her in her room with the TV on, but her face was turned toward the wall.

"Hey, beautiful, how are you?"

Instead of greeting him with her usual courageous, perky smile, the teenager kept her face averted. Then Frank noticed that the bandages on her head were gone. He swallowed hard against the tears that seemed to clog his throat at the sight of the red, scarred skin stretched taut over her cheekbone.

Drawing in a deep breath, he went around the bed and pulled up a chair. "Where's my smile?" he demanded, looking straight at her. "I thought you'd be glad to see me."

She tried to turn away again, but he touched her shoulder. "Don't," he said.

A tear slid down the unmarred side of her face. "But it's so awful," she whispered, pulling a pillow over her head. Her voice was muffled, but he could make out the rest of her heart-broken words. "I didn't know it was going to be like this. I'd seen the other patients, but I thought I'd be different."

Frank moved to the side of the bed, tugged the pillow gently away and forced her to face him. Then he opened his arms. With a sob, Pam launched herself at him and clung. "I'm never going to have any friends. Never. And I can't blame them. Who'd want to look at this?"

"I would," he said, his heart aching. "You know why? Because nothing that's important about you has changed. Inside, you're the same wonderful, funny, feisty girl you always were. You know what Jenny told me once?"

"What?"

"She said that how we react to our own flaws will determine how others react to them, too. If you're very brave, if you concentrate on how beautiful you are inside, then that's what your friends will see, too."

She sniffed and looked up at him hopefully. "Do you really think so?"

"I know so," he said, praying it would be so for her, praying that she'd chosen friends who wouldn't cruelly abandon her.

"My dad can't even stand to look at me."

"Oh, baby, I'm sure that's not true."

"It is. He was here when Doc Wilding took off the bandages. He walked out and he hasn't been back. That was hours ago."

Frank wanted to curse the man's insensitivity, even though he could understand what a shock it must have been to see his once-gorgeous, vivacious teenager so cruelly scarred.

"I think maybe he's just hurting inside because of what happened to you," he said finally. "He's probably feeling a whole lot of guilt that he didn't do something to prevent it from happening."

"But the fire wasn't his fault," she replied adamantly. "He wasn't even home when it happened. He was away on a business trip."

"That's exactly what I mean. He's probably telling himself if he'd been there, it wouldn't have happened."

"He always told Mom not to smoke in bed. He told her," she said, her voice thick with sobs. She stared helplessly into Frank's eyes, touching his soul. "Oh, God, why did she have to do it anyway? Why didn't she listen?" And then in a low, sad cry, "Why did she have to die? I tried to get to her, but I couldn't, I just couldn't."

Frank felt as though every breath was being squeezed out of him as Pam revealed what had happened at home the night she'd suffered these terrible, disfiguring burns. He'd never known, never realized what torment this poor child was dealing with. It made his own injuries seem insignificant. For the first time since the accident, he realized how truly fortunate he had been. Pam had the additional burden of grief and guilt weighing on her, when recovery alone would have been challenge enough.

He stayed with Pam for what seemed like hours, rocking her in his arms, wishing he had the words or the certainty to swear to her that things would be okay. Finally he noticed a man only slightly older than himself standing in the hallway, his face haggard, his eyes red-rimmed. He motioned to him.

"Pam, honey," he said gently. "You've got company."

Pam slowly faced the door. "Daddy." Her voice quivered with hope and fear. This time her father didn't flinch, didn't look away. He moved to the other side of the bed and sat on the edge. Pam eased away from Frank and held out her hand. Frank held his breath until finally the other man grasped Pam's hand

and pressed his lips to the scarred flesh. "I'm sorry I ran out before, baby."

"Oh, Daddy," she whispered.

Frank left them together, praying harder than he ever had in his life that they would be okay, that together they could handle the grief and anger and pain ahead.

He was greatly subdued when Jenny finally arrived at his house just after six. He led her into the kitchen, pointed out where things were, then sat at the table to watch as she immediately set to work. Her motions were efficient, yet he found them subtly provocative. Her quiet calm was soothing. There was comfort in her presence tonight, a comfort almost more important than the fierce longing that usually tormented him the instant she was near.

When the dinner was bubbling on the stove, she poured them each a glass of iced tea and sat down across from him. The look she directed at him was inquisitive.

"You've been awfully quiet ever since I got here. What's going on?"

"I saw Pam today after I left you."

She nodded, her own expression suddenly tired. "I heard you'd been visiting her regularly. She had a pretty rough time of it today. She said your visit helped."

Still troubled by the teen's anguish, he asked, "Will it get any better for her?"

"Not anytime soon. She has a lot of plastic surgery ahead."

Frank sighed wearily. "That poor kid. She could probably use some counseling as well. I had no idea how much she's been struggling to cope with."

"She's already seen the psychologist a few times. She'll make it. She's a fighter. She'll get past the shock of the scars and be ready to move on to the next step."

"That's what I told her. I found myself quoting you."

She grinned. "I'm glad something I said made an impression."

"Everything you said made an impression. I didn't always want to hear it."

"That's pretty much par for the course with burn patients."

He shook his head as he envisioned contending with emotional crises like Pam's day in and day out. "Jenny, why do you do this? How can you take it day after day? I know we talked about this before, but I'm just beginning to realize the toll it must take."

"It's what I do, the same way you're an artist. Can you imagine being anything else?"

"I suppose not, though I have been other things from time to time to help pay the bills."

"You've held other jobs," she corrected. "But only one career really means anything, right? I think maybe what I went through with my own surgery makes me even better able to deal with the fears patients have. I truly understand how scared they are, how damaged they feel."

The reminder of her cancer surgery surprised him. It was the first time she'd mentioned it since the day she first told him about it. He wanted to keep her talking, sensing that there were more things she needed to say, but probably never had. "Who's been there for you when you needed a shoulder to cry on?"

She dumped a spoonful of sugar into her iced tea and stirred it for so long he thought she might not respond. Finally she said with studied nonchalance, "Family, friends. Otis was with me when I went into the operating room. Usually the orderly just wheels you into pre-op, but he stayed right by my side until they put me under. I'll always be grateful to him for that."

Frank didn't even try to hide his dismay. "Your parents weren't here?"

She shook her head. "Actually I didn't tell them until after it was over. There wasn't any point in worrying them. There wasn't a thing they could do until I knew what I was up against."

Frank regarded her incredulously. "They could have been here for you. That's what families do. They share the bad times and make them a little easier."

She gave him a faint smile. "That's what *your* family does."

There was just a hint of envy in her voice. Frank wanted to say right then and there that it could become her family, too. The thought slammed into his consciousness like a car going sixty. In an instant of absolute clarity, he knew that was what he wanted more than anything else. He wanted to marry Jenny Michaels and teach her all about love and laughter and family, as she had taught him about fighting back and recovering. Although his physical wounds were not yet healed, thanks to her his emotional wounds were very nearly a thing of the past. He knew that no matter whether he carved again or not, he would be just fine as long as she was with him to make his blood race and his spirits soar. He could cope with whatever the future brought.

He also knew that she would run if he suggested it, if he dared to hint at what he was thinking. He couldn't imagine why she was so terrified of him. He'd never before encountered a woman so skittish. Megan had found being with him and his family totally comfortable. And his one or two other reasonably serious involvements had been with women who'd been quick to accept the idea of a relationship.

Not that he was such a prize, he amended quickly. But most women found him uncomplicated and nonthreatening. He tended to say what was on his mind. The directness and lack of pretense appealed to women who'd encountered too little of either. Jenny was clearly the exception. She regarded him every bit as warily as she might a snake…or a notorious Don Juan.

Who had created this distrust in her? Was he the specific target or was it all men? He had to understand her before he could expect to make any progress.

Jenny had moved back to the counter to roll out the biscuit dough she'd prepared earlier.

"Any special man in your life?" he inquired lightly, reopening a topic she'd successfully evaded in the past.

The rolling pin hit the dough with a thud. "I thought we'd discussed this."

"We did. Your answer wasn't very illuminating."

"Why do you want to know?" she said as the pin hit the dough again, sending a puff of flour into the air like late-afternoon fog rising on San Francisco Bay. Her gaze was carefully averted. Biscuit dough had apparently never been so fascinating.

"Curiosity," he admitted candidly.

"Prying is more like it."

"Let's try this from a different direction," he said. "How do you spend your spare time? You can't possibly read medical journals every night."

"Actually I could, but I don't."

"When you're not reading them, what do you do?"

He caught the subtle hesitation before she said, "I go to movies."

"Good. Now we're getting somewhere. I like movies." He listed several. She hadn't seen any of them. "What was the last movie you saw?"

She frowned, then finally named one.

"Sure," he said cheerfully. "I remember that one. It won an Academy Award."

She blinked at him. "It did?"

"Sure did." He paused, then added, "Last year."

"Oh." Her voice was meek. Her fascination with the biscuit

dough increased. If she rolled it any flatter there wasn't a baking powder in the world that could make those biscuits rise higher than a silver dollar.

"So far we've accounted for one night in the last year that you didn't read a medical journal. Anything else?"

"Aerobics class," she said in a rush, looking ridiculously pleased with herself. "I take aerobics."

"And?" he prodded.

"And what?"

"There has to be more, I mean for a woman with an active social life such as yourself."

"We go out to dinner after class."

"We?"

"A friend and I."

"Must be a woman friend."

She glared at him. "Why must it be a woman? Men take aerobics."

"But if it had been a man you'd have told me all about him ten minutes ago to get me to shut up and leave you alone."

Ignoring his comment, she cut out half a dozen very flat circles and slapped them onto a cookie sheet, then put the tray into the oven.

"They'll do better if you turn on the heat."

She whirled on him then, flour-covered hands on slim hips. "I don't have to do this, you know."

"I know," he said very seriously. "Why are you doing it? Why did you come?"

"Because you asked me to. You said you needed help."

"I need you," he corrected.

She was shaking her head in denial before the words were out of his mouth.

"It's true," he insisted. "In fact, I think if I don't kiss that smudge of flour on your nose within the next ten seconds I might very well die."

She stared at the floor until he reached out with the tip of his finger and tilted her chin up. Her gaze was defiant.

"Do it, then," she challenged. "Just do it and get it over with."

He grinned at her attempt to stare him down. "You're not going to shame me into backing off, by implying that I'm pushing you into something you don't want."

A reluctant sigh shuddered through her. "Who says I don't want it?" she asked.

Frank was taken aback by the hard-won admission. "Oh, Jenny," he murmured, drawing her slowly into his arms. With a sigh of his own, he settled his lips on hers. After an instant of stunned stillness, her arms circled his neck. Her body melted against his. Her skin was warm and flushed from bending over the stove. Her soft springtime scent drifted around them. She tasted of tea and sugar and a dusting of flour. It he held her in his arms like this for a lifetime, he knew his hunger for her would never be sated.

His fingers traced the line of her brow, the curve of her jaw. With each touch, she trembled. With each touch, his need built. One kiss would never be enough. He wanted to discover everything about her, every curve, every texture, every taste. His hand slid to her hips and tilted them up tighter until neither of them could deny the heat or the urgency. Then, without thinking of anything except the hunger to know every shape, every intimate detail of her body, he touched her breast, the caress as natural and needy as breathing.

With a startled cry, she broke free.

"No," she whispered tearfully, backing away. "No. This can't happen. Not ever."

And then she ran.

Chapter Nine

When the realization of what he had done slammed into him, Frank cursed himself for an insensitive fool. By the time he recovered from the shock of Jenny's anguished reaction to his touch, she had left the house, leaving the door wide open behind her. He raced outside and saw that in her haste to escape, she'd simply run, leaving her car parked halfway down the block. He took off down the hill after her.

He caught up with her at the corner. She was huddled under the street lamp, her arms hugging her middle against the chilly night air that plagued San Francisco even in May. She stood perfectly still, as if she couldn't make up her mind what to do next, where to go. With the silver mercury light filtering down on her through the fog, she looked lost and alone, so terribly alone. He reached out to her, but she seemed to withdraw to some safe and distant place he couldn't reach. As he put his hands in his pockets, Frank felt the painful wrench of her hurt deep inside.

"Jenny, please," he said urgently. "I'm sorry. I didn't mean to upset you. I wasn't thinking. I just knew how much I wanted you, how much I thought you wanted me. Let's talk about what happened, about why you're so scared. We can work this out."

"There's nothing to talk about," she said flatly. "Nothing."

The emptiness in her voice shook him, but the determination was worse. How could he fight that? "At least come back to the house," he urged as a first, crucial step. "It's too cold to be out here without a jacket."

As if to prove his point, she shivered. He pressed her then, afraid that she'd wind up sick if she stubbornly insisted on staying outside much longer. "I promise not to bring up what happened until you're ready," he said with reluctance. "And I won't touch you, if that's the way you want it."

Her eyes reflected her distrust and again he cursed himself. How much damage had he done in that one careless moment? In instinctively seeking to touch her breast, to discover every shape and texture of her, apparently he had reminded her graphically of her own fears of being an incomplete woman, her obviously deep-seated terror that she couldn't satisfy a man. Because she radiated such strength and self-confidence, he had forgotten that she was a special woman with a need for very special care, especially the first time they became intimate. He owed her all of the gentle tenderness that she had shown him when it came to his own scars.

Now he could only wait and pray that the damage of his gesture wasn't irreparable. Eventually a sigh seemed to shudder through her. Without a word, she began to slowly climb the hill. When she didn't stop at her car, Frank released the breath he'd been holding.

When they were finally outside his house, she stopped and looked up. The faint beginnings of a smile tugged at the sad, downturned corners of her mouth. "You did it," she said in a trembly voice. Tears she hadn't shed earlier sparkled in her eyes. "You painted it blue. I didn't notice when I came in."

"Jared finished yesterday. You chose the color, remember?"

She looked from the house to him and back again. "I was right," she said finally.

"About what?"

"It does match your eyes."

He chuckled. "So that's what Karyn's been gloating about. She guessed, didn't she?"

"She never said, but I think so."

"There's a touch of the romantic in you after all, isn't there, Jenny Michaels?"

She immediately shook her head in denial. "I'm a hard-headed realist. Ask anyone."

"You'd like to believe that, because it's safe, but it's not true," he said just as adamantly. "You have the same dreams as any other woman."

"What makes you think you know anything about a woman's private dreams, especially mine?" she said, a trace of anger in her voice, but an expression of undeniable yearning on her face.

"I know because you shared them with me in that kiss. We felt the same things, the same wanting not to be alone, the same need to love."

There was a spark of defiance in her eyes. "Chemistry. Pheromones. Lust. Not dreams."

"Oh, no," he said with certainty. "A woman like you could never separate the two. You would never let some casual lover get that close. You wouldn't take the risk of being rejected." He knew he was taking a risk himself by so bluntly stating the facts as he saw them.

For an instant, Jenny looked as though he'd slapped her.

Then, to his relief, she began to laugh. "Giving me a taste of my own medicine, aren't you? No man's ever been that direct with me before."

He stared at her for several heartbeats, then said gently, "Maybe no man has ever cared as much as I do." He held out his hand. "Come inside."

It was ten seconds, thirty, an eternity before she sighed deeply and slid her hand into his.

Inside, Frank was careful to keep his distance, to let Jenny set the tone and the pace. The thawing of icy tension was slow, but eventually they laughed about the hard-as-rocks biscuits and savored the rich beef stew. They talked about old movies— the only ones Jenny really had seen—and about sports. To his astonishment, she was both an avid football fan and an ardent baseball fan. Unfortunately she foolishly preferred the Boston teams to his own 49ers and Giants. She cited flimsy statistics in support of her imprudent loyalty.

"I hope you don't actually bet on your convictions with Otis," he teased, relieved that they were close to recapturing the earlier friendly tone.

"I don't bet anything with Otis," she reminded him. "Though goodness knows, he tried to convince me to wager against him by offering outrageous spreads. What the devil is a point spread anyway?"

"Considering your views on the evils of gambling, you don't want to know. You'd probably confiscate his paycheck and make him live on an allowance."

"I can just see him agreeing to that."

Frank laughed with her, then turned serious. "I doubt you have any idea just how persuasive you are. I think you could get a man to agree to just about anything."

She looked startled, then pleased. She held his gaze for just an instant before looking nervously away and getting to her feet. "Even helping with the dishes?" she said with the kind of rush born of deep-rooted caution. She was not going to make things easy for him. There would be no overnight burst of faith, no quick readjustment of her tendency to hide behind a brusque professionalism.

He wiggled his inept fingers at her. "I don't have enough dishes in the house for me to go tampering with the ones I do have."

"You could manage if you really wanted to," she countered, the mood settling comfortably at last into the light banter with which she obviously felt more at ease. "I seem to recall that you have a particular aversion to doing dishes. I think you're just using your injury as an excuse to get out of helping."

He grinned back at her. "But you'll never know for sure will you?"

"Maybe not," she said as one of his few good plates seemed to slide from her grasp. With his lightning-quick reflexes, Frank caught it in midair.

"Then, again," she observed, amusement dancing in her eyes, "looks to me like your recovery's a whole lot further along than you've been letting on."

"You little rat," he muttered. "You did that on purpose to test me."

She grinned. "You bet. You wash. I'll dry."

For the first time in his life, Frank actually enjoyed doing dishes. He was tempted to pull out every mismatched plate, every scarred mug and chipped cup in the cabinets just to keep Jenny around a little longer. He knew that the minute they were done, she'd go, fleeing her emotions, chasing the illusion of safety.

In fact, as it turned out, she had her jacket on and her car keys in her hands before he could drain the water from the sink. He didn't waste time arguing with her.

"I'll walk you to your car."

Wishing he could do the gallant thing and open the door for her, he stood by helplessly while she unlocked the car and got in. "Thanks for tonight," he said, when she'd rolled down the window.

Jenny nodded, her face upturned expectantly as if waiting for his kiss. Frank leaned down and brushed his lips across hers, fighting against the urge to linger and savor the velvet warmth. "It's not over, Jenny Michaels. Not by a long shot."

He whistled as he turned and walked back up the hill. It was a very long time before he heard the car start and saw Jenny drive off.

Frank made a resolution as he lay awake later that night. With the finely honed instincts of a man used to caring for others, he had seen through Jenny's veneer of steel to the fragility and insecurities underneath. For the first time he realized that the complexities of his own recovery were nothing compared to hers. She had taught him all about acceptance and fighting back. He was about to teach her all about joyous, unconditional love. Though his financial future was uncertain, he could offer her that much at least.

He would start his fight to overcome Jenny's shattered self-esteem with tender, potent kisses. He had seen the longing in her eyes, so much longing that it made him tremble. And, no matter what she said, there was no doubting that she had kissed him back. She would again. It would just take some old-fashioned wooing.

He might, he decided reluctantly, have to get a few tips on that from his experienced baby brother.

Tim was delighted to help out with some expert advice over lunch the next day. So, unfortunately, were Kevin, Jared, Peter and Daniel, who turned up en masse. The word that big brother had the hots for the therapist spread through the Chambers clan faster than a wildfire on a windy day. Even Karyn, still in Indianapolis with Brad for the Indy 500 trials, knew by dinnertime. She called just to stick in her two cents.

"I knew it," she gloated. "I knew that she was crazy about you the day she came out of your room all hot and bothered because you wouldn't do your therapy."

Frank groaned, tempted to hang up on her, but unwilling to give her the satisfaction. "Karyn, at that point the woman had spent approximately fifteen minutes with me and I was not especially charming. I don't think she was smitten. I think she was mad."

"Anger. Passion," she said dismissively. "They're both pretty powerful emotions. People get them confused all the time."

"Another five minutes of this and I am going to get passionately angry at you."

"Don't threaten me," she countered cheerfully. "It's payback time. You've been meddling in our lives from day one. Do you recall the night you stormed into Brad's hotel to rescue your precious baby sister from his evil clutches?"

"Only too well."

"I've never been so humiliated in my entire life. I may not rest until I've had a chance to get even."

"The man lied and said you weren't there," he reminded her. He was still none too pleased about that, but he had to admit that Brad was treating Karyn okay. The two of them were obviously crazy in love.

"He lied to protect my honor," she said. "It's about time you forgave him for that. Now let's talk about you. Forget anything Tim or the rest of those chauvinistic brothers of ours told you. Here's how you go about winning Jenny's heart. Trust me…"

Jenny did not sleep well, not that night, not for days. Like an old-fashioned newsreel, the scene in Frank's kitchen played through her head. Her panic was just as real in the middle of the night as it had been at the time.

Only once since the surgery had she allowed a man to touch her as intimately as Frank had. She had thought she loved Larry Amanti, thought he loved her. He had been warned about the scar. He'd told her it didn't matter, had sworn that he loved her just as she was. Then, when he had stripped away her clothes, when she was naked and vulnerable, she had seen the flicker of revulsion in his eyes, had shivered as he tried desperately to overcome his instinctive reaction and touch her anyway. Humiliated beyond belief, she had yanked the sheet around her and ordered him from her bed. He had fled, gratefully if the look in his eyes had been anything to go by.

In the days and months that followed, she'd realized that perhaps she was the one who had overreacted. With her insecurities close to the surface, she had never given him a chance to adjust to the disfigurement for which no amount of advance warning could adequately prepare a man. Even with that new self-awareness, though, she was not prepared to take the risk again. Rejection was always painful, but it would be doubly so if it came from a man like Frank, a man with whom she'd fallen hopelessly in love because of his kindness and sensitivity.

Although she couldn't bring herself to turn Frank's therapy over to Carolanne—it would be an open admission to him that she did fear what was happening between them—she did keep her distance. Not once over the next couple of weeks did she squeeze his shoulder in encouragement or place her hand on his to add pressure to his grip. The slightest contact seemed to stir desires she had no business having. It was better not to feel that flaring of heat, better not to respond to that tug deep within her, better not to experience the racing of her pulse.

To her chagrin, Frank seemed oblivious to the withdrawal

of physical contact. If anything, he was even more business-like than she was. He smiled. He joked. He even winked on occasion, a gleam of pure devilment in those wicked blue eyes of his. But his attention never wandered very far from the exercises. When the sessions were over, he thanked her politely and went off to visit with Pam, leaving Jenny vaguely discontented and out of sorts. He was doing exactly as she wanted, wasn't he? So why did she feel so damned lousy?

One day, feeling thoroughly abandoned, she followed him down the hall, then lingered outside Pam's room as the two laughed uproariously over stories she couldn't quite overhear. She hated to admit, even to herself, how much she missed that easy camaraderie, the teasing banter, the undeniable sexual overtones that made her pulse tremble.

"Eavesdropping?" Otis inquired from behind her.

Jenny backed up so fast she almost stumbled over his big feet. "No, of course not," she said.

Otis shook his head and rocked back on his heels. "You two got to be carrying on the strangest romance I ever did see."

Though her cheeks burned with embarrassment, Jenny retorted quickly and, she hoped, convincingly, "Romance? There's no romance between Frank and me."

Otis rolled his eyes. "You expect me to believe that? I've seen the way you've been mooning around here the last couple of months."

"Yes, I do expect you to believe it, because it's true."

"Oh, Jenny, Jenny. Are you just lying to me or to yourself, too?"

"Go away, Otis."

He grinned at her. "I'm going," he said. "By the way, I'm betting on a fall wedding. Don't let me down. I've got a bundle riding on it."

Horrified, Jenny chased after him. When she caught him, she

backed him against the wall, fire in her eyes. "Who would you make a bet like that with?" she demanded. "Otis, if you've been spreading gossip all over this hospital, you are history, dead meat…" She searched for a fate so terrifying it would put the fear of God into him.

"Don't go getting yourself in a dither. The bet's with Pam."

"Pam?" she repeated incredulously. Her friend, her pal, was engaging in bets with Otis behind her back? And about her wedding to a man she was barely even speaking to?

"She's betting on May," Otis said cheerfully. "Personally, I don't think either you or Frank is smart enough to make a move that fast. Only a few more days left in the month. Told her that, too, but the kid's a real romantic. She really wants a May wedding. She's probably in there right now working on Frank."

Jenny clenched her teeth. "There will be no wedding," she said slowly and emphatically. "Not in May. Not in the fall. Not ever."

Otis's smile spread across his face. "You want to make a bet on that, too? I'll give you great odds. Wouldn't even mind losing this one. I like the man. I think he's good for you. Puts a little color in your cheeks. Like now. Pink as can be."

Jenny groaned and went back to the therapy room, where she threw every piece of foam rubber in the place as hard as she could. When that didn't even dent her frustration, she started on noisier supplies. The door opened just as a jar sailed across the room. Frank ducked as it shattered mere inches from his head.

"Having a bad day?" he inquired lightly.

"A bad day. A bad week. A bad month."

"Something happen after I left?"

"No." Nothing that she was about to admit to him.

"Been to that aerobics class lately?"

"What aerobics—" She stopped herself as she recalled that

she'd told him about the way she spent her evenings. "Oh, of course, I told you about those. I forgot."

"Forgot you told me or forgot to go?"

She was very tempted to tell him to go to hell just to wipe that smug grin from his face. Instead she inquired testily, "Did you come back for a reason?"

"Sure did. I meant to tell you earlier that Tim got tickets for a Giants game tonight. He can't go. Want to come with me?"

Peanuts, popcorn and Cracker Jacks, all the lures of the song about the ballpark tempted her to say yes. "It wouldn't be a date or anything, right?"

He nodded agreeably. "Whatever you say."

How much trouble could she possibly get in with thousands of people around? Frank would be so busy yelling, he wouldn't even have time to notice her. Lately he hadn't seemed to notice her all that much anyway. "Okay," she said finally. "What time?"

"Now," he said at once.

"Now?"

"I didn't want to give you time to think it over and back out. Let's go."

During the first inning, Jenny was thoroughly self-conscious. She kept waiting for Frank's hand to squeeze hers, for his arm to slide around the back of her seat, for one of those bone-melting looks. His eyes never once left the ball field, and his hands were occupied with those peanuts and that popcorn she'd been daydreaming about earlier. She munched her own popcorn in oddly disgruntled silence.

By the third inning, she was just hoping for some small sign that he remembered she was there at all. When a soft-drink vendor passed by on the aisle, Frank actually blinked, glanced in her direction and inquired if she wanted anything. She was absurdly grateful for the attention and took a soft drink she didn't even want.

When the crowd stood for the seventh-inning stretch, Jenny decided there was no longer anything to fear…or hope for. Frank had brought her to a ballgame because he knew she liked baseball. It wasn't part of some grand seduction scheme. Why did that seem to irk her so when she had no intention of letting their relationship progress?

She was still pondering that when the game ended with a winning bases-loaded homer by the Giants center fielder. Suddenly Frank's arms were around her and he was swinging her in the air. His genuine exuberance was contagious. She was still laughing with him when the innocent embrace turned serious.

She slid slowly down the length of his body as he lowered her feet to the ground. She was aware of every inch of contact, every exciting flare of heat between them. Her breath left her as her toes touched down. Fortunately Frank showed no intention of releasing her. If he had, she was certain her knees would have buckled.

His gaze searched her face, his blue eyes darkening with desire. Her own heart was pounding.

"Oh, damn," she murmured finally as the strength for the battle with her own emotions ebbed.

Frank gave a low chuckle at her heartfelt sigh. "Yeah, I know what you mean."

"You did this deliberately, didn't you?"

"Did what?"

"Kept your distance until tonight, until just now?"

"I was advised by an expert that heightened anticipation can accomplish miracles."

Jenny felt something shift inside her at his hopeful expression. "Frank, don't," she warned, but without much force.

He grinned at her faint warning. "Don't waste your breath. This is one argument you will never win. I intend to prove to you that what we have isn't going to vanish overnight, that it isn't some quirk of the patient-therapist relationship. I love you, Jenny Michaels, and one of these days you're just going to have to accept that."

Jenny wanted to. Dear God, how she wanted to. But fate had dealt both of them a couple of low blows. She didn't trust it not to have another one in store.

Chapter Ten

It took Frank three weeks after the baseball game to convince Jenny to once again spend some time with him outside of the hospital. She displayed an inordinate amount of distrust of his motives. No doubt that had something to do with the undeniable arousal he was sure she'd detected when he'd taken her into his arms in the bleachers at the end of the game. It they'd been anywhere but in the middle of a stadium, she might not have escaped so easily. At the very least, he would have kissed her the way he wanted to, slowly and deeply and convincingly.

"Hey, I'm fighting for my life here," he teased, trying to overcome her reluctance with the humor she seemed to prefer to serious declarations. "What's one measly little afternoon? Surely you can trust yourself not to attack me and ravish me in that length of time."

Her brows rose a disapproving fraction. "I'm not the problem," she reminded him pointedly.

"Handcuff me," he suggested.

She chuckled at the outrageous option. "I don't think we need to go that far."

Frank seized the faint hint of surrender. "You're wavering. I can tell. What'll it take? A promise written in blood? A chaperon? I'll even ask Karyn to fly home and take your side. She'd love the chance to give me a little grief. She claims I made her dating life a living hell."

Jenny immediately appeared fascinated. "How? Too protective?"

"Maybe a little," he admitted ruefully. "She's itching to even the score. I will invite her, though. Just say the word."

"No," she said finally. "I guess I can trust you."

"Your faith is overwhelming."

"Don't pout. Besides, I'm not finished. I'll agree to see you, but only if I get to choose what we do. Something therapeutic."

Frank groaned, but agreed. "Anything you say. What's it going to be?"

"You'll see," she said with an unexpectedly impish little gleam in her eyes. "Sunday afternoon at three. Be ready. I'll pick you up."

Frank was so enthralled by the gleam in her eyes, so caught up in the seductive possibilities, that he forgot all about the Chambers Sunday dinner tradition. When his mother called that night to remind him, as she had every week since he'd moved out of the family home, he braved her wrath and announced, "Can't make it this time, Ma. I've got an important date."

Her startled silence lasted no more than a heartbeat. "Important?" she repeated with obvious fascination. "You'll bring her along. That's no problem."

"It's a problem. She's already made plans."

"What plans?"

"I don't know. It's a surprise."

"Well, you just surprise her and tell her you're coming here. Is it Jenny?"

"Yes."

"Wonderful. She'll fit right in. Four o'clock, same as always."

She hung up before he could argue. Maybe they could do both, he thought reluctantly. Maybe Jenny wouldn't mind at least dropping by for dinner, though the prospect of subjecting her to the fascinated examination of his family on a more concentrated level than the ones she'd been exposed to at their hospital visits was daunting. Tim and the others were not known for their subtlety. The already-skittish Jenny was likely to take off before dessert and never speak to him again.

He hadn't been off the phone five minutes when it rang again.

"Frank?"

From the sudden leap of his pulse, he would have known it was Jenny, even if he hadn't recognized that tentative note in her voice. The only time she ever sounded that uncertain was when she was talking to him about their relationship, rather than the progress of his therapy. "Hi. Didn't we just see each other? You aren't calling to cancel our date already, are you?"

"I'm not sure. I just had the oddest call from your mother."

Frank muttered a curse under his breath. He should have guessed she'd leave nothing to chance. "What did she want?" he inquired, though there wasn't a doubt in his mind that she'd taken that Sunday dinner invitation into her own capable hands.

"She said she wanted to personally invite me over on Sunday. She seemed to think you might not relay the message, something about a traditional family dinner."

"An astute woman, my mother."

"Frank, is your family getting the wrong impression about us?" Jenny definitely sounded troubled.

"I doubt it," he said. "It seems to me they've got it pegged."

"What?" She sounded even more alarmed.

"Never mind," he said quickly. "What did you tell Ma?"

"What could I say? I told her I'd be delighted, but Frank, I am not delighted." Each word was said with slow emphasis.

"Then we won't go. I told my mother we had plans."

He heard Jenny's deep sigh. "I tried that, too. She doesn't seem to take no for an answer. That's when I caved in and said yes. That woman should pick a charity and become a fund-raiser. She'd rake in millions."

"Believe me, I know the feeling. Trying to argue with her is like jogging straight into a brick wall. It's up to you, though. We do not have to go, no matter what you told her. I'll take care of it. I don't want you to feel uncomfortable," he said, though, now that he thought of it, the idea of watching Jenny interact as a part of his family held an undeniable appeal.

Now that she knew she had his support, she seemed to hesitate. "Is everyone going to be there?"

"Everyone. I think these Sunday dinners were part of the compromise when we all started to move out. We swore that we would always come back once a week."

"Then you can't very well back out of this one. You go. We'll do something another time."

Frank grabbed desperately at the first response that came to him. "And have my entire family know that you broke our date because you were scared of them?"

"I'm not scared of them," she countered. "Well, not exactly, anyway. I just don't want them to get the idea that there's anything serious between us."

"It might be too late for that," he admitted. "They all know how I feel. If you don't show up Sunday, I guarantee each one of them will probably pay you a visit to tell you what a great guy I am. I don't think any of them will beat you up…"

He allowed the possibility to linger before adding, "They're not usually violent. We all do tend to be pretty protective, though."

There was a long pause before Jenny said, "Are you saying I might have to listen to six separate sales pitches on your behalf?"

"Seven. Ma's a real tigress. Come to think of it, *she* might beat you up."

Jenny finally started chuckling. "You're teasing me, aren't you?"

"Oh, no, sweetheart. This is gospel."

"It might almost be worth it to stay home and see who turns up to list your attributes."

"You already know my attributes. Well, most of them, anyway. I'd be glad to share the rest anytime you're ready."

"I'll just bet you would. Okay, forget my surprise. We'll go to dinner with your family. But I swear to you, if the words wedding or marriage even creep into the conversation in a whisper, I'll turn you over to Otis."

"That's no threat," he scoffed. "He's on my side."

"I was hoping you didn't know that."

"I'm sure you were. See you Sunday."

Frank found himself looking forward to the prospect with a very odd mixture of buoyant optimism and gut-deep dread. The combined forces of all the Chambers would either win Jenny over, or scare her away for good.

Jenny stood outside the Chambers's small, unpretentious home, Frank beside her, and battled the flutter of a thousand butterflies in her stomach. A fresh coat of paint in sedate white lost its innocent air in the red trim. The combination reminded her of the family, old-fashioned with an intriguing hint of quirky daring. Frank epitomized those qualities, though she doubted he saw himself that way.

There was no mistaking the fact that he'd been courting her for all these weeks now, setting a pace that was just shy and patient enough to relax her guard. At the edge of all that caution, though, was the sly promise of dangerous desires about to be unleashed. Jenny was captivated, despite her best intentions to maintain a careful distance between herself and the man who was so trustingly offering her his heart.

She'd been lured here today by curiosity and longing. It seemed like forever since she'd felt part of a family. Never had she even imagined belonging to a clan as boisterous and tight-knit as this one. She'd been unable to resist the chance to spend one brief afternoon in an environment filled with warmth and acceptance and love. It might be the only chance she ever had to experience what it could have been like had she dared to believe in Frank's love, had she dared to make a forever commitment. Though she would never have admitted it to him, she was indulging herself in a dream, a dream that was both alluring and forbidden.

"You're shaking," he observed, snapping her out of her lovely daydream. "Scared?"

"Of course not."

"Then you're a braver soul than I am," he said fervently, making her laugh and forget her fears.

"They're your family," she reminded him.

"Then my reaction ought to tell you something. Are you sure you wouldn't rather go skydiving?"

"Absolutely not. I can't wait to see why they have a grown man like you quaking in your boots."

He grinned and held out his hand. "Then let's get it over with."

Before they'd made it up the front walk, the door was thrown open. Mrs. Chambers, wearing a simple navy dress with a prim, lacy, white collar under her apron, waited for them with a beaming smile. She wiped both hands on the apron, then held them out to Jenny. "Welcome, Jenny. Come in. We've been waiting for you. Everyone's here."

As they walked toward the living room, Frank leaned down and whispered, "I warned you. They've never been on time before. Today they couldn't wait."

His mother hushed him. "Maybe they just knew I was making pot roast."

"Ma, you always make pot roast on Sunday."

"I do not. Just last week we had chicken."

"Tasted like pot roast to me," Frank said.

"Me, too," Tim concurred, popping into the hallway. "Looked like it, too. Must have been all those carrots and baby onions you used to hide the meat."

Mrs. Chambers glared indignantly at the pair of them. "Keep it up and there will be no apple cobbler for the two of you."

"Cobbler again?" Peter chimed in with an exaggerated groan as he joined them.

His mother waggled a finger in his direction. "Just for that, you can set the table. Now. Jenny, you go on in the living room and sit down. Daniel, Kevin and Jared are in there. Don't let them gang up on you. If they start giving you a rough time, you can come hide out with me in the kitchen."

Jenny laughed. "I think maybe that's my first choice anyway. Can I come now? I'd like to help."

Frank's eyes widened in dismay. "Bad idea," he warned. "The woman will try to pry information out of you. No secret will be safe. She's going to want to know what your intentions are."

Mrs. Chambers patted Jenny on the shoulder. "Don't listen to a word he says. You come right along. The rest of you, play nice," she added in an echo of Jenny's own advice to Tim and Frank weeks earlier. Jenny understood now why Tim had teased her so over the comment.

Jenny had thought she'd feel safe in the kitchen, out of the reach of all those prying eyes, away from Frank's hopes and everyone else's expectations. And at first she did feel safe. At first it was comforting to be surrounded by the heavenly smell of the roast, the cinnamon-scented cobbler, the yeasty aroma of rising rolls.

"What can I do?" she offered.

"You can sit right over there and talk to me," Mrs. Chambers said, waving Jenny toward a curved breakfast area. She gave Peter a handful of silverware and shooed him toward the dining room. She brought over a bag of beans and began snapping them as she sat across from Jenny. "You've been seeing Frank for a while now, isn't that right?"

"At the hospital," Jenny replied cautiously, trying to decide if the question was innocuous or the start of an inquisition. She grabbed a handful of beans herself and clumsily tried to imitate Mrs. Chambers's quick, decisive motions.

Mrs. Chambers shot her a perceptive look. "Just another patient, right?"

"No, of course not. I mean…oh, dear," she murmured, falling neatly into the maternal trap set by Mrs. Chambers.

"Frank's a fine man," his mother reported.

"I know that."

"Took on a lot of responsibility at an early age."

"I know."

"Just look at this kitchen. He fixed it up for me, put in new cabinets, that fancy tile."

"It's beautiful," Jenny said honestly. The white, glass-fronted cabinets gave the room an open, airy feeling. The white tile floor and single row of red accent tiles amid the white on the walls added to the cheerful ambience. The built-in breakfast nook was a similar combination of white Formica and red seat covers. "Did Frank build this breakfast area, too?"

Mrs. Chambers beamed with pride. "Isn't it something? Used to be a pantry here. He knocked out the wall and the next thing you know the kitchen was nearly twice as big as it used to be. How many men would have thought to do that?"

Jenny admired all the extra touches that she was certain were Mrs. Chambers's, the framed prints on the walls, the bright dish towels, but Frank's mother wasn't interested in her own contribution. She was pushing her son's. In case Jenny hadn't gotten the message, she added, "He'd make a wonderful husband."

"Mrs. Chambers, really, Frank and I are just friends."

"Good way to start."

"Start?" Jenny said weakly.

"Of course. My husband and I started out as friends, too. Makes a lot more sense than the way kids do things these days. They fall into bed, get married and then discover they don't have a thing in common. Do things slow and you do them right. You two take your time, if that's what you need."

Suddenly the large room seemed to be closing in on Jenny. "But…" The protest was barely begun before it was interrupted.

"Of course," Mrs. Chambers said cheerily, "I always did think a fall wedding was mighty nice. The church could be decorated with bright yellow mums. Karyn would look real good in that coppery shade that you see in all the fancy fashion magazines."

"Karyn?"

"Of course, I don't mean to be pushy. I know you have your own friends, but I always think it's nice if someone from the groom's family stands up with the bride, too, don't you?"

"In theory," Jenny said, wondering desperately if there was any polite way she could escape to the living room or find a pit of vipers to throw herself into. If she stayed here much longer, she was liable to end up married before anyone heard her protests. She crumbled the beans in her hands into little, bitty pieces before she realized what she was doing.

The kitchen door swung open. "How's it going in here?" Frank inquired. "You two getting acquainted?"

"Oh, my, yes," his mother replied. "We were just discussing the wedding."

Frank's startled gaze shot to Jenny. His eyebrows rose a quizzical half inch. "Wedding?" he repeated. "Whose?"

"Why yours, of course," Mrs. Chambers said, back at the stove and still oblivious to Jenny's panic.

"Ma!"

She turned and waved a spoon at him. "It never hurts to give a girl a nudge, let her know she'll be welcome in the family."

A twinkle of amusement appeared in Frank's eyes as he scanned Jenny's face. She was sure she must be pale as a ghost. "You feeling welcome?" he asked.

"Very," she said, injecting the single word with ominous implications.

"Maybe you'd like to come back in the living room with me," Frank suggested hurriedly.

"I'd love to."

Mrs. Chambers gave them an approving smile. "You two go right along. I'm sure Jenny and I will have a chance to talk more later."

Jenny nearly moaned as she left the kitchen.

"I tried to warn you," Frank said, his arm circling her shoulder.

She twisted away from the embrace. "You're enjoying this, aren't you? You're letting your mother do your dirty work."

"What dirty work is that?"

"The woman practically proposed on your behalf."

His expression brightened. "Really? What did you say?"

"Say? She didn't want an answer. She took the answer for granted." Jenny knew her voice was climbing, knew that her attempts to cover her earlier irritation with humor were starting to fail her now. This was exactly what she had feared would happen. The whole Chambers family was going to sit around all through dinner staring at her, waiting for an announcement that was not going to come. And she was going to have to put up with it.

Why? she thought suddenly. Why shouldn't she just lay things on the line? Frank might be a little embarrassed at first, but wasn't that better than allowing this whole misunderstanding to get entirely out of hand? Or was the real problem that a tiny part of her wanted the charade to be perpetuated? If she were to be perfectly honest, hadn't she enjoyed sitting in that kitchen and playing prospective daughter-in-law?

Okay, yes, dammit! Was that so terrible? It wasn't going to happen, but couldn't she indulge herself for a few minutes or even a few hours in the fantasy of becoming Mrs. Frank Chambers?

She looked up at Frank then and caught the speculative spark in his eyes. It was as if he could read her mind, as if he knew that she was waging an internal war and laying odds on the outcome.

Before she could come to a final decision on whether to go or stay, the choice was taken out of her hands. Mrs. Chambers started putting food on the table and the next thing Jenny knew, she was seated beside Frank's mother and they were all holding hands to say grace. When Mrs. Chambers gave thanks that her oldest son had found such a pretty, kind woman, Frank squeezed Jenny's hand reassuringly. She caught herself blinking back the surprising sting of salty tears and trying desperately to hold back the flood of hope.

* * *

As they drove home, Frank marveled at the transformation that had come over Jenny during the afternoon and evening. From a shy, unwilling date, she had slowly fallen into the role of fiancée. Though he'd been ready to strangle his mother when he'd first walked into that kitchen, he had to admit now that he should be grateful. After a few token protests, Jenny had apparently taken to the idea. By the time they'd left she'd been teasing his brothers, beating them all at Monopoly and agreeing to return the following Sunday. He still wasn't sure exactly what had come over her, but he'd be damned if he'd complain about it.

"Did you have a good time?" he inquired as she sat beside him, her eyes closed, a pleased smile tilting the corners of her mouth.

"The best," she murmured.

"Did it have anything to do with me?"

She blinked and stared at him sleepily. "Of course, why?"

"Because a few hours ago, you were adamant about defining the parameters of our relationship in very businesslike terms. By the time we left my mother's, if I'm not mistaken, at least seven people were of the opinion that we're engaged. I'm one of them."

She sighed. "I never really said that, did I?"

"No, but you knew that was the impression and you didn't correct it. Why?"

Her lower lip was caught between her teeth as she obviously struggled with an answer. "I guess I just got caught up in a fantasy," she said slowly. "I'm sorry."

His heart thudding, Frank said, "It doesn't have to be just a fantasy. I love you, Jenny. You know that. I want to marry you." He pulled the car to the side of the road and touched her cheek, which was damp with unexpected tears. "I do love you, sweetheart."

Her fingers traced his jaw, then his lips as his breath lodged in his throat. "Oh, Frank, if only…"

"There are no 'if onlys,'" he said angrily. "All you have to do is say yes. One little word. Why is it so hard for you?"

"You know why," she said, her voice thick with tears.

"Then come with me, come home with me and let me show you that there is nothing, *nothing,* standing in our way."

Jenny's eyes were shining, her lips trembling, when she finally whispered, "Yes. I'll come with you."

He caressed her cheek, his thumb moving over the lush curve of her lower lip as his heart slammed into his ribs. Anticipation rushed through him, hot and sweet and urgent. Along with it came a faint anxiety that he was certain mirrored hers.

"You won't be sorry," he vowed to reassure them both. "You will never be sorry."

Chapter Eleven

Regrets and doubts rioted deep inside Jenny the instant she agreed to go home with Frank. But the temptation had proved too strong, the illusion too powerful. Caught up in it, she'd been unable to say no. She would give anything for this one night to be perfect. She didn't doubt, not for a second, that Frank would try to make it so. She didn't doubt that he loved her. Every considerate action spoke of the depth of his feelings.

But was love the only thing that mattered? She had doubts enough about that for the both of them.

Even so, there could be no backing out now, no second thoughts leading to a tearful withdrawal. When she had said yes, she had made a commitment, to him and to herself. It might last no longer than this one night, but it was a commitment just the same. And, like Frank, she believed in honoring her vows.

Inside his house, she caught him studying her, his expression thoughtful, worried. "Nervous?" he said.

Jenny nodded.

"Me, too."

It had never occurred to her that he might be every bit as scared as she was. His nervousness and his admission of it both charmed and reassured her.

"You can change your mind anytime," he said, his blue eyes serious. *"Anytime."*

Feeling stronger with each reassurance, she shook her head. "I won't change my mind," she said with absolute conviction. "I want to be with you more than I've ever wanted anything in my life."

He nodded and held out his hand. When she placed her hand in his, he rubbed the pad of his thumb across her knuckles, then lifted her hand to his lips, his gaze fastened on hers. Inside, she trembled with the magic of that tender gesture.

"Would you like a drink?" he offered. "I think I have some wine."

"Yes. Wine would be good," she said, though she wanted time more than she wanted the drink. She needed to accustom herself to being here, to the prospect of an almost-forgotten kind of intimacy. She needed to steel herself to the possibility of rejection. Though her heart told her that Frank would never ever hurt her intentionally, she knew that the faintest hint of revulsion in his eyes, the least sign of disappointment would be devastating. She had to prepare herself for that, had to be ready not to cast blame for something over which he might have no control.

As she waited for the wine, she walked down the hall to his workroom and flipped on the light. She breathed in the clean scent of the various woods, rubbed her fingers over the textures of his finished carvings. When she came to the unfinished blue jay, she recalled how she had guided his inept fingers in this very room, how she had badgered him until he began fighting back against his injury, fighting to regain his skill. Unless she was mistaken, there were fresh details on the piece, less delicate perhaps, but evidence that he was trying.

She sensed that Frank was standing in the doorway. Glancing over her shoulder, she smiled at him. "I hope you don't mind that I'm in here," she said, suddenly realizing that he might consider this an invasion of his privacy, a claim to intimacy that she didn't rightfully have.

"Of course not," he said, though his uneasiness contradicted the words. He came closer and handed her the wine.

"You've been working." She gestured toward the blue jay.

He shrugged, his expression unexpectedly vulnerable. "I'm trying."

"It's very good."

He shook his head and regarded the carving critically. "Not yet," he said, but there was a trace of hope even in the denial.

"I'm proud of you."

"I'm proud of you, too."

Startled, she stared at him. "Why?"

"For daring to take this step, for trusting me."

"It was time," she said simply, and knew it was true. She might have put off the action for a week or a month or a year, but emotionally she was as ready now as she was ever likely to be. No man was ever likely to be more right for her than this kind, gentle man who waited patiently for her to set the pace. She put down the glass he'd given her. "Frank, would you hold me?"

A slow smile trembled on his lips as he put aside his own glass. "I thought you'd never ask," he murmured, opening his arms then folding them around her.

Jenny rested her head against his chest, listening to the quickened beat of his heart and breathing in the faintly woodsy masculine scent of him. There was such comfort in his embrace, such a sense of coming home at last. And yet…

And yet there was the lightning-quick racing of her pulse. Warmth that had nothing to do with the comfort and everything to do with rising passion stole over her. When his lips finally, inevitably settled on hers, the lightning added thunder, the warmth became white-hot urgency. There was no rush to the kiss, no hurry to the slow exploration by his tongue, but deep inside her, need built feverishly, demanding more, demanding a more passionate pace. She appreciated the care he was taking, the gentle advances, but she hungered for desperate loving, loving that would carry her beyond thought to pure sensation, passion able to overshadow doubts.

Her fingers tangled in the dark midnight of his hair as she pressed him closer. Her now-sensitive lips brushed across stubbled cheeks, seeking, again, the velvet fire of his mouth. When one arm braced her back and the other tucked beneath her knees, she gasped in startled astonishment, then settled against his chest as he carried her down the hall and into his bedroom.

For a few seconds she registered the room's details, the clean, masculine lines, the cheerful colors, the clutter of framed family pictures crowded on the dresser, the haphazard toss of clothes scattered about by a man always in a rush...until now. Then Frank captured all of her attention, his eyes smoky blue with desire, his expression still anxious.

"You're sure," he said one last time.

Though her heart raced with something very much like sheer panic, Jenny nodded. "I'm sure," she whispered. Then, more loudly, "Very sure."

He stepped closer, his gaze locked with hers. With fingers that trembled, he traced the neckline of her blouse, leaving a trail of goose bumps along her neck. Scared as she had never been scared before, filled with a yearning deeper than any she had ever known, Jenny allowed him to slowly, carefully, unbutton her blouse. With the release of the first button, she stilled, but the press of his lips against the newly exposed flesh had her quivering with need. His touch was so deft, his kisses so potent that she forgot to watch for the revulsion in his eyes as first her blouse, and then her specially designed bra fell away. All she remembered were the nights she'd lain awake imagining being cherished like this.

When she first felt his lips against the scar, a cry of dismay gathered in her throat, but before she could utter a single sound, she was lost in the sensations he aroused, the fierce tug deep in her belly, the sweet, aching hunger below. She wanted nothing more than to go on feeling, but she had to know. She had to.

At last she opened her eyes. With a mixture of awe and dread, she observed him as he gently traced the line of the scar. With her breath caught in her throat, she waited for him to back away, but the only sign of emotion was the tear that tracked down his cheek and the faint trembling of his hand as he touched her. He lifted his head, though his hand continued to stroke and caress and inflame.

"I love you, Jenny Michaels," he said, his gaze locked on hers.

"I love you," he whispered again, as his gaze slid lower to the scar and lingered there. There was an instant when he seemed to freeze, and Jenny felt her heart go still. Then she realized that he was staring at his own fresh scars, seeing the cruelly reddened skin against the whiteness of her flesh. She captured his hand in hers and kissed each finger until he, too, believed in the healing power of love.

Her own tears falling, mingling with his, Jenny heard the tender endearments, felt the powerful stirring of her body responding to his touch. Eyes closed, she gave herself over to the feelings, savoring them as a treasure she would hold always. Even after he'd gone.

That these wonderful, wild sensations couldn't last seemed a certainty. She wouldn't dare to hope beyond tonight, beyond this sweet, thrilling moment. With the fascination of a woman capturing dreams enough for a lifetime, she studied the magnificent lines of his body, the sculpted flesh with its richness of texture. No wonder that he created perfection with his carving knife, when he'd been given such an example. She traced each hardened muscle, each curve and indentation until she knew him as well as she knew herself, until his body tensed with need.

When their touches grew more frenzied, when their blood flowed like warm honey, when their thoughts had given way to pure sensation, they came together at last. Years of pain and hurt and doubting vanished in one shuddering moment of exultation. Love, as fresh and new as springtime, flowered in Jenny's heart.

As she curved her body against his, she told herself that forever was within reach. With his hands curved gently over her disfigured flesh, she could believe that she was beautiful and that anything was possible.

Awakening to find Jenny still in his arms filled Frank with a joy so profound it was as if he'd been reborn. He stretched cautiously, trying not to disturb her, then settled back to study the perfect silk of her skin, the tumble of curls with highlights the color of amber caught in the muted rays of morning sun. She was even tinier than he'd realized. His hands could probably span her waist. He rested one hand just above the curve of her hip to prove his point.

Beneath his touch, her flesh warmed and she began to stir. As she rolled onto her back, his fingers moved from hip to belly in a slow, sensual caress that changed the pattern of her breathing from restful to hurried. Hesitant to touch her breast, fearful that she would perceive the touch as a need she couldn't amply fulfill, he stroked the scar instead. Jenny whimpered, then sighed, then came slowly awake.

Frank smiled down at her, her sleepy sensuality an incredible turn-on that had him instantly hard and wanting. For an instant she remained open to him, then as if realizing her vulnerability, the exposure in daylight that hadn't existed the night before, she grabbed for the sheet. He reached out to stay her hands.

"Don't," he whispered, trying to quiet the panic in her eyes. Meeting that fearful gaze straight on, he said, "You are beautiful, a beautiful, desirable woman. Inside and out. And I could not possibly love you any more than I do right now."

Her lower lip quivered, and he wanted desperately to cover that faint trembling with his own lips, but he held back, knowing that the best proof was in not looking away. She would only believe him if he acknowledged the defect and showed her time and again that it didn't matter. It would take words and actions and time.

"You must believe me, Jenny," he said. "You are all the woman I need, and I will spend the rest of my life proving it to you."

Tears gathered in her eyes, then spilled down her face. She captured his scarred hand in hers and held it to her damp cheek. "I know that," she said with a sigh.

There was a hesitation in her voice, a shadow of doubt. "But you don't entirely trust what we have, do you? Why not? How can a woman who spends her life teaching others to look beyond scars, not see beyond her own?"

She drew away from him then, both physically and emotionally. He could read the distance in her sudden stiffness, the dullness that took the lively sparks from her eyes.

"Frank, it's not just the scars. If it was, don't you think I would throw myself into your arms and never let go? Last night was the most perfect night of my life. I felt fulfilled and complete and desirable. You did that for me. But I won't be one of those people you gather in and protect. You've already raised five brothers and a sister. You deserve a life that is carefree and filled with happiness."

Frank struggled to follow what she was saying. It made no sense. How could she equate herself with his family? It sounded as if she viewed herself as a burden, rather than an incredible woman to be treasured. It sounded as if she planned to end things just as they were beginning.

"Jenny, this is crazy. I love you. I certainly don't think of you as some stray I have to take in and care for."

"But that could happen and I won't have it."

"Won't have what?" In his frustration, his voice rose to an irritated shout. "Dammit, talk to me. Make me see why you're willing to throw away what we have."

She turned pale at the thunder of his voice, but her voice was steady and bleak. "Because I don't trust it to last."

If she'd used the excuse that the sky might fall in a million years, he would have been no more confused. "Sweetheart, I know there are no guarantees, but why give up what we have now because of something that might never happen?"

"I don't like the odds."

"Odds? What odds? The fifty-percent divorce rate? What?"

"Stop yelling."

"I'm sorry. It's just that you're making me crazy," he said impatiently.

Her look quelled him. He took a deep breath. "Okay, talk to me. Make me understand. Are you worried about the way we met? Are you afraid that I've just grown dependent on you?"

Her expression softened. "No," she said, taking his hand and pressing a kiss to the knuckles. "You're strong now, and I know exactly what your feelings for me are. And I won't take advantage of that."

"Take advantage how?"

She did grab the sheet then and tug it around her. When it was snug, when there was nothing for him to see below her bare shoulders, she said quietly, "What scares me more than anything is the possibility that I might become dependent on you."

"Jenny…"

She touched a silencing finger to his lips. "No, listen to me. It's been just about four years since the surgery. Five years seems to be the magic number in cancer survival. I'm still a long way from that. Every day I live with the reality that the cancer could come back. I won't burden you with that, I won't ask you to live each day with the possibility of a death sentence hanging over us." Her gaze met his. "I won't," she said with finality.

Frank struggled with the horrible possibility of losing her to a disease he thought she had conquered. His heart ached for her as he tried to imagine living with that fear of recurrence. And, yet, weren't they losing even more by living now as if the merely possible were certain? He had to make her see that.

Gently he brushed the tendrils of hair back from her face. He searched his heart for words that would be convincing. "Jenny, my love, haven't you ever listened to the wedding ceremony? In sickness and in health, remember that? You're healthy now. We have this moment in our lives. We'll take each tomorrow as it comes. If we don't, Jenny, if we turn our backs on this, what sort of memories will we have? Loneliness? Fear? Longing? I don't want that for myself. I don't want it for you. Maybe we'll never quite stop being afraid, but we certainly don't have to be alone."

"It's not fair to you," she said stubbornly.

"It wasn't fair for you to get this disease. It wasn't fair for me to get burned. We both have to go on. It was your cancer and my burns that brought us together. Maybe we should concentrate on that and count our blessings."

"I'm scared, Frank."

"Of dying?"

"Of leaving you."

"Then don't do it now, not while you have a choice in the matter."

It was the most eloquent Frank had ever been, and he waited to see the effect of his words. For a moment as Jenny's arms slid around his waist, he thought he'd won. But then she rose, found the clothes they had tossed aside last night in their haste and, after sorting through them for hers, took them into the bathroom.

Frank wanted to throw something. He wanted to grab her by the shoulders and shout until she not only listened, but heard him. Instead he could only sit by helplessly as she did what she thought was right, what she thought was the noble thing.

When she came out of the bathroom, he held out his hand. "Jenny, don't go. I'll fix breakfast. We'll talk this out."

Swallowing hard, she shook her head. Then she kissed him one last time, with tears in her eyes, and left.

Chapter Twelve

Letting Jenny go, admitting that he didn't know how to help her grapple with her fears that obviously tormented her, was the most difficult thing Frank had ever done. He'd wanted to fold her in his arms, to hold her and love her until she couldn't walk away, but something told him that would only make the leaving harder, not impossible. He, better than anyone, knew just how stubborn and determined she could be. Yet knowing that he'd done the right thing didn't make the days any easier.

Boredom, worse than anything he'd faced in the hospital, set in and, combined with the loneliness, made him cranky. By the end of the week, he was snapping at anyone who dared to set foot near him. He tried carving again, but one slip of the knife had marred the blue jay he'd been struggling to complete and he'd tossed wood and knives into the trash. A day later he dug them out and tried again.

When Sunday rolled around, he begged off from the family

dinner. He felt as though a lifetime had passed since the previous week, and he wasn't up to the questions and teasing innuendoes about a relationship that no longer existed. As soon as the excuses were out of his mouth, though, he knew it had been a mistake. By four, instead of gathering at his mother's, the whole clan began descending on him. Tim and Jared were the first to arrive.

"You look okay to me," Jared said after a close inspection.

"I'm fine."

"You told Ma you were sick," Tim reminded him.

"I think I'm coming down with something," he amended hurriedly. "I'm sure it's not serious, but it could be catching. You two go over to Ma's."

"We can't," Jared said.

"Why not? She'll be expecting you."

"No, she won't," Tim said, just as the doorbell rang. "That should be her now." He glanced at Jared. "I'm betting on chicken soup. How about you?"

"Broth. Beef broth and custard."

Frank groaned. "This is ridiculous. I am not that sick."

"Then you shouldn't have told her you were. Now we're all going to have to eat wimp food," Tim complained grumpily. "Do you have any idea how much I detest custard?"

There was a deeply offended gasp from the doorway. "What do you mean, Timothy Chambers? You've always said you loved my custard."

"Cripes, Ma, you weren't supposed to hear that."

"Then you shouldn't have said it, should you?" she said, hiding a grin. "Go out to the car and get the rest of the dinner."

"Real food?" Jared inquired hopefully.

"Soup and custard are real food. Now, go." Once they'd gone, she observed Frank closely and, with her finely tuned maternal radar, zeroed in on the real crux of his problem. "You and Jenny have a fight?"

"Why on earth would you ask that?"

"Otherwise, she'd be here nursing you."

"Ma, I think you've gotten the wrong idea about Jenny and me."

She shook her head. "I don't think so. What was the fight about?"

"It wasn't a fight exactly."

"What was it then *exactly?*"

"It's private."

She nodded slowly. "Okay. You do what you think is best, but, Son, don't turn your back on your feelings just because things aren't so smooth. If you love her, then you owe it to both of you to fight. Don't let it slip away because of false pride."

Frank didn't think pride had anything to do with letting Jenny leave, letting her make her own choices, but maybe it did. Maybe it had hurt, thinking that she didn't love him enough to try to save what they had. On the chance that his mother might be right, he made up his mind to go by the hospital on Monday, to talk to her and pester her until she saw that they could face the future and whatever it held—good or bad—a thousand times better together than they possibly could apart.

Energized by a stubborn determination of his own, and filled with hope, he strode through the hospital the next day, poked his head into Pam's room to say hello, then marched on to the therapy room like Sherman taking on Georgia. He pushed open the door and stepped inside, glancing first at Jenny's desk, then around the room. It was empty. The desk was ominously neat. He was still standing there trying to decide what to make of it, when Carolanne returned. She looked puzzled at finding him there.

"You here for a treatment?" she asked. "I don't recall seeing your name on the list for today."

"No. I'm here to see Jenny."

Her friendly expression closed down. "She's not in," she said, her tone cautiously neutral.

"I see that. Where is she?"

"She took a few days off."

Frank's heart began to thud dully in his chest. "Why? Is she okay?"

Carolanne studied him with serious gray eyes. "Come on in and sit down," she said finally. "I think it's time we had a talk."

Frank's pulse began to race. "Dammit, tell me where she is. What's happened?"

With the same spunkiness he'd encountered in Jenny, Carolanne pointed toward a chair. "Sit. You want some coffee?"

"Fine. Whatever," he said impatiently, but he sat.

A lifetime seemed to pass before she handed him a cup of coffee, then pulled up a chair and sat opposite him. "Are you in love with her?" she asked bluntly.

"Yes."

"Does she know it?"

"Yes," he said, oddly disquieted by the personal questions, yet sensing that Carolanne really needed to know if she was to be equally honest with him. "I've told her."

She nodded thoughtfully. "That makes sense then."

"What makes sense? Dammit, would you stop hedging and spit it out? Is she okay?"

"I don't know."

Frank felt as though the air were being squeezed out of his chest. Before he could say a word, Carolanne looked contrite and held up her hand apologetically. "Sorry. I didn't mean to alarm you. I just mean that she's undergoing some tests. Bone scans, liver scans, blood tests, the works. It's routine in cases like hers, but that doesn't mean it doesn't scare the dickens out of her, out of all of us who love her. I don't know if you can imagine what it's like waiting out the results, waiting to find out if your life is hanging in the balance, if you're okay or doomed to undergo more surgery, more radiation, more chemotherapy, more hell."

Suddenly Frank made the connection between these annual tests and Jenny's departure from his house. "Did she know these tests were scheduled a week ago?"

Carolanne nodded. "I think she scheduled them three or four weeks back."

"Is she here in the hospital?"

"No, these are outpatient tests."

"Who's with her?"

"I'm not sure. I think Otis probably took the day off to drive her. He usually does, despite her arguments that she can do just fine on her own."

"What's her doctor's name?"

The therapist balked at that. "If she didn't tell you about the tests herself, then she won't want you turning up there."

"Don't you see? I have to be with her."

Carolanne continued to hesitate, then finally seemed to reach a decision. "Go to her apartment. She doesn't need you with her for the tests, but she will need you after. It's the waiting that's agonizing. She needs all the support she can get then." She dug in her purse and handed him a key. "Thank goodness I still have this from the first time I watered her plants, while she was back East. You know the address, right?"

"Yes. Thanks, Carolanne. I owe you."

"No. If you can make Jenny happy, that's all that matters. No one deserves a little happiness more than she does."

"I'm going to try like hell."

"You'd better. Otherwise, she'll kill me for giving out her key."

His first stop wasn't a florist, though that had been his first instinct. He'd dismissed the idea of filling the apartment with flowers as both too ordinary and too funereal. Frank opted instead for balloons, dozens of them in every color imaginable. Filled with helium, they floated in Jenny's living room like a rainbow sky. He ordered dinner from the finest restaurant in San Francisco and wine from the best Napa Valley vineyard. And, after determining that the test results would take days, he called a travel agent and ordered tickets for Hawaii to be delivered immediately by messenger. The impulsive, expensive vacation would dent his savings, but he couldn't imagine any gesture that would be a better use of his money. This was no time for caution. A little extravagance was called for.

With the tickets ordered, he sat back to wait, fully aware that his nervous anticipation was nothing compared to the dread that was likely to occupy Jenny's mind unless he could distract her. It was nearly five o'clock when he finally heard her key turning in the lock.

As the door swung open, setting a wave of balloons bobbing, an expression of delighted surprise spread across her face, wiping away the most obvious signs of weariness.

"Welcome home," he said softly, hiding his dismay at the shadows under her eyes, the slump of her shoulders that she couldn't hide.

"You did all this?"

Otis stood behind her, nodding in satisfaction. He gave Frank an approving thumbs-up gesture, then said, "Guess I'm not needed around here anymore. I'll just be on my way." When Jenny didn't even turn to look at him, his grin widened. "Tell her I said goodbye," he told Frank, feigning irritation. "If she happens to notice I'm gone."

"Bye," she murmured distractedly, apparently having caught

just enough of Otis's words to realize he was leaving. Her gaze was riveted on Frank. "Why?"

"Because it's time you and I came to an understanding," he said matter-of-factly.

She stared at him in obvious confusion. "About what?"

"About the way things are going to be from now on. You were there for me when I needed help, when I was facing the toughest days of my life. From now on I'm going to be here for you. That's just the way it is. Like sunrise and birds singing and tides changing. Don't fight it, Jenny. I can't let you win this one."

There was a spark of fire in her eyes, then a flicker of acceptance. She sighed heavily and sank onto the sofa. Her whole body seemed to slump with exhaustion. "I'm so tired. I don't think I could battle a feather and come out on top right now."

Sensing victory, though not especially happy about the cause of her token protest, Frank pressed. "Does that mean you accept this as a done deal? You and me? Together, always?"

"We'll see," she said weakly, her eyes drifting shut as she curled into a more comfortable position.

It wasn't the commitment he'd hoped for, but at least she wasn't fighting him. Worried by her lack of energy, by her pale complexion, Frank settled beside her and pulled her into his arms. With a quiet sigh, she rested against him. "Oh, Jenny," he whispered as he listened to the even rise and fall of her breath. "Don't you dare leave me."

She murmured something in her sleep, then was quiet. Holding her in his arms filled Frank with the greatest contentment he'd ever known, even as his heart ached with the uncertainty of the future.

Jenny only dimly remembered coming home from the day of medical tests. Nerves, rather than the tests themselves, always took everything out of her. By the time she got home she felt limp as a dishrag. She remembered coming in. She remembered collapsing onto the sofa. She remembered... A puzzled frown knit her brow. Had Frank been there? Had he issued some sort of crazy ultimatum or had that been a lovely dream? She drew in a deep breath and slowly opened her eyes. Then she blinked and blinked again. One part of the dream at least had been real.

Jenny had never seen so many balloons before in her life. Laughter bubbled up as she stared at the reds and greens, blues and yellows bobbing above her, trailing curls of matching ribbon. She reached for one and drew it down, then caught another and another until she held an entire bouquet of vibrant colors.

"Careful or you'll float away," Frank teased from somewhere just beyond the balloons. He ducked beneath them to sit beside her. So it hadn't been a dream at all. He was here. She was glad enough to see him not to ask how he'd gotten in. She could guess anyway. Carolanne had the only other key to her apartment, and Carolanne thought she'd been wrong to cut herself off from Frank, from a chance at love.

"How do you feel, sleepyhead?" he asked.

"Better. What time is it?"

"Nearly eight. Are you hungry?"

"Starved, but there's nothing in the house for dinner."

He grinned. "Ah, but there is. Veal piccata, pasta and a chocolate mousse cake that will make you weep."

Her mouth watered at the tempting descriptions. "If you prepared all that, maybe we do have something to talk about after all."

"Meaning?"

"Meaning that I will reconsider on the spot marrying a man who can make a chocolate mousse cake."

Frank didn't seem especially pleased by the concession. Either he hadn't made the cake or she was missing something. "You're going to marry me, cake or no cake," he reminded her. "That's been decided."

Her gaze narrowed. "Since when?"

"Since three hours ago, when you swore to stop fighting me."

"I don't remember that conversation."

"Then let me remind you. You and me. Together, always. Those were the exact words."

"Yours or mine?"

"Mine, but you agreed. How can I take you on a honeymoon to Hawaii if you don't say yes?"

"Honeymoon?" she repeated weakly. "Did I agree to that, too? I must have been more out of it than I thought."

"Just sensible, for a change."

"Frank, I can't get married and I can't go to Hawaii. I have to wait here."

"For the test results," he said matter-of-factly. "No problem. They can call us in Hawaii. I hear the phone lines are very modern. No more tin cans or drums."

"No," she said, feeling the pressure build in her chest. "I will not marry you. Not until I know for sure."

He waved the tickets under her nose. "Nonrefundable. For tomorrow. We're going, Jenny Michaels, if I have to sling you across my shoulder and carry you onto that plane. You deserve a break, you need a rest and I'm going to see that you get it. If you want to wait to get married until after the honeymoon, that's a little weird, but it's something we can talk about."

She stared at him. "You want to take the honeymoon first?"

"I don't want to do it that way, but I'm willing to compromise. Just to prove what an agreeable sort of guy I am, what a catch."

She touched a hand to his cheek. "You are a catch. Any woman would be proud to marry you."

"I don't want any woman. I want you and I mean to have you."

"By bullying me into it?"

He grinned and taunted, "I learned from a master."

Jenny saw her own tactics coming back to haunt her. But even as she fought the idea of marrying Frank or even taking this idiotic trip he'd planned without consulting her, she couldn't deny that Hawaii with Frank sounded like heaven. Would it be selfish of her to go? Would it be cruel to start something they might not be able to finish?

As if he'd read her mind, Frank said, "We are going to live every single day as if it's the only one we've got. We are not going to put our lives on hold for 'what ifs.' I won't have either one of us waking up one day with regrets."

He kissed her then, stealing away her breath, teasing her senses until her spirits were soaring every bit as high as the balloons she'd allowed to drift away. "I'll go," she said, when she could finally catch her breath. It might be wrong, it might be selfish, but oh how she longed for a few more days of magic.

A triumphant smile broke across his rugged face. "The wedding?"

"One step at a time," she pleaded. "I can't take any more than that."

He nodded slowly. "One step at a time. We start with the honeymoon of a lifetime."

Less than twenty-four hours later they were on the beach in Maui where the breezes smelled of frangipani and the sun caressed almost as seductively as Frank. For three days they rested and swam and made sweet and tender love. There was no forbidden talk of the future, only the here and now and the delicious thrill of Frank's most persuasive touches, the joy of

being together. Jenny felt healthier, more alive and more desperately in love than she ever had before.

On the fourth day when they came back to their cottage,
there was a message on her cell phone to call her doctor's
office. The brisk voice of the assistant was like a punch in her
midsection. All of the energy and hope seemed to drain out of
Jenny in the scant thirty seconds it took her to cross the room
and to the phone.

As she dialed the number of her doctor in San Francisco,
Jenny reached instinctively for Frank's hand. Instead of taking
her outstretched hand, though, he came up behind her and
wrapped his arms around her waist. He pressed a kiss to the
back of her neck, sending shivers down her spine, reminding
her of all that was at stake. It was no longer simply her own
existence that hung in the balance, but their future.

"I love you," he said urgently. "Marry me, Jenny. Say yes."

She stopped dialing and turned in his arms, meeting his
gaze. Her heart thundered in her chest, nearly breaking with
despair. Oh, how she wanted to say yes, wanted to believe in
the future, but she couldn't. It wouldn't be fair. "I can't answer
you now," she said, but the words were an uncertain, breathless tremble.

He shook his head. "I want it settled before you make the
call. I don't want there to be a single doubt that I'm asking
because I love you or you're answering because of what's in
your heart. Tell me now, Jenny. Do you love me?"

She wanted to do the right thing, the fair thing and deny it,
but she couldn't. "More than life itself."

"Then that's our answer, isn't it?"

With a wobbly smile, she touched his lips. "Frank, are you
sure? Really sure?"

"Absolutely. In sickness or in health."

She read the certainty in his eyes, heard the conviction in his voice, felt the love in his touch. "Then I guess that's our answer. I'll marry you."

Holding her tighter, giving her his strength, he said, "Now make the call."

When the nurse answered, Jenny had trouble even getting her name out. Her voice shook, but she took courage from Frank's embrace, from the commitment they had made only seconds before.

"Jenny," Dr. Hadley said in that low, soothing, bedside voice he had. "We have your results."

"And?"

"Everything looks good."

Hope, radiant and joyous, spilled over her like sunshine. "Everything?" she repeated.

"Not a sign of a recurrence. I'll want you in here a year from now, but I think there's every reason to be optimistic."

"Thank you," she whispered, her eyes locked with Frank's. Only one more year until that fateful fifth anniversary. One more. "You can't know how much this means to me."

"To both of us," Frank murmured huskily.

He took the phone from her grasp and replaced it in its cradle. With a sigh, he slanted his mouth over hers, filling her with an incredible sense of euphoria.

They had a chance, a real chance at a future, she thought as he tugged at the buttons on her beach coverup. When the gauzy material caught and tangled, he ripped it away with a fierce urgency that matched the rising tide of her own need. His hands were rough as he stripped her of her bathing suit, but the heated look in his eyes had her body shivering with the need for speed far more than finesse.

At the first daring touch of his tongue to her breast, excitement streaked through her like lightning. The last shred of self-consciousness between them shimmered, then disintegrated in a hot whirlwind of magical feelings. When he lifted his head to look in her eyes, cautiously seeking her reaction, she arched her back and drew him to her, wanting that exquisite, all-but-forgotten tug of need to go on forever. As pleasure built deep inside, she savored the bold strokes that told her again and again that she was woman enough for him. When his fingers sought the scar on her chest and his gaze locked with hers, she closed her hand over his and showed him the gentle caresses that inflamed and delighted.

There was no time to revel in each delicious sensation, because there were always more. Her body demanded and Frank gave, his lovemaking totally selfless. He reaffirmed the depth of his commitment again and again, building the aching hunger inside her.

With his kisses, slow, deep, passionate kisses that set her senses spinning.

With his caresses, the tenderest of touches, the boldest of claimings.

With his heart, his enduring love evident in his eyes, with the way he responded to her needs time and time again.

In moments, naked and filled with a wicked hunger, they tumbled together on the bed, a tangle of arms and legs, slick with perspiration, alive with desire.

"I love you," Frank said as he stilled above her, fulfillment an anxious heartbeat away. "I love you, Jenny."

"No more than I love you," she said fervently as their bodies at last joined together in a chaotic rhythm as old as time.

Never had Jenny been more aware of the rough and satin textures of his body, of the scent of saltwater and sweet air that surrounded them, of the way he tasted against her tongue or the way her body ached with need until the moment he slid inside her, making her whole, mending her dreams, reaffirming the sheer joy of living.

They were married on the beach a day later. She wore a white Hawaiian wedding dress, and he wore an impossibly loud shirt. She had a bright yellow flower tucked behind her ear and orchids for a bouquet. When they said their vows, Jenny stumbled over the words, but the commitment was etched forever in her heart.

When the brief ceremony was over and they were alone again, giddy on champagne and passion, Frank said, "You realize we're going to have to do this all over again in San Francisco?"

"Your family?"

"You bet. And it's our family now. Don't ever forget that."

"Don't you think with all those sons, your mother wouldn't mind missing this one wedding? My parents will be satisfied with a phone call."

"Not Ma. She'll be convinced we're living in sin unless she hears the vows for herself."

Jenny snuggled closer. "Could be fun," she teased. "It would add an element of danger, when things get too predictable."

"Things won't have a chance of getting predictable," Frank warned. "She's liable to move in with us until she's certain we've done the right thing."

"In that case, call ahead and line up the church. I am not going to give this up for a single night."

"I promise you, Jennifer Michaels Chambers, we will never be separated again. Never."

* * * * *

For my parents,
who've taught me the importance of family.

STAY...

Bestselling Author

Allison Leigh

ALLISON LEIGH

started her career early by writing a Halloween play that her grade-school class performed. Since then, though her tastes have changed, her love for reading has not. And her writing appetite simply grows more voracious by the day. She has been a finalist for a RITA® Award and a Holt Medallion. But the true highlights of her day as a writer are when she receives word from a reader that they laughed, cried or lost a night of sleep while reading one of her books.

Born in Southern California, Allison has lived in several different cities in four different states. She has been, at one time or another, a cosmetologist, a computer programmer and a secretary. She has recently begun writing full-time after spending nearly a decade as an administrative assistant for a busy neighborhood church. She currently makes her home in Arizona with her family. She loves to hear from her readers, who can write to her at P.O. Box 40772, Mesa, AZ 85274-0772.

Prologue

"Don't let him send me away." Her young voice was muffled against the saddle blanket hugged against her chest. "*Please, Jefferson, don't let him. I'll die in that school. I know I will.*"

His eyebrows lowered and he gently pried her fingers from the soft blue-gray plaid. "Don't say that."

Bereft of the blanket that he'd tossed over the stall door, she crossed her arms protectively across her chest. "If you'd just talk to him. I don't need some school to teach me how to be a girl—"

His eyes flickered over her short, dark brown hair and down her sweat-stained shirt to her torn jeans. Her rough 'n tumble appearance couldn't hide the developing curves. She wasn't the little seven-year-old anymore who'd been his constant shadow. Who'd followed his every step, asking a million questions, or just chattering away in her sweet little-girl voice.

She was fourteen now. And rapidly developing into a hellion that easily rivaled any one of his brothers. The problem was, she wasn't a *boy*. And something needed to be done. His father was at his wit's end. "It's not up to me," he said softly.

"But he'd listen to you—"

"It's not up to me," he repeated gently. Inflexibly.

Hot tears flooded her eyes and she turned away. "If I was a boy, he wouldn't send me away."

He cursed softly, but didn't disagree. He wouldn't lie to her. He couldn't change the situation. Hell, he had to catch a flight to Turkey first thing in the morning, and his mind was humming with the hoard of details involved. This brief stopover hadn't been in his plans at all.

He studied the young female. A sister. Yet not his sister. His cousin. Yet not. But family, nevertheless. "That boarding school might not be so bad, you know," he murmured, reaching past her hunched form for the bridle she'd thrown to the concrete floor a few minutes earlier in a fit of temper. "You'll meet kids your own age. Make some new friends."

"Tris's my own age," she replied, exaggerating only slightly. "And I have all the friends I need." She swiped her sleeve beneath her nose. "Matthew and Daniel—"

He sighed. "Girls. You'll meet *girls* your age."

The snort she gave was decidedly unfeminine. As was the explicit word she spat in opinion of his words. He raised one eyebrow. "*That's* one of the reasons you're going."

She swore again, and whirled around like a dervish, kicking her dusty boot against a wooden post. The metal bucket hanging from a nail in the post rocked loose and clattered to the floor, narrowly missing the dog who'd been sleeping in the corner near the tack room. The dog shot to his feet, barking furiously.

Frustrated…angry…but most of all scared, she kicked the fallen bucket and it crashed against the stone wall opposite them, toppling a pitchfork onto its side where it missed crowning the dog by mere inches. Yelping, the dog skittered for shelter. Every curse word she'd ever heard poured from her. And being raised among five boys, she knew more than a few.

Long arms wrapped around her waist, and Jefferson lifted her right off her feet. Twisting, she pushed at him. "I won't go," she gritted.

She was held firmly, high against his hard chest. His breath was warm against her ear as he whispered softly. Soothing. Calming her in the same way he'd often done whenever she'd awakened from a bad dream when she was little. She wasn't so little now, though, and the wide chest pressed against her cheek set off all sorts of new feelings.

"You'll go."

Her head reared back, ready for another round. But his dark blue eyes met hers steadily and the words died. Her head collapsed against his chest and she sobbed brokenly.

In the end she went.

Chapter One

Twelve years later

Emily Nichols downshifted the car's gears and nudged her sunglasses a speck up her nose. She checked her mirrors, but the traffic on the freeway's four lanes was solid. And stopped, dead cold. So much for getting home in time to make a trip out to the stable before dark.

She shifted into neutral, and rolled her head slowly from side to side, working out the kinks from sitting at a computer all day long. Grimacing at the traffic report coming from the car radio, she flipped open the case containing an assortment of CDs.

Tristan kept telling her to switch to MP3s. But she'd been collecting these CDs since she'd been fourteen when she'd received the first two as a Christmas gift. More than a decade later, and she was still cherishing each and every one. She sighed at that thought and popped in Zeppelin, turning up the volume.

Since the sun was still high in the cloudless blue sky, she thought about putting up the top of her convertible and turning on the air-conditioning. The cars in front of her began inching forward before she could put the idea into action, and she shifted into gear to follow suit. With one hand she twisted her long hair off her neck and held it up, hoping for a whiff of cool air. But she let go after a moment. Sitting in the middle of a gridlocked freeway in downtown San Diego during rush hour wasn't the likeliest place to catch a fresh ocean breeze.

The traffic continued inching forward, and though she was still miles away from the exit ramp closest to the house she shared with Tristan, she flipped her turn signal on and worked her way off the freeway. Driving surface streets, even with all the congestion and stoplights, was better than sitting like a lump on the freeway.

Maybe she'd also stop and pick up a pizza for supper. Tristan wasn't likely to be there, anyway. And even if he was, he wouldn't be likely to turn up his nose at pizza. Even frozen pizza. It was food, after all. Cardboardlikeness notwithstanding. And he could pack it away like nobody she'd ever seen.

A few miles away from home, she pulled into a grocery store and put the top up on her precious Mustang. She shrugged out of the off-white jacket she'd worn and tossed it over the seat before heading into the store. When she emerged again, she carried more than a mere box of pizza, and by the time she had arranged the half dozen grocery bags in the trunk, the sun was lowering toward the horizon. And the air had begun to cool. Thankfully.

The weather in San Diego was usually pleasant year-round.

But the middle of August was generally miserable. No matter what part of the country you lived in. Even Matt, who was running the Double-C Ranch up in Wyoming, had been complaining recently about the sweltering temperatures.

Emily stood beside the trunk, looking over the sea of cars parked in the huge parking lot of the supermarket complex. Deep, bone-thumping vibrations suddenly accosted her, and she looked over her shoulder at the old sedan slowly driving past. The car's stereo was so loud it made her chest hurt. The driver sneered at her, pitching his cigarette out his window and right at her feet.

Staring right back at the driver, who probably wasn't more than seventeen years old despite the world-wise look in his dark eyes, she slowly ground her foot over the burning cigarette. Her keys were locked between her fingers, jutting out in four jagged weapons. Sighing faintly, she turned away from the car, aware of it continuing on its way. She climbed into her own car, switched the music to a soothing Mozart and drove home.

An unfamiliar black car sat in the driveway, blocking the garage. "Girlfriend number 310," she muttered, and whipped the car into a U-turn to park on the street along the curb. Tristan must be home after all. And since he couldn't get his girlfriends to park in the street, as Emily was forever asking, he could carry in the darn groceries himself.

She shoved open the car door, reaching back for her slender gray briefcase and the jacket. The massive black front door opened as she headed up the terraced steps. A dark blond male head appeared as she stooped to pick up that morning's newspaper. "I don't know how that kid always manages to nail the flowers," she complained as she extracted the half-buried paper from a glorious display of white petunias. She straightened and picked a velvety bloom out of the rubber band. "Groceries are in the car," she called out. "You can have the honors, since it's your fault I'm parked on the street."

"You've developed a bossy streak," the man said, stepping outside and into the fading, golden twilight.

Emily's fingers loosened spasmodically at the man's voice, and she nearly dropped the newspaper right back into the flowers. Her heart clenched and she was grateful for the sunglasses shading her eyes as they flew to him, shocked.

Jefferson Clay was back.

Her fingers dug into the newspaper, tearing jagged little holes in the outermost page. She didn't notice. It was all she could do to contain the urge to turn tail and race back to her car. Instead, she stood rooted right where she was, her greedy eyes not willing to look away from him.

His hair was longer than it had been the last time she'd seen him, more than two years ago. On most men, it would have looked feminine. But not on him. Not with his face. Hard. Masculine. And thinner than it had been the last time she'd seen him. In fact, he was probably fifteen pounds thinner. It made him look even more carved. More unapproachable than he'd seemed before.

"Aren't you even going to say hello, Em?"

She drew in a steadying breath, gathering her composure, then climbed the last few steps leading into the house. "Hello, Jefferson," she said, managing to present a slight smile. Even in her high-heeled pumps, she had to reach up to drop a light kiss on his cheek. Her lips tingled from the impact of his five-o'clock shadow, and she slipped past him into the house, telling herself she wasn't breathless from just that little peck. "What are you doing here? Is Squire okay?"

She set the paper, her jacket and the briefcase on the narrow hall table and pretended to study the pile of mail that Tristan had left lying there.

"He's fine. As far as I know."

Her eyebrows rose and she looked over her shoulder at him.

"I haven't talked to him in a while," he said.

She nodded, unsurprised, and turned her attention back to the mail. But it was Jefferson's image imprinted on her mind that she saw. Not the collection of bills and circulars she was paging through.

No man had a right to look that good. It simply wasn't fair to the women of the world.

"Your hair's grown." His voice was low. Husky.

She closed her eyes for a moment. "So has yours." She gave up on the mail and tossed it beside her jacket. "Is Tristan here?"

"He's on the phone."

She nodded. Finally she simply gave in again and let her eyes rove over him. From the tailored fit of his pleated black trousers to his narrow waist to the single unfastened button of his white shirt at his brown throat. She wanted to ask him where he'd been all this time. Why he hadn't called. Written. "When will you be leaving?"

The corner of his mouth tilted, causing the slashing dimple in his cheek to appear briefly. "Here's your hat, what's your hurry," he murmured.

Emily felt the flush rise in her cheeks. Considering that Jefferson's presence in her life for more than ten years had been a brief series of arrivals *always* followed by an indecently hasty departure, she wasn't, however, feeling inclined to apologize. Her lips twisted. Facts were facts.

"Ah, Em…"

His soft voice seemed filled with regret. She wondered if he'd known she was living here before he'd come. A fanciful, wishful thought on her part, no doubt. Annoyed with herself, she pulled off her sunglasses and dropped them alongside the mail before turning toward the kitchen. What was she going to fix for supper? Jefferson was a meat-and-potatoes kind of guy and she wasn't sure they had anything—

"Darn it," she grumbled, swiveling about on her heel. The groceries.

Jefferson stood right behind her, and he warded her off with a raised hand, keeping her from plowing into him. "Whoa."

Then she noticed it. The carved, wooden cane. She stared at it. At his long brown fingers, curved over the rounded handle. How she'd ever missed it in the first place was a testament to how stunned she was to see him at all. "Oh, my God," she fell back a step. "What's happened?"

His lashes hid his expression, and his lips compressed. "Little accident."

Swallowing an abrupt wave of nausea, Emily strode across the foyer into the great room and flipped on a lamp. In the light, she studied him more closely. He'd been collecting little scars on his face ever since she could remember. But he'd added a few new ones since she'd seen him last. The thin line slicing along his angular jaw was still faintly pink. As was the crescent outlining the corner of his right eye. "How little?"

She watched his expression deliberately lighten. And the grin that flirted with his lips almost convinced her. But she'd known him too long. "Jefferson?"

He shrugged and moved across the room to lower himself onto the long caramel-colored couch. "Cracked some ribs." He lifted his left leg onto the coffee table and propped the cane on the couch beside him. "Broke a few bones. All healed up now."

He was making light of his injuries. She knew it. And he

knew she knew it. "What did you do? Fall off some bridge you were building or something?"

He was quiet for a moment. "Or something."

Shaking her head, she crossed over to him and grabbed a throw pillow. She bent over him and tucked it beneath his knee, scooting the table closer to the couch to provide more support. Her long hair fell over her shoulder and drifted across his pant leg and he tucked it behind her ear. She froze, half-bent over him.

"It's good to see you, Emily." His finger skipped from her ear to her bare arm, then away.

Irrational tears burned behind her lids, and she straightened abruptly, moving away. Far away. "I've got groceries in the car," she muttered, and left the room.

Jefferson watched her practically run from the room. He'd have offered to help, but in his shape, he'd be more of a hindrance. He closed his eyes wearily and dropped his head back against the butter-soft couch. He didn't like second-guessing his decisions, but maybe it had been a mistake for him to come here. Even after all this time. Wasn't there a saying somewhere that you could never go home?

"You look like someone rode you too hard then put you up wet."

Jefferson opened one eye and stared at his brother. Tristan was the youngest of the Clay brothers. And the biggest. At six foot five, his blond head practically brushed the top of the wide doorway leading from the foyer into the great room. "You sound like Squire."

Tristan grinned. "Flattery'll get you nowhere." He dropped his hulking length into an oversize leather wing chair and draped one leg over the arm.

"Wasn't flattery."

Tristan chuckled soundlessly. "No kidding." He swung his leg. "Speaking of our father, have you talked to him lately?"

"No."

"Plan to?"

"No."

Tristan snorted softly. "I guess that's clear then. How about Matt? Daniel? Sawyer?"

Jefferson shook his head at each mention of their other three brothers. When he could feel his baby brother's eyes drilling into him, he lifted his head and cocked one eyebrow. "They're all okay."

"How would you know?" Tristan asked mildly. "We haven't heard from you in more than two years."

Jefferson closed his eyes and leaned his head back again. "I've kept track of them." Except for those nine months, anyway. Then, before Tristan could poke his nose in, he said, "I've kept track of you, too." Jefferson rolled his head to one side and looked at his brother. "You've done well for yourself." He lifted his chin, indicating the comfortably spacious house that his baby brother called home. "I saw an article in *Time* a few months ago. 'Bout that hacker you tracked to Sweden."

Tristan shrugged. "It sounded more exciting than it was. How'd you get all busted up?"

"Emily's bringing in some groceries," Jefferson pointed out abruptly. "Why don't you get off your butt and go help her."

"And butt out of your business." Tristan concluded accurately. He tugged on his earlobe, then straightened from the chair. "You'll spill it eventually." His good nature was still evident.

"Don't count on it," Jefferson warned.

His brother's mouth curved in silent laughter and he went out to help Emily, leaving Jefferson to wonder when the hell his baby brother had gotten all grown up. His leg was aching, and his toes were numb, but he pushed himself slowly to his feet and crossed the room to the wide bay window overlooking the front of the house. The sun still hadn't fallen below the horizon, and through the delicate, off-white lace, he watched his brother lope down the shallow brick steps to the street level where Emily was pulling grocery sacks from the trunk.

As he watched, she set a bag down on the first step and leaned against the cherry red car. A picture of weariness. She was shaking her head to something Tristan was saying, then she raked her long hair back from her face and stared off down the street. Even from a distance, Jefferson could see the fine arch of her cheekbone. The sculpted curve of her lower lip. Her upraised arms tightened the loose-fitted suit across her chest, and Jefferson knew that his little Emily was grown up, too.

The last time he'd allowed himself to really look at Emily had been when she was nineteen. His gut still tightened, thinking of that time. She'd been incredibly lovely then. Sweet. Fresh as a spring flower. And way too innocent. His jaw tightened.

She was still incredibly lovely. But she was seven years older. And he should be shot for the dog he was for wondering if she was still the innocent she'd been back then.

Her arms lowered, and her hair, heavy glistening strands of dark brown silk, settled about her shoulders. She shook her head again, her hand slicing through the air. But Tristan caught the hand and pulled her to him. Tristan's size engulfed her slender form and, mouth tight, Jefferson turned away from the sight.

Emily pushed out of Tristan's arms. "I'm okay," she insisted.

Tristan stopped her from reaching for the grocery bags sitting on the step. "He probably won't stay long."

"He never stays anywhere for long." She avoided Tristan's eyes. They were shades lighter than Jefferson's dark blue, but they could be every bit as piercing. She stepped away from his reach and hefted up the grocery bags. "I'll be fine," she insisted. "I'm not going to fall apart simply because Jefferson has returned." She could read Tristan's thoughts almost as well as he could read hers. "And I won't fall apart when he leaves."

"Something is wrong this time." Tristan removed one of the bags from her arms and started up the steps. "Deep down. He's changed."

Emily didn't question how Tristan was so sure about that. Tristan just *knew* things. Always had. And she'd given up, years ago, asking him how, since her curiosity always met with glib non-answers. And now, regardless of Tristan's uncanny insight, Emily didn't want to think about whether Jefferson had changed. She didn't want to worry about how he'd gotten himself into such a bad condition. She didn't want to think about him at all. She wanted to drive to the stable where she boarded her horse, Bird, saddle up and ride for hours until she could manage to tuck away the ultimately futile feelings that Jefferson's presence always roused within her.

"He'll tell you about it if he wants," she said, stooping at the top of the steps to thread her fingers through the handles of the plastic bags she'd already carried that far. "Jefferson will tell you things he never tells any of the rest of us."

"He didn't tell me about what happened between the two of you," Tristan said as he grabbed up the rest of the sacks. "Not that I couldn't figure it out for myself."

Emily stopped in her tracks. "There's nothing to tell."

"Right."

"Tris—"

"All right." His big shoulders lifted innocently. "Don't get your shorts in a knot."

"Charming," she remarked, shouldering her way through the

door and heading down the hall toward the kitchen. "It's no wonder you can't get a decent woman to go out with you."

He laughed. "Honey pie, when I'm on a date, I'm not looking for *decency*."

Rolling her eyes, Emily felt her mood lighten a fraction. Tristan was good at that. He dumped the grocery bags on the pristine white-tiled counters and she waved him off. "Go bug your brother," she ordered, pulling out the rectangular boxes of frozen pizza and turning toward the wide freezer. "Supper will take a while."

Tristan stepped between her and the refrigerator and pulled out two apples from the crisper. "Whenever." He buffed one of the apples against his faded T-shirt and removed himself from her way.

Once he was gone, Emily's hands slowed and she closed her eyes. She could get through Jefferson's visit, she told herself. She *would*. A day or two at the most, and he'd be off again on some adventure or other.

An hour later she set the steaming pan of enchiladas she'd decided to make instead of pizza in the middle of the kitchen table, alongside a large, tossed salad. She'd had to force herself not to set supper in the dining room. When her traitorous thoughts had swayed toward setting the table with china and crystal, she'd resolutely plucked a package of paper plates from the pantry. She and Tristan never ate in the formal dining room. To do so now would only heighten the man's insatiable curiosity.

She eyed the table. Then, with a huff, she snatched up the paper plates and hastily replaced them with their casual white stoneware.

"Smells good," Tristan remarked, appearing in the doorway. She hastily shoved the plates in the garbage beneath the sink.

Jefferson, sans cane, followed more slowly. Emily turned to

the refrigerator but not soon enough to miss the way he favored one leg as he pulled out a chair. "What do you want to drink? We've got iced tea, lemonade—" she said, automatically reaching for a bottle of beer for Tristan. He passed behind her and she shoved the cold bottle into his hands. "Grape juice, soda, coffee, milk, beer, wine…"

Jefferson's lips twitched. "Beer's fine."

She shut her mouth and reached for two more bottles and elbowed the refrigerator closed. Tristan was sitting in his usual chair and reaching for the enchiladas when she pointedly placed a glass mug in front of him. As usual, he ignored it and deliberately picked up his bottle to take a long drink.

"Squire should have sent *you* to school to learn manners," Emily announced, and started to pull out her own chair, but Jefferson, leaning over, did it first. She aimed a small smile in his direction, happy that she could do so without actually looking at him.

Jefferson slowly unfolded a napkin and dropped it in his lap. Emily had slapped Tristan's hands away from mangling any more of the enchiladas, and she deftly scooped a hefty portion onto Tristan's plate, then Jefferson's. All she put on her own plate, however, was salad, at which she proceeded to pick.

Jefferson silently watched his brother and Emily. And wondered.

"I take it that's a rental parked in the driveway?" Tristan asked.

Jefferson nodded, gingerly taking a forkful of the steaming enchilada. The temperature was nothing compared to the spiciness, and it scorched all the way down. He almost knocked over the mug of beer when he abruptly reached for it. "Geez," he muttered when he could draw breath. "Think it's peppery enough?"

Tristan caught Emily's gaze and grinned sadistically. "Getting soft in your old age?"

Jefferson smirked. "You wish." Prepared this time, he forked another bite of enchilada into his mouth. By his fourth bite, he didn't even have to wash it down with a chaser of ice cold beer. "Is this the type of cooking they taught you in that fancy school in New Hampshire?"

Emily shook her head and carefully laid her fork on her mostly full plate. "No. There, they taught me how to set a fine table and serve *Cordon Bleu*. Squire got what he paid for," she assured Jefferson dryly. It had been a long time since she'd gotten over her anger at Jefferson's father for sending her to boarding school when she was a teenager. She nodded toward the enchilada dish. "I took a Southwest cooking class a year ago at the community college to learn how to do that."

"Thank God, too," Tristan inserted. "I was getting sick of watercress and—" The telephone rang, and he leaned back in his chair to grab the cordless unit with a long arm. "Yup," he answered lazily. His eyebrows rose as he listened. "Well, sweetheart, I can't think of a single thing I'd rather do than have supper with you this evening." Tristan grinned wolfishly at whatever "sweetheart" had to say, and he rose, ignoring the fact that he'd just packed away a good portion of supper already.

"You want me to wear *what?* Why you naughty girl...." Ignoring Jefferson and Emily, he wandered out of the kitchen, the phone tucked at his ear.

Emily rolled her eyes at Tristan's back. "Girlfriend 372." She smiled faintly and reached for her own beer.

Without the easygoing presence of his overgrown baby brother to provide a buffer, Jefferson silently concentrated on his meal. "I was surprised to discover you're living out here," he said finally.

Emily sipped her beer. Well, now she knew for certain that he hadn't come to San Diego to see her. "Here, as in San Diego? Or here, as in Tristan's house?"

"Either. Both."

"I'm an accountant," she reminded.

"I know. I'd have thought you'd return to the Double-C. Help Matthew with the books or something like that. Start your own business, even."

She shrugged, pleased with her nonchalance. "Pay's better here. Besides, Matt handles the books just fine on his own. I'd have been bored stiff." She studied her beer.

He frowned. "Liar."

Emily glanced at him, then lowered her gaze. She wasn't about to tell him that he was the reason she hadn't returned to live at the ranch that had been her home since she'd been seven years old. She lifted one shoulder and sipped at her beer. "Think what you want. But the fact is, once I passed the CPA exam, I was offered too good a job to turn it down. The corporate office just happened to be in San Diego. Tristan was already out here. Living with him is…convenient."

His jaw ached. "Convenient."

Emily smiled mockingly, and Jefferson caught a glimpse of the spirited teenager she'd been. "Yes. Convenient."

"What does Squire think of this?"

Her delicately arched eyebrow rose. "Do you think he wouldn't approve?" Her lips twisted as the past suddenly twined between them. A bittersweet, tangible thing. "He figures that by living with Tristan, my…virtue…is well protected."

"Does he?"

"What?"

"Does Tristan protect your virtue?"

Emily's dark eyes narrowed until only a slit of pansy brown remained. "I don't need any one of the infamous Clay brothers to protect my virtue. I can do that just fine, *when I choose to,* on my own, thank you very much." She rose and began clearing the dishes.

Jefferson wiped his mouth with the napkin and crumpled it in his fist. "I hope you're being smart about it," he warned softly.

She looked over her shoulder. "Excuse me?"

"When you're *choosing*."

Her lips curved. "Good Lord, Jefferson. Are you trying to tell me to practice safe sex?" She laughed abruptly. Harshly. "That's just *too* sweet."

"You never used to be such a brat."

Emily flipped on the water and began rinsing plates. "Yes, I was. You just weren't around to notice." She shot him a flippant smile and bent to stack the dishes in the dishwasher.

"I wasn't always gone."

Emily paused, then straightened and reached for another plate. "That was a long time ago," she said brusquely.

He held out his empty mug and she reached for it. "Feels like yesterday." He held on to the mug as she tugged at it. "Sometimes."

Her short-lived bravado died a quiet death. "I'm not going to talk about this with you."

"I didn't plan on talking about it, either."

Her eyes, when they rose to his, were pained. "Then why are you? We've managed to see each other a few times since—" She could count on half the fingers of one hand the few times they'd seen each other since the week of her nineteenth birthday. And she could count on the other hand the number of words they'd exchanged.

"You can't even say it, can you."

Emily let go of the mug. She reached for the green-and-white dish towel hanging from the oven door and slowly dried her hands. Staring blindly at the smoked-glass oven door, she felt him moving around the island counter to stand behind her. "What do you want from me, Jefferson? Do you want me to tell you that Tristan and I aren't involved?" She folded the towel in a neat rectangle. "Is that what's bugging you? Well, we're not. He's my best friend. My brother."

"He's no more your brother than I am."

"Well." She refolded the towel. "I guess that puts me in my place, doesn't it. My last name is, after all, Nichols. Not Clay. I'm just the kid your father took in when my parents died in the crash. Because of some absurdly remote familial relationship we have. What was it? His great-grandfather's second wife was my mother's second cousin's aunt's mother-in-law's uncle?"

"Dammit, Em. That's not what I meant."

She flipped the towel over the oven door handle. She knew that wasn't what he meant. But this was far safer than touching on *that*. Waving her hand, she stepped away and went back to the table to continue clearing the dishes. "Just forget it, would you, please?"

He leaned back against the refrigerator and crossed his arms. Emily stifled a sigh as she couldn't help noticing the way he'd rolled up the sleeves of his shirt. The way his sinewy forearms tapered into long, narrow wrists. They were golden brown. Just like the rest of him. She'd never known a man with such intrinsically strong wrists. Just looking at them made her want all sort of indecent—

She blinked and began gathering up the used napkins.

"The men in California can't be blind," Jefferson finally said. "There must be someone you're involved with."

Flattening her palms on the table, Emily bowed her head. "For God's sake, Jefferson. Your nosiness exceeds even Tristan's."

"It's not being nosy to want to know what's going on in my sister's life."

She shook her head. "We've established already that you're not my brother."

"I'll just find out from Tris."

She moistened her lips and dropped into a chair. "Let me just get this straight. Are you asking me if I'm dating anyone? Do you want their names, addresses and phone numbers so you can personally check them out to find out if they are suitable for your nonsister? Or are you asking me if I'm sleeping with anyone?"

His eyes were dark. Inscrutable. "Are you?"

"Are you?" She fired back.

"No."

"My condolences."

His eyes never wavered. "Save 'em. I answered. Now it's your turn."

"I'm not sleeping with anyone," she announced slowly, deliberately. If it had been anyone but Jefferson questioning her this way, she'd have told them to take a flying leap. "Are you satisfied? Is the inquisition over? May I be excused now like a good little girl? Though, first perhaps I should ask a few questions, too." She turned her face away. "Like where have you been for the past two and a half years? Building bridges, still? Or working on an oil rig? Not that you've ever told us *exactly* what you do.

"How did you injure yourself? Why didn't you even call Squire to let him know you were okay? Alive." She hesitated. "Or have you lost that sense of *family responsibility* that used to be so all-fired important to you?" She looked at him.

He silently looked back, a shadow coming and going in his deep blue eyes. After a moment, he turned and slowly limped out of the kitchen.

"Dammit," Emily buried her head in her arms on the table. This is what happened when she and Jefferson talked too much.

If they'd just keep their exchanges in the realm of "nice weather we're having" and "what team do you think will make the Super Bowl" everyone would be happier. She couldn't put all the blame on Jefferson, either. She shared the responsibility.

"Hey, squirt, where's Jefferson?"

Emily lifted her head and shrugged. "I expect he's not far, considering the way he's favoring that leg." She was accustomed to seeing Tristan in various attires, but this time she was surprised. "Since when do you wear a tie?"

His hand ran down the silk material. "Is it straight?"

Emily shook her head and rose to help him pull it neatly to center. "Where're you going?" He stood still long enough to let her finish. Barely.

"Coronado."

"So, I, uh, shouldn't wait up for you?"

He grinned, and slipped his arms into a finely tailored black suit coat. "Like you've ever bothered to do that."

Emily smiled faintly and leaned back against the island, her arms crossed.

"Hey." Tristan chucked her chin up with a long finger. "You and Jefferson could come with us."

Her eyebrows shot up. "I bet that's not what 'sweetheart' had in mind."

He shrugged. "So, come anyway. It'd do you good to get out and have some fun for once."

"I don't think so."

"Why not?"

Faintly exasperated, she shook her head. "We don't all work in our own homes, at our own leisure, you know. I do have to go to work in the morning."

"Consider it a celebration that Jefferson's back."

Emily heaved a sigh. "Tristan—"

"Okay, okay." He dropped a kiss on the top of her head and pulled her hair. "Behave while I'm gone."

"That's a laugh," she murmured. "Why don't *you* behave for once?"

Tristan just smiled and with a wave he left. He must have found Jefferson easily, because she heard their deep voices, if not their words, soon followed by the slam of the heavy front door.

After a deep, cleansing breath, she went in search of Jefferson. The huge great room was empty, and she peeked in Tristan's office and the den. She finally found him in the rear of the house where Tristan had glassed in a high-ceilinged atrium.

She watched from a distance as he seemingly examined the leaf of a fern. He slowly moved along the brick-paved floor, disappearing behind a ficus, then reappearing on the other side. He'd folded up the long sleeves of the loose white shirt another couple of turns, and a second button was loose at his throat, hinting at the strength of his chest. She watched him silently, filling up an empty place inside her with just the sight of him. Longing, sweet and bitter, flooded through her.

Why did she have to feel this way about Jefferson, of all people? Why couldn't she have picked an easier man. Like Stuart Hansen, a manager from her office whom she occasionally dated. Or Luke, the man who owned the stable where she kept Bird. Or even Tristan, for that matter. Why Jefferson? It was a question that had plagued her for years.

Unfortunately, she was no closer to an answer than she'd ever been.

Sighing, she pushed open the French door leading into the atrium. "I'm going to put fresh sheets on the bed in the guest room," she told him, attracting his attention. "There's a bathroom attached. With a whirlpool tub. It might feel good on your leg."

Jefferson gently snapped a tiny white flower from its stem. "Fine."

"Well." Emily flipped over her wrist to look at her watch. It wasn't the least bit late. Maybe she should have taken up Tristan's offer. Then at least she wouldn't be *alone* with Jefferson. "It's the first room to the left at the top of the stairs."

"Tris showed me when I arrived."

"Oh." She fiddled with her watch again.

He crushed the bloom between his fingers. "If you've got somewhere you need to go, don't let me keep you."

"Hmm? Oh, no. No. I'll just go take care of those sheets." She spun around and headed for the stairs.

At the top, she snatched a set of clean sheets from the linen closet and went into the guest room. A single duffel bag sat at the foot of the bed. The bag had probably once been black leather, but now was worn nearly colorless in most places. She reached out to move it, pausing over the collection of airline stubs hanging from the handle. There must have been a dozen or more, and with merely a glance knew she didn't recognize any of the abbreviations.

Closing her fingers over the handle, she moved it to the top of the dresser, out of her way. It hardly weighed enough to warrant the size of the bag. Jefferson obviously had perfected the art of traveling light.

She flipped back the dark blue down comforter and smoothed the fresh white sheets in place. She had the edge of a plump bed pillow caught between her teeth when Jefferson silently appeared in the doorway. Ignoring him, or at least pretending to, she finished pulling on the pillowcase and dropped the pillow next to its twin at the head of the full-size bed. With a flick, she pulled up the comforter once more and, reaching across the bed, smoothed a wrinkle.

"I remember when you used to refuse to make your own bed."

Emily tossed several decorative pillows back onto the bed and straightened.

"You insisted that it was a waste of time, when you were only going to mess it up again when you had to go to bed."

"It was good logic," she answered lightly. "Squire never climbed on you boys when any of you didn't clean your room. Or didn't make your bed each morning. Apparently that was something he reserved for *girls*."

Jefferson crossed to the opposite side of the bed and stooped to pick up a small square pillow that had fallen to the floor. His fingers hovered over the deep blue and maroon needlepoint pattern. "Was it so bad, then? Being raised by Squire?"

Emily shook her head. This, at least, was something she could be perfectly honest about. "No. It wasn't bad." She smiled faintly. "What could be bad about being raised on a ranch? There were dogs and cats. Horses. The swimming hole. And several big 'brothers' to tag after. It wasn't bad." She headed back into the hall and the linen closet. It had been heaven on earth to a lonely little girl. It would be heaven on earth to a lonely woman, too.

He followed her to the doorway and leaned against the doorjamb. "How often do you get back to the ranch?"

She pulled a couple of oversize towels from the closet and turned back to the bedroom. "Two or three times a year, I guess. I've tried to get back each Christmas, but with work and all…" She passed by him and hung the towels over the brass rods in the bathroom. "When you're the low man on the totem pole, other people usually get first crack at holiday vacations."

"Squire doesn't celebrate much at Christmas, anyway."

"Considering that your mother died on Christmas Eve, who can blame him?" She halted and squared the edge of his duffel bag against the corner of the dresser. She glanced at him. "You were never around on Christmas, either. Even when you still lived at home, you went to the cabin rather than stay in the big house. Sawyer was in Europe by then. Dan was—"

"Off raising hell," Jefferson finished. "And Matthew was either closed up in the office or out on the range somewhere. Just one big happy family." Jefferson watched her, his eyes brooding. "And Tristan—"

"What?" She prompted when he broke off.

He shrugged. "Nothing."

Emily leaned her hip against the dresser and absently caught her hair back to weave it into a loose braid. She could take a stab at what Jefferson was thinking.

"Your mother died giving birth to him. Naturally that left a mark on him." She dropped the braid and headed for the door. "If you want to watch a movie or read, you'll probably find something to your taste in Tristan's room. He's got everything under the sun."

"What are you going to do?"

Escape. She cupped the side of the doorjamb with one palm. "I brought home some work from the office." It wasn't strictly a lie. "You, um… Let me know if you need anything." Her lips sketched a smile and she fled.

Jefferson pinched the bridge of his nose and collapsed on the side of the bed. Arms outstretched, he gingerly lifted his leg until he sprawled across the bed diagonally. His toes tingled as sensation returned. His head was pounding and his hip ached worse now than it had six months ago when he'd first been discharged from the hospital in Germany. Even his shoulder was kicking up a protest. Due, no doubt, from the horrendously long flight from Amsterdam. He had some pain medication in his duffel bag, but just then he didn't have the energy to retrieve it from across the room.

Restlessly he shifted, and his hand brushed against the pillows. He nudged aside the assortment of ruffled and tucked shapes until he reached the plain white bed pillow. Slowly his fingers closed over the edge and he pulled it to him. When it was near his face, and he could almost smell Emily's clean, pure scent on the pillowcase, he closed his eyes with a sigh.

And slept.

Chapter Two

When her head jerked upright just before hitting the edge of her laptop, Emily blinked, owlishly. She stared at the garbled spreadsheet displayed on the screen. Her fingers must have been pressing on the keyboard. Blinking, she erased the gobbledygook, closed the file and shut down the computer system.

A huge yawn made her eyes water, and she rubbed her eyes. Another yawn.

Still functioning, barely, she remembered to put the computer in her briefcase so she wouldn't forget it in the morning. Standing up from the leather chair she'd been perched in, she set the computer on the coffee table and arched her back, wiggling her bare toes. The antique clock sitting on the mantel chimed softly, and she realized it was after three in the morning. Yawning yet again, she padded out to the kitchen and retrieved a cold bottle of water from the refrigerator.

Before shutting off the light and heading upstairs, she

peeked into the garage. Jefferson's rental was parked neatly beside her Mustang. His work? Or Tristan's?

She twisted off the cap to the bottle and shut off the few remaining lights, checking the front door and the back French doors that overlooked the swimming pool beyond the atrium. In darkness she moved back through the great room and up the stairs. The door to Jefferson's room was open and the light was still on.

Pausing at the head of the stairs, she sipped on the water, studying the rectangle of light cast upon the dark green and maroon carpet runner that ran the length of the upstairs hallway. The house was quiet in the way that houses were. She could hear the quiet tick of the clock on the downstairs mantel. The gentle sighing of wood as it settled for the night.

She set the bottle on the square newel post and moved over to the doorway, peering around the edge. Jefferson was stretched across the bed at an awkward angle. One leg, obviously the one he'd injured, was flat on the bed, but his other leg was bent at the knee and hung over the edge of the bed, the worn slanted heel of his leather cowboy boot flat on the floor. His face was turned away from her, tucked in the edge of the pillow that sat beside, rather than under, his head.

She bit the inside of her lip and leaned against the door frame. Who was she kidding? To pretend that life would just continue on as normal, now that Jefferson had returned. However temporary his return might be. "Oh, Jefferson," she murmured, watching him sleep for a long moment.

Without a sound, she went to her own bedroom, turned on the light, retrieved the softly nubby afghan that usually sat folded at the foot of her bed and returned to his room. She snapped off the lamp and decided against trying to remove his boots for fear that he'd waken. She leaned across him, lightly spreading the blanket across his chest.

He didn't stir. She began to straighten and her fingers grazed the thick ends of his hair. She froze, her fingers tingling. Swallowing, she curled her fingers into a fist and snatched her hand away before she could succumb to the temptation of running her fingers through its heavy softness.

She didn't know what happened then. One minute she was tucking her hair behind her ears and backing away from the bed. The next, Jefferson sprang at her with a feral growl, his large hands gripping her upper arms like manacles. He swiveled and pushed her onto the bed hard enough to jar the breath from her chest.

Speechless, she stared up at him.

His breath was harsh, and his hands tightened painfully as his weight pressed across her midriff. "You're dead," he growled.

Shock held her immobile as surely as his hands around her arms. "Jeff...er...son," she gasped faintly.

Even in the pale light coming from her room down the hall she could see his teeth bared. Her heart was pounding painfully, and her head ached with the adrenaline shooting through her veins. "Jefferson. It's me."

His eyes, blackish pools, looked down at her, unblinking. In another time. Another place. A terrible, dark, painful place.

"It's me. Emily," her soft voice shook, but he held himself still for a long moment. "Shh," she whispered faintly. "It's okay, Jefferson."

His arms seemed to sway, and he loosened his iron grip.

"It's all right now," she breathed, and closed her eyes on a faint sob when he lowered his head to the curve of her breast. As gentle as they'd been painful, his hands slid up her arms to her shoulders. Wide-eyed, she lay stiffly beneath him, looking down at the crown of his head as he seemed to just collapse. As abruptly as he'd charged.

Biting down on her lip, she closed her eyes tightly. Tears

burned their way from beneath her lids anyway. Oh, Jefferson, what's happened to you?

She hauled in a shaky breath, half-afraid that he'd rouse again, in Lord-only-knew what kind of state. But he was still.

After long minutes she lifted her hand and smoothed his heavy hair away from his forehead. Letting the tears come, she lay there, still trapped beneath his weight. Her hand gently stroking through the silky blond strands.

"It will be okay, Jefferson," she whispered. "Everything will be okay."

A few hours later, her eyes were gritty with the snatches of sporadic sleep, and the gray light of dawn was slipping through the slats of the cherry shutters hanging at the windows. The arm trapped beneath Jefferson's shoulder was completely numb. But he seemed to be sleeping easier now. More naturally, if the deep breathing that wasn't quite a snore was any indication.

Grimacing against the pins that immediately began stabbing her fingers when she gradually worked her arm from beneath him, she edged away from his weight until she was free to slip from the end of the bed.

He sighed deeply and turned back into the pillow, one hand eclipsing an entire corner of it.

Hunched against the furious feeling returning to her arm, she found herself reaching for the afghan that had fallen to the floor at some point. Far too disturbed to wonder at her daring, she slipped the covering over his shoulders before leaving the room and closing the door softly behind her.

The bottle of water was right where she'd left it on the newel post, and she swayed, fresh tears clogging her throat. Gritting her teeth, she grabbed the bottle and closed herself in her own bedroom. She poured the water among the various plants growing in her room, and the empty bottle she dropped on the pristine white eyelet bedspread. Her clothes landed haphazardly where her hands dropped them, and she stood there, numb. Unthinking. Sleep would be impossible. Goose bumps danced across her skin, and she automatically pulled on softly warm sweatpants. She covered the T-shirt she pulled on with an oversize sweatshirt that Tristan had cast aside.

Her cold fingers nimbly pulled her hair into a braid and she tucked a house key and five dollars into her pocket. In minutes, she was quietly letting herself out the front door, into the chilly dawn. The afternoons in mid-August might be sweltering. But the crack of dawn in San Diego was bound to be cool. And, that morning, foggy as well.

Emily eyed the house as she methodically warmed up her cold muscles, and then stretched gently. When she set off up the block in a slow jog, all she could see in her mind were Jefferson's eyes. Wounded. Black with pain.

Her shoes thumped steadily as she rounded a curve in the street and began the ascent that would eventually, after exactly 2.4 miles, lead to the stable. And Bird. But she didn't hear the slap of her shoes against the pavement. Nor did she hear the gradual awakening of the neighborhood. Car engines starting. Front doors slamming as morning newspapers were retrieved. She heard nothing. Only the memory of Jefferson's deadened voice.

"You're dead."

It was afternoon when Jefferson finally woke. And he probably wouldn't have even then if it weren't for his baby brother standing over him, shaking the toe of his boot hard enough to rattle his teeth.

Jefferson peeled open his eyes, squinting at the bright California sunshine blasting through the windows. "What?"

"Rise and shine, bro. The day is awastin'."

Wearily, Jefferson closed his eyes again. He bunched the pillow beneath his head and scratched his chest. "Says who."

"Me. Come on, Jeff. You keep sleeping the way you are and we're gonna have to call in the paramedics just to see if you're still alive."

"Go surf the Net. Or whatever the hell you do on those computers of yours."

"No work today," Tristan said cheerfully. "We're going out." He yanked the pillow from beneath Jefferson's head.

"Speak for yourself."

"Or we can stay here and you can tell me what the hell's been going on with you the past few years."

Jefferson pushed himself up until he was sitting. A blue knitted thing drifted across his lap. A stray thought hovered at the edge of his mind as he looked at it. Frowning, he shoved it aside and held out his hand. "Help me up."

"Damn, buddy," Tristan said as he pulled Jefferson to his feet. "You're really gettin' decrepit, aren't you."

Jefferson planted a hand on Tristan's chest and shoved him out of the way. "I can still whip your butt," he warned. Pulling his shirt free, he balled it up and dropped it on the foot of the bed.

"Holy sh—"

Jefferson ignored Tristan's muffled curse as his brother obviously saw the scar on his back and continued into the bathroom. He sat on the closed lid of the commode and studied his boots. He wiggled his toes. At least, he *thought* he wiggled them. They'd gone numb again. Grimacing, he bent his knee and began tugging.

"Maybe you should just get it over with," Tristan said as he appeared quietly in the doorway. "Ain't nothing you can say that's going to outdo what my imagination is coming up with."

"Don't be too sure." Jefferson's teeth clenched as he managed to pull his foot free from the high boot.

"You ought to stick to bedroom slippers at that rate," Tristan advised. "They're a whole lot easier to get on and off."

Jefferson politely told his brother what he could do with the advice.

Tristan watched Jefferson struggle with the other boot for a long minute. "Oh, for crying—" He bent down and pulled the boot off himself, dropping it to the marble-tiled floor with a heavy thud. Then he turned and flipped on all four faucets full blast. The Jacuzzi tub began to fill. He watched the water rise. "How long you been out?"

Jefferson went still for a moment. "Out of where?" He slid open drawers until he found a disposable razor and a toothbrush still in the plastic package.

"The hospital."

Relax. He ripped off the plastic wrapping and tossed it aside. "Long enough."

Tristan grunted and left the bathroom. He returned moments later, bearing a tube of toothpaste. "Here."

"Hope you give Em more privacy than you're giving me," Jefferson commented blackly as he squeezed toothpaste onto the new toothbrush.

"I'm not likely to be overcome with lust at the sight of your bod, if that's what's bugging you," Tristan assured dryly.

"At least California hasn't warped you completely." Closing his eyes, Jefferson enjoyed the simple act of brushing his teeth. For too long he'd not had access to such simple things. And then when he did have access, he'd been unable to do it himself.

Tristan flipped off the water as it neared the top of the tub. "What kind of gun makes a hole like that," he wondered after a moment.

Jefferson spat and rinsed his mouth. Slowly, he set the toothbrush on the side of the sink. He cupped cold water in his hands and doused his face with it, running his fingers through his hair and away from his face. He looked into the mirror and saw his brother watching him silently.

"The same kind that I'm never gonna carry again," Jefferson finally said.

Tristan's eyes narrowed, but he didn't comment on that. After a moment he nodded. "I'm glad you made it back," he said simply.

Jefferson eyed himself in the mirror. He looked every day of his thirty-six years. And then some. For the first time in more than a year, though, he could honestly say the words. "I'm glad, too."

The two brothers shared a look. Then abruptly Tristan nodded. "Well, holler if you need help crawling out of that swimming hole when you're done." He cupped the back of Jefferson's neck in his big palm for a brief moment. "Then we're gonna go have a beer. Maybe admire a few lovelies along the way," he said gruffly. He dropped his hand. Nodded once. And left.

Jefferson slowly shucked his pants and lowered himself into the tub, thinking how much Tristan had grown to be like their father. It was both a curse and a blessing.

He groaned aloud when he flipped on the Jacuzzi jets and the water began churning. In that moment, the five-by-eight dirt-floored room in Lebanon, the hospital in Germany and the doctors in D.C. all seemed very far away.

Eventually Jefferson, clean and muscles and joints loosened somewhat from the soothing water, climbed out unaided from the tub and dried himself. He ran a comb through his tangled hair, thinking it was high time he got a haircut. He rummaged through the drawers again, but gave up when he couldn't find any rubber bands. Back in the bedroom he unzipped his bag and pulled out some clean clothes. His eyes were on the blue blanket as he tucked the long tails of his shirt into his jeans and buttoned up the fly. He leaned over and picked it up by the edge, his thumb and forefinger absently smoothing the fluffy softness.

"You ready yet?" Tristan yelled from somewhere in the house. Jefferson took a last look at the blanket and dropped it back on the bed. He shoved his wallet in his pocket and grabbed a clean pair of socks before retrieving his boots from the bathroom.

Tristan's heavy feet pounded up the stairs. "Come on, Jeff. It'll be dark at the rate you're going—"

Jefferson stepped into the hallway, ignoring his cane where it was propped next to the dresser. "I'm ready." He waved his boots at his brother who thundered back down the stairs. He followed more quietly, then sank down on the last step to pull on his socks.

"Want to borrow some shoes?"

Jefferson tucked his tongue in his cheek as he glanced over at the huge white sneakers Tristan wore. "I'll wear my boots. Thanks." Lips tight, he shoved his foot into the worn-soft leather and tugged. Thank God they were easier to put on than take off.

He pulled himself up by the banister and stomped once. Once a pair of boots were broken in, they were more comfortable than any other kind of footwear. He'd believed it since he'd been eleven years old.

The corner of Tristan's lips curled slightly and he turned for the door. "Gonna die with them things on, aren't you."

"Yup."

Jefferson waited while Tristan set the security system and securely locked the door. In minutes, they were hurtling down the freeway in Tristan's battered half-ton pickup. Jefferson edged a stack of books out from beneath his boot. They started to slide and he bent over to shove them away so his feet had somewhere to go. He sat up again, and hunched his shoulder so as not to knock over the computer that occupied the middle portion of the seat. Atop the computer was a beaten-up leather deck shoe with half the sole missing. "You know," he pointed out as he pulled the leather lacing from the shoe. "We could've driven the rental." He reached up and pulled the annoying hair away from his face and tied it into a ponytail with the lace.

Tristan looked at the conglomeration of stuff as if for the first time. "Push it behind the seat if it's bugging you."

Jefferson's chuckle was rusty. Then he watched in amazement as a tiny little compact car sped around them and pulled right in front of them, slowing down abruptly. He caught the computer just as it began to slide when Tristan hit the brakes, swearing. In seconds everything was back to normal, and Jefferson shook his head. The traffic heading the opposite direction was already heavy. "Driving in this would do me in," he muttered.

Tristan grunted, switched lanes, slowed down and switched lanes again. "You get used to it. I couldn't do what Em does, though." He maneuvered around a lumbering panel truck and headed for the exit. "She drives about forty miles round-trip every day."

"Does she like her job?"

Tristan pulled up at a stoplight. He checked the traffic, then turned right and right again, coming to a halt in a nearly deserted parking lot. The beach was merely yards away, a jumble of umbrellas and kids and kites. "She's as happy there as she's going to be anywhere, I'd guess." He climbed out of the truck.

Jefferson got out too, eyeing Tristan over the dusty roof of the cab. "Meaning?"

Tristan turned, his eyes squinting in the late afternoon sun.

After a brief moment, he shrugged. "Meaning nothing." He rounded the truck and headed for the weather-beaten wooden building. "Come on. Beer's getting warm while we're sitting here yakking."

Jefferson tucked his fingers in his pockets and followed his brother into the dimly lit bar. He'd been in a hundred similar establishments in a hundred different cities.

Tristan held up two fingers as he passed the bartender. "Hey, Joe. How's it hanging?"

The bartender slid two foaming glasses of beer toward Tristan. "Can't complain."

Tristan tossed a couple of bills on the bar. "Say hi to my big brother," he told the other man.

Joe nodded and held out his beefy hand. Jefferson reached over and shook it. "Joe Pastorini," he introduced himself. "Your brother here's a good man. Helped my daughter out of a jam a while back." He pushed the money back toward Tristan. "That's no good here, boy."

Silently, Jefferson watched Tristan grab up a few peanuts from a brown bowl and pop them into his mouth. He noticed that Tristan didn't take back the money.

"How's little Emily doing? Haven't seen her in here for a while."

Tristan picked up one of the glasses and handed it to Jefferson. "She's fine." He grinned. "I think that CPA she's dating from the firm frequents the finer establishments."

Jefferson zeroed in on that. CPA?

"No finer place than this," Joe was defending.

"That's why I come here, Joe," Tristan assured dryly. He waved and headed toward the back of the room where a pool table sat. He placed his glass on the wide edge of the table. "Rack 'em up, Jeff."

Jefferson hadn't played pool in years. But he easily recognized the good-natured challenge in Tristan's eyes. Pushing aside thoughts of Emily and her CPA, he racked them.

Four games and two beers later, Jefferson placed the cue on the wall rack. "Enough."

Tristan sipped at his diet cola. He'd switched after the first beer. "Can't take the heat?"

"What heat," Jefferson asked lazily. He perched against the high stool he'd dragged over to the table from the bar after the first game and stretched his long legs. "I've won the last two."

Tristan seemed to consider that. He walked over to the wall rack and placed his cue there, also. "You know," he said, absently watching a young blond woman enter the bar, "Squire was the only one who could ever beat us hands down."

"Except for Daniel."

Tristan chuckled soundlessly. "Dan spends all his free time in the pool halls. He's practically a pro." He waved his nearly empty glass. "So he doesn't count."

Jefferson drained his glass and plunked it on the side of the pool table. It felt good. Not the beers, necessarily. But the easygoing company of his brother. Talking about their other brothers. His head was buzzing ever so slightly. "Who's the CPA?"

"Huh?"

"Emily's CPA."

Tristan stood up. "Come on. Let's go home."

Jefferson waited.

Tristan's lips compressed. He noticed the curvy blonde was staring at them. He lifted his chin in her direction. "Why don't you go say hello. She's interested."

Jefferson couldn't care less. The woman could have paraded around the pool table naked, and he wouldn't have cared. "Is it serious?"

"I'd say so, considering the way she's licking her chops over there." Tristan smiled faintly.

Jefferson waited.

Tristan returned Jefferson's stare with one just as silent. Just as long.

It was the blonde who finally interrupted. "Excuse me—" she glided to a stop next to Tristan, her green eyes sharp and her painted mouth smiling "—aren't you that cyberspy guy?"

Tristan raised his eyebrows. "Cyberspy?" He shot Jefferson a confused look, the picture of a befuddled male. "What's that? Some new kind of deodorant?"

The woman's eyes narrowed faintly. "You are," she insisted. "Your picture was in the *New York Times* a few weeks ago."

Tristan hooted. "New York? Geez, baby," he leered down at her, giving a good impression of a rather sun-baked beachboy. "I stick to the Pacific side of the states. Too uptight over there, I'd bet."

The avaricious interest in the woman's eyes waned slightly. But she wasn't ready to give up just yet. She turned to Jefferson. "I bet you're brothers," she said. "Am I right?"

Jefferson shrugged, amused at the way his brother was sidling away from the blonde.

"So, tell me," she ran a long red fingernail along the arm of the bar stool where Jefferson leaned. "Are you into computers, too?"

"Not lately."

She looked over her shoulder at Tristan. "He is that guy," she insisted. "I hear he's loaded. Pity he doesn't want to…play." She turned back to Jefferson and leaned forward, encasing him in a cloud of her spicy perfume. "But I can see that you—" she flashed him a long look "—are more experienced." She moistened her lips and cocked her hip, bending forward just enough that he could have looked straight down her loose shirt, had he been interested.

He wasn't. "This boy doesn't want to…play. Either," he assured her politely.

She straightened. Flipping her hair over one shoulder, she shrugged and wandered over to a man sitting alone in one of the booths.

Tristan pretended to shiver. "Scary," he muttered, and headed for the door, sketching a wave toward Joe as they left.

This time Jefferson shoved some of the books behind the seat before climbing into the truck. "Why'd you throw her off the scent?"

His brother coaxed the engine to life and headed them home. "You kidding? Even if I ever touched her, she'd be crying palimony, or abuse or some kind of garbage like that inside of two weeks. Just until she got a nice fat check." His lips twisted. "Amazing how money brings 'em out. Like worms after a rain."

Jefferson shook his head. He thought about telling his brother that he was too young to sound so jaded. But he saved his breath. "So who is the CPA?"

Tristan just shook his head.

When they let themselves into the house a while later, Tristan still wasn't answering. And Jefferson had quit asking. For now.

The house was quiet, and Jefferson knew instinctively that Emily wasn't home. Tristan headed for his office almost immediately, and Jefferson went to the kitchen. He drank down a narrow bottle of fancy water from the fridge and tossed the empty container into the sink. Frowning, he paused next to the counter, his palm flat on the white tile. He closed his eyes and imagined her.

Emily.

Moving around the kitchen. Cooking. Loading the dishwasher.

Laughing with Tristan over one of his stupid jokes.

His fingers pressed into the cold tile.

When the phone rang right beside his hand, he nearly jumped out of his skin. He bit back a violent curse. He hadn't quite been able to lick it yet. The unexpected attack of nerves. The jumps.

Maybe he'd never be able to.

The thought of which was almost more than he could bear. Swearing again, he flipped on the water and bent over the sink, throwing water over his face with hands that weren't quite steady.

"Jefferson?"

He froze, still hunched over the sink. He lowered his forehead in his hands. He hadn't even heard her come in, much less walk up behind him. Damn.

Emily slowly reached around him and shut off the gushing water. She settled her weight against the counter and leaned to the side until she was at his level. "What is it, Jefferson? What's wrong?"

Her scent. So cool. So clean. It matched her voice. Gentle. Soft.

Without looking, he knew her long brown hair would be pooling on the stark white tile. That her large eyes would be velvety brown and filled with emotion. He straightened abruptly, raking back the hair that had fallen loose from the shoelace tie.

He watched her straighten, also. The severely tailored dress that covered her from neck to knee shouldn't have been flattering on her slender figure. But it was. The black color suited her. As did the narrow lines that followed each curve and valley. His fingers curled.

"I shouldn't have come here."

She flinched. As if he'd physically struck her. It took her a moment before her expression smoothed out. "Then why did you?" Her voice was steady. "Never mind. I know why," she continued when he said nothing. "You came to see Tristan. So go ahead and tell him what it is that's eating you up inside."

She blinked her long lashes and aimed her glance somewhere around his shoulder. "Then maybe you'll get some peace."

"There's no peace left anymore," he said, the words dredged up. "Not for me."

He could hear her breath hissing between her teeth when she drew it in. Suddenly her palm, cool and smooth, cupped his cheek. Her brown eyes captured his gaze in their liquid depths. "Yes, there is," she promised him. Her thumb gently stroked his jaw. "It's just hiding from you right now," she spoke softly. "But it's there, Jefferson. You'll find peace again."

Her hand started to slide away, and he caught it with his own. "Where?" His gut hurt. "Where is it hiding, Emily?" He shook his head once. "Nowhere. That's where."

"You're wrong." She paused. "You know you're wrong. That's why you came here in the first place. To get rid of this—" she shook her head, unable to put a word to whatever *this* was. "Because you and…and Tristan are connected."

He released her fingers and put his hand to her shoulder to nudge her away. But his palm closed over the curve instead. "You're a dreamer, Emily," he didn't mean the words unkindly. It was just that he didn't have any dreams left. Only nightmares.

His hand slid down, cupping the upper curve of her arm through the black fabric of her dress. She bit her lip. "Maybe I am," she agreed sadly. She shifted and his hand dropped away. She caught it between her own and looked down. "You'll find peace," she assured him again. "It's hiding underneath the pain. The tears."

He gently touched her head. Silky. "I don't have any tears left, Emily."

She lifted her chin and looked him full in the face. A tiny droplet slipped from her eye, leaving a silvery trail in its wake. "I have tears," her words were barely audible. "I'll give you my tears." Her gaze skittered away from his, then returned. Another drop slid past her long lashes.

His jaw ached. With his thumb, he caught the next tear before it fell to her cheek. Then his hand slid behind her neck and he hauled her into his arms. Her hands slipped behind his shoulders, holding him tightly. Securely.

Her face turned into his neck and he could feel her tears. Groaning, he lowered his head to her shoulder and held her as she wept.

For him.

When the phone rang this time, Jefferson didn't flinch.

But Emily stiffened at the sound and pulled away a few inches. After that first, single ring, the phone was once again silent. She backed away a few more inches. She carefully removed her fingers from their clutch on his wide shoulders and tried to wipe her face. But Jefferson stopped her. His hands cradled her head and she felt tears clogging her throat anew at the tortured expression darkening his blue eyes until they were nearly black.

She closed her eyes, swallowing. "I'm sorry," she whispered. Why did she think *she* would be able to help him?

He shushed her so quietly she wasn't sure he'd actually made a sound. But his hands were lifting her chin, and, helpless, she looked up into his hard face. Her eyes fluttered closed when he dropped the lightest of kisses across her lids. She trembled when he softly kissed away the traces of tears still on her cheeks.

His breath whispered over her brow. Her temples.

"Sweet Emily," he murmured.

The floor seemed to sway beneath her feet and she clutched his arms for support. That deep, aching longing that had been her heart's constant companion for years nearly overwhelmed her. To be in his arms again.

A soundless sob rose in her throat and she pulled away from

his hands. A strand of her hair caught on the rough bristles blurring his carved jaw and she froze. A single strand of hair. Binding them together, for however brief a moment.

He slid a finger into her hair, slipping it behind her ear, then pausing to circle the small pearl stud earring. "Sweet, sweet Emily," he whispered again. His jaw clenched and he closed his eyes. Then he opened them. Watched her. Lowered his head.

Emily couldn't move. His lips grazed hers. Lifted. Lowered to sample once more.

His face blurred in her vision, and she instinctively closed her eyes, lifting toward him when he seemed to retreat.

"Jefferson," she whispered his name against his lips. "Let me help you."

He pressed his forehead against hers, struggling with the need that thundered in his blood. It wasn't just a sexual thing. He'd long grown accustomed to the fact that Emily aroused him, like no other being on the face of the planet could arouse him. For just as long he'd been beating down that flame. Knowing that it should never be allowed to freely burn.

She lifted her cheek, pressing it against his. He felt her tremble against him. Yet he knew she wasn't weak. She was strong. So strong he could let her take his pain, if only for a little while. That was the need that nearly overwhelmed him. But he didn't deserve the respite that only she could provide. He didn't deserve the freedom.

And he wouldn't sully her with the filth. It was, perhaps, the only thing in this damned world that he could do for her.

He clasped her arms gently and set her away. "No."

Her mouth opened soundlessly. Shut again. "It's always the same, isn't it, Jefferson," she managed eventually. Her arms crossed protectively across her chest, and he was abruptly reminded of the sweetly defiant teenager she'd once been.

"What's the same?"

She shook her wispy bangs away from her eyes, sending her hair rippling over her shoulders. "You don't want anybody getting too close. You don't…want…*me*…getting too close." She blinked her eyes away from his, rocking slightly on her heels, cupping her elbows in her palms. Regret curved her soft lips.

"Em—"

She looked back at him. There was simply too much emotion between them. The things she'd wanted from him. That he couldn't…wouldn't give. She blindly focused on the way his loose cotton shirt draped across his wide chest. "I used to think," she mused softly, "that you always—" Her lips trembled and she sniffed, dredging the depths for some control. "That you always left because you didn't care enough about the things you left behind. The people. The ranch." *Her.* "Because you cared more about the adventures waiting for you in some god-forsaken country."

"Em—"

"Sooner or later you'll have to stop running, Jefferson." She blinked rapidly. Enough tears had been shed today. "That's really what you've been doing all along, isn't it? But one day you're going to have to stop running. And come home again."

His jaw tightened. He could have disagreed with her. Could have denied it. He heard her quick, harsh breath, her delicate features drawn tight with pain.

"Coward," she accused softly. Swallowing, she bit her lip and looked away. Another tear slipped down her cheek and crept along her jaw. Spinning on her heel, she walked away.

Jefferson reeled. Swearing, he slammed his flat palm against a cupboard door. It bounced open violently and jounced shut. He dug his fingers into his temples, reining in the impulse to hit something again. "Dammit," he whispered. "Dammit!" He wrapped his fingers around the edge of the tile, his head bowed. Still, he couldn't contain a low growl. He shoved away from the counter and rounded it, his leg tight and most of his foot numb, as he stalked unevenly out of the kitchen. He headed through the great room and ended up slumped on the brick bench in the middle of the soaring atrium.

The violence drained away, leaving him tired. Weary beyond words. And what did he have to be so angry about, anyway? Emily spoke only the truth.

He heard a soft footfall. He stopped wiggling his foot. He picked up a leaf that had fallen to the ground and twirled it in his fingers.

"I'm sorry, Jefferson." She halted a few feet away. "I had no right to say what I did."

"Forget it."

Emily watched his fingers outline the delicate edges of the drying leaf. "I can't forget it." As soon as she said the words, he dropped the leaf. It landed near the toe of her shoe.

"Yes." He looked up at her, his expression closed. "You can."

Moth to a flame. That's what she was. Drawn to his light, no matter how deadly. Over and over again. In a single motion, she crouched at his feet, her hands lightly resting on his knees. "We used to be friends, Jefferson," she reminded him.

She bit back a protest when he carefully lifted her hands from his knees. He didn't even hold her hands, but circled her wrists with his fingers. As if he didn't even want to touch her. He shook his head, and her heart, already beaten and battered, received a fresh bruise. It was one thing to sense that their friendship was gone. It was another to have him confirm it. "Not family. Not friends." She was hardly aware that she spoke the thought aloud. "Not even old…"

"Lovers," he supplied the word when she couldn't.

"No. Not even that."

"I don't mean to hurt you, Emily." His fingers tightened gently on her wrists. "That's the last thing I've ever wanted."

She forced the corners of her mouth upward. "Forget it."

"Touché."

Somewhere in the depths of the house, the telephone rang again. Jefferson let go of her wrists, and Emily straightened. She smoothed down her dress. Without a backward glance she left him alone.

Through the open door to his office, Emily saw Tristan hunched at his desk, the phone at his ear. She passed by, retrieving her briefcase and her laptop, which she carried upstairs to her bedroom. She couldn't allow herself to think. For thought brought a fresh stab of pain. And with each stab of pain, she wanted to turn to the only one who could bring comfort.

But how could she do that when the source of her greatest comfort was also the source of her greatest pain?

Chapter Three

That night found Emily, once again, prowling around downstairs. Her eyes were beginning to sting from this second night of disturbed rest. But each time she'd tried to lay her head down in her own bed, her eyes had refused to shut. Her mind had refused to relax. Eventually, she'd simply given up and headed downstairs. Her restless wandering finally easing when she ended up in the kitchen.

Nothing like baking in the middle of the night. Opening up the refrigerator, she took out the carton of eggs and set it on the counter. She added the eggs to the mixture she'd started. Her toe absently tapped the base of the cabinets in time to the music playing softly on the radio. In her present state of mind, she'd be lucky not to eat the whole darn pan of brownies.

Sighing, she reached for the pan of melted chocolate, which she'd left to cool, and poured it in a slender stream into the batter. Her thoughts drifting, she scraped the edges of the pan with a spatula and began mixing once more.

She remembered the first time she'd tried her hand at cooking. She'd been nine years old, and she'd misread the recipe. The results had been practically inedible. Squire had turned nearly green when he'd taken his first bite. Tristan had comically started to make gagging motions. Matthew, bless his loving heart, had stoically eaten a small portion, as had Daniel.

But it was Jefferson who'd taken her aside the next day to help her read the recipe. It was Jefferson who'd stood by in the kitchen when she'd been determined to make that stupid casserole. He'd stood there, answering her questions as best he could. But never interfering. For he had known how important it had been to her to do it on her own. And when she'd presented the casserole again the next night, Squire and the boys had eaten every last bite.

Emily reached for the flour-dusted pan and filled it with batter, then slid it neatly into the oven. Returning to the counter, she perched her hip on the edge of the bar stool and slid her finger around the edge of the bowl. The dark chocolate was sticky and sweet and she savored the taste as she licked her finger clean. Then, before she could polish off the rest of the batter clinging to the inside of the glass bowl, she stuck the whole thing in the sink and rinsed it with hot water before shoving it into the dishwasher.

She absently set the timer on the oven and finished cleaning up the kitchen. There wasn't much to do. Tristan had been called out on some computer thing before supper and Jefferson had never reappeared. Emily had been torn between relief and despair when she'd sat down alone to the salad she'd prepared for herself.

In minutes the kitchen was completely restored to its usual

pristine state. The dishwasher was humming softly below the low music from the radio, and the first warming scent of baking brownies filled the room. She returned to the bar stool and leaned her elbows on the counter, cupping her chin in her hands. The smoked-glass door of the wall oven threw her reflection back at her.

She stared. Hard. But in her mind she wasn't seeing herself. She was seeing the tall, broad shape of a man. His heavy hair was a streaky golden mass that fell, shaggy, past his shoulders. His brows were darker than his hair and straight over his deep blue eyes. His jaw angled sharply to his chin where a long-ago adventure had left a tiny scar marring its otherwise perfection.

Emily rubbed her eyes wearily. But the sight of Jefferson was engraved in her mind. His broad shoulders. His wide chest, all bronzed and smooth. The corrugated muscles narrowing to—

She caught herself and blinked. Reaching out, she snatched up an apple-shaped pot holder and went to the oven, needlessly checking on the baking brownies. As soon as she cracked the oven door, a waft of heated chocolate escaped and she carefully shut the oven, tossing the pot holder aside as she turned.

Seeing him standing in the door, Emily wasn't sure she hadn't conjured him up from her imaginings. But her imaginings, no matter how detailed, didn't speak.

"Can't sleep?"

Emily shrugged, abruptly—painfully—aware of the brevity of the ruffled white nightshirt she wore. Aware of how thin it was.

Jefferson grimaced and leaning heavily on the cane, crossed to the bar stool. He lowered himself onto the round seat and propped the cane against the counter. "Neither can I," he admitted. He folded his arms on the bar, much as Emily had done earlier, and his unbuttoned shirt separated several inches.

She sank her teeth into the inner softness of her lip. "Do you, uh, want something to eat?" Her bare toes curled. "You didn't come down for supper."

She couldn't read a thing in the dark gaze he ran over her. She managed not to tug on the hem of the shirt, and he looked away, shaking his head. "No, thanks."

The low throb of music filled the kitchen. Swallowing, Emily stepped over to the wide pantry and, opening it, reached to the upper shelf for the powdered sugar. A strangled sound startled her, and clutching the package to her chest, she swiveled. "What?"

Jefferson had risen and, moving faster than she'd thought him capable, now stood beside her. His eyes burned as he lifted her arm above her head. The loose ruffles serving as a sleeve fell back to her shoulder.

Emily, confused, tried to pull away, but his hand gently detained her.

Jefferson took the package of sugar and placed it on the counter. He let her lower her arm, only to shove up the fabric at her other arm. "How?"

"What?"

His lips tightened, his teeth baring for a moment. White. Clenched. His hand flashed out and suddenly the button holding the loose shirt at the neck was unfastened and the fabric slid off her shoulders.

She gasped and grabbed at the fabric before it fell away. Color stained her cheeks. "What are you doing!"

He tugged on the fabric, pulling it well below her shoulders and she backed away, only to be brought up short by the cool surface of the refrigerator door. Soundlessly he smoothed her hair back from her face and, looking down, she realized what disturbed him so.

Angry blackish bruises circled her upper arms. Bruises in

the perfect shape of a hand. A hand that he was even now care-fully fitting around her arm, matching up exactly the dark marks marring her pale skin.

He drew back, as if the contact burned. "I did this." He backed away, his hands raking through his hair.

The lingering soreness of her upper arms was nothing compared to the stark expression in his eyes. She reached for him and he seemed to scramble backward, warding her off with an outstretched hand.

"Don't," he growled. Begged. He turned away, as if he couldn't bear the sight. But his eyes kept swiveling back to her, his long lashes not quite guarding his horror.

"It was my fault," Emily told him softly. "I shouldn't have disturbed your sleep last night." She took a step toward him. "I only meant to cover you." Another step. "You were having a bad dream."

"Nightmare," he corrected dully. "One huge, long, unending, goddamned nightmare."

She stepped forward an inch more and caught his hand in hers.

"Why, Jefferson? Why the nightmares?" She couldn't help the question. She wanted to know why he'd muttered "You're dead" in his sleep. Even though she knew he wouldn't say.

"I frightened you," he said, grimacing. "Marked you."

"You would not have hurt me." She clasped his hand close and dropped a kiss on his whitened knuckles. "No matter what your nightmare."

"You're foolish," he ground out.

"No." It was imperative that she get through to him. On this, if nothing else. Her heart beat unsteadily. "You listen to me, Jefferson Clay. I know that you would not have hurt me. And *yes,*" she said, keeping a grip on his hand when he would have turned away. "I was frightened last night. But frightened for you. For whatever hell that you've been through. I was not frightened *of* you."

"Then you truly are a fool," he pronounced, bending over her. "If you had two ounces of sense in that beautiful head of yours, you'd be heading for the hills, instead of sticking around me."

"I won't run away from you, Jefferson," she said deliberately. "Running isn't my style."

Twin embers seemed to burn deep in his eyes. "It should be," he warned her.

The fine hairs on the back of her neck prickled. The hand clasped in hers suddenly wasn't tugging away. It was nudging forward. Her mouth ran dry.

"You should be running fast and furious, Em."

She swallowed and shook her head. His palm had flattened against her collarbone, his fingertips resting on the mad pulse beating in her neck. "I'm not a child, Jefferson," she whispered. "I can take whatever you dish out."

"Can you?" His fingers grazed across her skin to her shoulder. With the flick of a finger, the loosened collar fell off her shoulder. "I wonder."

Emily shook her bangs out of her eyes then stood, unmoving as his heavy-lidded eyes studied her bare shoulder. The ruffled fabric was halted by her bent elbow, preventing it from completely baring her breast to his eyes.

His hand moved to her other shoulder, to nudge away the fabric there also, she thought. But instead, he adjusted the collar upward, securely over her shoulder. His fingers drifted across the wide ruffle running down the neckline to the valley between her breasts. Up again his hand went, this time pulling the fabric taut. The heel of his palm brushed against the dark shadow of her nipple clearly outlined against the thin white cotton.

Emily's breath stopped. Her eyelids flickered, but she didn't lower her gaze when he pinned her with his.

"Ready to run yet, Emily?" His hand brushed over that tight peak once again.

"No." Her voice was steady, though her heart was not.

He bent his head suddenly and his lips burned her neck where it curved into her shoulder.

Her legs weren't steady when he ran his lips up her neck to her ear. His breath wasn't quite steady, either. "Now?"

She swallowed. Moistened her lips. "No."

His head hovered next to hers, and his breath was warm across her skin. She jumped a little when his teeth scraped gently over her collarbone, and her head fell back, weak, as his head passed beneath her chin. She didn't sway, however. Not until he captured her pebbled nipple in his mouth, wetting the light fabric.

And then her knees did buckle. He was there, though, one long arm sliding around her waist, holding her up, her back arched. An offering to him.

"Now?"

If it had begun as a game to him, then he was surely caught. Just as she was. He held her so closely she could feel the unsteady beat of his heart. Could feel his arousal pressed against her.

The knowledge gave her strength. She willed her heart not to give way on her and she let go of her grip on the shirt. It slipped from her shoulder. Drifted down her back, held in place by his arm and their bodies pressed together at her waist.

"No," she said clearly. "I'm not running, Jefferson." She placed her hands flat on his chest, nudging beneath the edges of his shirt. "I'm not running until we finish what we started when I was nineteen years old." Her fingers slipped up his chest to his throat. Curved behind his neck. Grasped a handful of silky, thick hair. Tugged. Pulling his head down to hers.

It wasn't easy. He resisted. He wasn't going to kiss her. She knew it. Rising on tiptoe, she pressed her mouth to his. She tasted. She nibbled. She let out all her pent-up feelings for him as she delicately plundered his lips. But he didn't kiss her back.

Maddened, frustrated, she lowered her heels. Her hands raced to his shirt and jerked it wide. Then she nearly reeled, and bit down on her tongue to keep from crying at the sight of that gilded chest. The sleek muscle. The narrow strip of white briefs visible where the top buttons of his jeans hung loose. Mindless, she pulled her arms out of the nightshirt and she pressed herself, bare, to his chest.

"God!" His hands closed convulsively over her shoulders and he thrust her away. Without his arm wrapped around her, the last barrier was gone and her nightshirt drifted to her feet, leaving her clad only in a minuscule scrap of lace that hid nothing from his eyes. His lips parted as if he couldn't get enough air.

She'd been lovely at nineteen. All sweet, young, innocence. Now she was older. Still young. Still sweet. But ripe now. A woman. A woman who was still too young for the likes of him.

Jefferson told himself to turn away. Knowing that the pain he'd cause her by turning away would be far less than if he didn't. He knew all that. He'd been living with that for years now. His hand reached out, and he ran his fingertips down her shoulder, past the bruises on her arms. He felt the shivers dance to the surface of her silky skin. He placed both his hands on her waist and she didn't shrink away. She just continued watching him. Her large brown eyes luminous. Unblinking.

He could hear her breath tumble past her slightly parted lips. The tip of her tongue peeped out and left a glisten of moisture on that sweet, sexy curve.

Who was teaching who a lesson, he wondered with that minute portion still capable of coherent thought.

Her mouth formed his name, though she said not a word.

His jaw tight, he lifted her slight weight. Lifted her right out of the nightshirt pooling about her feet to set her on the counter. Her knees were smooth. Her thighs smoother. His hands, damn them, anyway, lingered without his permission and somehow he found his fingers had slipped down. Nudged apart her legs, so he could stand between them. So he could slip his palms around to the firm curves barely covered with lace.

He'd misjudged. Badly. He knew it right down in his bones just moments before she placed her warm hands on his chest and lifted those long, sleek legs to his waist. Wrapped around him. Pulled him against that intimate spot where he wanted, so badly, to be. Where he could never allow himself to go.

Her breath was a little sob that hitched in her throat, and he knew she could feel him through the barriers of denim and lace. For he could feel her. He dragged his hands from the curve of her bottom and reached for the wooden cupboard above her head. He closed his eyes tightly and tried to summon a vision of his father. But Squire's disapproving expression wouldn't appear.

All he could see, eyes open or closed, was Emily. Her long, silky dark lashes casting shadows on her cheeks where a flush of color rode high. Her heart beating so rapidly that he could see it shimmering through her creamy skin.

His eyes opened at the touch of her hand on his face. Her palm lay gently, soothingly, against his cheek. A diamond-bright tear hovered on the tips of her eyelashes. "Please," she whispered, stroking his stubbled cheek. The tear glided downward.

She trembled against him. The hand left his cheek, and her knuckles glided down his chest and brushed against his stomach when her fingers closed over the top unfastened button. He sucked in his breath harshly, looking down and wishing he hadn't. The memory of her lithe fingers tugging apart his half-loose jeans was one which wouldn't soon leave him.

Her fingertip scalded him as it traced the edge of elastic. "Please," she whispered again. This time leaning forward, obscuring his downward vision with the silky crown of her head as she pressed her lips to his chest.

Her hand, unseen now, but felt to his very soul, moved. Lightly covered him. Shaped his length through the worn denim. The pain was more than physical. His eyes burned. But he had to do it. He closed his hands over her silky shoulders and gently, inexorably, pushed her away.

He took a step backward, and her legs loosened, seeming to fall away from his waist in slow motion.

Her eyes had the expression of a doe he'd once had in his sights. Soft. Sadly accepting. He found himself wondering if Emily's eyes ever smiled anymore. The way they had years ago. Before.

And knew himself damned for all eternity that he was the cause of all this.

But she wasn't so accepting after all, it seemed. "Why?" Her head was bent, her expression hidden. "Why do you pull back, Jefferson?" Her hands clasped the counter on either side of her hips. "Do you really not…want…me?" With a little shake, her hair rippled out of her eyes and she looked up at him. Her lips stretched in a macabre imitation of a smile. "Is the notion so distasteful?"

Jefferson swore. "Dammit, Emily—"

"No, really. I, uh, I want to know. Obviously you're not, um—" she staved him off with a raised hand "—unaffected by me," she enunciated carefully, even while her eyes grew red rimmed. "I might be stupid, but I'm not *that* stupid."

"You're not stupid."

She chuckled humorlessly at that. She blinked rapidly and stared off to the side, sniffed and abruptly dropped from the counter.

Jefferson felt like he'd been gut kicked. Her rose-tipped breasts swayed gently with the impact. He couldn't have moved if his life had depended on it.

She leaned over and picked up the nightshirt. He supposed she felt more secure by presenting him with the long curve of her back as she pulled it over her head. He could have told her that the vision of her smooth, taut skin, narrowing into a tiny waist then flaring out gently was as disturbing to him as the front side. The white fabric settled about her thighs, hiding that glorious expanse of creamy skin as she turned back.

"What do I do that makes you turn away from me?" Her fingers toyed with the pot holder sitting on the counter, and she shot him a defiant glance. "If you'd just tell me, then maybe I won't make the same mistake with someone else."

His teeth clenched. "The CPA, you mean?"

Her eyebrows contracted. "Who? Oh." Her expression smoothed out. "Perhaps."

"Don't even *think* about it."

"Why not, Jefferson?" She seemed to be as pained with the words that she spoke as he was by hearing them. "Why shouldn't I think about it? You all but made love to me before. That time when you visited me at school. You had an excuse then when you stopped. That I was barely nineteen. And that claptrap about us being family and all. Well, I'm twenty-six now. We still don't have a drop of common blood running in our veins, and you still turn me away. Why shouldn't I find a man who won't turn me away?" The pot holder crumpled in her fist. "Why should I go through my life waiting for something you'll never share?"

The oven timer went off. For a long moment she stared at him while the annoying buzz went on. And on.

She went over to the oven. Shut off the buzzer. Pulled out the pan and set it on the square wooden chopping block.

Finally, she carefully hung the pot holder on a hook beside the oven and turned back to him. When she looked at him this time, there were no tears in her eyes. "You want to know the ultimate irony, Jefferson? I want somebody in my life. I want my own home. My own family." She touched her temple. "I have a picture in my head, you know?" She dropped her hand. "Me, sitting at the breakfast table. One child working on his homework at the last minute. One trying to stuff cereal in her little face, but managing to spread more of it on the floor."

Her expression was soft. Dreamy. Jefferson found himself picturing exactly what her words conjured. A boy with her brown hair. The baby girl with blon—

"And at the other end of the table," her voice went on, "should be my husband. My lover. My…my…soul mate. But he's not there. I can't picture him." She frowned faintly. "I wish I could picture him, Jefferson. I wish I could find a man who wouldn't turn me away. Who would share his life with me. Who'd be the father of my children." She seemed to rouse herself then and abruptly turned off the oven. "You've never even taken *me*, Jefferson. But you've taken away all the rest. Because I can't bear to share myself with any other man but you. And the one person you refuse to share yourself with…is me."

She pressed her lips together, and he knew the effort it took her to maintain her control. He knew the effort it took him. To not reach for her. To not take her to him and make her his. To let her turn and walk away. From him.

Emily was shaking so badly that her legs wouldn't even carry her up all the stairs. Several steps shy of the top, she sank down, her forehead pressed against the carved wooden rail. She had no idea how long she sat there. All she knew was that she never saw Jefferson come out of the kitchen. And eventually, when her feet had grown cold and her legs gone stiff, she heard the front door open and close. Then Tristan was there, trudging up the stairs.

Midway up, he stopped, peering at her in the dark. He seemed to sigh and then he was carefully stepping past her, lifting his briefcase over her head. In minutes he returned and stood a few steps lower than the one where she still sat.

"Come on," he said softly.

"Why does it have to be him, Tristan?"

He lifted his shoulders. Understanding everything without needing the words. "Just is."

He stood over her silently, then sighed again and reached down. "Come on," he said, and lifted her into his arms.

Emily's head lolled against Tristan's shoulder as he carried her up the rest of the stairs. "I wish it was you instead," she murmured.

He seemed to find that amusing. "No, you don't."

"It'd be so much easier."

"No." He shouldered his way into her bedroom. Holding her in one arm, he straightened her blankets slightly and then lowered her to the mattress.

Emily clutched at him when he would have straightened and moved away. "What is it with us, Tristan? You go through women like there's no tomorrow and—"

"I don't 'go through women,'" he objected. He tucked the covers beneath her chin. "And you'll find what you're looking for."

"I don't think so."

"Don't give up on him just yet, squirt."

"I don't know that I have a choice. He won't give an inch, Tristan. Not where I'm concerned."

"It'll be different this time."

"How do you know?" Emily pushed up on her elbow. "If I could just believe there was a possibility…oh, who am I kidding?" She sighed. "It doesn't matter what I believe. Jefferson isn't about to let me into his life. Not that way. And even if he remotely considered it, he'd be haring off on some adventure before we'd even have a chance."

"I have a feeling he's tiring of his traveling days," Tristan murmured. "Just hang in there."

Emily brushed the hair out of her eyes. "He didn't even know I was living here, Tris. I have to be realistic."

"Since when is love realistic?" He flicked the tip of her nose with a light finger. "Get some sleep."

Emily lay back on the pillows and watched Tristan leave the room, closing the door softly behind him. "Realistic," she murmured, staring into the dark. It was a lofty goal. And one she could never hope to attain. Rolling onto her side, she punched the pillow into shape and closed her eyes.

Jefferson lifted his head, hearing a door close along the hall. He dropped the corner of the soft blue blanket he'd been holding onto the seat of the chair. Silently, he lifted his duffel from the dresser and placed it on the bed. The zipper sounded loud when he opened the bag. He eyed the single pair of jeans sitting in the bottom of the bag. The weight of the footfalls heading closer warned him of Tristan's approach.

"Are you unpacking? Or packing?" Tristan said quietly from the doorway.

"Wish I knew," Jefferson muttered to himself. He reached for the clothing that he'd worn the day before and rolled them into a ball. "Packing," he said, and stuffed the bundle into the duffel.

"Why?"

Jefferson snorted. "Why not?"

Tristan sighed and moved over to the bed. He dropped down onto it and circled his head wearily. "Don't be an ass, Jefferson. Cutting out now isn't going to make it go away."

Jefferson hesitated, but continued gathering his meager possessions to place in the duffel. "Stay out of this."

"You brought me into it when you came here," Tristan countered.

"I came to see you."

"She thinks you didn't even know she lived here."

"So?"

"So." Tristan's lips tightened. "We both know that's not true. You knew, and you came, anyway. So don't try to tell me to butt out. Jesus, Jefferson...she'd die for you!"

Jefferson viciously shoved another shirt into the bag. "Do you think I don't know that?"

"Then what the hell are you doing? Why can't you two just get your act together and be happy for the rest of your lives?"

"There's too many reasons to list them all."

"That's a cop-out."

Jefferson glared at his younger brother. "She's off-limits. Okay?"

"Why?"

"Have you lost your mind? Why do you think?"

"So, she was raised with us. Big deal."

"It is a big deal." He ran his hand behind his neck. "A very big deal. And even if it weren't..."

"What?"

"I'm too old for her." And way too beaten up.

Tristan just shook his head. "You're a fool."

"Yeah, well, I may be a fool." Jefferson zipped his bag shut. "But my coming here has only hurt her."

"What's hurting her is knowing that you're going to leave again."

He shook his head, remembering the bruises he'd inflicted. "It's better this way."

Tristan obviously thought differently. He fingered the ragged airline tags hanging from the strap of the duffel. "So, where will you go?"

Jefferson shrugged. It didn't matter where he went, and Lord knew the ranch wasn't an option. His nightmares would follow wherever he went. But at least he couldn't hurt Emily anymore.

"What about money?"

That amused him as much as anything could, just then. "What about it?"

Tristan shrugged and let the matter drop. "You going to tell her goodbye? Or just let her wake up in the morning to find you've left."

"You can tell her." He lifted the bag and slung the strap over his shoulder. "Don't pretend that she'll be shocked I left, Tris. It's exactly what she expects."

His brother nodded. "Don't worry about the CPA," he said abruptly.

Jefferson stopped shy of the door.

"She's not seriously interested in him," Tristan added.

He didn't feel relieved. It just added to his mountains of guilt. "Take care of her."

Tristan sighed again. Jefferson heard it all the way by the door. "You're sure about this?"

Jefferson looked over his shoulder. "Yes."

He watched Tristan nod again and stand. His younger

brother ran his long fingers through his blond hair and stretched. Tristan rubbed his chin and looked back at Jefferson through narrowed eyes. "Then I guess the way is finally clear for me."

"I'm not in the mood for games, Tris."

"Neither am I, Jeff," Tristan said steadily.

There was a sick feeling swelling in the pit of Jefferson's stomach. "You're not interested in her that way."

Tristan cocked his head slightly. "Says who?" His eyebrows rose. "You? You're not even going to be around by tomorrow. Emily and I *do* live together."

Jefferson's knuckles whitened. "She's not interested in you, either, Tris, so just forget it. It's not working."

Tristan's jaw tightened, and he stepped closer to Jefferson. His voice was very low. "Listen up, Jefferson, and listen good. Em and I aren't kids anymore. We've been sharing this place for a good while now. We'll be sharing this place after you leave again. She wants a life you're not going to give her, and I'm tired of watching her wait. When I take her into my bed you can take it to the bank that she won't be thinking about you. She'll be thinking about me." He leaned closer and his voice dropped another notch. "She'll be thinking about the babies I'm planting in her flat little belly."

Jefferson's duffel hit the floor. "You so much as lay a hand on her and I'll—"

"You'll what?" Tristan straightened and his lips twisted. "You're not going to be around to witness anything. But if you leave some sort of address, I'll be sure you get a wedding invitation."

His palms itched. The hair on the back of his neck stood at attention. If it had been anyone but his brother standing before him, he'd have reduced the man to a pulp. "She'd never share her bed with you, much less marry you," he drawled. "And we both know it. So drop the act."

Tristan smiled humorlessly. "You want her to spend her life as alone and miserable as you are? That's one hell of a love you've got for her."

Jefferson bent and picked up his duffel to stop himself from weakening and planting his fist in Tristan's face, brother or not. His head knew that his brother was trying to manipulate him, but his gut churned at the very notion of Emily with someone else. Even Tristan. Or, perhaps *particularly* Tristan.

"She deserves some happiness," Tristan said.

"Do you think I don't know that?" Jefferson growled. "I *want* her to be happy. I want her to be safe, too. And if I stay, she won't be safe." His head pounded and his breathing grew harsh. "She won't be safe from me."

Tristan frowned. "You'd never—"

"Take a look at her arms, Tris." Jefferson kept his eyes open, knowing as soon as he closed them he'd be seeing those black bruises. Bruises that *he'd* inflicted. "You'll see for yourself why I have to go."

"She could help you through this, if you'd let her."

"No."

"She's a strong piece of work," Tristan continued. "Just tell her what happened."

"Nothing happened," Jefferson ground out the blatant lie.

Tristan sighed. "Until you can admit that something *did,* I guess there's nothing more to say, is there."

"Exactly."

Tristan picked up the cane beside the dresser and held it toward his brother. "Except that while you're off denying what's gone on in your life, Emily might just decide to move on with her own."

Chapter Four

Emily rose the next morning and mechanically moved through her morning jog to the stable. She had to force her mind to stay on her riding, however, lest Bird toss her onto her backside in the bushes lining the dirt trail. By the time she turned back for the stable, she was fully awake and Bird had worked out his jitters. If only the rest of her life were so easily controlled.

Jefferson was gone.

She hadn't needed to peek into the guest room to see if his duffel was still sitting on the dresser. Nor had she needed to look into the garage to see if the black rental car was still there.

She'd instinctively known.

Her steps dragged as she walked back to the house. He'd only been there two days, but she knew the house would feel empty without him. As empty as she felt herself.

She'd survive. Just as she'd told Tristan she would. She'd had plenty of practice. She'd been surviving for years now.

So she prepared for the day and drove off to work, telling herself that she was going to get on with her life. She would, once again, hide away her hopeless feelings for Jefferson. Maybe this time she'd even be able to move past them.

It was with that thought in mind that the next day she accepted Stuart Hansen's invitation to join him and a few of his friends for the weekend. They were driving down to Mexico, he told her. They'd leave Friday after work and return Sunday evening. Just some guys and girls getting together for some sunshine and seafood. No pressure, he assured. She could bunk with the other two women who were going.

Tristan frowned at her when she told him that night over supper that she'd be gone for the weekend. "I thought you weren't serious about the bean-counter."

"I'm a bean-counter," Emily responded smoothly. "And who says I have to be serious about Stuart? We're just going to Rosarita Beach for the weekend with some other people."

"Why now?"

"Because he invited me now, that's why."

"Where will you be staying?"

Emily shrugged. She wouldn't be surprised if they ended up camping on the beach. "We'll wing it, I'm sure. Don't worry," she smiled tightly, "I'm not going to do anything foolish. Like elope on the rebound or something."

"Not with that dope, at least." Tristan shuddered.

"You're awful. I thought you liked Stuart."

Tristan shrugged and leaned his chair back on two legs. "He's okay. He's just not…"

Emily's lips tightened. "Not Jefferson," she finished. She rose and took her plate to the sink. Her appetite was nil, anyway. She meticulously rinsed off the uneaten casserole and placed the dishes in the dishwasher. "Look, Tristan, Jefferson is gone. I knew he'd leave. So, I'd just as soon we not talk about him."

"You're the one talking, sweet pea. I was just going to say that Stuart isn't real exciting."

Emily flushed. "Maybe I don't want exciting," she said. "Maybe I want someone nice and steady. Reliable."

"Jefferson's reliable."

She laughed abruptly. "Right. You can always rely on Jefferson to leave." Tristan just watched her and her eyes began burning. "I'm going to Mexico tomorrow night," she said flatly. "We're leaving from the office, so I won't see you until we get back, I guess."

"I'd feel better if I at least knew where you'd be staying."

"Perhaps you'd like to come along and play chaperone," Emily suggested tartly. "But somehow I don't think you'd qualify for the part."

Emily didn't want to call him. But she would. Only because Tristan seemed to think it was important. "Fine," she agreed tiredly. "It's your turn to clean up," she reminded Tristan. "I'm going to pack." She turned and left before he could find another concern to latch on to.

At the top of the stairs, she looked at the open doorway to the guest room. Closing her eyes, she wished with all her heart that she'd never heard of Jefferson Clay. And then promptly retracted the wish. Mentally squaring her shoulders, she strode into the room and yanked back the comforter, causing pillows to tumble every which way. She pulled off the sheets and bunched them in a heap, then remade the bed with fresh linens. With the ones she'd removed balled up in her arms, she clumped down the stairs and through the kitchen, straight to the laundry room.

* * *

"Don't pussyfoot around," Jefferson warned, his temper short. He'd been sitting in this bloody office for an hour, waiting for the surgeon to return. "The fragment's moving. Right?"

The doctor, who looked young enough to still be in high school, moved past Jefferson and rounded his desk to sit down. He opened a thick file and seemed to study it for a while. He nodded. "We knew it was a possibility that the shrapnel would eventually begin to shift. That's what's been causing the numbness in your toes and foot." He folded his hands across the file and watched Jefferson across the paper-strewn desk. "You're going to have to decide, soon, Jeff. The surgery to remove the fragment is risky enough right now. The closer it moves to your spinal column—"

Jefferson waved his hand, cutting off the surgeon's words. He'd heard the spiel so many times he knew it by heart. "You know how many surgeries I've had since I…"

The surgeon nodded. He knew full well what Jefferson had been through. The thickness of the medical file his arms rested upon testified to that fact. "Nevertheless," he continued steadily, "you're going to have to go through one more."

"One more that could leave me paralyzed." Or dead.

"You may become paralyzed without it," the surgeon countered. He sighed and leaned back in his chair. "The possibility that the fragment wouldn't move did exist. That's why I didn't push the issue of the surgery when I met with you in Amsterdam. But it's obviously not the scenario we're looking at now. It is moving. And it will get worse. You could die, Jeff."

Either way, the odds weren't in his favor. Unable to sit in the high-backed leather chair another minute, Jefferson rose, and moved over to the wide window. He looked out on the expanse of neatly groomed grounds. No one looking at the sprawling building located in upper Connecticut would take it for anything other than what it appeared. A commonplace industrial complex.

Except the trucks that periodically entered and left the grounds weren't carrying your everyday goods. Jefferson himself had arrived at the center thirty-six hours ago safely hidden away in the trailer of a semi that for all the world appeared to be carrying paper products. Toilet paper, to be exact.

Considering his life seemed to be in the toilet, it was a fitting touch. "I don't want to get cut on again," he said. Never mind the weeks and weeks of therapy he'd have to undergo once, *if,* the surgery was a success.

"Your foot's numb right now, isn't it?"

Jefferson didn't answer.

"Pretty soon, your calf will feel the same way. Then the rest of your leg. You won't be able to move your knee. Already the reflexes in your other leg are diminishing." The surgeon tapped his finger against the file.

Jefferson pressed his fist against the windowpane.

"You'll never be able to return to the field, unless you do something soon."

"I don't give a good goddamn about getting back in the field," Jefferson said, gritting his teeth. He'd given enough of his life to the agency. Whatever time he had left would be his own.

The other man closed the medical file. "What about the nightmares?"

Damn that psychiatrist bitch. Nothing was private in this place. "What about 'em?"

"The therapy sessions would help, Jeff. If you weren't so damn stubborn."

"You know what kept me alive in that hellhole?" Jefferson

queried. "Stubbornness." It was also what had kept him going in the months since.

"Okay. You've no plans to return to the field. What do you plan to do? Transfer to a different sector? Sit at a desk? Teach? Assuming that you even last more than a year or two. What? Regardless of what you choose to do with your future, Jeff, the surgery is still a necessity." The surgeon swiveled his chair around so he could face Jefferson directly. "What about marriage? Children? Why cut off the possibility of those things if you don't have to?"

Every muscle in Jefferson's body tensed. He couldn't let himself think about that. Not when those thoughts were irrevocably twined with thoughts of Emily. It was a road he simply couldn't travel down. "How long before I can get out of here?"

"You know the routine. Seventy-two hours."

Leaving him a day and a half before he'd be transported back to the city by, in all probability, another toilet paper truck. He raked his fingers through his hair and pressed the heels of his palms to his eyes. Thirty-six more hours of people probing his mind and his body. Invading his dreams and his thoughts.

The other man sighed. He might look like a kid, but he was one of the top men in his field. And he'd known Jefferson Clay for years. Pretty much knew what made the man tick. Jefferson Clay had been the best in the business. He'd had a golden touch for so long, that it had gotten pretty darn spooky. People stood in line to be on one of his missions, because despite the danger, everyone knew that when Jefferson Clay was the lead man, bloodshed on his team was nonexistent.

The man had pulled off more successful missions than any other agent, and he'd only once failed. And it was that very single failure that even now continued torturing the tense man standing across the room. "Jeff, it wasn't your fault that Kim died. You have to accept that. He knew the risks."

"Cold comfort for his wife." Jefferson wheeled around and began pacing the length of the office. "Or for his little son." His partner...*his friend*...had had every reason to live. Yet he'd died in that little square of a room that he'd been held in. The whole mission had been a fiasco from start to finish. But they'd waited and planned. And endured. Until the day had arrived when they made their break. The day their plans got shot to hell once again.

It hadn't gone the way they'd planned at all. Kim wasn't supposed to have died. He'd been just a kid, practically. Hardly old enough to be married with a son of his own.

"Are we finished here?" Jefferson asked abruptly. He knew the futility of just walking out. They'd find some way to drag him back.

The surgeon sighed again and scribbled out a note. "Here," he said as he shoved it into Jefferson's hand. "Have it filled at the dispensary before you leave. It'll help with the pain."

Jefferson stuffed the prescription in his pocket. He still had a nearly full bottle of pills from his last exam. He could handle the physical pain. It was that damned numbness that unnerved him.

"I hope you change your mind about the surgery," the man said as Jefferson prepared to leave the office. "Your chances are better with it than without."

Jefferson didn't respond. He left the office and headed downstairs. If he didn't show up in the cafeteria and eat something, he'd just be visited by that nurse-from-hell upstairs who had myriad ways of wearing a man down.

The cafeteria more closely resembled a quiet, elegant restaurant than a person's idea of a hospital cafeteria. He found himself a table that wasn't occupied and dragged a second chair around so he could prop his leg on it. Then whittled away the next hour by nursing a bottomless cup of strong coffee and pushing a ridiculously mild enchilada around his plate. The chef could have used a few tips from Emily.

"You should have ordered the roast beef," a deep voice said next to him. "It's overcooked and dry, but it's a lot better than that crud."

Jefferson's head swiveled. He looked up at the dark-haired man who'd seemingly appeared out of nowhere. Shock held him still for a long moment. "Well," he finally mused. "Fancy seeing you here."

Sawyer Clay, eldest brother of the Clay crew, grinned wryly and clapped his brother on the shoulder. "Good to see you, too." He turned away briefly to signal the waitress for a cup of coffee. Then he took over the chair that Jefferson's boot had kindly vacated. He shook his head. "Damn, Jefferson, you look like something the cat dragged in."

"Another bit of Clay wisdom," Jefferson grimaced. He knew he looked beat. He *felt* beat. "I have a feeling your presence here is no coincidence. So cut to the chase. Why are you here?"

Sawyer's dark head turned as he leisurely studied the room. "It's been a while since I was here," he said. "But I see nothing's changed. Do they still have that nurse upstairs…what was her name? Bertha?"

Jefferson noticed the gold insignia on his brother's dark blue uniform. Yet another notch up the ladder. He also noticed the way Sawyer hadn't answered his question. "Beulah," he supplied grimly.

"Beulah," Sawyer repeated. He grinned wickedly. "I've never seen a nurse who filled out her uniform like that."

"You're crazy. She might look like something out of a teenage boy's fantasy, but she's got the temperament of a...geez, I can't think of anything bad enough to describe that devil-in-nurse's-white."

"You just don't know how to handle her."

"Who wants to handle her? I see her coming and head the opposite direction."

Sawyer chuckled softly. He removed his coffee cup from the saucer and poured about half the cup's steaming contents into the saucer.

Jefferson watched his brother drink his coffee from the nearly flat saucer. "I haven't seen anybody do that in a while," he commented, putting away for the moment the questions he had for his brother. Questions like why his big brother, Mr. Navy-All-the-Way, was here at this private medical complex. Like why Sawyer even knew of its existence, much less Beulah's existence.

Sawyer set the saucer down, managing not to spill a single drop. "Proving that you haven't been home in *a while,*" he said. "Squire never drinks coffee from the cup. It's the only way to inhale hot coffee the way he does."

"Well, I've known other Swedes who don't insist it's the only way to properly drink coffee. Despite what Squire maintains," Jefferson said. He'd never gotten the hang of drinking out of saucers. Oh, he'd tried it often enough when he was a kid, trying to be like his older brother and his father. But he'd always managed to spill it or burn his fingers or something. He liked his coffee in a mug, thank you. Not in his lap.

Sawyer finished the coffee and nudged the empty saucer to one side. The time for chitchat was over. "What did the doc say about your back?"

Jefferson squared the end of the knife with the end of the spoon. He wondered exactly how much Sawyer knew about his activities. About the events that had brought him here to this medical facility in the first place.

His lips twisted. Knowing Sawyer, he probably knew it all. His brother had the ability to find out anything he wanted about anybody. Apparently, even a brother who'd been so far underground that rumors had had him dead and buried. "I'm surprised you haven't read the medical report yourself." He leaned back in his chair, crossing his arms over his chest. Despite his casual pose, his eyes were sharp on his brother's face. "Or have you?"

Sawyer shrugged. "I know the gist of it," he admitted. "What are you going to do?"

"I've just been this route with the good Doctor Beauman. I really don't feel like getting into it again."

"So you're still refusing to have the surgery. Well—" Sawyer waved off the waitress before she could approach the table "—I can't say I'm surprised. You always were stubborn. Nobody ever could tell you what to do. Have you talked to Tris about it? No. I'd guess not. You obviously know where Emily's been living, too. That must have been interesting." He continued speaking, clearly not expecting an answer from Jefferson. "Do you have plans? No? Well, good. Because I came to take you home."

Jefferson's eyebrows shot up.

"Not my home," Sawyer elaborated. "My apartment isn't big enough for two Clays. I'm taking you to the ranch. Tonight."

Jefferson straightened abruptly. "The hell you are. I don't want to see Squire just now. Thanks all the same." Even if it did mean an early escape from the white-coats.

Sawyer studied him. And Jefferson felt his stomach clench.

"It's time to go home, Jefferson. Not just for your sake, either." Sawyer's lips tightened. "Squire's in the hospital. He had a heart attack a few days ago."

Emily's hand shook as she held the note up to the light, reading it through once again. "Oh, my God," she whispered.

Her legs gave way and she sank onto the kitchen chair. The note fell from her fingers and drifted to the floor.

Squire was in the hospital, Tristan had written in his messy scrawl. He'd had a heart attack, and Emily should get to Wyoming as soon as she could. He'd tried calling her but hadn't been able to get through. Eventually he'd gone ahead and flown home.

Of course he'd not been able to reach her on her cell. Emily looked over at the bag she'd dropped just inside the door. After she'd called him to say they'd arrived, she'd turned it off and forgot about it in her bag.

Brushing her hair out of her face, she tried to think. She had to pack a few things to take with her. She had to let her office know that she'd be away for a while. She had to—

Please, oh please, oh please, let Squire be okay.

She reached for the phone and punched out the main number at the ranch. It would be nearly midnight there. She let it ring and ring, but no one picked up. Which probably meant that no one was at the big house. They were all at the hospital.

Her fingers trembled, but she managed to hang up and dial the airline. She booked herself on the last flight out that night. Which left her about twenty-five minutes to clean up and leave for the airport.

The shortage of time was a blessing. It didn't leave her any time to worry. But once she was on the plane…

The plane was only about a third full, and most of those people had tucked pillows under their heads, sleeping all the way to Dallas while she worried.

As soon as she got off the plane the hospital's information desk and was informed that Squire was in ICU. His condition wasn't available.

Emily closed her eyes and sat down in a nearby chair.

Nausea clawed at her stomach. "Could I speak with the nurse's station in ICU, at least?"

"One moment," the disembodied voice told her, then the line clicked several times. She was treated, ever so briefly, to a moment of piped-in music. The line clicked once again. And the phone went dead. Rather, the connection went dead, since the dial tone told her very neatly that the phone itself was still operating.

Emily huffed, and glanced over her shoulder at the clock on the wall. She had about twenty minutes before her connecting plane should be boarding. She began punching in the numbers once more that would connect her to the hospital.

"ICU, please." No more wasting time with information desks.

After just a few rings, the phone was picked up at the nurses' station. "This is Emily Nichols. You have a patient there, Squire Clay. Could you tell me what his condition is please?"

"Just a moment." On hold again. "Are you immediate family?"

Emily thought she might throw up right there. She swallowed. "Yes." It was close enough to the truth.

"Just a moment." Hold, once more. "Ma'am? Mr. Clay's condition is critical—"

Oh, God, please—

"—but stable. He has some family in the waiting room. Would you like me to connect you?"

Emily barely had time to answer before the nurse had transferred her call and it was ringing again. And ringing. And ringing.

Finally it was picked up. But the woman who answered told Emily that there was no one in the waiting room beside herself. Though she did say that there had been a few men in and out earlier. Emily thanked the woman and hung up. She glanced at the clock again and tried dialing the house once more. But her efforts were futile.

Swallowing a wad of tears, Emily gathered her tote bag up and returned to the gate just in time to board.

The morning sun was steadily rising when Emily finally neared the main gate of the Clay ranch. Her tired eyes absently noticed the new iron sign proclaiming the boundary of the Double-C, and it was second nature for her to drive up next to the big metal mailbox alongside the road. She reached through the window and pulled out a large stack of envelopes, packages and circulars, which she dumped on the seat beside her. The newspaper box was on a sturdy post next to the mailbox, and she inched forward in the car and with her fingers snagged the bound-up paper. Tossing it onto the mail, she turned sharply and drove through the open gate.

Dust billowed and rolled behind her car as she left the pavement for the hard-packed dirt road, and she rolled up the windows and turned on the air-conditioning. She still had a few miles to go.

When the buildings came into sight, the car was covered with a film of tan dust. Emily coasted to a stop and for just a moment she didn't worry about Squire. Didn't worry about Jefferson. She didn't worry about anything. She just sat, her arms folded across the steering wheel, as she looked through the slick sheen of threatening tears.

Directly ahead stood the big house. Its sturdy stone and wood lines meandered from the central two-story structure to the right and the left with the additions that had been added here and there over the years. A porch ran the entire width of the front, and geraniums bloomed from the window boxes. Lilac bushes clustered at the south corner of the house. A grouping of aspens stood off to the side in the circular lawn situated in front of the house. Even from her distance, she could see the golden retriever sleeping in the soft green grass beneath the trees.

She was home.

She blinked and took a long, deep breath. She drove up around the circle drive, parking between the lawn and the house. The car door squeaked faintly as she pushed it open, and she climbed out, arching her back. She looked around, but all was silent. It wasn't a usual sight for the Double-C. Even the dog didn't raise her head.

The worry was back, and she grabbed the mail and paper, shut the car door and headed for the house, automatically by-passing the wide double-doored front entry. Her tennis shoes crunched over the gravel drive then sank into the soft green grass surrounding the house as she headed past the lilac bushes to the rear.

She entered through the mudroom, where the wooden screen door slapped closed behind her with an achingly familiar sound. Cowboy hats hung from the rack on the wall, and there were several sets of cowboy boots lying in the mudroom all in varying states, from dusty to muddy, to— Her nose wrinkled and she pushed open the door to the kitchen.

"Well, there she is." Matthew Clay rose from the oblong oak table that had held center stage of the spacious kitchen for as long as Emily could remember. He swung his long leg over his chair and reached Emily in just two steps before engulfing her in his big hug. "Tris said you'd make your way here one way or the other." He dropped a kiss on her cheek and lifted his head to study her with his nearly translucent blue eyes. "How ya doing, peanut?"

She shrugged, sharing his feeling smile. "About the same as you, I suppose." He let her go, and she tossed the mail onto the table before heading for the commercial-size steel refrigerator across the room. "How's Squire?" She pulled out a cold bottle of apple juice and drank nearly half of it in one swallow.

Matthew ran his hand over his closely cropped blond hair. "He's alive," he said bluntly.

Emily's teeth chattered before she clenched her jaw. She looked away from Matthew's piercing eyes and stared blindly out the wide uncurtained windows looking over the recently mown backyard. She swallowed the lump blocking her throat. "Is he going to stay that way?"

"Damn straight he is," another voice said.

Emily looked over her shoulder to the doorway leading into the dining room. "Hi, Daniel." She set her apple juice on the counter and went over to receive another Clay hug.

"Hey, babycakes," the fourth Clay son said as he swung her into his arms. He planted a kiss on her lips before letting her feet once more find the floor. "Don't you worry about Squire, hear? He's a stubborn mule and not about to leave this earth before someone starts giving him grandkids to spoil."

Matthew snorted and Daniel shrugged. "It's true, isn't it? 'Cept it'll probably be up to Em here to have the babies. Since none of us seem inclined to procreate."

Emily's smile faded at the corners. She tilted her head, and her hair slid forward as she retrieved her apple juice. She swallowed the rest of the juice and cradled the squat round bottle in the palm of her hand. "Does Sawyer know about Squire?" *Does Jefferson?*

Daniel nodded and plucked the coffeepot from the stove. He filled his mug and topped off Matthew's before returning the blackened enamel pot to the stove. He seemed about to say something, but he just nodded again and sank down into one of the sturdy chairs at the table. Matthew joined him at the table.

"Where's Tristan?"

"Right here." He appeared through the same doorway as Daniel had. He bussed her cheek and poured himself a mug of coffee. "How was Mexico?"

"Fine, I guess."

"I tried to get hold of you."

"I know." Emily grimaced. "I turned my phone off," she admitted. "If only I'd checked it…I could have…"

"Could have been here a day earlier, is all," Tristan finished. "And Squire's been unconscious the whole time. Don't sweat it, Em. Sawyer's plane didn't get in until last night, and then—"

"We all spent most of the night at the hospital, cooling our heels in the damn waiting room," Daniel put in.

"I tried calling both places." Emily told them of her efforts to get hold of somebody. "Once I landed, I couldn't decide whether to go to the hospital or come here first." It was sheer cowardice that kept her from going straight to the hospital.

"We'll drive down to the hospital a little later this morning," Matthew told her. "It'll give you a chance to rest up while we finish off a few chores."

"Where is everybody?" Emily asked. "I expected you all to be in the middle of combining."

"We've got a crew coming in day after tomorrow. Between trips to the hospital and the work around here, we're keeping busy. Joe's a big help."

Emily knew Matthew was referring to Joe Greene, the foreman he'd hired a couple years ago. Joe and his wife, Maggie, who served as housekeeper and cook, lived in the tidy brick house situated on the far side of the ranch buildings.

"Speaking of chores…" Matthew lifted his coffee mug again for a long drink, then plunked it onto the table. It seemed to be a signal for his brothers to also rise as there was a general exodus.

Even Tristan, computer hacker extraordinaire, followed.

"Tristan?" Emily called him just before he disappeared after his older brothers. "Squire…you said he's been unconscious? Is he—" she broke off.

"He had a triple bypass, sweet pea. He's in tough shape. But he's a tough old man. And the tests they've run are promising." He smiled encouragingly, even though his eyes couldn't quite match the smile. "The best thing for him is the rest he's getting. And knowing we're all here for him." He smiled again and went after his brothers.

With the absence of the men, the kitchen loomed large, empty and silent. Emily hugged her arms to her and rubbed her elbows as she looked around her. The room hadn't changed much since the day Squire had brought her home. She'd been terrified. Feeling like her world had ended.

Squire had brought her into the kitchen, and the boys had all been sitting around that big oak table. All except Sawyer, anyway. He'd already gone off on his own by then. But the rest of them had been sitting there. Shoveling down their supper with a small semblance of manners, even while they boisterously tried to top each other's accounting of their day. They'd eyed her curiously for a few moments. Then Jefferson had pushed out the empty seat between him and Tristan, and Emily had climbed onto the chair. She'd been a part of their family ever since.

Swallowing, Emily ran her fingertips over the chair at the head of the table. Squire's.

"Seems strange for the old man not to be sitting there telling us how to live our lives, doesn't it?"

Emily whirled. She smiled faintly at Sawyer, nodding. "Very strange." She glanced at the eldest Clay son. His hair was going silver at the temples, and he very much resembled the father they spoke of. The Clay men were nothing if not striking. "It seems we've all been called back to the ranch," she murmured. Where was Jefferson?

Sawyer passed by for the coffeepot, dropping a kiss on the top of her head. "Where is everybody?"

"Chores. Sawyer…"

He turned, raising his eyebrows as she hesitated.

Emily bit her lip, flushing. "Never mind."

He turned back to pouring a mug of coffee and grabbed a saucer from the cupboard. "Spit it out, Emily."

"You sound like Squire."

His wide shoulders rose and fell. "So I've been told." He laughed shortly. With his usual economy of movements, he sat at the table and poured the coffee into the saucer.

Emily closed her fingers over the top of one of the chairs. "You know everything about everybody…"

Sawyer's lips twitched. "Well, not quite."

"But, you uh, well…oh, hell. Do you know where Jefferson is? He left San Diego just last week, and he was in terrible shape, Sawyer. He wouldn't tell me…not that I expected him to, of course, I mean, he never does…but he didn't even talk to Tristan…and I'm just really—"

"Whoa!" Sawyer lifted his hand and she fell silent. "Take a breath before you pass out. And yes, I do know where Jefferson is. He's here."

Emily caught her breath. "Then he *did* come here when he left California."

"No. He didn't get here until last night. He flew in with me."

"Then where—"

"You'll have to ask him that." He sipped his coffee, watching her over the rim of the saucer.

Emily looked away from Sawyer. "Is he, uh, in his room?"

He shrugged. "Have no idea."

The screen door to the kitchen squeaked and Daniel appeared. "Hey, Em…oh, great, Sawyer, come out here for a minute, will ya? That damned horny horse of Matt's kicked out half his stall trying to get to the mares and we need your help for a sec."

Emily followed the men out. But she turned toward her rental car to retrieve her suitcase when they headed for the horse barn. She'd have time to grab a shower and freshen up before they went to the hospital. She also needed to call her office, knowing that the hasty message she'd left on Stuart's voice mail had barely been coherent. She tried focusing her thoughts on the simple tasks. But her tangled thoughts were on Squire. And Jefferson. Lord, how was she going to face Jefferson?

As she headed back to the house, a breeze kicked up. She paused for a moment, squinting against the dust swirling through the air, and grabbed her hair with her free hand. In a moment the breeze had passed and she let go of her hair, shaking the bangs out of her eyes. She supposed it was the faint squeak of the screen door that caught her attention. Or maybe it was just instinct.

When she looked up, Jefferson was slouched in the doorway. He wore jeans faded white, and a raggedy beige cotton-knit shirt clung softly to his shoulders, which despite his thinness, were as wide as ever. His wet hair was dark and combed starkly away from the sharp angles of his face.

He was beautiful.

Emily's fingers tightened on the suitcase handle. Part of her wanted to throw the luggage back in the car and hightail it out of there. The other part, the stronger part, wanted to run into his arms and never let him go.

Hardly breathing, she climbed the two steps into the mudroom and was silently relieved when he shifted, giving her room to pass. There would be no "Clay hug" from Jefferson, brotherly or otherwise. She couldn't think of a single thing to say. Not without embarrassing herself, anyway. She stepped across the mudroom and into the kitchen.

"Emily."

She swallowed, schooled her expression and glanced back at him over her shoulder. "Yes?"

His own expression was inscrutable. "Are you all right?"

"Fine," she said evenly. "You?" She watched a muscle tick in his jaw.

"Fine," he returned.

He didn't add anything, and Emily turned once more to head upstairs to the room she'd used since childhood.

"Emily—"

Her shoulders tightened, and like a coward she pretended not to hear as she hurried up the stairs, the suitcases bumping her legs.

Jefferson watched her hair swish against her back as she raced up the stairs. Her denim jeans were well washed and lovingly fit her curves. He stood at the foot of the stairs until long after she'd disappeared. Until he heard the sound of water rushing through the pipes, and he knew she was taking a shower.

The knowledge brought all sorts of visions to his mind. None of them decent. And none of them wise, particularly when he was under Squire's roof. Biting off a curse, he went back to the kitchen and limped his way outside.

Two hours later, Emily propped her hands on her hips and glared at Tristan. "Why on earth shouldn't I drive myself to the hospital? I've been driving these roads for half of my life! I'm no more distraught over Squire than you are. And I'm not likely to drive myself into a ditch because I'm worried. Good Lord, Tristan, I managed to get myself to Wyoming without your overbearing assistance—"

"Stop arguing," Matthew ordered abruptly, walking up behind them. "You've been sniping at each other for ten minutes. Tris, you know darn well there isn't room for all of us to go in one vehicle, so quit bugging Emily. She can go to the hospital however she wants, and she's already said she doesn't want to be cooped up in the Blazer with the rest of us. She could drive one of the pickups if she wanted."

The screen door squeaked open and slammed shut and Tristan suddenly capitulated. He shrugged, tugged a lock of Emily's hair and opened the passenger door to the rental. "I'll ride with you, then," he announced.

"What a nut," Emily grumbled as she went around to the driver's side of her rental. Then she noticed what she hadn't before, because Tristan had been acting so impossible. Jefferson stood several feet away, his legs braced and his weight obviously leaning on the cane. The sunlight struck him full in the face and his eyes were narrowed as he watched Emily.

Her throat went dry. He looked so...*alone.* Even standing mere feet away from his passel of brothers. She moistened her lips. His name was a whisper on her lips.

"Yo, Jeff!" Daniel called as he climbed into the rear seat of Matthew's Blazer. "Load it up, man."

Jefferson's head slowly swiveled to the other vehicle. Emily could see the muscle ticking in his jaw, and he finally moved over to the truck, climbing into the front passenger seat. His door slammed shut and Emily lowered herself into the rental.

Tristan's knees were practically buckled up beneath his chin. "You just gonna sit here, or are we going to follow Matt to the hospital?"

She started the engine and placed her hands on the sun-heated steering wheel, flexing her fingers. "I don't know if I can handle this," she muttered.

"Seeing Squire in the hospital?" Tristan reached around under the seat and managed to scoot it back a few more precious inches. "You'll manage just fine." He reached over and flipped on the air-conditioning.

"I don't mean just Squire," Emily admitted as she followed the Blazer away from the ranch.

"You'll manage Jefferson, too, sweet pea."

She choked on a miserable laugh. "That'll be a first."

Chapter Five

The visitation policy in the Intensive Care Unit would allow only two family members in at a time. Emily was shaking so badly that she thought she might be sick, and she was glad when Matthew and Sawyer went first. She, Jefferson, Daniel and Tristan remained in the waiting room located around the corner from ICU. The room was nearly full of people, and they had to split up in order to find a seat.

It took Daniel all of two minutes before he rose again, obviously restless. He murmured something to Jefferson and strode out of the room. Minutes later, she saw him outside through the windows that overlooked a small grassy area behind the hospital.

He stood with his back to the building, his dark gold hair ruffling in the faint breeze. He lit a cigarette, then moved abruptly and strode out of sight.

Emily looked down at her hands, twisted together in her lap.

She smoothed the cuff of her off-white linen shorts. A teenager turned on the television situated in the corner of the room. The phone rang. The two people sitting to her left continued discussing an article they'd read in that morning's newspaper.

She looked up, her gaze colliding with Jefferson's. His expression inscrutable, he didn't bother hiding the fact that he'd been studying her. She wished that she'd worn something with sleeves. The tank top was cool and comfortable. But it also revealed the fading yellow outline of the bruises he'd left on her arms. A movement in the doorway caught his attention, and he looked away briefly. Long enough for her to see that muscle in his jaw. Still ticking.

Matthew and Sawyer returned. Emily looked closely at them, her stomach clenching anew at their expressions. She rose nervously, and Sawyer closed his palm over her shoulder.

"Daniel went in a minute ago," Sawyer told them. Tristan rose instantly and headed to ICU. Sawyer squeezed her shoulder once more, then left, saying he needed some coffee.

A middle-aged couple departed, emptying the two seats next to Jefferson. Matthew nudged her toward them, taking the seat in the middle between her and Jefferson.

"What's he like this morning?" Jefferson asked.

"The nurse said he had a good night," Matthew answered. "And his color's quite a bit better."

Jefferson twirled his cane between his palms. "Still unconscious?"

Matthew nodded. His chest rose and fell in a deep sigh, and he leaned his head back against the wall behind the chairs.

Emily twisted the narrow leather strap of her small purse into a knot. "How did it happen? I mean, has Squire been having heart problems all along? He never said anything. Did he?"

"Not a word." Matthew stretched his legs out before him and

crossed his ankles. He clasped his hands together across his flat stomach and looked down at his thumbs. "But we all know Squire. He never gives anything away. Turns out he's been seeing a cardiologist here in Casper for the past couple years. Anyway, he'd ridden Carbon out to do some fishing."

Jefferson's head lifted at the horse's name. He himself had bought the ornery young colt many years ago. Back when he'd still been in Squire's good graces. Before he'd made the mistake of sharing his conflicting feelings toward Emily with Squire.

"Near as we can tell," Matthew continued, "he found some downed fence. Stock was probably straying." He pressed his thumbs together. "Instead of riding back and sending someone else out to round 'em up and fix the fence, he stayed and did it himself." He pinched the bridge of his nose. "Carbon came back alone. When we found Squire, he was unconscious. Lying next to the fence he'd repaired. The wire cutters were still in his hand." He shook his head. "Damned stubborn old man."

Suddenly his legs jackknifed and he stood. "I need some fresh air."

Emily glanced across the empty seat at Jefferson. His chin was propped on his fist, his thumb moving across his tight lips. His bad leg was stretched out straight, the tip of his boot rhythmically ticking an inch or so back and forth. His attention was focused ahead.

She wished he'd say something. Anything. And called herself a coward for not being able to say anything herself. Tears threatened again and she blinked rapidly. Crying was not going to do anybody a bit of good. She pulled a tissue from her purse and surreptitiously wiped her eyes and nose.

Jefferson's arm reached across the empty space between them and he took her hand in his, threading her fingers through his own. She shot him a startled glance. His attention was still focused forward. But his palm was warm and dry against hers.

For now, it was enough.

Before long, Daniel returned. "Tristan went to talk to the cardiologist himself," he told them. "You guys can go in now."

Jefferson let go of her hand, and Emily tried not to feel bereft. She drew in a steadying breath and rose. She placed the strap of her purse over her shoulder. Without waiting for Jefferson, Emily walked over to the swinging doors leading into ICU. She paused, then straightened her shoulders and pushed through the doors. She hadn't been raised like a Clay for nothing. She knew Jefferson was right behind her but didn't let herself focus on that. If she did, she knew she'd fall apart.

The nurses' station was situated in the center of the unit, with the beds radiating out like spokes of a wheel. Glass walls separated the beds from each other, but only heavy white curtains separated the beds from the nursing station. Squire was in the very first "room." She saw him as soon as she cleared the double doors, and stopped short.

Jefferson nearly bumped into her, and he closed his hand over the back of her neck.

Emily swallowed and moved out from his touch, entering Squire's cubicle. Tubes snaked out of his nose and his arms, and machines surrounded his bed. If it weren't for all that, she'd have suspected that he was merely sleeping. His thick silvered hair sprang back from his chiseled forehead, and he was slightly pale beneath his permanently tanned skin. A stark white bandage covered most of his bare chest and a pale blue sheet covered him to his waist.

"Do you think he knows we're here?"

Jefferson nodded and moved around to the opposite side of the bed. He was leaning hard on the cane.

Now that she'd seen Squire, Emily didn't feel quite so terrified. Her instincts told her that everything would be all right. Hoping that those instincts weren't leading her astray, she sank into the chair situated next to the bed and gently touched Squire's hand.

She leaned over to kiss his weathered cheek. "Squire, it's Emily. You didn't have to go to all this trouble just to get us home for a visit, you know." She looked up at Jefferson. His lips were pursed and his eyes narrowed as he looked down at his father. She positively ached with his buried pain. Squire wasn't the only Clay man who found it hard to "give anything away" as Matthew had put it earlier.

All too quickly, their allotted five minutes were up, yet Jefferson hadn't said a word to his father. Emily felt like crying. Or hitting him. Either one would have made her feel better. She squelched both urges and pressed a gentle kiss to Squire's cool cheek, promising him that she'd return soon to see him.

The rest of the men were back in the waiting room. Emily took one look at Tristan, and the tears started squeezing out of her eyes again. He enclosed her in his gentle bear hug, and she only cried harder. As much as she loved Tristan, it was Jefferson's arms she wanted around her. But he was standing over by the window, his expression brooding as he watched the rest of them.

"Why don't we head across the street to that restaurant and grab some lunch. Then you all could go on back to the ranch," Sawyer suggested, his eyes playing over his brothers and Emily. "I can stick around here, and somebody can come and get me tonight when visiting hours end."

Daniel needed no second urging. He was nodding and heading outside almost before Sawyer finished speaking. Matthew was obviously torn, wanting to stay. Needing to go. He had work to take care of.

"Emily?" Tristan nudged her for her opinion.

She swiped her cheeks and nodded tiredly.

Sawyer caught Jefferson's glance, who shrugged. "Okay then."

They all trooped out and headed for the restaurant. It took several minutes for them to set up a table to accommodate all six of them. Despite Emily's best efforts, she ended up seated next to Jefferson. That's what she got for stopping first at the rest room to freshen her face.

Tristan sat directly across the table from Jefferson, and he smiled blandly. She could have kicked him, knowing that he was responsible for the seating arrangement.

The young waitress took one look at the men sitting around the table and brightened. Emily had to bite back a chuckle when, after returning with their orders of iced tea all around, the girl, "I'll be your server—call me Candy," had freshened her pale lipstick and loosened the top few buttons of her fitted pink uniform.

She opened the laminated menu and automatically glanced over the selections, even though she wasn't sure her stomach really wanted food. She closed the menu and laid it on the table alongside her tea.

"Decided already?" Daniel's menu was lying on the table also and he nudged the container of artificial sweetener toward her. "Let me guess. French dip. Right?"

She took a little packet and ripped it open, pouring it into her tea. "Call me consistent."

"Consistent!" Tristan chuckled. "She's ordered that for lunch or supper in damn near every restaurant we've ever been in since she was ten years old."

"So?" Emily wasn't fazed in the least. "I can't help it if I know what I like."

She felt Jefferson shift beside her. When she glanced at him, he was leaning over to retrieve his napkin from the floor.

"Well," she pulled her attention back from the way his navy blue shirt stretched taut across his long back, "you'd better decide yourself what you want mighty quick. Before Candy, there, comes back to get the order."

Daniel sipped his tea and looked across the room to where the waitress was taking an order from a young family. "Whatcha want to bet she's gonna have another button undone when she comes back?" He set his glass down and leaned slightly forward. "She'll lean over your shoulder again, Tris, and give you a real view."

Matthew shook his head. Sawyer looked bored. Tristan laughed. Jefferson shifted again, and his knee brushed against hers.

When Candy returned, Daniel won the bet.

That day set the pattern for the ones that followed. They'd all go to the hospital in the same two vehicles. They had lunch at the same restaurant each day. Then they'd all return to the ranch, with one of the brothers staying behind. The second day, Daniel volunteered to stay. On the third, Matthew. And so it went. For the next several days.

Five days passed since she'd first seen Squire in the hospital before she found herself back in Squire's cubicle with Jefferson. Somehow, between the two of them avoiding each other, they'd managed to not say three words to each other since that first day at the hospital. She'd been sure not to sit next to him at the restaurant. Only, she'd found it nearly as heartbreaking to watch him over lunch as it had been to sit beside him.

She'd nearly fallen off her waiting room chair when Jefferson said he'd accompany her to ICU that morning.

Tristan shot her a brows-raised look, but nobody else seemed to think anything of Jefferson's quiet comment.

So that's how she came to be sitting once again in Squire's room, with Jefferson holding up the wall on the opposite side of the bed. It no longer surprised her that he didn't seem inclined to say anything.

But she was determined not to brood over Jefferson. At least not in Squire's ICU cubicle. "Squire, we really want you to wake up," she said in a clear voice, after kissing him hello. "Matt needs to know about an invoice he got for some equipment it looks like you ordered. And I'm sure I saw Daniel trying to sneak a smoke earlier. You know how hard it was for him to quit last year." She pushed out her lip and glanced toward Jefferson. He wasn't looking at the man in the bed. He was staring at Emily, his eyes dark and unreadable.

She swallowed and moistened her lips. "I'm going to run out of leave time from work next week and I expect you to be up by then," she continued. "Joe Greene's got a crew in now. Combining should be done this week."

She picked up his cool hand and smoothed her thumb over the back. "There's a pretty nurse just a few feet away," she wheedled. "If you'd just wake up, I'll bet you'd have her swept off her feet in no time at all with just one look from those blue eyes of yours."

She slid a glance over her shoulder at the two nurses manning the desk just a few feet away. One was very definitely a man. The other nurse's gray hair was so tightly curled next to her head that it almost looked like wool, and she looked about two days away from retirement. "She's got long auburn hair, Squire."

She ignored Jefferson's raised eyebrows. "And beautiful green eyes," she added for good measure. "But you should wake up and see for yourself."

She fell silent for a few moments. Jefferson still said not a word. "Bird's looking real good," she said. "You were right about his temperament when we picked him out at that auction. But I'm still glad we didn't have him gelded. His bloodline would be good to breed. You're gonna have to get well quick, though, or by the time I get back, he won't be fit to ride for a month of Sundays."

She fell silent as the male nurse entered the room. He smiled cheerfully and after looking at the machines, made a few notations on the chart at the foot of Squire's bed, then left again.

Emily lifted Squire's hand and held it to her cheek. She closed her eyes. "Jefferson's here too, Squire," she finally said. "He's right here on the other side of your bed. Actually, he looks almost worse than you do." She opened her eyes, defiantly ignoring the glint that had appeared in Jefferson's. "He's added a couple of new scars to his ugly mug. Maybe if you'd wake up, he'll tell you what he's been doing the past few years."

Jefferson snorted. "Not likely."

"Ah, he speaks," Emily quipped. Squire's fingers flexed against hers, as if in agreement. Startled, she looked at the man in the bed. "Squire?"

"What is it?"

"He moved his hand, Jefferson." She leaned closer to Squire. "Squire, can you hear me? Squeeze my fingers again. Oh, please Squire, just squeeze my fingers again."

She nearly shot out of the chair when she felt the faint pressure against her fingers. She leaned forward and kissed Squire's cheek again. "I'm going to get the nurse," she said and gently laid Squire's hand back on the mattress.

Jefferson readjusted his grip on the cane. He could see Emily talking urgently to the older nurse. "Come on, old man," he said softly. "I didn't come all the way here to keep watching you lie in that bed like a sack of feed."

Emily stuck her head back in. "Has he moved again? Oh, for God's sake, Jefferson, sit down and hold his hand!" She went back to the nurse's station.

"I guess she told me, didn't she." Jefferson couldn't help the slight grin on his face as he did as she'd ordered. Well, he sat down, at least. He didn't hold his father's hand. He knew it wouldn't be what Squire wanted.

"She can be pretty bossy, you know. Emily. Must be the Clay influence." He looked for a long time at his father, then propped his elbows on the edge of the bed. "I know you can hear me, Squire. Maybe hearing me talk to you will be annoying enough that you'll get your old carcass up and out of this place."

He raked his fingers through his hair, his eyes skipping over the monitors. God, he hated hospitals. Hated the antiseptic smell. The quiet noises. "I know I heard every damned word they whispered around me when I was in the hospital a while back." It was amazing how easily the words came when Squire was helpless to respond. "Blasted medical people," he continued. "Talking about you like you're dead, when all along you know exactly what's going on. Even if the old bod doesn't let you get it across to them."

Emily stepped up behind him, her clean scent enveloping him. She laid her hand across his shoulder as she leaned forward. "Squire, your doctor's going to be here soon. Promise me that you'll prove to him that I didn't imagine you squeezing my hand."

Jefferson's jaw clenched. Her hair drifted across his shoulder. Touched his cheek. If he turned his head a few inches, his lips would touch her shoulder, left bare by the sleeveless white sweater she wore. She'd been torturing him all week wearing an assortment of skimpy, sleeveless things.

Squire's lashes moved. Once. Twice. Then lifted infinitesimally until a pale blue narrowly gleamed from between his thick, spiky lashes. His lips parted, and, still leaning across Jefferson, Emily held the plastic cup with the bendable straw to

Squire's lips. His eyes closed again as he gathered the energy to sip water through the straw.

Squire sighed and relaxed, and Emily put the cup back on the table beside the bed. Her fingers dug into Jefferson's shoulder, and she pressed her head against the top of Jefferson's. He knew she was trying not to cry. Just as he knew, as Squire's eyes opened once again, the picture his father saw looking at the two of them beside his bed.

Jefferson's fingers were already closing over the handle of his cane, when Squire's lips moved.

"Get...away..." he mouthed.

Emily's head shot up, and Jefferson rose, his lips twisted. "Welcome back, old man." The chair scraped back with a sharp screech, and Jefferson limped out of the room.

Dismayed, Emily's eyes went back and forth between Jefferson's departing back and Squire's squinting eyes. "What—"

"Emily," Squire's voice could barely be heard. She stepped next to the bed, looking over her shoulder. Jefferson stopped only to say a brief word to the male nurse, who rounded the counter immediately and headed toward them.

"I'm here, Squire." She lifted his hand again and turned her attention back to him. His eyes were closed once more.

The nurse checked the monitors, flashed a light in Squire's eyes. "Looking good," he pronounced. "I'll notify his doctor that he's conscious. He needs some rest," he told Emily. "Why don't you come back this afternoon."

Emily jerked out a nod. She kissed Squire's hand, saying a silent prayer of thanks when he squeezed hers in return. She laid his hand on the bed. "I'll see you later, Squire."

She practically raced back to the waiting room. They were all there, except for Jefferson. She knew that he'd been there, however briefly. Obviously Jefferson had told his brothers that

Squire was conscious. She knew that, just by looking at the collected relief on their faces.

"Where'd Jefferson go?"

"Back to the ranch," Tristan said.

"The Blazer?" She didn't understand why he'd leave the lot of them stranded at the hospital.

"He said he was going to find a cab or walk."

"Oh, for Pete's sake," Emily scraped her hair out of her eyes. "You can't be serious." Clearly, he was. "Why didn't he just wait until the rest of us went or have one of you drive him back?"

"If you'd hurry, you'll probably catch him down in the lobby," Daniel murmured close to her ear as he headed to the door.

"Stupid, stubborn Clays," Emily muttered. "I'll see you guys later." She decided not to wait on the elevator and raced down the stairwell instead. Her heart was pounding when she burst into the lobby, and she made herself take a huge, calming breath when she saw him leaning against the wall outside the hospital's main entrance.

One way or another she was going to find out what was going on between Jefferson and Squire. She might as well start with the son.

She straightened her purse strap and took another cleansing breath. When she walked through the automatic sliding glass doors, she knew her expression was calm. Jefferson didn't even glance at her when she took up a similar position right next to him.

Silently she stood beside him and watched a small bird hop around the grass growing beneath a young tree. It pecked at something unseen in the grass. A car slowly drove by, looking for a parking space, and the bird flew off. Emily took a faint breath. "You want to tell me what that was all about up there?"

"No."

"Come on, Jefferson. I know you weren't even surprised at

what he said in there. It was like you expected it. Good grief, you were already half out of your seat when he…when he, um—"

Jefferson looked at her, his expression bland. "When he told me to get out."

"You don't know that's what he meant."

His eyebrows rose slightly. As if he couldn't believe she'd even suggest such a notion. He shook his head. "I know."

Emily moved around to face him. "Okay, so then why did he say it? Why on earth wouldn't he want you to be there?" There was no point in suggesting that Squire hadn't directed his comment straight at Jefferson.

"Leave it alone, Emily."

She crossed her arms. "I won't leave it alone." If he insisted he was simply a brother figure to her, then she'd treat him the way she would any of the rest of the Clays. At least she'd try. "Did the two of you argue? I know it can't have been recently, since until you showed up at Tristan's, you'd pretty well dropped off the face of the planet for more than two years. Is *that* why you were gone so long? Did you and Squire have some major falling out or something?"

"I said to drop it." Each word was bitten off between his teeth.

"Jefferson." Unable to contain herself, she reached up to touch his cheek. "Whatever it is, it can be fixed. I know it can."

"There is nothing to be fixed."

"You're just like him, you know." Emily folded her arms once more. "Completely inflexible." She shook her head, disgusted. She opened her purse and rooted through its narrow confines for the single key to the rental. "Here," she held it out to him when she found it. "You can drive the rental back to the ranch. I'll ride with Matthew and the others when they leave."

He didn't take the key from her hand.

"You'd rather spend a fortune on a cab than use *my* rental?

Assuming that a cab would even make the trip." She rocked back on her heels. She should have known she couldn't come out of a conversation with him unscathed.

"Don't do that." He bit off a curse. "Don't look at me like I just shot your puppy."

"I can't help it," she snapped. "Some of us haven't stomped out all semblance of emotion from our lives." She flipped open her purse and dropped the key back inside. "Get yourself back to the ranch however you want to." She spun on her heel.

He swore again and grabbed her arm before she'd gotten two feet. Angrily, she shrugged off his touch.

"I can't drive."

She stopped in the entryway to the hospital. Surely she'd misheard. His voice had been so low, she'd barely heard him. "What?"

Jefferson's jaw clenched. The glass doors slid shut. Opened. Shut. Opened. Emily finally stepped off the entryway, and the doors slid closed. She moved closer to him. "What did you say?"

His jaw set. "I said…I can't…drive."

She blinked. Talk about male pride. "Well, good grief, Jefferson, why didn't you just say so?" She extracted the key once again and headed toward the parking lot, still speaking. "Come on, then. I'll drive you back. Is it because the rental's a manual? The car you had in California was an automatic. Your knee won't let you work a clutch yet, I'll bet. How long is your knee going to take to heal, anyway?"

Jefferson closed his eyes briefly. "A while," he said grimly, earning himself a quick look from Emily. But she didn't comment or question further, and he stepped away from the wall, following her slowly. She was cutting diagonally across the parking lot, slipping between two cars.

He followed, then nearly fell flat on his face when his boot caught on a cement parking stop. Swearing a blue streak, he shot his arm out and latched on to the side of the truck bed of the pickup backed into the parking space beside him. His hip banged painfully against the side of the truck, but he kept himself from landing on the ground. His cane rolled under the car on the other side.

Emily whirled around, gasping when she saw what had happened. She rushed back and went to grab him, but stopped cold at the expression in his eyes. Vulnerability wasn't something he'd chosen to share lately.

Giving him a moment, she dropped to her hands and knees and fished around for his cane from beneath the car. With it tucked under her arm, she stood and brushed the dust from her hands.

Fearing that he'd bite her head off if she tried to assist him, she silently handed him the cane and made herself turn around and continue to her car. She managed not to look back to see how he was progressing. But she did suck in a relieved breath when she went around to the passenger side to unlock the door and casually glanced across the top of the car to see that he was heading her way.

How on earth was she supposed to stick to her decision to move on with her life? How could she when every fiber of her soul was telling her that Jefferson needed her? Whether he admitted it or not.

Worrying the inside of her lower lip, she unlocked her side and climbed behind the wheel, starting the engine. She kept silent when Jefferson awkwardly maneuvered himself into the passenger seat. She turned up the radio when he stifled a groan. And she didn't offer to help him out of the car hours later when she pulled to a stop in front of the big house.

The back door was unlocked, as usual. She went into the

kitchen, her ears perked to Jefferson's uneven gait. But the path around the house from the front was grass, and she heard nothing. She quickly raced into the dining room and peeped through the lace curtains hanging at the tall windows just in time to see him round the corner toward the back of the house. When the wooden screen door squeaked open and banged shut, she was standing in the kitchen, one arm propped on the counter near the sink.

She glanced up casually, her heart beating unevenly, then turned her attention to the leather sandal she was sliding from her foot. The piece of gravel that she'd picked up from the drive fell out, and she slid the shoe back on and tossed the little pebble in the trash.

Watching him from the corner of her eye, she headed for the refrigerator and pulled out an apple juice. "Want one?" She held up the bottle for him to see.

He shook his head, appearing as if he would just pass through the kitchen. Then he seemed to change his mind and abruptly pulled out a chair and sat down.

Emily closed the refrigerator door and joined him at the table. It was then that she noticed the blood streaking the palm of his right hand. She caught his wrist in her hand and turned his palm upward. "You've cut yourself."

He curled his fingers shut. "It's nothing."

"Don't be a mule," she muttered, pushing at his closed fist with her fingertips. "Let me see."

"I snagged it on the truck. No big deal."

Her eyebrows lowered and she let go. With a shrug, she picked up her juice and left.

Jefferson grimaced. He opened his hand and poked at the cut with his other. Fresh blood spurted through the shallow cut. He reached for the basket of paper napkins sitting in the center of the table and pressed a few to his palm. He'd get up and wash it off in a minute.

He lifted the wad of napkin, to see if the bleeding had stopped. It had. Pushing his left hand flat on the table, he began levering himself up off the chair, abruptly changed his mind and sank down.

Maybe he'd wash it off in five minutes.

He crumpled the napkin and left it on the table. It wasn't the cut on his palm that had him concerned. It was the unexpectedly sharp pain arrowing from his hip down toward his thigh. Hopefully he'd just bruised himself knocking into the truck and hadn't done any damage to the artificial hip he'd received in Germany.

He glared at his boots. As if they were to blame for catching on that parking stop. When he knew full well why his foot had dragged. His brain had told him he'd cleared that damned block of cement. The message just hadn't extended to his foot. Something that was happening more often than he liked.

Which was why he hadn't put himself behind the wheel of a car since he left San Diego. He'd probably end up killing someone if he did.

Emily came back into the room. Her bare feet padded softly across the wood-planked floor and she set a rectangular white box on the table. She opened the first aid kit, her attention on its contents. She'd pulled her hair back into a loose braid, and he could tell by the way her smooth jaw was drawn up all tight that she wasn't as calm as her expression indicated. She ripped open an antiseptic wipe and waited.

"This wasn't necessary." But he held up his hand, anyway. "I was going to clean it."

"Shut up."

For some reason his humor kicked in. He squelched the grin wanting to spring free. "Mule, huh?"

Her head tilted slightly to one side, and she firmly pressed the wipe to the cut.

"Ow!" He jerked his hand away, but she grabbed hold. "That stuff stings."

She spared him no mercy. "You're Mr. Macho," she said. "Surely you can stand a little antiseptic."

When the cut was clean, she dried it with a gauze pad and covered it with a plastic bandage. His palm still stung when she let go of his hand. "Brat. Squire should have spanked you more often."

"Huh! Squire never laid a hand on me, and you know it."

"Obviously."

Emily gathered up the trash and dropped it into the trash can beneath the sink. "The only one who ever dared to spank me was you, mister. That time when—"

"—you filched one of Squire's cigarettes and tried smoking it out in the barn. You nearly set fire to the loft trying to light that stupid thing."

"I did not nearly set fire to anything," she defended lightly. She remained at the sink, looking out the window. "You would never have even known I was up there if you hadn't taken that…that…*girl* in there to, um, make out."

"You were pretty pissed off. Such a dinky thing, too. Damned if you didn't punch me right in the stomach after I took away that cigarette and swatted your butt."

Emily's lips twisted. She rinsed out the dishrag and needlessly wiped down the sink rim. "I was fourteen," she said. And she had been angry with Jefferson for daring to bring that girl with him on his brief stay. So angry that she'd have done almost anything to get his attention away from that tall, blond, *curvy* female. She'd succeeded, all right. Just not in the way she'd planned. Jefferson had been disgusted with her, calling her careless and immature. He'd left the next day, taking Miss Curves with him.

"Fourteen or not, you were still dinky. That was the summer you went off to school, wasn't it?"

"Mmm." She began wiping off the counter. "I thought my bacon was saved when you came back unexpectedly." She rinsed the cloth again and squeezed the water out of it, watching the water drip into the white sink. "It seemed like fate to me. I was so sure you'd change Squire's mind about sending me." It had broken her heart that Jefferson hadn't even tried.

He'd breezed in and breezed right back out again within less than twenty-four hours. And though she received a tattered postcard from him now and then over the years, and the cassette tapes each and every Christmas, she'd seen him only once in person from the time she'd left for boarding school and the time she'd been in college.

She closed her palms over the edge of the sink, curving her fingers down. For a long minute they were both silent. "Jefferson?"

"Yeah?"

She closed her eyes, willing her heart not to jump out of her chest. "Why did you come to see me at school that time?" She heard the creak of his chair as he shifted his weight. "When I was nineteen," she added unnecessarily.

"You'd just had a birthday. You hadn't made it back home yet that year. Squire wanted to give you—"

"Yes," she said, interrupting his bland explanation. "I know all that. Squire wanted to make sure I received that pearl necklace of your mother's safely, and he didn't trust the mail. But he could have brought it himself when he came to visit me, or just waited until I came home for vacation." She looked over her shoulder. "Why *you?*"

He was fiddling with the scissors from the first aid kit. "Just turned out that way. I'd been by here. Saw Squire. When he found out I was on my way to Washington, he asked me to stop off and give you your birthday gift."

She'd heard the story before. Yet she kept hoping… "You stayed in New Hampshire nearly a week."

"I had some time on my hands." He turned the scissors point down and balanced his hand atop them.

"So you were just…passing the time, then." She didn't know why she kept at this. It was like picking at an old wound. Painful. Yet morbidly fascinating.

"What do you want me to say?" He sighed and flipped the scissors into the box. "Well, Emily? Are we talking about the fact that I visited you at school, or are we talking about the fact that I practically stole your innocence while I was there?"

Emily's breath dissipated, leaving her light-headed. She moistened her lips and slipped into a chair across the table. "It wasn't *stealing*," she managed. They'd spent five solid days together. Walking together. Talking. Laughing. Falling in love, or so she'd thought. Each night when he'd left her to return to his motel room, it had been harder and harder to let him leave. And then that night, when his chaste kiss on her forehead had turned into something more…

"Why do you insist on rehashing this?"

"You never answer!"

He stifled a curse. "You were barely nineteen."

"Is that why you stopped? Because I didn't have any experience and wasn't any good at it? Did you get bored? You wanted to find some other way to kill some time? What?"

He made an exasperated sound. "For Pete's sake—"

"Wait!" She scrambled out of her chair, kneeling before him before he could get up and leave. "I have to know, Jefferson.

Can't you understand that?" Her hands closed urgently over his legs, her fingers pressing into him. "I have to know!"

"You want to know?" His eyes darkened and the muscle in his jaw twitched. "Then know this." He moved suddenly and Emily found her face captured between his hard hands. He covered her mouth with his, forcing open her lips and sweeping inside.

One hand went to her nape and held her still while he ravaged her mouth. By the time he lifted his head, Emily was trembling. She could taste the faint coppery tang of blood from her lip yet refused to cry. Though she wanted to throw herself on the floor and weep. Weep for all the pain she sensed in him. Pain that he kept hidden behind his rough actions.

"I wanted to do that," he said baldly. "When you were nineteen." His hand was like iron about her neck. "Just looking at you made me hard." He watched her cheeks pinken. Watched the tip of her tongue sneak out and touch her upper lip.

"I wanted to tear off your shirt," he growled. "I wanted to do this." He dropped his hand to her breast and molded the fullness with a less-than-gentle touch. He leaned over, and his breath was harsh against her ear. "I wanted to tear off your panties," he said, running his hand from her breast to the flat of her stomach. "I wanted to touch you." He rotated his palm and his fingers arrowed lower. "*There*. I wanted to taste you. *There*." His hard hand slipped between her thighs. "You were dreaming of roses and candlelight and all I wanted was to find a bed and bury myself in you. Right there. Hell, a bed wasn't even necessary."

Emily swayed. His touch branded her. Then, just as suddenly as he'd swooped over her, he sat back, withdrawing his hands. His warmth.

"You damn sure weren't prepared for that when you were nineteen." He picked up the scissors once again, not looking at her. "You still aren't."

Shivers danced across her shoulders. They weren't shivers of fear. "You're not frightening me, Jefferson. You didn't frighten me when I was nineteen. You didn't frighten me in San Diego. *And you're not frightening me now.*" She rose smoothly and walked away, dignity gathered around her like a cloak.

The room was empty. Lifeless without her presence.

Jefferson stared at his hands.

"I frighten myself," he murmured.

But there was no one there to hear him.

Chapter Six

"What do you mean you're not going to the hospital today?"

Frowning, Emily finished securing her ponytail and hurried out into the hall. Tristan had just stepped out of his room, looking curious.

"Did you hear that yelling?" she asked.

"Who didn't?" he answered. "Sounds like someone got up on the wrong side of the bed. Betcha I know who's planning to stick to the ranch today, though." He dropped his arm across her shoulders and herded her downstairs. "You look very nice today," he said as they entered the kitchen. He dropped a kiss on the top of her head and headed for the coffee.

Emily glanced down at her well-worn blue jeans and thin, cropped white shirt. The clothes were clean, but hardly on the cutting edge of fashion. Just about to ask Tristan what had gotten into him, raised voices sounded just outside the mudroom.

The screen door banged shut as Jefferson stalked in,

Matthew charging after him. "I don't care what Squire said," Matthew yelled.

Jefferson swiveled on his heel, stopping his brother short. His fingers were white over the handle of his cane. "Back off!"

Emily hastily filled a mug of coffee and stuck it into Matthew's raised hand. "Have some coffee," she muttered.

He looked at her. At the mug of coffee. Some of his anger drained away. Despite its scalding temperature, he drank half of it down and set the mug on the table. "Look, Jeff, we've all got stuff we need to be doing. I've got fifty things that I've let slide since Squire went into the hospital. This place doesn't run itself, even with Joe Greene's help. But I'm going to the hospital this morning. Just like usual. We're all going. *And so are you.*"

Jefferson looked terrible. Emily could tell just by looking at the lines bracketing his eyes that he hadn't slept much the night before. Tristan caught her glance and shook his head slightly, as if he knew she was ready to move between the two men. To take Jefferson's arm and—

"Not today," Jefferson stated softly. He turned around, his eyes colliding with Emily's. Lips tight, he looked away and went back outside.

Matthew swore, but Tristan caught his shoulder before Matthew could take off after Jefferson. "Let him be." His eyes sent the same message to Emily.

It wouldn't have mattered if Tristan had pinned her to the floor; if she'd wanted to follow Jefferson, she would have. Unfortunately, she didn't have a clue what she'd say to him, so in the kitchen she stayed. Well, the mudroom, at least. Where she watched him walk toward the bunkhouse.

Matthew shrugged off Tristan's hand. "Does he think this is easy for any of us?" His fingers raked through his hair. The phone jangled and he yanked up the receiver. "Yeah? Oh, sorry,

Maggie. What's up?" Matthew's expression tightened as he listened. "No, sure, that's fine. Yeah…fine…okay…yeah. Bye." He waited until he'd hung up before losing his temper. "First Squire. Then Jefferson, and now this?" He slammed his palm flat against the door frame. "How much is a person supposed to stand?" Without looking back, he headed outside.

"Well, that was enlightening," Tristan commented, tongue firmly in cheek. The phone rang again and he picked it up. He spoke briefly, then hung up just as Daniel came in. "Hey, Dan, isn't Jaimie Greene Joe's little sister?"

"Yeah." Daniel flipped on the faucet and stuck his head beneath the cool water. Emily pushed a dish towel into his groping hand. "Ahh," he sighed thankfully, catching the dripping water with the towel. "Damn but it's already hot out there. What's this about Jaimie?"

Tristan nodded toward the telephone. "That was Maggie just now on the phone. She said she forgot to give Matthew Jaimie's flight number."

Daniel lowered the towel from his face. "Jaimie's coming? Here?" His lips pursed and his eyes lit with an unholy gleam. "And Matt knows?"

"Apparently. He's picking her up at the airport this afternoon."

Daniel started laughing. "Man, oh, man, this ought to be good."

"*Who* is Jaimie Greene?" Emily asked.

"She's Joe's little sister," Dan said. "Oh, that's right. You guys haven't met her. Well, anyway, she worked here for a while last summer. I'll bet Matt's shorts are in a knot but good." He laughed again, shaking his head. "Never thought she'd come back here," he said, once he'd gotten control of himself. "I guess you could say that she and Matt rubbed each other all wrong."

"I didn't know there was anybody that Matthew didn't get along with," Emily said.

"Normally I'd agree," Dan answered. "But, I swear, those two took one look at each other—" He broke off when a horn blasted through the air. He tossed the towel on the table and looked out the window to see Matthew leaning on the horn. "He acted like a wet hen all summer long, and it looks like we're in for more of the same this year." He grinned again and headed for the door. "Didn't help his mood any that he couldn't look at her without slobbering all over himself. Tris, you coming?"

"Yup," Tristan quickly drank down his coffee and left the mug in the sink. "Don't know why though," he grumbled, following in Daniel's wake. "I *hate* haying."

Truck doors slammed and they drove off, leaving an unnatural silence behind. Emily peered out the window for a long moment. She knew that they wouldn't have turned down an offer of help from her, if she'd expressed one. She also knew that they didn't need her help, and if the truth were known, she hated the hot chore worse than Tristan did.

Turning her attention to the kitchen, she busied herself washing and putting away the few dishes the men had left in the sink.

It was still early in the morning, and they wouldn't be driving out to see Squire for a few hours yet. Retrieving her organizer from her bedroom, she returned to the kitchen and opened it to her calendar. Settling at the big table, she called her office in San Diego. It wasn't a particularly satisfying call. She made a few notes on the calendar, and called Luke Hawkins where she stabled Bird. He assured her he was exercising Bird regularly and that the horse was doing just fine.

She hung up, tapping her pen against the open calendar. You'd think that her horse, at least, would have the decency to miss her. Tossing down the pen, she slammed the organizer shut, grabbed an apple from the bowl on the counter and went outside. The

ever-present breeze drifted over her and she breathed in the distinctive scent of open fields. Of cattle and horses.

Her mood lifted somewhat. Who needed offices and computers and spreadsheets when a person had all this? The horse
barn was the closest building to the big house and that's where
her boots took her. More than half the horses were out, but she
found a nice gray mare. Crooning to the sleek animal, she fed
her the remainder of her apple and slipped into the stall.

Within minutes, she'd made a fast friend and the horse willingly let Emily slide a halter on and they went out into the
sunshine. The mare was the picture of good health, but Emily
wasn't about to just take her pick of a horse without checking
with Matthew or Dan first. Unfortunately they were nowhere
in sight, obviously out on the tractors somewhere.

She led the horse past all the buildings. She found Maggie in
the huge, commercial-type kitchen attached to the bunkhouse.

They visited for a while and then Maggie asked about San
Diego and her job.

Emily shrugged. She didn't want to talk about work. If her
employers had their way, she'd be returning to it all too soon.
"Do you know where the guys are working this morning?"

Maggie dragged a large stockpot off a high shelf. "I think Matt
and the boys were headed out toward Dawson's Bend." Puffing
a lock of pale blond hair out of her eyes, Maggie maneuvered the
big pot into the extra deep stainless steel sink. She pressed her
palms to the small of her back and straightened again, seeming
to sway for just a moment. "They'll probably be back in an hour
or so. You all are heading out to the hospital, then, aren't you?"

"Mmm-hmm." Emily reached out and touched Maggie's
elbow. "Are you feeling all right?"

A wan smile spread across the other woman's face. "Yes.
Just a bit of morning sickness."

"You're pregnant?" Emily stared at the gargantuan pot the woman had just wrestled all by herself. "What on earth are you doing moving things like that around? Does Matt know?"

"I'm doing my job," Maggie said dryly. "As for Matt, I have no idea. Joe and I just found out a couple weeks ago. Don't worry. I'm fine."

Emily wasn't so sure, but she held her tongue. For now. But she'd make darn sure Matthew knew what kind of strenuous tasks Maggie was completing. Lord, there were enough men around the place that she shouldn't have to be pulling pots and pans off ten-foot-high shelves.

She reminded herself of the reason she'd come into the bunkhouse in the first place and looked out the long side window overlooking the corrals situated across the gravel road. "Do you know anything about that gray? I thought I'd take her out for a ride."

Maggie followed Emily's pointing finger. "Oh, sure. Daisy's the mare Jaimie used last summer. I ride her pretty regularly, myself, now." Her hand touched her still-flat abdomen. "Well…" She smiled faintly. "Take her out," she encouraged. "She's a real sweetie."

Emily watched Maggie turn toward the double-wide freezer and pull out a large package. She plunked the butcher-paper-wrapped bundle on the wide butcher block. "I'm fixing roast beef for dinner tonight," she said. "I'll bring it up to the house before six, if that's all right."

Emily tugged at her earlobe. "You know, Maggie, I could cook for us…." The other woman's expression fell slightly, and it occurred to Emily that Maggie Greene was probably only a few years older than herself. "Not that your cooking isn't wonderful," she added hastily. "But, you know, if you're not feeling well, or…or something. I'd be happy to, uh, help out."

Level blue-green eyes looked out from Maggie's pale face. She seemed to relax slightly and a smile flitted across her mouth. "Thanks. I'm sure I'll be fine. But…thanks."

Nodding, and still feeling like she'd just taken a huge bite of her own foot, Emily left Maggie to her duties. Using a rung on the fence for a boost, she slipped onto Daisy's bare back. Emily didn't really have a destination in mind. But she gave Daisy her head and after a meandering romp, ended up at the swimming hole that lay about two miles east of the big house.

She dismounted and let the reins fall. Daisy didn't wander. Obviously familiar with the spot, she bent her graceful head and nibbled at the lush grass surrounding the tiny lake, affectionately termed the hole. To please his wife, Squire had fenced it off from the stock, and as far as Emily knew, he'd only had to bring cattle down for the water once or twice.

It had been Sarah Clay who'd planted the lilac bushes that still grew in such profusion around the spring-fed swimming hole. She'd nurtured the clover and wildflowers that still came back each spring, almost before the snow was gone. It was a place that Squire's wife had obviously loved. It was fitting that her headstone lay on the far side.

Not for the first time, Emily wondered about the woman who had borne Squire's five sons. Her portrait hung in the living room above the fireplace. She'd been a lovely woman with golden blond hair and deep blue eyes. With a gently rounded chin and a dimple in one cheek. It was Jefferson and Tristan who resembled her the most, at least coloringwise. All the Clay sons, as anyone with a speck of vision could see, had acquired their strong facial features from Squire.

Emily kicked off her boots and socks and stepped up on the flat boulder that stuck out over the water, serving as a rough-hewn diving board. She sat on the end, letting her toes dip into the cool water. Her eyes were on the opposite bank, and even though she couldn't see the small granite headstone because of the bushes and trees, she still felt the aura of love and happiness left behind by Mrs. Squire Clay.

"How did you handle all these males, Sarah?"

The only answer she received was the ripple of water as she lifted her feet up to rest on the rock. Sighing, she lowered her cheek to her knees. She had no idea how long she sat there before the sound of a twig breaking brought her head up. She looked over to Daisy, but the horse was contentedly munching her way closer to the water's edge.

"You always did like it out here."

Her breath caught and held. She swallowed and turned around to see Jefferson leaning against a tree. "Yes. I did."

His hand wrapped around the thick rope hanging from one of the high branches, and he swung it out over the water. "You used to swing on this rope and drop off right in the middle of the water. You and Tristan. You were like two little monkeys playing in the trees."

"I remember." Through her lashes, she watched him step over a fallen branch. If he could behave like their encounter in the kitchen the day before had never happened, then so could she. "You did your share of swimming here, too."

"That I did." Ducking beneath a branch, he walked over to the boulder.

"How'd you get out here?"

"Walked." He grimaced. "Limped."

"Where's your cane?"

The corner of his mouth twisted. "Somewhere in the middle of a field, where I pitched it."

Her eyebrows rose. "You threw it into the middle of a field."

"Yup." He lowered himself onto the rock and lay near the

edge projecting farthest over the water. A solid foot of space separated them. "'Course I'll be regretting it come this afternoon when I get all stiffened up again."

Emily found herself responding to his faint, dry smile. "Perhaps you should have taught Matt's dog to play fetch-the-cane before you went off and did it."

They both smiled, then fell silent. Emily's teeth worried the inside of her lip, and she looked at him over her arms, folded across the tops of her knees. Before she knew what she was doing, she'd reached out to run her finger along his angled jaw. "What's this scar from?"

Jefferson caught her finger in his. "My stupidity," he answered. Which was no answer at all.

She tucked her hand back over her knee. "Jefferson—"

"Shh," he said, his eyes dark pools. "Don't."

"You don't even know what I was going to say."

"Yeah, I probably do. And it's a bad idea."

"Your ego is monstrous." She turned her head to look out at the water. She'd only been toying with the idea of trying to persuade him to go to the hospital.

"Don't." He tugged lightly on her ponytail. "Let's just enjoy the morning."

"Oh, so you *can* enjoy something, can you? How refreshing."

"Snot."

"Yup."

Jefferson sighed. He shifted on the boulder until he was lying on his back. Just to see if he could, he wiggled his toes. And was relieved when he felt the inside of his boot. The numbness seemed to be gone. For now. "Tell me about your job," he said.

"My job."

"Your job."

"Ohhh-kay," she murmured. She stretched out her leg and dipped her toe in the water. "Well, let's see. I've been there a few years now. I guess you know that already." She went on to tell him a little of her daily routine.

"And who's the CPA you're dating?"

"Stuart? I'd hardly call it dating. Well, of course we did go to Mexico just before I flew up here, but that hardly—"

"You went to Mexico with him?"

Emily chastised herself for the twinge of satisfaction she felt at Jefferson's obvious displeasure. "Just for the weekend," she elaborated.

"Just you and this *Stuart* guy? What the hell was Tristan doing, letting—"

"Hey," she shot him a glare. "Tristan doesn't *let* me do anything. I make my own decisions."

"And smart ones, too. Haring off to Mexico with some joker. What if he—"

"What? What if he what? Put the *moves* on me? What if he did? What if I wanted him to? What if I *liked* it?"

Jefferson's jaw ticked. Then abruptly he smiled. So broadly that the dimple in his cheek broke free. He folded his arms behind his head and lay back. "Nothing happened."

She wasn't sure who she was more disgusted with. Jefferson for his ridiculous attitude. Or herself for almost falling off the boulder after one glance at his little-used megawatt smile. She clambered to her feet. "How do you know? There are some men on the face of this earth who do find me attractive, you know."

"Oh, I don't doubt that," he agreed, his low voice whiskey smooth. His lashes shaded his eyes partially as he ran his glance up and down her slender figure. "You grew up real nice, Emily."

"Gee," she replied as she propped her fists on her hips, "thanks. I'm so touched."

"Anytime."

Huffing, Emily shook her head and looked to the sky, then back down at Jefferson's sprawling body. She stepped back onto the rock and crouched down beside him. "You know what occurs to me, Jefferson?"

His eyes were closed, a half smile still hovering about his lips. "What?"

"It occurs to me, that you probably *haven't* had a good swim in a while." With that, she pushed at his waist. Off balance, he rolled right off the boulder into the swimming hole.

Water splashed over her feet and calves. Satisfied, she looked down at him as he slowly rose. Standing on the bottom, the water lapped at his shoulders. He shook his head, and his drenched hair flipped away from his face. He wiped the water from his eyes.

She was several feet above him. Yet, even from that safe distance, her feet edged backward, away from the water. "Wait, no, wait, Jefferson," she shook her head as his hands closed over the edge of the boulder. "You deserved that," she insisted, backing up another step.

Water sluiced from his shoulders as he heaved himself up onto the boulder. He looked down at his feet. "My boots are wet," he observed.

"Well, yes, I guess they are." She bit her lip and backed up another step, eyeing the short distance between her and Daisy out of the corner of her eye. Her bare heel felt grass beneath it. "They'll dry. Or—" she replied, backing up another step "—or, I'll buy you another pair."

"Do you know," he asked as he slicked dripping water away from his forehead, "how long it takes to break in a pair of boots? Years." Jefferson started to sit down and groaned.

Instantly Emily decided against escape and went to him. And

found herself flying through the air. She barely had time to close her eyes when she splashed into the water. Her toes skimmed the gravelly bottom and she surfaced. "Hey!" She treaded water, wishing for a few more inches in height. She shoved her palm across the surface, sending a cascade of water flying in his face. "Faker."

Jefferson laughed.

Stunned, she forgot to tread and went under again. When she came up sputtering, he was still laughing.

It was a glorious sound. Bemused, she smiled up at him. But eventually, the goose bumps could no longer be ignored and she swam over to the boulder. "Much as I'd like to listen to you laugh yourself silly, it's getting a tad cold in here." She reached her hand up.

He linked his fingers with hers and hauled her out of the water. She shook her hands, and droplets of water splattered everywhere. Not that it mattered, what with the puddles surrounding their feet. "I can't believe we used to swim in that sometimes until the middle of September." She grinned and looked up. "Then we only had to wait a few weeks, it seemed like, and we'd put away the swimming suits and break out the ice skates."

His laughter had faded, though the smile still lingered in his eyes. The leaves in the trees rustled and the breeze set off a fresh crop of goose bumps. Autumn was definitely coming. She plucked at the hem of her shirt and wrung out the water as best she could.

Jefferson swore softly.

"What is it?"

He shook his head and began unbuttoning his shirt. Shrugging out of it, he handed it to her. "Here."

"I hate to tell you this, Jefferson, but I'm not going to warm up any by putting your wet shirt on over my own wet shirt."

"No, but at least I can't see right through the fabric of mine." He dangled his shirt in front of her. "And I'm not missing any little pieces of underwear this morning, either."

Her eyes flew down and she realized how transparent the cropped top had become. The wet shirt clearly displayed the bare curves beneath. "Oh."

"Yeah. *Oh.* Give me a break, would you?"

Emily eyed the bare expanse of chest right in front of her nose. She wanted more than anything to press herself right up against that hard plane. She wanted to explore each ridge of muscle. Kiss each nick. Each scar. "Give *me* a break," she returned, trying to sound unaffected. But she took the shirt and slid her arms into it. Even though he'd folded the sleeves up to just below his elbows, they hung nearly to her wrists. Wrinkling her nose at yet another layer of wet fabric, she wrung out the shirttails as best she could, then tied them at her waist and shoved the sleeves up her arms.

Jefferson was busy pulling off his boots. "These used to be my favorite boots," he informed her as he upended them. A thin stream of water poured out.

"They're still your favorites," Emily assured him, trying desperately not to gawk at his golden chest.

"They're ruined."

"They're wet."

"Ruined."

She finally turned and looked toward the middle of the lake. "You've worn them in the rain, haven't you? And in the snow, probably. You'd walk through puddles in the middle of the street, rather than walking around them. What's the difference?"

Jefferson pulled the boots back on. "The difference, angel-face, is that on those occasions, the wet was on the *outside*." He grimaced as his socks squished when he stood. "Now it's on the inside." A quick sharp whistle from between his teeth brought Daisy ambling over. He caught the reins and with one swing of his long leg, mounted up. He reached his hand down for her. "Come on, let's get you back for some dry clothes."

He pulled her onto the horse, sitting her in front of him. Though still soaking, his body heat blasted through her sodden layers. She felt, rather than heard, the groan that rumbled through his chest. His arm slipped around her waist, and he turned Daisy through the trees back toward the big house.

There was simply no way for two people to ride one horse bareback and keep any distance between their bodies. Emily didn't even bother trying. She smoothed her palm across the hard arm holding her firmly against him. She leaned back and enjoyed.

"So why aren't you out haying with the rest of them?" she asked as Daisy meandered through the long grass toward the gravel road.

"They didn't need me."

"Me, either." Her fingertips feathered through the hair lightly sprinkled across his wrist. It seemed perfectly natural to tilt her head and kiss the biceps curving past her shoulder. She barely stopped herself from pressing her lips to his warm skin.

He snorted softly. "Angelface, the last time you went haying, Squire ended up hauling you to the doctor's for six stitches in your leg. But if you want to think that Matt wants your assistance, you go on ahead and keep dreaming."

"I could do it," she insisted halfheartedly. "If I put my mind to it. *If* I wanted to."

He clicked his tongue, and Daisy picked up her pace. "If you put your mind to it, you can do anything. But perhaps you'd best keep your interests trained toward the horses rather than the tractors, hmm?"

"I like horses better, anyway. I do miss Bird." She leaned

forward and patted Daisy's strong neck. "Although this pretty lady is a nice one, isn't she? Remember how you used to talk about having your own spread? Do you still want that?"

His palm pressed her backward until she nestled, once more, against his chest. "I talked about a lot of things. I was young then."

Emily choked on a laugh. "You're not exactly decrepit, you know. You talk as if you have one foot in the grave."

He stiffened slightly against her back. "You need some dry clothes," he said abruptly, urging Daisy into an easy lope that rapidly ate up the last several yards. He halted near the rear entrance of the big house. "Go in. I'll take care of Daisy."

The bright, happy morning they'd spent together ended. Just like that. Silently she slid to the ground. He waited just long enough for her to move away before wheeling Daisy around and heading for the horse barn.

For about the millionth time, she wished she knew what thoughts whirled in Jefferson's head. What caused his silent torment. She wiped a drip of water from her forehead and turned to the house.

Since there was no one about, in the mudroom she shucked off all the wet clothes except her panties. After wrapping herself in a big blue towel that had been folded atop a stack of clean laundry, she dumped her clothing into the washing machine.

The few items were hardly worth running a load, but she started one, anyway. It was purely habit that took her upstairs to the bedrooms where she found empty hampers in Matthew's and Daniel's rooms. She nearly tripped over the faded black duffel bag laying on the floor of Sawyer's room.

She frowned, wondering why Jefferson's duffel was in Sawyer's room. Then she noticed the luggage tag clearly printed with Sawyer's name and address. She picked it up and tossed it onto the bed, watching the tangle of airport tags bounce. Sawyer had almost as many tags hanging off the bag as Jefferson had hanging on his. Sawyer's duties with the navy were obviously keeping him as busy as ever.

She headed to Tristan's room after finding Sawyer's hamper empty. She gathered up the meager collection in Tristan's hamper. Then, since she'd already checked the other rooms, she made herself walk into Jefferson's room.

Like Sawyer, his duffel was lying in the middle of the floor. Brothers. She shook her head and, balancing Tristan's bundle on one hip, leaned down and plucked the items out of the wicker hamper. Quickly, she nipped down to the mudroom and started tossing Tristan's clothing in, her fingers automatically searching through his pockets. The man was notorious for leaving pens and pencils stuck in his pockets. She'd ruined more than one load of clothing before she'd learned her lesson.

Sure enough, she found two ballpoint pens. Shaking her head, she set them on the shelf above the washer and dumped the jeans into the agitating tub. Tucking the edge of the towel more securely between her breasts, she bent down and picked up Jefferson's jeans. Paper crinkled from inside one of the pockets, and she fished it out, then added the jeans to the load. She absently noticed the small square of paper was a prescription. She'd have to ask him if he needed it filled, then realized he'd had ample opportunities to do so at the hospital when they visited Squire.

She reached for the shirt lying on the floor, turning when the door squeaked open. Jefferson stepped in. He'd found a faded denim shirt somewhere, though it hung unbuttoned over his chest.

"Here," she handed him the prescription. "It was in your pants pocket."

Jefferson automatically pocketed the slip. "What are you doing?"

"Oh, a load of wash. Might as well make a full load. Want to throw your wet stuff in, too?"

"You're wearing a towel."

"No kidding." She rolled her eyes. Turning back to the washing machine, she dropped in his shirt and closed the lid. "I wasn't going to track water all through the house."

"You're parading around a house full of men, wearing nothing but a towel."

Good Lord, the man was furious. "You can't be serious. For Pete's sake, Jefferson, I'm more covered now than if I were wearing a bathing suit. Besides, nobody is even around. Except you."

"Is this the way you behave in San Diego?"

"Behave?" She echoed. "Behave?" Her voice rose as she repeated the word. Tires crunched over gravel and through the window she saw Daniel, Matthew and Tristan pile out of the truck. *Great. Just great. So much for being alone.*

Matthew and Daniel passed through, hardly giving her a second glance, though Daniel seemed ready to make some remark about Jefferson's wet jeans. But he took one look at his brother and reconsidered, choosing instead to follow Matthew back to the office. Tristan, of course, wasn't nearly so cooperative.

He took one look at Jefferson's wet pants, and Emily's lack of them and whistled. "Well, lookee here. While the cat's away…"

"Can it," Emily snapped without even glancing Tristan's way. With her hands on her hips, she continued glaring up at Jefferson. "What exactly are you implying? Does it bother you to think that I might," she clapped dramatic palms to her cheeks, "oh, my, dare I say it, actually *wear* a towel in my own home?" Oblivious of Tristan's interested observance, she lifted furious hands to the knot holding the towel in place. "Lord, Jefferson, you'd probably have a coronary if you thought I might actually find myself nude once in a while. I hate to shock you, of course, but it's easier to bathe that way."

Tristan choked on his snicker and at the twin glares he received, turned around and went right back outside. Emily transferred her attention back to Jefferson. Turmoil bubbled within her. "All my life, *all* my life, I've been surrounded by men who find it perfectly acceptable to walk around in their underwear. But *Heaven forbid* if I should present myself in anything less than a nun's habit." She flipped loose the knot in the towel and shoved it into Jefferson's chest. "Well, there. This is about as bad as it gets." She waved her arms. "But wait, the roof isn't caving in. Oh, dear."

Jefferson whipped the towel back around her shoulders faster than a ladies' maid. "That's it," he muttered. Bending down, he grabbed her up, flinging her over his shoulder. A hard arm clamped over her thighs, holding her, and the towel, in place as she struggled. "Cut it out."

Emily pounded on his back. "Put me down! I'm not a child."

"Then stop acting like one." He shouldered his way through the door, striding through the empty kitchen and not stopping until he reached her bedroom. He let her go, unceremoniously dumping her onto the bed. The towel that had been wrapped about her shoulders flew free. The pillows at the head of the mattress bounced madly. "You're asking for it, Em."

"Promises, promises," she taunted.

He leaned forward suddenly, his arms braced on the mattress to either side of her. "Acting the tart doesn't impress me, Emily."

He caught her palm before it could connect with his cheek. She struggled, and he settled the matter by pinning her arms above her head.

"Let…me…go." She twisted against his hold but he easily subdued her efforts. His eyes closed, as if in pain, and she suddenly stilled. "What's the matter?"

He grunted. "You've got to be kidding. Even *you* are not that naive."

Insulted, she renewed her efforts to wriggle out of his hold.

"Dammit," he cursed, quickly evading her knee aimed at emasculating him. She was slicker than a greased doorknob. But he managed to subdue her legs with one of his. And then had to look away at the planks in the wood floor, the beam of sunlight shining through the opened curtains. Anything rather than her taut, creamy skin. Her slender waist. Her rose-tipped breasts.

He bit off another curse and abruptly released her, moving so fast that the mattress bounced all over again. "Cover yourself." He tossed the towel at her.

She caught it and threw it at his head, scrambling off the bed. "If you don't like the sights, then take your chauvinistic carcass out of here."

The towel hit the wall behind him. Ignoring it, he pulled open a dresser drawer. Then another until he found what he wanted. Turning back to her, he held out a long-sleeved T-shirt. "Put it on." He felt a peculiar satisfaction as her hackles bristled all over again at his shamelessly autocratic order.

She arched a flippant "make-me" eyebrow and crossed her arms. Her nipples peeked out over her arms. And she knew it, the little witch. He yanked the shirt over her head, pulling it down over her shoulders. Her arms were caught inside. "You're trying my patience," he warned.

"Too damn bad."

He tugged on a bunched fold of shirt, jerking her off balance, but she set to wriggling again, earning himself a painful elbow in the ribs. "Dammit, Em. Be still."

"Don't order me around." She twisted, trying to make sense of the shirt tangled about her neck and shoulders. "Just because you say *jump,* doesn't mean I'm going to ask how high." She made a frustrated face then yanked off the shirt rather than try to make sense out of the twisted mess.

His jaw locked. She shook out the shirt, seeming to take an inordinate amount of time with it. "I warned you," he gritted, anchoring his hand in her hair. Then he kissed her.

She bit his lip.

He slowly lifted his head and touched a finger to the tiny bead of blood. "Like it rough, do you?"

Her cheeks flamed. No other person in existence had the ability to drive her beyond the borders of reasonable behavior. She looked everywhere but at him. For the truth of it was, she liked *it* any way it came as long as *it* was from him. She fumbled with the shirt trying to pull it down, but his hands blocked hers.

Going still, she looked up at him. Her breasts swelled from the heat blazing in his eyes. Without conscious thought, she swayed toward him and groaned low in her throat when his fingers brushed across her flesh. Thumb and finger circled a peak and she lost her breath. His fingers lightly pinched the taut nipple, and desire arrowed sharply to her core. Then his mouth replaced his hand, his teeth scraping over her hypersensitive skin.

Her hands knotted in his hair. Her breath hissed between her teeth. Before she knew what she was doing, her hands had dropped her shirt and were sliding into the neck of *his*.

Just that fast, he shoved himself away from her, raking his fingers through his hair.

Reeling, she spied the alarm clock on the bedside table. "Get out. I want to get ready to see Squire," she said, hating the way her voice shook.

At the mention of his father, Jefferson's eyes darkened. His face went curiously blank, and he inclined his head. "By all means."

Then he was gone.

Emily sank onto the edge of the bed, absently aware of the way the quilt was all bunched and wrinkled beneath her. Her heart was thudding so unevenly she felt dizzy. She pulled on the stupid shirt and, tilting to her side, pulled her legs up onto the mattress and waited for the room to stop spinning. And then she cried.

Tristan, walking past the open door several minutes later, glanced in. He silently took in the tumbled bed and the soft snuffles from the hunched figure facing away from the doorway. As silently as he'd approached, he retreated.

He strode down to the kitchen. Clapped his hand over Jefferson's shoulder and pulled him around from where he stood at the sink. Water spewed across the floor from the glass in Jefferson's hand.

"Dammit, Tris. What the hell's wrong with you?" Jefferson growled. He dropped the glass in the sink.

Tristan straightened to his full height, topping Jefferson by a few solid inches. His fists curled. "You *stupid* son of a bitch."

The screen door slammed, and Matthew trotted in, his eyes taking in the scene. In a flash he went between the two angry brothers, lifting a steadying hand, even as he grabbed for one of the chairs he'd bumped. Ignoring Matthew, Jefferson scooted out of the way to avoid the wooden chair skittering crazily toward him.

Matthew planted his palm on Tristan's chest, keeping him from moving toward Jefferson. "Come on, guys."

Tristan shook off Matthew. "Get out of my way," he warned.

Daniel barely paused in the doorway, taking in the tumult. "For God's sake," he muttered. "Somebody not have their prunes this morning?" Starting forward, his boot slipped in the water pooled on the floor. Arms waving, his momentum carried him against a tipped chair and he went down with a racket and a curse. Bright blood spurted onto his shirt. Matthew muttered under his breath and tossed his brother a dish towel.

Jefferson looked at Tristan. "Look what you started, you idiot."

Tristan, shoving past Matthew's not inconsiderable barrier, went nose to nose with Jefferson. "*I* started? You're the one breaking Emily's heart. I never thought you'd be the type to tumble her in bed and leave her crying. You're my brother, but I swear to God, Jefferson, you'd better do right by her. Or, I'll—"

Jefferson's eyebrow lifted.

"What do you mean *tumble* her in bed?" Daniel's voice was muffled through the cloth held to his dripping nose.

"What do you think?" Tristan said sarcastically.

Suddenly, Jefferson found himself the object of not just one angry brother, but three. All he needed was for Sawyer to join the fray. "I didn't *tumble* Emily," he said stiffly, aware that he'd wanted to do just that. He bit back a stream of vicious words and shouldered his way past Matthew and Tristan, stepped over Daniel, and stomped outside.

Matthew wearily righted a chair and plunked down on it. "Well, this was fun," he said to no one in particular.

"Jefferson's sleeping with Emily?" Still sprawled on the floor, Daniel shook his head in disbelief. "She's practically our baby sister!"

Emily stepped into the room. She'd heard most of the fracas from the staircase, but it had begun and ended so abruptly she'd not had a chance to step in. "Jefferson is *not* sleeping with Emily," she said bluntly, garnering several startled looks. "But not for lack of trying on her part," she added for good measure. "So, if you're going to be horrified at someone's behavior, aim it at me. Not Jefferson. He deserves better from you."

With her hands propped on her hips, she studied the motley collection of Clays. They were, at the moment, a pathetic bunch. And she loved them all. "Now, I'm going to the hospital to see Squire. So if you're coming, get a move on."

Matthew slid back his chair and rose. Daniel retrieved a fresh towel and shirt from the stack in the mudroom and Tristan righted the rest of the chairs. Silently they followed Emily out to the Blazer. Sawyer came out from the horse barn, his steps faltering as he saw his brothers' expressions. But he held his tongue. They piled into the truck, with Emily taking the driver's seat.

There was no more talk of Jefferson accompanying them.

Chapter Seven

Squire was awake when they arrived. The nurse on duty even said they could all go in together to see him. Propped back against a stack of pillows, his vivid blue eyes tracked their entrance.

Emily dropped a kiss on his cheek. "You're looking much better."

He grunted. "Can't say the same for Daniel there. You been picking on my boys again, missy?" He folded his arms across his chest, studying his sons. His eyes narrowed when no explanation was forthcoming. "Where's Jefferson?"

Emily sat in the single chair and scooted closer to the bed. "He's feeling under the weather," she murmured, sliding a warning look toward Tristan.

"How are you feeling today?" Sawyer asked, smoothly taking Squire's attention.

The older man harrumphed. "Like a damn pincushion. Ever'

time I'm ready to snooze, that battle-ax out there comes in disturbin' me. The least they could do for a dyin' man would be to provide some pretty nurses."

"You're not dying," Sawyer countered.

"Although you certainly seemed to try," Emily commented. She slid her hand into Squire's. "You gave us quite a scare, you know."

He just harrumphed grumpily. But his fingers gently squeezed hers, and she smiled and fell silent as he ordered Matthew and Dan to bring him up to speed on affairs at the Double-C.

"And when're you coming home to stay?" Squire said, seeming satisfied with the ranch report and turning his startlingly translucent blue eyes on Emily.

"Squire, you know I have a job in San Diego."

"So? Don't tell me you're happy with it. I can look in your eyes, girl, and tell that something's pluckin' at you. If it ain't that damn boring job you got, then what is it?"

"My job isn't boring," she defended lightly. "In fact, there's been some indications that I might get to do more consulting, and that will mean I get to travel. How bad can that be?"

"Airports and more airports. Pretty soon it'll seem like all you see is the inside of airports," Sawyer answered quietly.

"Airports, oh, geez," Matthew shoveled his fingers through his hair, making the short strands stand on end. "What time is it?" He grabbed Daniel's arm and turned it around to see the watch. "Great. That's just great. I forgot all about Jaimie. I knew there was a reason we were supposed to drive separately. Now I'll have to make an extra trip back home to take her up to the ranch from the airport."

"What's this about Jaimie? You talking about Joe's sis?" Squire pushed himself up against the pillows, grimacing against the pull of the adhesive tape covering his chest.

"One and the same," Daniel answered, a faint grin playing with his lips.

"Just come back here with her before driving to the ranch," Emily suggested to Matthew. "Then you guys can go on, and I'll stay here until later. Somebody can come back and get me."

"That boy's sure got his shorts in a twist," Squire commented after Matthew had left, grumbling something about a stupid waste of driving time. "All 'cause that girl's coming back. Never did see what the beef was between them. She seemed kinda sweet, if ya' ask me."

The question of Jaimie Greene's sweetness had to go unanswered when the nurse on duty came in and shooed them out. "This is ICU, you know," she reminded them needlessly. "Besides, we're moving Mr. Clay to a regular room this afternoon."

Sawyer suggested they hit the café for lunch, and they left after Emily promised Squire she'd track him down, regardless of where they stuck him in the hospital.

As usual, Candy was on duty and her young face perked up markedly as they trooped into the café. She hastily splashed coffee into her present customer's cup, then plunked the pot right onto the table in front of the woman. She snatched up several menus and rushed over. "Hi," she greeted them breathlessly, her eyes wide on Tristan's face.

He smiled slowly, and color rushed into Candy's face. Blinking, she turned, nearly bumping into another waitress, and led them back to their usual table.

"You're mean." Emily pinched Tristan's arm.

"What did I do?"

"You know."

"What? I smiled at the girl. What's so bad about that?"

"You're twenty miles out of her league," Emily said under her breath as she slid into the chair Tristan held out for her.

"Relax, would ya? There's nothing wrong with—"

"She sees you smile at her, and she's going to think something's going to come of it. And we both know that nothing will."

"Hey," he said as he tapped her nose with his fingers, "don't take out your problems with Jefferson on me. All I did was smile at the girl. She's pretty. She's worth smiling at. So relax." He turned just as Candy reappeared. "Bring a pitcher of beer," he told her. "We're celebrating. Our father is getting out of ICU today."

"How wonderful," she gushed, then fumbled with the apron tied tightly about her hips for the pad to write down their orders.

They were more than halfway through the meal when Matthew arrived. A tall, slender redhead followed him, her dark green eyes shooting daggers into Matthew's back. But when he stopped beside their table and introduced her around, her expression lightened and she greeted everyone with a musical voice.

Emily scooted over so there was room to pull up a chair beside her, and Jaimie slid into it, dumping her huge shoulder bag over the chair back. She turned down the offer of food and declined a mug of beer, softly asking Candy to bring her a glass of iced tea instead.

The table fairly rattled when Matthew plunked himself down onto the chair between Sawyer and Daniel. He reached for the pitcher and poured the last of it into an empty water glass. He lifted the glass to his lips and steadily drank it down, his eyes watching Jaimie as he did so. "Ahh," he said when finished, and thumped the glass onto the table. "Nothin' like a cold beer."

Jaimie sniffed and turned toward Emily. "How is Mr. Clay doing? My brother told me what happened."

Emily instinctively liked the other woman. And despite the sullen looks they received from Matthew, the two women visited their way through the meal that Candy hurriedly brought for Matthew and the dessert that Tristan indulged in. Sawyer had excused himself quite a while earlier to use the phone, and Daniel was reading the newspaper he'd purchased from the machine in front of the café.

"I can't wait to see Maggie," Jaimie was saying. "What with her pregnancy and all, I'm hoping to stay until the baby comes—"

Daniel's and Matthew's heads came up simultaneously. "What?"

Jaimie jumped faintly at the twin demands. Eyes rounded, Jaimie looked toward the brothers. "What?"

"What did you say about Maggie?" Daniel asked.

"Well, I thought you'd all know. But I suppose what with your father and all…"

"What about her," Matthew interrupted.

Jaimie's eyes narrowed at Matthew's arrogant tone. "She is preg…nant," she announced slowly, as if to a dim-witted child.

But Matthew waved off that point. "About staying."

"And I hope to stay until the baby is born," she obliged, her tone dulcet.

Clearly, this did not thrill Matthew Clay. But he contained himself. Emily figured it was only because they were in a public place. Matthew was the least flappable of all the Clay men. Yet the news that this lovely redhead planned to be around awhile obviously jangled him.

"Pregnant?" Daniel touched Jaimie's hand, taking the woman's attention from his older, disgruntled, brother. "Maggie's pregnant?"

Matthew grunted and shoved back his chair. "That's what she said, Dan. More than once. Can we get a move on here? Where'd Sawyer go, anyway?" He snatched up the check and his wallet in one motion and headed toward the front of the restaurant.

Tristan pointed toward the windows at the rear of the restaurant through which Sawyer could be seen leaning against the glass-enclosed public phone. He scooped up the last of his gargantuan slice of apple pie.

"Why don't you just lick the plate," Emily suggested on a laugh.

Tristan shrugged, unrepentant, and waved her off. "You going across to the hospital now?"

Emily nodded. "I'll see you guys later. Don't forget to come back and get me, or else I'll have to take a room at the motel next door." She turned to Jaimie. "We'll have to go riding soon. Tomorrow," she suggested, having learned the other woman also loved horses.

"I'd like that," Jaimie's smile wavered as she looked past Emily's shoulder. "As long as I have time," she finished.

"We'll make time," Emily insisted, fully aware that Matthew was standing just a few feet away. "It's long past time there were more women around the place, and I intend to enjoy every minute of it." She smiled again, waved goodbye and sailed past Matthew, just daring him to make some comment.

She looked over her shoulder as she pushed through the café door. A person could practically see the sparks arcing between Matthew and Jaimie. Biting back a laugh, she returned to the hospital.

Squire had been moved to a room on the third floor. He was sleeping when she peeked in, so she backed out quietly and wandered down to the gift shop. But a person could only kill so much time looking at infant gifts, get-well cards and magazines. She ended up purchasing a paperback and a can of soda and slowly made her way back to Squire's room. She'd plowed through four chapters of the book before Squire's eyes opened.

She closed her book and looked at him.

"What? I been drooling in my sleep?"

"No," she chuckled. "It's just good to see you." She helped him situate his pillows and adjust the head of the bed up. "Want some water or something?"

"What I want," Squire said as he caught her hand, dropping his good ol' boy routine, "is for you to tell me what's bothering you."

His expression could have been Jefferson's. Or Tristan's. Or any one of his other sons. And though she might be able to hold her own with each one of her nonbrothers, it was a different matter with Squire. This was the man who'd been the only father she'd known since she was seven years old.

Her natural parents were such a hazy image in her memory that she had to look at her old photo albums now and then to remind herself what they had looked like. And though there was a touch of sadness in that reality, Emily had been raised by the gruff man propped up in the hospital bed, and he'd done it with love.

"Well?"

Emily perched on the edge of the hard chair. She tucked her hands between her knees and pondered the wisdom of bringing up the subject. Finally she gave up and took the bull by the horns. "I want to know what's wrong between you and Jefferson."

Squire's expression went stony. "Who said anything's wrong?"

Emily tucked her tongue between her teeth and counted to ten. "The first thing you said to your son," she said eventually, "after you woke up in ICU was *get away.*" She sighed slightly and had to fight with herself to maintain eye contact with the stubborn, intimidating man. "A son you hadn't seen in over two years," she added softly. "I'd like to know why."

"Ever think it might be none of your concern, little lady?"

"I'm concerned about Jefferson. And you," she said steadily.

"I'm gonna be as good as new."

She nodded. "I believe that. I do. But that's not what I

meant." And he knew it. She could tell. "Squire, I lo— I can help him." Her fingers twisted together. "I know I can. But not while I'm floundering around in the dark."

"Who says he needs help?" Squire barked. "What's he gone and done?"

Emily caught his shoulders as he leaned forward. "Relax," she nudged him back against the pillows. "He's not in any trouble," she assured him soothingly. And hoped like fury that it wasn't a lie.

"Then what the hell you going on about?"

Smothering her frustration, she sat back. "It hurt him terribly, Squire, when you told him to leave."

"I didn't tell him to leave," he said abruptly.

"Oh, Squire, for Pete's sake! I was there."

His expression was set. And Emily knew she would get no further with Squire than she had with Jefferson. She wanted to howl with frustration. But a hospital room occupied by a newly recovering Squire was no place to vent it. "Okay," she said in a tight voice. "You win."

He seemed to soften slightly. "There's no winning or losing here, girl."

"We're all losing," she murmured sadly, unaware of the sharp look Squire shot her way. Standing up, she loosened her neck and shoulder muscles. "I'm going to walk a bit. Can I bring you back anything? Some magazines? A book?"

"How 'bout that red-haired nurse I vaguely remember some-one telling me about?"

"No one could ever question where your sons inherited their stamina from." Emily shook her head, a reluctant smile tilting her lips. "You're incorrigible."

"Go," he said, waving her off. "Don't want you watching me drooling while I sleep."

Squire had eaten dinner and was soundly beating Emily at checkers when the hospital room door swung inward with a telltale whoosh. "I told you not to move that one," Squire was saying. "Now I'm gonna have to capture this one. And this one." He set aside her two pieces. "I told you."

"Yeah," Emily snorted. "Like you've left me a whole lot of choices on where to move." She looked over, expecting Tristan. Or Sawyer, perhaps. She'd *never* imagined that Jefferson would be the one standing just inside the door. Her fingers accidentally scattered several checker pieces across the board. "Hi."

He nodded, but didn't move from the doorway.

"Did you drive?"

His lip curled mockingly. "Tristan's waiting in the parking lot."

"Oh."

Squire tapped Emily's arm with the box that had held the checkers. "Wake up, girl."

She tore her eyes from Jefferson. "Hmm? Oh, right." Heat engulfed her, and she scooted the pieces into the box, the game obviously over, and set it on the stand beside Squire's bed. "Next time I'm gonna stomp you."

"Sure you are," he agreed dryly. "Go on with you. Let an old man get some sleep."

"Old man my foot," Emily muttered. She glanced at him briefly, wondering again what was between the two men. Then she leaned over and kissed his bristly cheek. "See you tomorrow evening."

He grunted, tugged on a lock of her hair and settled back against his pillows.

Emily tried to draw up some of her anger with Jefferson from that morning. But it wouldn't come. It was always that way. She gathered up the nearly finished paperback and her purse and went over to Jefferson. Her eyes clung to his, but he merely moved a few inches out of her way, holding the door open.

"Son."

Jefferson stiffened and nudged Emily through the door. "I'll be right down."

"I'll w—"

"Go." He didn't want her around to hear whatever it was his father would sermonize about this time. "Go on." He cut off the protest forming on her soft lips.

She went silent and wheeled about, hurrying down the corridor, leaving Jefferson feeling as if he'd just kicked a puppy. "Dammit," he muttered.

"Close the bloody door, son."

Jefferson pulled his attention from Emily, who was now pacing in a tight square as she waited for the elevator. He looked over at his father. Except for the darkening shadow of whiskers and the wrinkled hospital gown covering the man's shoulders, Squire looked almost like his old self. Right down to the autocratic expression in his icy blue eyes.

Jefferson folded his arms across his chest and leaned against the wall. "What do you want?"

Squire looked from the still-open door to his middle son.

"Get to the point, old man. I'm no more thrilled with hanging around hospital rooms than you are to have me here."

Squire looked pained. "That's not true, son."

Jefferson's eyebrow climbed. A movement in his peripheral vision alerted him to the fact that Emily's elevator had finally arrived. He watched her until she disappeared from view.

"You still can't keep your eyes off her, can you?"

His eyes turned back to his father. "If that's all you wanted to keep me up here for, you're wasting your time and mine." Jefferson straightened and took a step for the door.

"Just hold on there," Squire said testily.

"I'm not going to listen to your lectures about Emily," Jefferson warned.

"I never lectured—"

"Bull."

Squire glared. Then coughed. And coughed. His color went pale.

In two quick steps Jefferson pushed his father's water within easy reach, and after a few sips, Squire quieted. When he leaned back against the pillow, he looked as though he'd aged a few years. Jefferson pinched the bridge of his nose. "Hell, Squire, I don't want to fight with you."

Squire sighed heavily. "'Cause you figure I'm too old now to take it?"

"You're out of your tree, you know that?" Jefferson shook his head. "What did you want? Spit it out, or I'm going home."

"Home. Well now there's an interesting choice of words." Squire's long fingers tapped the mattress. "Does it mean you've finally come home? Quit wandering?"

"Why? You worried that I might decide to hang around here for a while? Afraid you're gonna have to kick me off the ranch again? I'd think you'd be glad I might stay here in Wyoming, considering Em lives all the way out in California."

"Stop twisting my words, boy." Squire's voice rose.

Jefferson's voice lowered. "Then stop wasting my time. If you just want to rehash your disapproval of me, I'm not interested."

"Dammit, boy, I never said I disapproved of you!"

"Gentlemen!" The stern voice interrupted them and Jefferson turned to see a nurse standing in the doorway, her hands propped on shapely hips. "Would you kindly keep it down? We can hear you down the hall!"

She strode into the room, rounding Squire's bed. She flipped the bedclothes smooth with a brisk hand. "Visiting hours *are* over, you know."

"You should've closed the door like I told you to," Squire groused.

"I'm not the one yelling," Jefferson pointed out.

"You shouldn't be exciting yourself," the nurse chided. Looking across the bed, she smiled brightly. "I'm assuming my patient here is your father, yes? Well, you can visit your father tomorrow."

Squire opened his mouth to say, "I'm not finished—"

"Yes," she interrupted. "You are finished. For tonight, anyway. Be a darling and let me do my job."

Jefferson felt an unwilling smile tug at his lips. "Good night then. Miss...?"

"Mrs. Day," she provided.

Squire looked up at the white-clad curves standing over him. His eyes met Jefferson's and despite the dissension between them, they shared a simple moment of purely male appreciation. "Pity," Squire murmured.

There wasn't a thing wrong with Mrs. Day's hearing, and a cloud of pink suffused her high cheekbones. She merely arched an eyebrow and shook her head, making a few notes on Squire's chart. With a nod toward his father, Jefferson left the nurse and patient to their business.

The minutes ticked by while he waited for the elevator. He eyed the entrance to the stairwell and stifled a curse. He should've been able to manage three measly flights. He even began to step toward the door, but his knee chose that moment to begin throbbing. Almost like a taunt.

Biting back a curse, he leaned his weight against the wall and tried to be patient. Each passing minute seemed to take longer and longer, until finally the elevator doors ground open and he stepped in. Something in his expression must have startled the couple already inside, for they both scooted right back against the wall.

Well, that suited him fine, too.

Tristan was behind the wheel when Jefferson made his way out to the truck. And he remembered why he'd suddenly told his brother he'd ride back to the hospital with him. Because he didn't want Emily and Tristan cooped up, all alone, in the pickup cab.

And he'd accused his father of being out of his tree. Hell, Jefferson was already sprawled at the base of the tree, figuratively speaking. He jerked open the door. "Scoot over," he ordered.

Emily, who'd been leaning back against the door, nearly fell out. "For crying out loud," she said as she righted herself and slid to the middle of the seat. "Got a burr under your saddle?"

Jefferson pulled himself up into the cab and slammed the door shut. The yellow gleam of the parking-lot light glinted through the windshield, and he looked down into her face, surrounded by a silky cloud of dark hair. Desire slammed into his gut. It was all he could do not to kiss her right then and there. His fingers dug into his thigh, but he hardly noticed. "What're you waiting for?" He looked over Emily's head toward Tristan. "The first snow?"

His little brother grinned. "Snow might cool things off a bit," he said as he started the engine.

The parking lot was riddled with speed bumps and Tristan jerked and rocked over each and every one. Emily tried not to slide on the seat, but it was nearly impossible, and more than once she found herself bumping over against Jefferson's increasingly stiff form. Her legs angled toward Jefferson's side, leaving room for Tristan to get at the gearshift sticking up from the floor. She tried holding on to the dashboard, but it did no good. Tristan jounced over the next bump, and her hips nudged against Jefferson's. She felt, more than heard, him swear under his breath.

"I'm sorry, all right?" She snapped at him. "There's no seat belt. Maybe you'd be more comfortable if I sat in the truck bed."

The truck rocked again. "Pothole," Tristan announced. Gleefully, Emily decided. She shot him a look, but he was oblivious.

They bumped over yet another bump and Jefferson's arm darted in front of her, holding her against the back of the cab seat. "Cut it out, Tris," he said.

"Hey, I can't help it if the parking lot needs paving again," Tristan said in defense. He turned out onto the smoother street and headed for the highway. "Is that better?"

"Much," Emily ground out. Jefferson took his arm away, and she held herself still, trying to keep her knees from touching him.

After several miles Jefferson muttered beneath his breath and lifted his arm behind Emily's shoulder. He shifted her until she was leaning gently against him. His firm hand on her shoulder told her not to budge. By the time Emily dared look up at him, his head was leaning back against the rear window, his eyes closed.

She tried swallowing the lump in her throat and tried to breathe more slowly. Hoped that her racing heart would slow. But his slackened fingers hung past her shoulder, grazing the upper curve of her breast, and her heart continued tripping along a path bumpier than the hospital's parking lot.

Tristan caught her eye, and his teeth flashed as he grinned. Turning up the radio a notch, he shifted slightly, seeming to take up even more than his share of the bench seat and pushing her farther against Jefferson.

"Stop it," Emily jabbed him in the ribs viciously. She hastily looked up, but Jefferson slept on.

Tristan made a face, covering his ribs with his other hand.

"Brat," he accused fondly. "So tell me about that consulting garbage you were talking about this afternoon."

"It wasn't *garbage*," Emily muttered. "Well, it wasn't," she added, when he shot her a disbelieving look. "Stuart told me that the 'suits' are going ahead with the reorganization."

"I thought that was dropped."

"So did I. But apparently the board of directors was more serious than anyone expected. You know they booted John Cornell out of the presidency not too long ago."

"Have they replaced him yet?"

"Not permanently. Anyway, the board wanted to downsize and they're doing it. Once John was out of the way, they were able to push their plan forward."

"Which means…what?"

Emily felt a pain take root in her temple. "Bottom line? It means that unless I agree to travel, I'm going to effectively be out of a job." She grimaced. "So much for job security, huh?"

"So, tell them to take a hike. You haven't been happy there, anyway."

"I've been perfectly content there," Emily argued.

"Right."

Jefferson listened to their soft conversation. What was it like to have someone to share your day with? To talk the simple and not-so-simple things over with? Envy curled through him, closely followed by disgust for being envious of his very own brother. Who was he to wish now for things he'd never wanted in the first place? Lord knew he didn't deserve them. He certainly didn't deserve Emily. He'd bring her nothing but pain. Just like he'd been doing for the better part of ten years now.

Beneath his arm, Emily shifted, and her cool fingers slipped through his, throwing his thinking offtrack for a long moment. He drew in a slow breath, feeling the faint scent of her hair fill his lungs, and recalling that it was the memory of that very same freshly innocent scent that had kept him sane when he'd been locked in a room the size of a closet.

His throat closed, and he cut off that line of thinking. But it didn't matter whether he was thinking about it or not. The fact was that he didn't deserve Emily. One way or the other, he'd end up hurting her.

But he absolutely could not stomach the thought of Emily with someone else. Not even his own brother. Particularly his own brother.

At long last the tires left the paved highway, crossed a series of cattle guards and crunched along the gravel drive. Emily slumped against him, genuine in her sleep, while he was not. Tristan parked and turned off the engine. Jefferson opened his eyes to meet his brother's steady gaze. Jefferson might have fooled Emily, but not Tristan.

The brothers eyed each other, while the cooling engine ticked softly. Finally Tristan palmed the truck keys and reached for the door. "See you in the morning," was all he said before he pushed the door closed with a quiet click and walked around to the back of the house.

Jefferson's head fell back wearily against the seat. Emily was a sweet, warm weight against his side, and he could have happily stayed there for hours while she slept so trustingly against him. Sighing, he pushed open his door, gently dislodging Emily from his shoulder. "Come on, sweetheart, it's time to wake up."

She murmured unintelligibly and scrunched up her face when the interior light came on.

"Emily, honey, come on." He started to take his hand from hers but her fingers convulsed over his.

"Don't," she murmured sleepily.

He lowered his boots to the ground and jiggled her hand. "Em, we're home."

"Mmm-hmm." Still more asleep than awake, she scooted toward him, looping her free hand over his shoulder. Her nose found its niche in the curve of his neck and shoulder, and she sighed deeply.

Jefferson stifled a curse even as his palm slid around her slender hip. Somehow or other he ended up standing outside the truck with Emily's thighs hugging his hips as her cheek lay on his chest. It took every fiber of decency in him not to nudge her down onto the seat. Not to grind his aching hardness against her.

"Emily," his voice was sharper than he intended, and her eyes flew open, staring blankly at him. She blinked a few times and cleared her throat. Brushing a strand of hair out of her eyes, she pushed his shoulder and he moved aside while she slipped out of the truck. She weaved toward the house, then abruptly stopped, seeming to wonder for a moment where she was before correcting course for the back door.

Jefferson shut the truck door and followed her, scooping his arm around her waist as she nearly wandered into the side of the house. "Over here," he murmured, guiding her up the steps and into the mudroom. By the time they made it through the darkened kitchen and halfway up the stairs, Emily was leaning against him again, all but asleep. He gave up the fight and scooped her off her feet to carry her the rest of the way.

It wasn't smart. All this carrying her around. But what was a sharp pain in his hip or the dull throb in his back, compared to the gentle weight of her in his arms. He turned sideways and carried her into her bedroom and deposited her in the middle of the bed.

"Jefferson," she whispered sleepily, her fingers tangling in his hair.

He knew he was a weak man when he let her pull his head

lower until her lips found his. Her kiss was soft and sleepy and utterly bewitching.

His forehead met hers as he took a long, shuddering breath. Finally, he pulled her hands away and pressed them gently to the pillow beside her head. "Sweet dreams," he told her softly as he allowed himself one last chaste kiss.

He straightened. Watched her sigh and turn onto her side, curling against the pillow. Turning on his heel, he went into his room, bypassed the bed and headed straight for a cold shower.

Sweet dreams, hell, he thought.

Chapter Eight

Emily woke well before dawn. She pulled off her shoes and slipped out of her clothes then climbed under the blankets again for a few more minutes of sleep.

The few minutes stretched into a few hours. When she finally pushed the pillow off her head and looked around her, she knew the house was empty. Her face split in a yawn as she swung her legs over the side of the bed and stood. Outside her window a dog barked. An engine rumbled to life.

After a hasty wash and a tug or two with the brush, she pulled on a loose pair of shorts she'd made long ago by cutting the legs off an old pair of sweatpants. She added a sport bra and a muscle-T and with socks and running shoes in hand, headed downstairs.

She was standing in the mudroom, stretching her calf muscles, when the phone rang. She went into the kitchen and picked up the phone, but someone else had already answered on another extension. Maggie, she realized and hastily, quietly, hung up before she could overhear anymore of the softly hissed, angry conversation between Maggie and the caller. Joe. Emily returned to her stretching. When she felt loosened up, she headed down the porch and jogged past the barns and the bunkhouse, slowing ever so slightly as she heard the heated voice coming from within. Seemed like everyone was arguing these days. And judging from the clearly audible one-sided phone conversation that was obviously continuing, even Maggie and Joe were.

Turning a deaf ear, Emily picked up speed and returned the way she came, heading instead in the direction of the swimming hole. She hadn't planned on going that direction. In her mind the spot was too closely linked with Jefferson. So she kept her eyes on the ground in front of her as she thumped past the trees and bushes. Eventually, winded and sweaty, she turned and headed back. But this time her eyes wouldn't stay in front of her and she found herself crunching through the fallen leaves and twigs to the edge of the water.

Stretching, she lifted her clinging hair off her neck and eyed the water. Yesterday, it had been freezing. But she hadn't been drenched in sweat, either. If she had more nerve, she would strip off and dive in. After a mental shrug, she pulled off the loose T-shirt and contented herself with dunking it in the cold water and pulling it over her head. It served the purpose of cooling her down, and she began walking back to the house.

Tristan was in the kitchen, the phone at his ear, and when he saw her, he held it toward her. "Stuart," he told her.

Emily pondered the receiver. She didn't really want to talk to Stuart. He wanted a decision from her regarding her job, and she didn't want to give it to him. Taking the receiver from Tristan, she covered it with her hand. "Too bad I wasn't a few minutes later."

"Just tell him what you want to do."

"If I only knew," she muttered. Pulling a clean dish towel out of the drawer she draped it around her neck and dabbed her face. Then she sat down at the table and lifted the phone to her ear. "Hello, Stuart," she greeted.

Ten minutes later Emily wasn't sure if she still had a job or not. She hadn't agreed to take on the consulting position. But Stuart hadn't fired her, either. She supposed it was a good sign. She set the phone on the table, then picked it up again when it suddenly rang. It was for Matthew, so Emily took a message, then went to find him to deliver it.

It was no surprise that he wasn't around, but Emily went to check the bunkhouse just in case. Through the open door she saw Maggie and called out her name.

Maggie whirled around nervously, her fingers brushing her cheeks.

Emily forgot the slip of paper tucked in her palm. "Maggie? What's wrong?" The snatch of argument she'd overheard flitted through her head.

Maggie shook her head. "Nothing." She turned away and pulled an apron around her waist, clearing her throat. "Did you need something?"

"Just looking for Matt. Um, Maggie, you're feeling all right. Aren't you?" It was so obvious the other woman didn't want to talk, that Emily felt like an intruder for even expressing her concern. But she couldn't ignore the fact that Maggie had been crying. No doubt a result of the argument Emily had inadvertently overheard.

"Matt's out with the vet," Maggie answered.

Emily could take a hint. "I'll leave this in his office, then," she wagged the slip slightly. "I sort of made arrangements to go riding with Jaimie this morning, but she's probably given up on me by now. Is she around somewhere?"

"She's with Matt, also. She did mention riding, but that it would need to wait until she finished her chores."

"She surely doesn't need to be tied up every minute with chores. She's a guest, for heaven's sake!"

Some of the tension eased from Maggie's drawn face as she shrugged. "Jaimie wants to do the work. She likes it. Of course it drives Matt up—" she broke off, seeming to realize that she was speaking to a member of Matt's family.

"Up the wall," Emily finished easily. "Good. He needs someone to shake up his world a little. Well, we'll get together later. If you can, perhaps you'll join us? That is if it's all right for you to be riding, what with the baby and all."

The smooth skin around Maggie's eyes seemed to draw up tight. "Maybe," she allowed. She turned to the large refrigerator and yanked open the door. "Let me know later when you're going," she added, her voice muffled by the door.

"Sure." Emily hesitated a moment longer, watching Maggie bend over the deep shelves of the refrigerator. What more could she say? She didn't see any reason on earth why she couldn't become friends with Maggie. They were similarly aged. They were the only women living at the Double-C. Well, add Jaimie to that, for now, Emily amended silently.

Feeling edgy, Emily made her way to Matt's office and left the message on his desk. Then, putting off her shower for a few more minutes, she headed into the horse barn. Daisy greeted her with a soft nicker, and Emily retrieved a brush and currycomb and let herself into Daisy's stall.

She missed her own horse. Missed the morning rides when Bird was frisky and full of sass and vinegar. Missed the regular, soothing ritual of grooming him. Emily ran the brush over Daisy's back. "But you're not too bad, either," she assured the horse softly. "You and Bird would make some pretty babies, too.

Wouldn't you?" Daisy's tail flicked. "Of course with him in San Diego and you here, there's not much chance of that." She switched to the comb and smoothly worked on Daisy's mane. "In fact, you have about as much chance with Bird as I do with Jefferson." Daisy's head bobbed. "You agree with me, don't you?

"But," Emily continued, "if I end up with no job, maybe you'll end up meeting Bird after all." Emily hung her arm over the horse's neck and sighed. "What am I going to do, Daisy? I know you're a smart girl. I can see it in your eyes. So what do you think I should do? Hmm?"

"Stop asking horses for advice for one thing."

Emily whirled around, tangling the comb in Daisy's mane. "Dammit, Jefferson, don't sneak up on me." She turned back to the horse and worked the comb free. He was still standing there when she finished, and she shot him a look over her shoulder. "What do you want?"

"Crabby today, eh?"

"So? Did you think you had a corner on that market?" She let herself out of the stall, expecting him to move aside. But he didn't. Her brow rose. "Do you mind?"

Silently, he let her pass. She returned the comb and brush to the tack room and came out to find him still standing by Daisy's stall. His faded jeans were wearing through at the knee, and his denim shirt had been washed nearly colorless. She knew people who paid fortunes to obtain the "distressed" look. But Jefferson wasn't trying to be vogue. He simply looked mouthwatering no matter what he wore.

Next to him, Emily felt like a dirty dishrag in her baggy shorts and wet T-shirt. She probably smelled like something that needed shoveling off the floor, too. Great, just great. She shoved a limp tendril of hair away from her face, wishing like everything that she'd hit the shower instead of—

"Why didn't you tell me you were worried about your job?"

"What?" Her brain sluggishly switched tracks.

"Yesterday, when we were out at the pond."

She shrugged, studying the dusty toes of her running shoes. "It didn't come up."

He lifted her chin with a long finger. "I specifically asked you about your job," he chided. "You didn't say much of anything."

As they were wont to do, Emily's thought processes grew muddled when she looked up into his azure eyes. Her teeth worried the inner corner of her lips. "It, um, didn't seem important," she heard herself say faintly.

"It was important enough to tell Tristan."

Emily blinked away visions of those mobile lips pressed to her skin and concentrated on his words. My Lord, he'd sounded almost jealous. Her mouth went dry, and she slowly moistened her lips. "I'd have told you if I had thought you were really interested."

He went still, his shoulders stiff beneath the denim shirt.

"I'd *tell* you anything," she added softly. "I'd *listen* to anything you said to me. If you...were—" she hesitated when his finger dropped away from her chin "—interested," she finished, feeling stranded.

She ached at the glimpse of torment in his eyes before he turned away.

His fingers whitened when he closed them over the top rail of Daisy's stall, and his back bowed as he lowered his head. "Leave."

She tentatively touched his hand. "Jefferson—"

He yanked away from even that small touch. "Dammit, Emily, *go.*"

Her mouth opened soundlessly, and she snatched her hand away, clasping it at her waist. She closed her eyes for a moment. Looking anywhere but at him, she instinctively turned toward escape, praying that she wouldn't embarrass herself further by tripping over her wooden feet.

She hurried past the stalls, flinching when she heard his soft curse. Her stomach churned, the need to somehow help him warring with the need to protect herself from more pain. She kept her focus on the sunshine beyond the yawning entry, determined not to turn back. Not even when she heard the sharp crack of something hard and unyielding strike something else equally hard and unyielding.

She heard his footsteps, yet wasn't prepared for the arm he scooped about her waist, pulling her around to him.

She pushed at his arms. "Let me go," she pleaded. Being in his arms was a double-edged sword. Easing distress. Adding tension. Making her crazy.

"I'm sorry," he breathed against her temple. His palms cradled her head as his lips covered hers. "Sorry," he murmured, "so sorry."

She could no more resist his gentle kiss than she could stop breathing. She reached for him, but he caught her hands in his, pressing them to his chest.

"I don't deserve your touch," he muttered between short, burning kisses that left her quaking for more.

She wanted to know what he meant by that. She wanted him to tell her what was in his heart. In his dreams. His nightmares. But his hands were sliding up her arms, into the oversize armholes of her wet shirt. Seeking the swelling curve of breast. The tight crests.

"I can't think," she whispered, her fingertips frantically catching over the buttons on his shirt.

"Just feel." His low growl rustled along her neck as he gently tugged on her ponytail, revealing the curve of her throat to his lips.

She swallowed a moan. He held her arched so tightly to him

that she couldn't move her hands from his chest. His heat seared through their clothing, and she strained even closer. Their breath sounded harsh in the silent barn before he closed his mouth over hers.

His large palms molded her shoulders. Moved down her back. Glided over her hips and tilted her against him, rocking against her. His lips fused to hers, his kiss deep, thrusting, and Emily felt it down to her toes. Colors were swirling in her head as he slipped his fingers up the loose leg of her raggedy shorts. He swallowed her cry when he brushed his thumb across her smooth hip. Her naked hip.

He groaned her name as his hand shifted, cupping her bare bottom.

Daisy snorted, and Jefferson's head shot up.

"No," Emily cried faintly. Her knees were so weak she could only sag against him. But she heard the same thing that Jefferson did. The sound of boots crunching across the gravel. Definitely drawing closer, accompanied by the indistinct murmur of voices.

Jefferson slowly withdrew his hand and adjusted her shorts. Wordlessly he set her away from him, and moments before Daniel rounded the yawning entry to the barn Jefferson disappeared out the back.

She fruitlessly smoothed her ponytail. Her body hummed with yearning, and no doubt Daniel would know with a single glance just what was what. Sawyer appeared just moments behind Dan, but the men merely greeted her with lifted arms before veering off to the side and heading down the other row.

She sagged. Relieved. Frustrated. Her legs were none too steady when she walked toward the back side of the barn, but when she looked out, Jefferson was nowhere in sight. Damn the man, anyway. She kicked the side of the barn, but it didn't help. And she was left with a set of throbbing toes.

She stomped back to the house, not even pausing when she heard the raised voices coming from inside. She let the screen door slam nice and loud as she entered and walked in to find Jaimie and Matthew squared off on either side of the big table. "Stop arguing," she said wearily. "Can't anyone around here carry on a normal conversation? Can't any of us have normal relationships with each other?"

Matthew snorted, but his eyes were trained on Jaimie. "If people were *reasonable,*" he began.

Jaimie huffed, clearly girding herself for another skirmish. "Reasonable? Look who's talking! I was perfectly capable of handling that truck—"

"Capable! You backed it into a fence."

"Then why were you waving for me to keep going?"

"I was waving for you to stop," he gritted.

Emily raked her fingers through her hair. "I am going upstairs," she announced, even though it was perfectly obvious that the other two had already forgotten her presence.

After showering, Emily changed into a deep blue sundress. Still restless and out of sorts, she dried her hair and pulled it back into a loose braid, then smoothed on some makeup. She might feel like a wreck on the inside, but at least from the outside she appeared perfectly controlled. It was some small comfort.

She tidied up the room, then headed downstairs. She heard the clang of the bell from the bunkhouse kitchen. Maggie, announcing the noon meal. Her bare feet were soundless as she entered the blessedly empty kitchen. Propping her chin on her hands, she leaned against the counter and looked through the window at the activity Maggie's summons had spurred. A pickup rolled by and a group of young men hopped out, heading straight for the bunkhouse. They looked like high school kids.

Probably were, since it was still summer vacation. Matt would've hired the kids, giving them a chance to earn some money. Within minutes, it all quieted. Everyone was probably seated at that huge long slab of a table, tucking in to the rib-sticking meal that Maggie, most capably, would have laid out for them.

Operations at the Double-C were running as always, smooth as glass.

So where did she fit in?

There was not a lick of work around this place that wasn't already being handled by someone else. And from the way things were progressing at her office, she was either going to have to agree to the type of job she'd never wanted, or look elsewhere.

Knowing that she was sinking into a depressing mood, she sighed deeply and straightened. It wasn't as if she weren't capable of finding a new job, she reasoned with herself as she began opening cupboards and pulling out ingredients.

She was well qualified and had an excellent employment history. She even enjoyed her work. Found it satisfying to make everything balance out in the end. Numbers were numbers. They could be counted on. Oh, sure, you could manipulate them just like anything else, but the numbers themselves? They were always constant. Unlike some things.

She thumped a bag of flour on the counter and a little puff of white floated into the air. *Be honest, Emily, my girl. You are never going to be completely satisfied. Because what you really want is a family. A husband. Not just any husband, either.*

"What on earth are you planning to make? Pickle-flavored cookies?"

Tristan's voice startled her, and she accidentally knocked the box of unsweetened chocolate off the counter with her elbow. Aware that he'd bent to pick up the box, she blinked at the conglomeration of items she'd gathered. Sure enough, among the flour and sugar, butter and vanilla, sat a huge jar of dill pickles. Grimacing, she returned the jar to the refrigerator.

"Okay, squirt, what's bugging you?"

"Aside from my entire life?" She answered flippantly. "Not a thing." She pulled out a small saucepan and automatically began melting butter and chocolate squares.

"Now, come on." He poured himself a glass of water and drank it down in a single gulp, then refilled it and did it again. "It can't be that bad," he finally said.

"Says who," she muttered. She lowered the heat and turned around, her arms crossed. She cocked her head and cast a considering eye his way. "You know, Tristan, you really are an attractive man."

His eyebrows shot up.

"No, I'm serious." She considered him for a few more moments. "How come you've never…you know." She flapped her hand.

"You know?" He echoed warily. "What, *you know?*"

"You know," her eyes widened meaningfully. "You. Me. It's not as if you don't like women."

"Cripes, Em! We don't feel that way and you know it. Geez…" He shook his head, and headed for the back door.

"Wait a minute," Emily stopped him with a hand on his arm. His white T-shirt was sweaty and his jeans were covered with dust. His golden tan had deepened to an even darker hue from working outside, and his familiar blue eyes looked warily down at her from his towering height. The man had a brain that was darn-near frightening, and he had looks that rivaled Jefferson's. If there was a single man on the face of the earth who could measure up to Jefferson Clay, it would be his youngest brother.

But to her, Tristan was simply her best friend. Nothing more. Nothing less.

"What? If I don't hurry up, there's not gonna be any food left."

"Forget your stomach for a minute." She frowned. "I'm serious. Tell me why."

"Em—"

"Come on. Consider it research."

"Gee, thanks."

"Tristan—"

"Oh, hell." He flipped the hair off his forehead, clearly aggrieved.

"You're impossible." She turned back to the stove. "It was just a question."

He sighed abruptly and plopped down onto a kitchen chair. "The things you ask of me," he muttered. "Never let it be said that I disappointed a woman."

"Just forget it, will you? I changed my mind. I don't *want* to know."

"Well…inquiring minds want to know and all that."

She shot him a look.

He shrugged, dropping the sarcasm as she slumped into a chair. "You know what your problem is?"

"I'm sure you'll tell me."

"Lack of sex."

She groaned and dropped her head to the table. "Tell me something I don't know," she said, her voice muffled. Her shoulders heaved with a huge sigh and she sat up. "Tell me what to do, Tris. I'm at a loss. And I'm not referring to sex," she added hastily.

"Thank God. I love ya squirt, but lessons in sex are not something I'm willing to give you. I prefer pupils who have some…personal…interest in me."

She made a disgusted sound and rose to remove the chocolate from the stove. "I live with you," she reminded him. "I've seen your *pupils*."

"Okay, this emotional quandary is either about your job, or about Jefferson. I'll pick door number two and choose my big, bad brother. And much as it pains me to say it, I don't have a clue what you should do."

"There's a first."

"Snottiness will get you nowhere, runt."

"Being a good little girl isn't getting me anywhere, either." She cracked an egg and tossed the shell into the sink, then followed it with two more. "I'm not sure I should stay here any longer," she said, voicing the unpalatable idea that had been swimming in her mind.

"Emily, this is as much your home as anyone's."

She smiled sadly, clearly showing that she had very nearly made up her mind. She heard him stifle a curse.

"It's ironic, Tristan. All these years of enduring Jefferson's departures. And this time, I'm going to be the one to leave."

"You'll go back to San Diego, then."

Her lashes kept him from seeing her expression, but she worried her lip.

"Emily?"

"Maybe it's time for a change," she whispered. "Past time."

"Dammit! I don't want to lose my best friend because my brother's too stubborn to see what is right under his nose!"

Emily turned back to the batter, stirring blindly. "Don't be angry with Jefferson. He can't help the way—"

Tristan stopped her with a blunt word. "He's in love with you, Emily. Pure and simple."

"If he loves me," she nearly choked on the words, "he'd stop pushing me away." She gave up trying to mix the batter. "I know he has feelings for me," she acknowledged. "That he's attracted to me." Color rose in her cheeks, but she made herself continue. "But I need him to share himself with me. You know? His thoughts. His dreams. His past. But even more, *he* needs someone that he can share himself with that way." Her jaw worked. "That person isn't me. It's time I faced that." She looked up at Tristan.

"So you're going to use his example and run away from the people who love you?"

It hurt Emily to hear Tristan phrase it so bluntly. "That's probably what I'm doing," she admitted. "But I can't go on this way. Maybe a complete break will help."

"It's not gonna help me," Tristan argued. "It's sure as hell not going to help Jefferson. And what about Matt and Dan? What about Squire? What are you going to tell Squire?"

"I don't know!" She cried. "But Jefferson *is* a Clay. And he needs you all so much. He just doesn't know how to say it. I can't bear for him to be so unhappy, and my presence here is only making it worse!"

"Neither of you has to leave. And you're a Clay, too," Tristan said firmly. "That fact is half of Jefferson's problem."

"What?"

"It's stupid, as far as I'm concerned," Tristan continued. "And he'll probably break my legs for me when he finds out I said something. But he's gotten some crazy idea about his feelings for you not being appropriate. What with Squire raising you and all."

"But that's ridiculous. Jefferson knows we're not related." Her lips twisted. "We've even talked about it."

Tristan shrugged. "Have you told Jefferson that you're planning to leave?"

"Not yet."

"Promise me one thing, then."

"What?"

"Promise first."

She rolled her eyes. "I promise."

"Don't tell Squire or anyone else that you're leaving until after you've told Jefferson." He yanked open the door. "I swear, Emily, you're not going to give up your home and family, even if I have to make good on my threat to Jefferson and marry you myself."

Emily blinked. After a moment's delayed confusion, she jogged out to the mudroom and swung out the screen door, looking at his departing back. "What's that supposed to mean? Tristan?" She yelled after him, but he ignored her.

"Remember your promise," he yelled back, moments before swinging up into the back of the pickup that had rolled to a stop behind him.

Through narrowed eyes she watched the crew head back out to the fields.

What had Tristan gone and said to Jefferson?

Chapter Nine

Emily had halfway planned to ask Sawyer what he thought about employment prospects back East, but her promise to Tristan kept her silent. Instead, she found herself counting the minutes of each hour of the day until after their early supper, when they'd all troop to town to visit Squire. All of them except Jefferson.

The man who'd basically kept to himself all day long, she reminded herself as she followed Daniel outside to the vehicles, a plastic-wrapped plate of brownies in her hand.

Sawyer and Jefferson were standing several yards away. Another arguing pair. Emily watched them openly, though she couldn't hear a word.

"Are you planning to stand there all day?" Tristan nudged her arm toward the car. "I'd drive that little tin can you rented, but your seat doesn't go back far enough."

"What do you suppose that's all about?" She hunched her shoulder in the direction of Sawyer and Jefferson.

Tristan dropped his arm over her shoulders. "Hard to say. Maybe wise old Sawyer is giving Jefferson some advice on his love life."

Emily elbowed Tristan in the ribs. "Very funny." She rounded the car and yanked open the door. Across the roof of the vehicle she watched Sawyer gesture. Jefferson suddenly lifted his head, and across the distance his eyes searched out Emily. She found herself holding her breath.

Jefferson said something to Sawyer who shook his head sharply. But after a moment, the two men shook hands. Jefferson stood watching as Sawyer returned to the Blazer. A faded duffel bag sat on the gravel near the truck, and Sawyer picked it up and tossed it into the rear before going around to climb in beside Matthew.

She looked at the spot where the bag had been. The pang that shot through her left her knees weak. "What's the bag for?" she asked Tristan.

"Hmm?" He noticed her expression. "What's wrong?"

"Is Jefferson leaving?"

Tristan started. "Hell no, he's not leaving! You're the one talking about that nonsense."

"But the duffel—"

Tristan squinted and looked over to the truck. "Oh, that was probably just some clothes of Squire's. He wanted us to bring him some of his own stuff. Relax, would ya?"

"So why didn't Sawyer use Squire's suitcase?" she asked as she placed the brownies on the floor in the back seat.

"What?"

"The duffel," Emily said impatiently. "Why would Sawyer take Squire's stuff in Jefferson's duffel? Or it could be Sawyer's duffel, I guess."

"Well how on earth should I know? Maybe he couldn't find Squire's suitcase. Geez, Emily. Get a grip would ya?"

"You'd tell me if Jefferson was leaving, wouldn't you?"

Tristan heaved a sigh. "I'd tell you," he promised. "And he's not leaving."

Emily bit the inside of her lip. Her eyes went from Tristan's exasperated gaze to Matt's truck. Jefferson was the only one not inside the truck. "Okay, I believe you," she mumbled and climbed into the car. She started the engine and pulled in behind the Blazer, far enough back that they weren't choked in the dust stirred up by the other vehicle.

In her rearview mirror, she caught sight of Jefferson as he lingered by the aspen trees, watching their departure. After a moment he turned away and walked out of sight behind the big house. Suddenly she took her foot off the gas and coasted to a stop.

"What are you doing?"

Emily's fingers tapped on the steering wheel and pinned Tristan with a firm look. "You didn't really tell Jefferson we were involved, did you?"

Tristan looked uncomfortable.

"You didn't." She wanted to throttle him. "Tristan, what am I going to do with you? No wonder Jefferson keeps giving us strange looks."

"He didn't believe me," Tristan assured her. "I was just trying to light a fire under him. For all the good it did," he added darkly. "Hey, what are you doing?"

Emily unsnapped the safety belt and got out. "You'll have to drive. Legroom or not. Tell Squire I'll see him tomorrow," she said. "And give his nurses the brownies, please. Don't eat them all before you get there."

"What are you planning to do?"

"Get some answers," she replied. "Or make a complete and utter fool of myself." She shrugged. "Take your pick."

Tristan got out and rounded the car. "Tell him about your crazy idea of leaving," he advised as he began folding himself into the driver's seat. He knocked his knee on the steering wheel and grunted. "Maybe I should just stay behind," he muttered.

"Don't you dare," Emily pushed his head inside and closed the door on him. "This is one evening the place isn't crawling with people, and I plan to take advantage of it." Color rose in her cheeks. "I mean—"

Tristan chuckled and started the engine. "Don't let him scare you off," he said, sobering. "You're exactly what he needs." He gave her a thumbs-up and shifted into gear.

Emily hastily backtracked so she wouldn't get an eyeful of dust. "Exactly what he needs," she repeated, wishing that she could be as confident of the notion as Tristan seemed to be.

She drew in a deep breath and brushed a strand of hair out of her eyes. With her heart in her throat, she began walking back toward the house.

It took a little longer than she'd expected. And she felt hot and sticky by the time she walked into the kitchen. She prowled through the rooms of the main floor, but Jefferson was nowhere in sight. Nor was he upstairs or in the den or in the basement. In fact, Emily finally gave up and acknowledged that the man wasn't anywhere in the house at all.

Feeling anticlimactic, she retreated to her room. When she freshened up and looked at herself in the mirror, she knew she was being cowardly. Jefferson had to be somewhere. If she wanted to find him, she could. She would.

She let herself out through the front door, narrowing her eyes against the fiery sunlight that hovered just above the horizon. Streaks of red and orange blazed across the sky in a magnificent sunset. The wooden swing that had always been on the front porch was empty, swaying gently in the warm breeze. She went down the steps and headed around the side of the house, scanning the grounds for some sign of Jefferson.

She stuck her head inside the horse barn. But the only sounds that greeted her were the soft nickers from the half dozen horses enclosed in their stalls. She walked around to the corrals, but the only one who paid attention was the golden retriever that slowly rose from her sprawl in the fading sun to join Emily. "Hey, Sandy," she softly greeted Matthew's dog and bent down to scratch behind her ears. "Where's Jefferson?"

But the dog merely cocked her head and looked back with her gentle eyes.

Emily gave the dog a final pat and stood. To her right lay the gravel road that led toward the machinery barn. Voices and music rang from the bunkhouse as the men finished up their evening meal. She headed that way and stuck her head inside the side door. Many heads turned her way, smiling and nodding and calling out greetings. But Jefferson's blond head wasn't one of them.

She returned Maggie's wave and left.

Situated farthest from the big house, was another set of corrals used primarily during branding. The foreman's home was west of the corrals. She could just see the back side of the brick house. She propped her hands on her hips. Still no sign of Jefferson.

Pursing her lips, she began walking back the way she'd come. She passed the horse barn again and paused. In a smooth curve, the gravel road led to the swimming hole.

She set off for the trees, forgoing the gravel for the softer knee-high grass alongside the road. When she came upon the lilac bushes growing lush and thick among the trees surrounding the natural spring, the sun was casting its last efforts of daylight. Twigs crackled beneath her sandals as she slipped between two trees.

A slender shaft of sunlight arrowed through the trees, highlighting the man's shaggy golden mane. Emily stopped cold, her hand pressing flat to her stomach. Jefferson was sprawled on his back atop the flattish boulder that jutted out from the bank.

His head was toward the water, his sun-gilded hair drifting from the rock toward the still water. Almost like a dream, she watched his eyes turn directly toward her. As if he'd been expecting her.

Desire clenched inside her. Low and demanding. This was no dream.

She stepped forward.

In just the moment it took to cross the few yards to the boulder, the shaft of sunlight flickered then slid away to nothing. Twilight still hovered in the air, holding back the evening darkness, and she saw his chest slowly rise and fall.

"I thought you were going to see Squire," he said.

"I was," she toed off her sandals and stepped closer. Beneath her foot, the boulder was still warm from the day's heat. "I'm here to see you instead." She looked down at him.

He opened his eyes and looked up at her, silent. She couldn't tell what he was thinking. It was too dark now. Not that she'd be able to tell even if it were broad daylight.

"Squire'll miss you," he murmured.

"I'm sure he misses you, too. No matter what the problem is between you. But he's doing much better and his cardiologist is talking about releasing him soon."

He lifted his arm and bent it across his eyes.

"Aren't you glad he'll be home soon?" she asked.

"Of course I am." It was true. He was glad his father was improving. Glad that the man would be returning to his own home soon. It also meant, though, that Jefferson would have to be moving on soon. And the thought of leaving the ranch again brought on a curious sense of grief.

"Pardon me, but you don't look overjoyed."

He deliberately forced his hand to relax before it could curl into a fist.

"I know, I know," Emily said. "None of my business."

He heard her walking around the boulder and then felt the warmth of her against his knee when she sat down beside him. He watched her from beneath his arm. She stretched out one leg until her toe broke the glassy surface of the water. Drawing in her breath, she retracted her foot. It was one thing to go for a dunking during the middle of the day. But the evening was another matter entirely.

"I remember when Squire taught you how to swim out here. You were like a little fish. It didn't matter how cold the water got, you still wanted to go swimming."

Beneath the full skirt, she propped her foot on the rock and clasped her arms around her bent knees. "You do that a lot, you know," she pointed out. "Veer our conversations back to my childhood."

She lowered her cheek to her knees and continued speaking softly, amazed that her voice was steady when her heart was thundering so unevenly. "As if by putting my existence in that context you won't have to deal with me. You won't have to acknowledge what's going on between us. You won't have to give up any of those precious secrets you keep hoarded so close to your chest.

"There is nothing going on between me and Tristan. I don't know exactly *what* he said to you. Only that he said *something*. But he and I are just friends. Exactly like I told you in San Diego. He was just…just…" She broke off.

"I know what he was doing."

Emily nibbled on the inside of her lip and was grateful for the gathering darkness. She softly cleared her throat. "Would it have mattered to you? If it had been true?"

Jefferson took the question like a blow to his midriff. He wanted to tell her. Tell her exactly how much every little thing about her mattered. He wanted to spill his bloody guts and let her sweetness wash over him. But it all came back to those damned secrets she accused him of hoarding.

Secrets. He was so sick and tired of secrets. Of partial truths. Of cover stories. But he didn't think he was up to the aversion he'd see in her pansy brown eyes if she knew the truth. He didn't even know if he knew how to get the words out anymore.

She made a frustrated sound at his continued silence and pushed up from the rock. She bent and picked up her sandals. "One of these days," she murmured bitterly as she walked back toward the trees, "I'm going to learn how to leave you alone." Her voice went slightly hoarse, but he still heard her words. "I'm going to finally get it through my head that you don't want, or need, anything from me."

Jefferson sat up and watched her pick her way back through the trees. He even called her name, but she didn't hear. Or perhaps she did. Calling himself a fool, he pushed himself up from the boulder and went after her.

She was leaning against a tree trunk, pulling on her sandals. "Emily."

She looked over her shoulder at him, and he realized she was crying. "Go away."

"That's my line." He took the other shoe from her and bent over. He brushed away the crushed leaves from the sole of her foot before sliding on the sandal. She went to step away from the tree, but he moved, blocking her from leaving. He brushed his thumb across her cheek. "I'm sorry."

"I'm sorry, too," she sniffed. "I'm sorry you're a sorry, stubborn, mangy, moth-eaten, mulish, jackass—"

He shut her up the simplest way he knew. He kissed her.

Her breath was tumbling past her lips when he raised his head. But at least she was quiet. "Moth-eaten?"

"Damn you, Jefferson Clay," she muttered, curling her palm behind his neck. She pulled his head down and kissed him back.

His breath was uneven when he raised his head. He pulled her hands from his neck, and with one hand he anchored them safely above her head, against the tree. "We can't do this."

"So you've said."

She tugged at her hands, and he adjusted his grip accordingly.

"Over and over again," she added, renewing her efforts to unleash herself.

Her squirming succeeded in arching her back away from the tree trunk, and had he been a gentleman he'd have stepped back when her curves thrust up against his chest. Of course, had he been a gentleman he wouldn't have her trapped against the tree, either.

She seemed to realize her position and suddenly ceased struggling, choosing to plaster herself back against the peeling tree bark. A good half foot out of touching range. "Let me go," she ordered.

He had to look away from the dark eyes bravely staring him down. He stifled a curse. "I wish I could," he muttered.

She let loose a stream of invectives he hadn't heard her use since she was a teenager. "Impressive," he said, dryly applauding her efforts. But he still didn't let her loose.

She sagged. Her head drooped like a broken flower. "*Please,* Jefferson. Don't toy with me."

He gently cupped her satin-smooth cheek. "Ah, Em... *oof*...dammit!"

She'd punched him in the stomach! Hard enough to get his attention. Surprise held him still for the minuscule moment it took for her to slip around him and stalk off toward the house.

He set off after her, and uneven though his gait was, he soon overtook her. "Hold it," he muttered, scooping an arm around her waist.

She pushed at his hands, trying to move forward. "Shove it," she spat. "I hate you!"

"Oh, hell," Jefferson grumbled and simply took her to the ground. He cushioned her fall with his body, but she was scrambling about so that he twisted until she lay pinned beneath him.

His body's reaction was all too predictable.

"I hate you," she repeated, even as her hands slipped over his shoulders.

"Good. It's safer that way."

A broken laugh escaped, and her softly ragged breath struck his throat, followed by the butter-soft glide of her tongue, then her lips. It was torturous heaven. He pushed up on his arms, painfully aware of the way her thighs, beneath the flowing dress, relaxed to cradle him. Painfully aware that they were fully out of sight of the buildings. That, lying here in the darkness, hidden in the long grass, they could do exactly what they wanted, with no one to see.

Her breath hissed in sweetly when he pressed against the juncture where their two bodies collided. Her head fell back in the long grass, exposing a silken line of throat to the rising moon.

He had to taste that skin. His hunger for her was killing him. He pressed his open mouth to her throat, feeling her throat work. She was sweeter than honey. He slid his hand to her cheek, and she turned into his touch, burning his palm with her kiss.

Angling his weight to the side, he slid his leg over hers, running his palm along her hip and across the flat of her stomach. Her dark eyes were bottomless in the shadowed moonlight. His palm glided upward and cupped her breast. Gently plucked the pebbled peak.

"I watched you drive away this evening," he said, barely audible. He lowered his head and took the nipple between his teeth, fabric and all. She arched against him. "I knew I'd never seen anything so beautiful as you. And then you showed up here, by the water and it was like I'd conjured you out of my thoughts."

His name whispered from her lips.

"I knew—" he lifted his head and looked up at the stars beginning to sparkle overhead "—I knew what you were thinking."

He felt her fingers tangle in his hair, pulling it from the leather string holding it back. When he looked back down at her, she was still again.

And he knew she was bracing herself. Waiting for him to push her away again.

"You were thinking about us together. About me touching you. Filling you." He closed his eyes and prayed for forgiveness. "I was thinking it, too." He opened his eyes to see her swallow. "God help me, I can't stop this," he admitted, his voice raw and as quiet as the night.

Her heart was so full, she thought she'd burst. "Maybe God doesn't want you to stop," she whispered. She knew she was praying that Jefferson wouldn't.

His teeth flashed when he threw back his head. "You should be properly married."

It was what she'd been taught all her life. But the only one she would *ever* marry would be this man. And he'd never put his head in that particular noose. A peculiar calm spread through her. "I should be loved," she said steadily. "Truly loved."

He flinched, as if she'd punched him in the stomach again. "Don't."

"Jefferson—"

His hand left her breast and touched her lips. "Shh."

Emily took the hand in hers and kissed it. The stars twinkled dizzily above their heads. She wondered why on earth it had taken her so long to admit the truth to him. "I love you, Jefferson."

He shook his head slightly, his lips tight. "No."

"Yes." She held on to his hand when he would have pulled back. "I love you."

"You don't mean it."

She pressed his palm to her heart. "I do."

His fingers curled into the cool cotton. "You're just…caught up in the moment."

She pushed herself up until she sat, facing him. Her resolve was already shaking. How many times had she wanted to tell Jefferson what was in her heart? How many times, faced with his displeasure, had she backed down?

Not this time. Not yet. "I've loved you for as long as I can remember, Jefferson. If I'm caught up in *the moment* as you say…" She had to swallow before the words would emerge. "Then so are you." On her knees, she leaned forward and speared her fingers through his hair. She kissed his brow. His temple. The now-familiar scar at the corner of his eye.

His breath was warm on her cheek, and she moved until her lips were a hair's breadth from his. "You don't have to say it back, Jefferson," she whispered. "Just don't pretend that I'm too young, or too naive or too whatever to know what my own feelings are."

Her tongue flicked out to lightly taste the corner of his lips. "I *do* love you." She kissed his jaw, ran the tip of her tongue along the narrow ridge of scar tissue. "And I believe, if you'd let yourself, that we could be happy together. But what I want most right now is just you. And me."

She caught his earlobe between her teeth, then soothed it with her tongue. "I want you to make love to me," she murmured against his ear. "More than I've ever wanted anything in my life." She held her breath and forced herself to sit back on her heels. "But if you tell me right now that you...don't...want me," she said as she drew in a shaky breath, "then I'll leave you alone." She didn't know how she'd be able to keep the promise. But she would. She'd go away, just as she'd told Tristan she would. She'd leave. So that, if only this one time, Jefferson could stay.

Her heart stopped when he sat up, too. She was going to have to keep her word. Oh, God, please.

She looked back over her shoulder toward the buildings. The spotlight high on the corner of the horse barn threw its bright light over part of the corrals. Someone, Joe, probably back from wherever he'd been earlier, was working a big dark horse. Squire was lying in a hospital bed, and life at the ranch still moved on. Somehow or other, she would, too.

The thought did nothing to stop a hot tear from squeezing out the corner of her eye. Dammit, she wasn't going to fall apart. She just wasn't! "My love for you isn't going to go away. It hasn't even after all these years." Emily realized she'd said the thought aloud and she dashed another tear from her cheek. Sniffing, she looked down at her hands. "Seeing you, being near you and not...not—" She broke off, swallowing another wad of tears. "I know you're hurting inside and you won't let me help." Her hands moved helplessly. "It's tearing me apart."

She felt, more than heard, the rough sound he made. He raked back his hair with one hand. "Poor Jefferson," she murmured.

"This is exactly the sort of thing you hate. I'm sorry," she managed to push herself unevenly to her feet and turned instinctively toward the buildings. She was so cold inside.

"Emily, stop."

Hardly daring to breathe, she hesitated, then turned back. Her heart filled her throat when he rose to his feet. She searched his expression, but the night shadows made it impossible. The breeze stirred, lifting his hair across his face. The cool air danced around her bare shoulders.

He turned his face into the breeze, letting it wash over him. "I'm too old for you, Emily. I always have been.

"Wait," he said as her shoulders drooped. "I'm not finished yet. There's an eon of living. Existing." He took a step closer. "My entire life separates us. But that doesn't keep me from wanting you." Squire's anger…his disapproval…his threat to have Jefferson drawn and quartered if he so much as laid a hand on Emily…hadn't kept him from wanting her. "I don't want to hurt you, Emily, and I know I will."

"So it's better to hurt me now, than later. Right?" She hugged her arms close.

"No! Dammit, that's not what I'm saying." He reached for her shoulders and pulled her to him. "I'm saying I want you so badly I ache to my back teeth with it. And right now I'm too damn tired and too selfish to push you away again."

He'd pulled her off balance, and her arms were trapped between them. "Be very sure, Emily," he warned. "Because once I start, I'm not going to stop."

Time slowly ticked by. A rogue cloud drifted across the moon, briefly obscuring the cool light. She moistened her dry lips. "I'm sure."

The rigidity left his shoulders. He ran his thumbs over her cheeks, drying the trail of tears. She could barely breathe, her heart thudded so slowly and painfully. He stepped back, slipping her hand into his.

"We're not going back to the house?" She looked over her shoulder toward the lights shining from the big windows. When she looked back at him, his gaze seemed trained on the house. "Jefferson?"

"No. Not there." He continued toward the swimming hole, tugging her hand gently. "This way."

Emily followed, brushing a strand of hair out of her eyes. He led them back through the trees and across to the opposite side of the swimming hole where the thick grass vied with a heavy mat of clover for supremacy. The water's edge was only a foot away, still and reflecting the faint sliver of the moon. A frog croaked. The leaves in the trees rustled. She'd never heard such sweet music.

Jefferson began unbuttoning his shirt and she swallowed, suddenly nervous. He tugged the tails loose from his jeans and shrugged out of it. He tossed it to the side, away from the water, then crouched at her feet.

"Lift," he instructed softly. She obeyed and he removed first one sandal. Then the other. The grass was cool and soft beneath her feet. His palms circled her ankles and she trembled. Her fingers found his shoulder, steadying her. His hands smoothed the full skirt about her calves, slipped beneath to glide across her bare legs, curving behind her knees. He held her there for a long moment, looking up at her, giving her time to steady. Her fingers went from his shoulder to his forehead, pushing his hair back, letting the moonlight find his features.

His eyes captured hers, holding them steady when his fingertips slipped up to her hips and slowly, so slowly, eased beneath the lacy edge of her panties. The fabric of her dress rustled as he drew them away. She knew her love for him was in her own eyes. Could he *see* the truth of the words he didn't want to believe?

Her panties slipped to her feet, and she automatically stepped out of them. Jefferson tossed the lacy scrap over by his shirt and slowly pushed himself upright. Tall and straight, he seemed to tower over her, even blocking out the cool white moonlight.

For a moment he seemed carved from stone. The long, roping muscles in his arms, the broad, hard plane of his chest, down to the lean stomach. She reached out to touch the ridge of muscle just above his waistband. He was almost too perfect to be real. But the washboard muscles flexed beneath her touch, and she knew he was real. Real, and so very, very warm.

Her fingers meandered up over his taut skin, which gleamed golden even in the moonlight. She felt the ridges of his ribs. An indentation in his skin. Another scar, she realized. Her hand skimmed up, over his chest. Felt a flat male nipple rub against her palm. Stopped directly over his heart. Rejoiced that his heartbeat was just that little bit uneven. That little bit too hard.

Her breath was tumbling past her lips, and her fingers trembled. Jefferson nudged her chin up and gently captured her lips. She swayed and grabbed hold of his belt loops, vaguely aware of his fingers guiding down the zipper at the back of her dress. His lips left hers and forged trails of heat as he worked his way to the curve of her shoulder. Her head felt heavy on her neck, and she blinked at the stars shining overhead. The zipper made a soft rasp, and her dress drifted loose, barely held in place by the narrow straps over her shoulders.

He drew a blunt finger up the ridge of her spine, setting off all manner of shivers. His name escaped her lips as his finger grazed the pulse beating at her neck, then dipped beneath the fabric barely covering her breasts. The strap slipped from her shoulder, baring one full breast to his eyes. Then he slid his finger up, finding her achingly hard nipple.

It was torture, the way he circled and taunted. With a soft cry, she covered his hand with her own, pulling until it covered her, surrounded her soft skin with his warm touch. She looked down to see his big hand molding her breast, her smaller hand resting atop his. Unbearably aroused, she could only look at him. He smiled faintly.

"Kiss me," she whispered. He did. On her temple. Her jaw. Her shoulder. She sank her hands into his hair and tugged. "Kiss me," she begged. He responded by capturing her ponytail in one hand and gently tugging her head back. He tasted the pulse beating at the base of her neck. "You're making me crazy," she accused breathlessly.

"I want you crazy," he whispered. "Crazy and as bloody desperate as I've been all these years."

His tongue explored the shell-like curves of her ear, and shivers danced down her entire body. She squirmed against him, enjoying the way his skin leaped when she ran her palms across his abdomen. His lips were traveling again. Exploring her other shoulder. Her head bent over his when he passed beneath her chin, replacing the coolness of the night air with the warmth of his breath. Then his mouth trailed over the slope of her breast and closed over the rigid peak. A soft moan filled the night, and she realized it was coming from her.

He slipped his arm behind her back, holding her steady when her knees went lax as he gently suckled her. She trembled violently as he meandered to her other breast and plucked at the aching peak through the fabric still covering her. She gasped his name when he went onto his knees before her.

Leaning back on his heels, Jefferson looked up at her. At the sheen of wetness on the jutting curve of her breast. His hands slipped beneath the dress. Her fingers were digging into his shoulders, but he barely noticed. Just as he barely noticed his hip and knee protesting at his position. "Do you have any idea how much I want you?" He leaned forward and pressed his lips to her belly. He felt her trembling. "How often I've dreamed about you?"

Her fingers went to his hair, tangling in it. And he realized why he hadn't cut it all off, just yet. He'd been waiting for her touch. Waiting for this.

He should be shot for what he was doing. There was no future for them. No future for him.

"Jefferson?" Her soft voice glided over him.

He gritted his teeth, forcing himself to keep his touch gentle. Slow. She deserved that much from him, at least.

"Jefferson, you, uh, you're not, um…oh, *please,*" she broke off on a little cry when his kiss burned through the dress to her abdomen. To her thigh. "Tell me this isn't just for me."

"Hmm?" He barely heard her, his attention was so focused on the heated vee beneath the blue fabric. How he wanted to touch her there. Kiss her. But not yet. Not yet.

She trembled beneath his hands and sank to her knees. He saw the way her hands twisted together. The way she hesitated. His jaw clenched as he managed to beat down the urge to tumble her onto her back and have her. Once and for all.

He should take advantage of the moment and stop this madness. He should. But he didn't. He lifted her chin with a finger. "Hey," he asked as he cocked his head so he could see her face. "What is it?"

It was his gentleness that undid her. If he'd been his usual taciturn self, she might have gotten the words out again, without feeling her entire being flush with embarrassment. She closed her eyes, desire twisting through her, fighting against the wave of mortification. "You're not doing this because you feel sorry for me, or something, are you?"

He went so still, that she *had* to look at him. "Jefferson?"

His mouth twisted wryly. "The only one I'm gonna feel sorry for is me, if we don't stop all this jabberin'."

"That's not exactly an answer," she pointed out, flushing anew.

He moved suddenly, catching her shoulders in his hands and pushing her back against the fragrant clover. His momentum carried him right on top of her, where he pressed himself against her. "Is this answer enough?" He slipped a hand behind her, tilting her hips toward him. "You think I get this way because I feel *sorry* for you?"

She'd annoyed him. She could tell. Her breath stuck in her throat as he moved again and her knees lifted instinctively to hug his hips. "Well, excuse me," she murmured tartly. "I just want to be clear on where we stand here. Oh, my…"

Jefferson lifted his head from her neck. He took a few slow breaths. "By all means, Emily. Let's be clear here. I want you. That *point* is glaringly obvious." He added dryly. "And you," he said, slipping a hand wickedly down her abdomen, making her breath whistle between her teeth, "want me. I think seven years of foreplay is long enough."

She could have slugged him again. Would he really reduce their relationship to just sex? Her hand even clenched into a fist. "Put this to better work," he murmured, pulling that hand to his button fly.

Her heart raced. "I'm going to have sex with you because I love you," she ground out, her fingers busily fumbling over the buttons strained beyond their normal capacity.

"I'm making love with you because I want you," he returned. His fingers curled into the folds of fabric caught between them. He gave a tug and the dress flew over her head.

She clenched her jaw and forced the last few buttons loose. With one hand on either side of his hips, she yanked down his jeans and briefs in one fell swoop.

Breathless, she fell back, looking up at him.

"Losing your nerve now?"

Her eyebrow shot up. Without stopping to think, she closed her hand over his rigid length. "What do you think?" She demanded.

"Geez—" he rolled onto his back, pulling her with him. She sprawled across him, all curving limbs and sweet skin. He pushed away the dress strap that somehow had twisted about her wrist. She wriggled out of his grasp. "What are you doing?" he asked.

"If you think I'm going to sit here," she broke off, to tug at his boot. "Buck naked all by myself, *oof,* then you're dreaming." The boot came loose and she tossed it aside.

A laugh strangled in Jefferson's throat. She was a slender nymph. Creamy skinned, bending over his feet and presenting him with a glorious view of her nude figure. "I am dreaming," he muttered. The other boot slid free, and he pulled her back into his arms, finding her lips with his. "You deserve candle-light and wine," he said finally, all toying aside.

Pressing her hand against his chest, she pushed herself up until she was straddling his waist. The seductive breeze drifted over them and she lifted her arms to pull her ponytail free. Her hair swung down over her shoulders. "We have moonlight and clover," she told him, encompassing their private moonlit haven with an outstretched arm. "Nothing could be more perfect," she added, her voice low.

Her hands flitted over the jeans that were still more on than off. She was an enchanting mixture of bravado and shyness. He knew he didn't deserve this stolen moment with her. He'd end up hurting her. No matter what emotions she spoke of, no matter what she believed, or felt, or *thought* she felt, he knew she should be saving it all for a man worthy of her. Lord knew that he wasn't that man. Sooner or later she'd learn that and it would destroy him. He wove their fingers together. "Come here."

She leaned over him, her eyes widening when her breasts pressed against his chest. Swallowing a groan, he rolled them to their sides. But for tonight, at least, she was his.

Emily didn't even notice the edge of fabric beneath her back as Jefferson nudged her over. The dry humor had left his face. As had the tinge of annoyance, leaving his sharply etched features taut with desire.

This was Jefferson, she reminded herself. The same man she'd always loved. Her nervousness subsided, and she reached out to pull at his jeans. He helped her and then tossed them out of the way.

Leaning on his arm, he looked down at her. She knew he took pleasure in the sight. His dark eyes burned over her just as surely as his hands. As surely as the unyielding flesh brushing her thigh. This time the color that burned beneath her skin wasn't from embarrassment. She slid her palms over his biceps, feeling the muscles bunch.

"Close your eyes," he whispered.

She did, and drew in her breath when he laid his palm low over her flat stomach. She had to bite her tongue to keep silent the thought that whirled through her mind. What if she became pregnant? What if they created a baby that would nestle and grow right there inside here, beneath the very spot where his hand now rested? Like a flowering vine, the idea grew. Bloomed. A whimper rose in her throat.

His head lowered over her breast, and his palm slid across her thigh. Her smooth legs impatiently sought out his hair-roughened ones.

"Easy," he murmured, notching his thigh between hers. Then his hand moved, lingering over the patch of soft curls, and unbearable tension coiled within her as his palm gently pressed, his fingers slowly delved.

Her breath carried his name.

It took every ounce of self-control within him to keep the pace slow. Soft sounds fell from her lips and her hands clutched at him, pulling him down. She cradled him sweetly and he bit back a groan as he brushed against that wet heat. He was not a small man, and she was so little in his arms. So delicate. Bracing his weight on his arms, he paused at her entrance, seducing them both with the tantalizing contact.

"Now, look at me," he whispered. He wanted to see her eyes when they joined. His heart in his throat, he watched her heavy lids slowly lift. Bottomless pools looked up at him, so trusting. So filled with love that his throat tightened. Slowly, so slowly, he pressed forward into that heavenly heat.

Her teeth closed over the tip of her tongue and her eyes widened. Her fingertips dug into his arms. He felt the barrier guarding her virginity. He sucked in his breath. "Why didn't you say…"

"I told you there was no one. Don't stop," she pleaded. "Oh, Jefferson, please don't stop."

He folded his arms next to her head and leaned his forehead against hers. His chest heaved under his restraint. "Honey, I couldn't stop even if a bomb exploded next to us." He flexed his hips infinitesimally, and her breath became a hiss.

"Please." Her hands slid over his hips. "I need you inside," she cried.

Jefferson needed it, too. More than his next breath. He slipped his hand behind her knee, pulling it up.

Instinctively, she bent her other knee, opening herself to

him. Her hands scrabbled at his hips, slipping over the hard curve of buttocks. She lifted herself to him, gasping against his chest as if she'd impaled herself on his flesh. But the pain was a minor companion to the thunderous pleasure.

In his head Jefferson began counting backward. By sevens. When he thought he could speak coherently, he asked if she was okay.

Wordlessly, she nodded. And moved in such a way that rockets went off behind his eyeballs. Sweat broke out on his brow. He'd never last. And she deserved far more from him. He shifted his weight, pulling her over him. Once again, she straddled him. With one obviously major difference this time.

"You like?" His hands settled on her hips as he gently guided her movements until her instincts soon took over.

She nodded, jerkily. She felt like a cork in a champagne bottle, wrapped way too firmly. Far too tightly. She rocked against him, feeling his strength deep inside, reaching right up to her heart. She cried out his name. Her arms and legs trembled.

"I...can't... Help me..."

"It's okay," he soothed, even though his voice was rough. On her hips, his hands were strong. Safe.

She bit her lip. She couldn't breathe. She moaned his name, nearly incoherent.

"Ah, honey," he growled, sitting up, keeping her firmly in his lap. Her inner muscles gloved him, and he guided her, ruthlessly controlling himself. It was her. Always her. He worked his hand between them and slid his finger over that sweet spot.

His name was a keening cry from her that he swallowed with his lips as she convulsed over him. Lights exploded in his head as her pleasure ignited his. "Emily—"

She trembled against him, her mouth open against his chest.

His control flew out the window and he rolled her over, burying himself within her.

She was everything he wanted in this world.

It was his last coherent thought before he spilled himself deep inside her.

Chapter Ten

They'd slept. The knowledge hovered in the back of Emily's mind as she slowly drifted awake. There was no sense of unfamiliarity. No moments, however brief, of wondering where she was. Or why a long, masculine arm was lying heavily across her waist, its wide palm cupping her breast. At some point he must have covered them with their discarded clothing. Her lips tilted into a soft smile, and she turned to face him, huddling against his warmth as the sky slowly lightened with the approaching dawn.

Jefferson breathed deeply and pushed her head down onto his shoulder. "Quit squirming," he mumbled sleepily.

"I thought you were sleeping." She pressed a kiss to his collarbone.

"I was."

She smiled again and curled closer to him. She loved the way he held her. Loved the way he'd rinsed her panties in the swimming hole to gently wipe her thighs after the first time. Loved the way he'd tenderly woken her later with a slow, easy loving as different and fulfilling as the first time had been. She slipped her hand behind his neck and ran her fingers through his hair.

"Ow," he complained a moment later when her finger caught in a tangle.

"Sorry," she whispered.

He opened one eye. "I'm cutting it all off," he informed her balefully.

"I'll still love you," she warned him lightly. "I'd love you even if you were bald."

"Empty promises," he grunted. "Squire's still got a full head of hair, and if heredity has anything to do with it…"

At the mention of his father, the teasing glint in Emily's eye died. "Jefferson—"

"No," he warned abruptly, knowing what was coming.

She frowned at him and sat up, pulling the skirt of her dress over her shoulders like a shawl.

Jefferson saw that she had sprigs of grass and pieces of crushed leaves stuck in her tangled hair. And even though they'd already made love twice, he found himself wanting her all over again. Worse than ever.

"Why won't you tell me what's going on between you two?"

Jefferson just shook his head and reached for her. But she eluded his grasp, falling to her back and rolling away. He caught the strap of her dress and pulled. She abruptly let loose and he tossed the dress aside. "Come here."

"No," she laughed, dodging his hands. "I'll make a deal," she offered.

His eyes narrowed. "I don't do deals."

Her lips pursed. "Ooh, don't you sound the tough man."

"Don't you sound the brave woman, sitting safely five feet away."

She grinned. "I'm no fool." She scrambled back another foot, avoiding his quick reach. "Ah-ah-ah."

Jefferson shrugged and lay back. He folded his arms beneath his head and relaxed, for all the world like a man sunning himself on a beach instead of sprawling alongside a small swimming hole in the early Wyoming dawn.

"Here's my deal," she said, her dark eyes studying him.

Beneath his lashes, he watched her watch him. Saw the way her eyes glided, stopped, held, then glided again. It was the most amazing thing. The way he got turned on by seeing her get turned on.

"I'll come over there," she pointed to the crumpled grass where she'd lain next to him. "And you'll tell me why there's such a rift between you and your father." She picked a leaf out of her hair and slowly tore it into little pieces.

"Okay," she tossed the leaf aside when he didn't respond, and crawled a foot closer. "I'll come over there, and you'll tell me what you've been doing for the past few years. Why you're having nightmares."

The ground was getting hard. He rolled onto his side and propped his head on his hand. Her nipples were the color of delicate strawberries. Now he knew they tasted even sweeter.

"Okay," she offered again, her cheeks coloring as she realized the direction of his avid stare. "I'll come over there, and you'll tell me where you went when you left San Diego."

He smiled faintly.

She huffed and crawled closer yet. "Okay. I'll come over there, and you'll tell me why you have that scar there on your hip."

He glanced down, absently noting the surgical scar.

Her lips pursed. "*Okay,* I'll come over there, and—"

His hands closed over her waist and he pulled her down beside him. "You're already here."

"*And,* you'll tell me that last night was the absolute-best, most-fantastic, most-incredible experience you've ever had."

"Ah, well that's easy, then," he smiled. Then chuckled. And realized it was an unfamiliar sensation. "Last night was the absolute-best, most-fantastic, most-incredible experience you've ever had. Both times," he added.

She punched him in the shoulder. And dragged his head down to hers. "You should smile more often," she murmured against his lips.

He kissed her until she clung to him like a wet blanket. "Last night," he told her, tumbling her onto her back, "was the most incredible experience I've ever had in my life."

"And you want to do it again and again and again," she grinned even while her cheeks flushed pink.

"And I want to do it again and again and again," he repeated obediently. Truthfully. "But you," he said as he touched her intimately, "are probably sore."

She blushed even brighter. "Geez Louise, Jefferson—"

"Don't be embarrassed." He kissed the curve of her neck. "There're other ways, you know."

"Oh?" Her voice was faint, and he liked to think it had something to do with the delicate marauding down below. "I, uh, suppose," she broke off, her throat working as she swallowed. "You're going to show me?"

"Mmm-hmm."

She moistened her lips, her eyes glittering between her narrowed lashes. "You're decadent," she murmured.

"You're beautiful," he returned, kissing the curve of her breast. Delightful moments later, she dug her fingertips into his unyielding back. "Inside," she begged softly. But he held himself back, filling her gently with a long finger instead.

"It's not the same," she protested faintly, arching into his palm and closing her fingers over him in return.

He groaned on a half laugh. "No. But it's not bad."

Long, exquisite minutes passed. And eventually, Emily collapsed breathlessly onto the grass. Just before she slipped back into sleep, she had to admit that he'd been right.

"Hey. Time to wake up, sleepyhead."

Emily opened her eyes, squinting against the sunlight. Jefferson was standing above her buttoning up his jeans.

She yawned and stretched.

Jefferson groaned and glanced aside. "Don't tempt me," he said and tossed her dress onto her belly.

She pointed her toes, then flexed them. Lord, she was stiff. "This camping-out stuff has some drawbacks," she grumbled. She pulled the dress over her head and stood up. "Where's the rest of my, uh…clothes?"

Jefferson looked around. "Back there," he pointed to the splash of lace hanging haphazardly from a small lilac branch. He left them hanging there though, and picked up her sandals instead. "Here," he said, turning back to her, grinning slightly.

She was staring at him, aghast. Ignoring the sandals in his hand, she pushed at him, scooting behind him. "What the *hell* is that?"

Jefferson mentally kicked himself. He glanced at his denim shirt, lying uselessly beneath a tree. He'd been so wrapped up in her that he'd stupidly forgotten the vicious scar on his back that he'd kept her from seeing so far.

She slipped underneath his arm, her fingers running frantically over his ribs. "Emily, don't—"

But she'd already found it again. The small circle of scar

tissue riding just beneath a rib. "That was a bullet wound," she realized aloud.

She went behind him again and traced the ragged edge of scar tissue below his shoulder blade. He flinched, as if burned. He turned to see her hands lifted in bewilderment. "How…what?" She asked.

Just a little while longer. He wanted more time before the rich, shining trust that filled her eyes each time she looked at him would disappear forever.

"Don't you *dare* tell me it's nothing," she warned, her tight voice shaking. "Or that you got that…that *thing* in some little accident. People don't usually shoot at bridge builders, do they?"

Had it been too much to ask for just a little more time?

"Of course they don't!" She answered her own question. "And if you've spent so much as a minute helping to build a bridge, I'll eat my hat. I'll bet you weren't really on that oil tanker, either."

"Find a hat and start nibbling," he said.

She shot him a look tight with disbelief. And hurt. "Who pays your salary?"

"Whoever I happen to be working for."

"Do you ever give a straight answer to anyone?"

"Ah, Em—"

"Don't 'Ah, Em' me," she snapped. "I want to know whether the man I'm in love with really exists. Or whether *this* Jefferson," she waved her hand at him, "is just another persona you've assumed. *Who are you?*"

"I exist, all right. I warned you, but you wouldn't listen. What you see is what you get, sweetheart. And if you don't like it, then that's too damn bad. Did it ever occur to you that it might not be any of your business?"

She jerked as if he'd slapped her. Suddenly all the barriers that were between them, all the distance *he'd* created over the past several years, all came crashing to place between them. As if they hadn't just shared the most momentous night of their lives together. He cursed himself for ten kinds of a bastard.

Her hair slid over her face as she snatched the shoes from him. But whether she hid it from him or not, he knew the expression of pain that would be in her eyes.

Emily ached to ask him the million questions flying in her mind. She pushed her feet into the shoes. Jefferson had been shot. She wasn't particularly knowledgeable about wounds of that nature, but having been raised on a ranch, she wasn't entirely naive about firearms, either. Judging by the angle of the scar on his chest and the exit wound on his back, it was a wonder he hadn't died.

Just the idea was enough to send nausea careening through her. She reached out and leaned her head against a tree. Only by slowly breathing in through her nose and out through her mouth was she slowly able to conquer the nausea. When she could raise her head without it spinning, she turned around to see him standing in the same spot, watching her. "When…how long ago, did you," she whispered, "get shot?"

His beautiful, deeply blue orbs were flat. Expressionless.

"How long?" Her voice rose and she strode over to him, shoving his chest. "You can at least answer that!"

The corner of his lips tightened. "Two years ago."

Two years. "And this?" She touched the crescent scar near his eye. "And this?" Her fingertip traced the narrow ridge on his jaw. "Are these from two years ago, also? How about the scar on your hip? That one was a surgical incision. Wasn't it? What happened to you? Oh," she said, waving her arms in frustration. "Don't bother. I know you're not going to answer me."

Pleading filled her dark eyes, despite her caustic words. He wished he could tell her. He wished he were a better man. A braver man.

"Tell me this, Jefferson," she said as she turned away abruptly, but not before he'd seen the sheen of tears in her eyes.

"What?"

"If that bullet had killed you two years ago, would we have ever known about it? Or would we have just gone on believing that you were still going around the globe, working yourself from one adventure to the next?"

Kim's wife had been told by a chaplain appointed for such tasks. A man who'd been unable to divulge much more information than he'd been told to say. "They'd have notified you," Jefferson said quietly.

He watched her slender shoulders tremble. *"They."* Her shoulders firmed and she turned to face him. Her arms twined about her waist and she looked anywhere but at him. "Whoever *they* are."

"Em, we need to talk."

Emily couldn't believe her ears. What did the man think she'd been trying to do with him since he came back into their lives? "That's rich coming from you," she said, her lips twisting.

"About last night."

She shifted. From a distance she heard an engine crank to life. A dog barked. The Double-C gearing up for another day. "What about it?"

"We…*I*…didn't use anything. To protect you."

Squelching every shred of emotion from her face, she looked up at him. "From what?"

Something flickered in his eyes. Just for a moment. "Pregnancy."

"Oh. That."

"What did you think I meant?"

"How should I know? HIV?"

His teeth bared for a bare second. "You think I'd take a chance with you like that?"

"How should I know?" She sighed and recanted. "No, I don't believe you would."

"I've been tested," he said stiffly.

"Fine."

"You shouldn't be so casual about it."

"Fine."

"You need to check these things out beforehand, not afterward when it's way too late."

"Like you did with this pregnancy idea?"

His eyes flashed and were carefully banked. "Seeing that you were—"

"Incredibly stupid," she supplied.

"—a virgin," he continued as if she hadn't spoken, "I suppose you're not on the pill or anything."

She studied him. Anything was preferable to his unyielding, unsmiling, unflinching control. She knew he had feelings. Emotions. Lord, the man was a seething *cauldron* of emotion. If he'd only just let out some of it. As he had when there'd been nothing between them but the layers of skin on their bodies. She'd gambled everything in her heart on breaking through to him, once and for all. Had it all been for nothing?

"Emily?"

"Don't worry about it," she finally dismissed.

His eyebrow twitched. "When's your period due?"

A tide of color burned its way up her neck to her cheeks to the tips of her ears. "That," she snapped angrily, "is none of *your* blasted business." Spinning on her heel, she took off, twigs snapping under the stomp of her sandals.

"The hell it's none of my business," he grated, starting to take after her. But their night on the ground had taken its toll and a sharp pain seared its way down his spine. Swearing, he stood stock-still, waiting for the pain to abate. And watching her slender figure moving farther and farther away.

By the time the pain eventually subsided, he was drenched with sweat. Emily was nowhere in sight. Moving slowly, he went back to get his shirt. Using a tree for support, he bent at the knees and snagged the denim between two fingers. He started to straighten and noticed the panties that still hung from the lilac bush.

He slowly reached out and untangled the bit of lace, unaccountably sad when the lace snagged and a tiny tear formed. Carefully, he worked them free. They were still slightly damp from when he'd rinsed them in the spring water. He laid them over his thigh, fingering the torn lace. Ruined. Just like so many things he touched lately.

He started to rise again. The pain that shot through him this time told him that the first one had merely been a mild warning. Nausea clawed at him and his back ached too badly to even swear. Eventually, when the stabbing pain had mutated into a stiff, throbbing pain, he slowly began walking back toward the house.

Naturally, the first person Emily saw when she slipped in through the front door of the house was Tristan. He'd set up his computer in the little-used front room. Why couldn't he still have been sleeping? Then she could have made it up to her bedroom in privacy.

He looked up when the door opened and he leaned back against the couch. "What's this? Emily, I do believe those were the very clothes you were wearing last night." He fanned himself. "Mercy me. Have you been out all night? How scandalous."

"Shut up."

His wicked grin lost some wattage. "I'm not exactly hearing the lilt of morning-after euphoria in your voice."

"Aren't you the genius," she marveled sarcastically, stepping over the electrical and phone cords stretching from the wall to where his equipment was laid out upon the gleaming cherry wood coffee table.

"Whoa," Tristan leaped off the couch and headed her off before she reached the staircase. He took her shoulders in his hands and marched her back into the living room. "Give."

She twisted out of his hold. "Not now, Tristan. I'm not in the mood."

"We've got enough people in this family who don't talk about what's bugging them. We don't need to add you to the ranks." Pulling her by the wrist, he nudged her onto the couch and set his printer on the floor to make room for himself on the coffee table facing her. "What happened?"

"Your brother happened." Her elbows propped on her knees, she buried her face in her hands. "I'm such a fool."

"No."

"*Yes.*"

He gently pried her hands away from her face. "Tell me."

Long-used to Tristan's brand of nosiness, she sighed. "It's none of your business."

"I'm wounded. This is you and my brother we're talking about here."

"Yes, well, it still doesn't concern you."

"Emily," he tsked.

She groaned and raked her hands through her hair. "Oh, all right. All right!" Her hands flopped down onto the couch. "For crying out loud, between the two of you…" She shook her head, then again plopped her face in her hands. Her voice was a muffled mumble. "Some things are just too private, you know?"

"So, tell me the parts that aren't so private." He sighed, patting her knee. "I'll start. Will that help?" In typical Tristan fashion, he plowed right on, despite the very plain shaking of her head. "Rather than visit the esteemed Squire Clay in the hospital last evening, we know you chose to seek out my stubborn brother. You found him. Knowing Jefferson, you talked while he probably sat there doing his imitation of a hunk of granite.

"Then, at some point, you probably got irritated with one another. There's no surprise there. It's what usually happens between you two. Then, one way or another, you guys ended up, shall we say, bunking down together? I know you didn't come back to the house."

"What did you do? Sit at the foot of my bed, waiting up for me?"

"No, I've been working all night. Right in this spot, squirt. I'd have heard you come in. So, how am I doing so far? Then, in the cold light of day, you or Jefferson…probably Jeff in his usual fashion…screwed it all up."

"He doesn't screw up." Emily's head lifted. "How can you say such a thing!"

Tristan smiled faintly. "Just seeing if you were listening."

"You…are…a…pig."

He smiled happily. "Yup. A Clay Pig." His big hands rubbed together. "So, what went wrong?"

Emily absently plucked a crushed leaf from the ends of her hair. "Has Jefferson told you what he's been doing the past several years?"

Tristan's eyes strayed for a moment to his computer. "Not exactly."

The leaf came free and she studiously placed it in the crystal ashtray sitting on the little round table next to the couch. "He's, um, got a scar. On his back."

"I've seen it."

"Did he tell you where he got it?"

"Nope."

"Did he tell you why he got it?"

Tristan shook his head.

"At least he's consistent," Emily pushed to her feet, stepped around Tristan's big feet and paced to the wide picture window. "He's had surgery, too. Did he tell you about that? He certainly wouldn't tell me."

She touched the spot on her hip where Jefferson's scar was located. Tristan's computer suddenly beeped softly, and paper began spewing from the printer. She bit her lip, staring sightlessly through the lace curtains. "I thought it would make a difference to him. After we—" She swallowed past the lump in her throat. "Well, it doesn't matter anymore."

"Of course it matters."

"We scratched an itch, Tristan," Emily said deliberately. So deliberately that perhaps she would actually believe that was all she and Jefferson had shared.

"Is that what he said?" Tristan slowly rose.

"No. But that's what it all amounts to, anyway." She twitched a lace panel into place. "What is it with you guys, anyway?"

"Are we talking guys in general?" he asked warily. "Or the Clay species?"

Her lips twisted. "I dunno. Clay, I suppose. You all hide so much of yourselves. You only give a little bit away."

Tristan only grunted in reply.

Emily swiveled on her heel and waved at the array of equipment spread about the room. At the paper silently sliding into the printer tray. "What do you do with all that stuff?"

He frowned, looking down at his equipment. "Consulting. Stuff like that. You know."

"No, actually I don't know. You've never really answered me whenever I've asked. And I just finally quit asking. Almost everything that I know about what you do, I've read in some magazine or newspaper article. You design software. You consult. You work for yourself, but you still work for someone else at times, or so it appears. I don't know who. You hardly take two steps out of the house without one of your little toys there at your side.

"You get calls in the middle of the night, and you'll take off for days at a time. You rack up more frequent flyer mileage than anyone I know. But I still don't really know what you do. And I *live* with you. You're almost as secretive as Sawyer, only I know he's with the navy. He, at least, wears a uniform. And then there's Jefferson. He's worse than all of you put together." She hugged her arms to her.

"We're not all operating in some cloak of secrecy, you know. Matthew and Dan are about as upfront as it gets. And you know confidentiality is an important part of my job. But a job is all it is."

"So what kind of job is it that gets Jefferson shot up with something that blows a hole through his back the size of my fist? He'd never be involved in anything illegal, I just know he wouldn't. Why does it all have to be such a big mystery?"

The window rattled under the force of Emily's open palm. "I just want him to open up to me! I thought if we…well, you know…I thought it would be a start. It's not like I expected him to propose or anything. I just need him to share himself with me. Instead, he gives me some song and dance about safe sex and getting pregnant."

Tristan's eyebrows rose slightly. "Uh, is that a possibility here?"

She gave him a stony glare.

"Sorry."

Emily sighed tiredly. Her emotions were heaving back and forth, riding a crazy roller coaster. "I love him, Tristan. I'd do anything for him."

"I know, squirt."

"I'd walk away from him if it was what he wanted."

"It's not."

"I'm not so sure." She didn't need to close her eyes to picture the way Jefferson had looked at her earlier. As if they were two strangers passing on the street. Discussing the weather, rather than the baby he might have created with her. So effectively denying her the right or privilege of sharing the trauma he'd experienced. He'd done it as easily as turning off a light switch. "I want to believe that last night wasn't a mistake."

"Loving someone the way you love Jefferson is never a mistake," Tristan said quietly. "And you also need to remember that Jefferson doesn't do anything he doesn't choose to do."

Emily nodded sadly as she headed for the stairs. "Exactly."

Emily was sitting on the window seat in her bedroom, looking out, when Tristan came up to her room a few minutes later, carrying a stack of papers.

"Here." He held out the papers. "Maybe this'll give you some answers."

Puzzled, Emily automatically took the stack in her hands. "What is this?"

"The story of Jefferson Clay." Tristan scrubbed his hands over his face, raking his fingers through his hair. "Don't read it at bedtime, though. It'll give you nightmares."

Unwillingly her eyes scanned the first few lines of the top page. She didn't recognize the name of the company, but she certainly could identify the type of information printed. "Tristan, this is a personnel file. How'd you get it?"

"I just did. Don't question it."

"You've been hacking?" She shot to her feet. "No way! Tristan, that's illegal! You're supposed to *catch* hackers! Not *be* one!"

"I wasn't hacking," he said quietly.

"Then how—"

"It's just one of the jobs I do, okay? Don't worry about it. I didn't do a single illegal thing to get that information."

"No." Shaking her head, she shoved the papers back at him. "I'm not going to read any of this. How'd you know where to look anyway?"

He heaved a sigh. "Look, it's not important how or why I came by the info. Let's just say that Jefferson wanted to keep his business private, and I saw no reason to disabuse him of that idea. It's only been since he returned that I've been nosing around."

"I thought Sawyer was the eyes and ears in this family. Are you secretly with the navy?" She eyed him sarcastically.

"No. Look, we're straying from the point here. Which is," he said as he pushed the papers back into her hand. "This."

"You're out of your mind if you think I'm going to read this."

"Why not?"

"It would be wrong, that's why not!"

"Wrong or not, it'll explain pretty much everything to you."

"I want that sort of thing to come from Jefferson's lips. Not some stack of papers you've managed to obtain! Here, take them back."

"No. Keep them. You might change your mind."

"I won't," she assured him, even though her curiosity was practically choking the life out of her. She firmly placed the stack of papers on the dresser. "You've wasted your time."

"We'll see," Tristan said. "We'll just wait and see."

"You'll just wait," Emily corrected. "Now get out of here. I want to take a shower."

He headed for the door.

"Tris, wait—"

Tristan turned. "I knew you'd change your mind. It didn't even take five minutes."

"I have not changed my mind. I was only going to ask how Squire was last night."

"Fine. They plan to release him tomorrow."

"So soon?"

"He'll have to take it easy here, for a while, of course. And his cardiologist has assigned a nurse to stay with him for the first week. Since we're so far from immediate care. But they really don't expect any problems."

"That's so wonderful." Emily blinked back relieved tears. But along with the relief came another dart of worry.

How long would Jefferson be able to stay under the same roof as his father?

Chapter Eleven

That night Emily cooked a celebratory dinner. She'd managed not to think, too often at least, about the stack of paper sitting upstairs on the dresser in her bedroom. She hadn't seen Jefferson in person since she'd left him that morning by the swimming hole, though she'd surreptitiously watched him from an upstairs window when he'd been working with a huge black horse. Carbon, she'd realized. For long minutes she'd watched him, drinking in the sight, even though she hadn't been able to see his face because of the battered cowboy hat tilted over his eyes.

It was the Jefferson she remembered. The man with an affinity for stubborn horses like no one she'd seen before or since. The man she'd fallen in love with before she'd been old enough to understand how that love would forever affect her life. She'd sat at the window, long after Jefferson had taken Carbon back to the barn, remembering every moment of the night they'd shared.

She'd sought out Maggie before noon and had shared her plans for the dinner, taking care not to step on any toes. As it turned out, Maggie had been feeling particularly nauseous. Jaimie had been helping with the huge noon meal, and it worked out perfectly that Emily would cook for the Clays that evening. It also gave Emily something productive to do.

She'd even managed to convince Maggie that she and Joe and Jaimie should join them. Emily dumped a tray of ice into the freshly steeped tea and glanced at the clock. In fact, the Greenes should be arriving any minute. Wiping her palms on the apron covering her sleeveless peach top and loose pants, she carried the crystal pitcher into the dining room.

"Hi, Matt. Could you get those glasses down from the top shelf of the hutch? I can't reach them without getting on a chair."

He opened the glass-fronted antique and began removing the delicate, fluted crystal. "They need rinsing," he commented.

"I know. Oh, you need three more," she mentioned.

Matthew didn't need to count the plates she'd placed around the linen-covered table to know there were too many. "Three?"

"Yeah," she took two of the champagne flutes in hand and headed for the kitchen. "Maggie, Joe and Jaimie are joining us." She stopped and looked over her shoulder. "That's okay with you isn't it?" She waggled one of the glasses. "We are celebrating, after all. I'd have invited the hands, too, except Maggie talked me out of it."

"Wouldn't have mattered," Matthew murmured. "The work's all done and everybody cut out this afternoon. Until spring, it's just us and the Greenes."

"And Jaimie, too, don't forget." Emily stifled a chuckle when Matthew's expression grew dark. "Bring the rest of the glasses, would you?"

He did. But when the sound of voices floated into the

kitchen from the mudroom, he grumbled something and stomped out.

Joe walked into the kitchen first, followed by Maggie, then Jaimie. Maggie held out a basket filled with summer flowers. "Here. I'm growing these out behind the house and thought you'd enjoy some, too."

"Oh, Maggie, they're beautiful. What a wonderful green thumb you must have." Emily set down the last of the champagne flutes and took the basket, burying her nose in the fragrant blooms. "Joe, I think there's a pool game going on in the basement, if you want to check it out."

Typically quiet, Joe plunked his dusty cowboy hat on an empty peg by the door and with a nod, clumped out of the kitchen.

Maggie watched him go, her expression hidden behind veiled lashes. Jaimie broke the vaguely awkward silence by asking Emily if she had a vase for the flowers.

Quickly Emily went back into the dining room and retrieved a vase. She set it on the kitchen table, and Jaimie began arranging the flowers. "You don't mind, do you?" she asked.

"Lord, no," Emily waved her on. "Have at it." She headed for the refrigerator, pulling a chair out from the table as she did so. "Maggie, sit down and relax. I take it you're feeling better?"

Maggie smiled faintly and sat down. She picked a daisy out of the basket and pinched off a browning leaf on the otherwise perfect specimen. "A bit," she said, handing the flower to Jaimie. "Fill in between the dahlias," she suggested. "Today has been my worst day yet. Just yesterday I visited my obstetrician. And that man had the nerve to tell me that morning sickness was all in the head. I'd have liked to have heard him tell me that while I was lying on the bathroom floor all morning. I'd have happily vomited on his wing tips."

Emily's eyebrows shot up. "That bad, huh?"

Jaimie nodded. "Made me wonder about wanting to get pregnant, I can tell you." She shuddered delicately and after a moment's consideration, added another flower to the arrangement.

Maggie laughed softly. She laid her palm on her as-yet-flat abdomen. "When you want a baby so badly you can't think straight, you'll endure anything. Even worshipping the porcelain goddess ten times a day."

Jaimie arched her eyebrows. "If you say so," she said.

"I can't imagine anything more wonderful than carrying the child of the man you love," Emily murmured, then felt her cheeks fire. It wouldn't solve a thing if she'd conceived last night. But it would be a blessing all the same.

"Spoken like a woman in love," Jaimie teased gently. "Who's the lucky guy?"

Emily's flush crept toward the roots of her hair. "It was just an observation," she said hurriedly. "Jaimie, you really have an eye for floral arranging. Have you taken classes or something?"

Maggie giggled. Jaimie looked at the lopsided bouquet and chuckled.

"Oh." Emily bit her lip as she really looked at the arrangement. "Perhaps a few flowers on the other side," she suggested.

In moments, all three women were giggling.

Daniel poked his head into the room. "You cooking supper in here? Or goofing off?"

Emily picked up the now-balanced vase and added water. "Put yourself to use and put this on the sideboard." She pushed the vase into his hands.

"Bossy little snot," he complained.

"Just put it on the table," she waved him toward the dining room. "We'll eat in about twenty minutes."

"Good. That'll give me enough time to win back my twenty bucks from Jefferson."

"You mean you actually lost money in a pool game?"

"Disgraceful, ain't it?" He leaned in the doorway, devil-may-care good looks stamped over his smiling face. "Jaimie, you're looking particularly lovely tonight."

Jaimie returned his grin, full measure. "And you're sounding particularly full of it tonight, Daniel."

His smile widened. "It's always a pleasure to have three beautiful women gracing our humble kitchen. What more could we ask for? We have a petite brunette. A leggy redhead—" he cocked his head Jaimie's direction "—and an angelic blonde," he added, turning his attention to Maggie. "How's our little mama doing?" he asked lightly.

Maggie's slender fingers scattered the little pile of discarded leaves they'd just been collecting. "Fine," she answered abruptly.

Jaimie glided over to slip her arm through Daniel's and guide him out of the kitchen. "Get rid of that vase, Daniel Clay, and give me a five-minute lesson on how to become a pool shark."

They could hear her musical laughter as Daniel led her to the basement.

"I'm so glad that Squire is coming home tomorrow," Maggie said. "We've all been concerned for him. I imagine he'll be happy to get home. He doesn't strike me as the type of man to take kindly to hospital life."

Emily smiled and nodded, but her mind was on the look in Daniel's eyes when he'd been looking at Maggie. The buzzer on the oven timer sounded and she shook off her vague disquiet as she checked the bubbling lasagna. "This has a few more minutes," she decided. "Why don't we go down and see if Daniel has any luck winning his money back."

"Sure."

They headed through the dining room to the stairs leading down to the basement. "How long have you and Joe been married?"

"Ten years."

Surprised, Emily looked at Maggie. "You're kidding! You must have been a teenager when you got married."

The other woman shrugged, smiling faintly. "Seventeen and fresh out of high school. Joe came along and swept me right off my feet."

A raucous cheer floated up the stairwell. "Sounds like they're taking sides," Emily said. "When I was seventeen, I was attending boarding school in New Hampshire." She looked up toward Maggie, who was following her down the stairs. "I hated it," she confided lightly. "I wanted to be home with Squire and the boys. Calving and haying and all that was much more to my liking than learning how to waltz and speak French."

Tristan heard the last of her comment and hooked his arm around her waist to swing her into the room. "You can't speak French."

"And you can't waltz," she tossed back as he stepped on her toe. "Let me go, you nutball."

Music was blasting from the sound system and Tristan handed Emily off to Matthew, who took over. "I can waltz," Matthew assured her. "Mom taught me."

"You mean she *gave up* trying to teach you," Daniel corrected, taking Emily into his arms.

"I thought you were trying to win back your money," Emily protested, getting dizzy with all the whirling about.

"Darlin', I already did," he said with a grin. "Plus another twenty from old Sawyer, there."

"Who're you calling old." Sawyer adeptly took Emily into his arms. He swept her into a graceful waltz.

Emily breathed a sigh of relief and smiled up at Sawyer. "Now here's a man who can truly waltz," she pronounced.

Jefferson propped the end of his pool cue on the floor and watched Emily gracefully revolve around the huge room. A tiny smile tugged at the corner of his lips. Tristan reached past Jefferson to pull a cue from the rack hanging on the wall. "Looks like it's your turn to dance with Emily," he said.

Jefferson reached for the little cube of chalk. "Shut up."

Daniel changed the song and Jimmy Buffett started singing about Margaritaville.

"Hey," Emily protested. "You can't waltz properly to this."

Sawyer simply picked up his pace, until Emily begged off, laughing. "Give someone else a chance."

His eyes smiling, Sawyer turned to Jaimie and swung her into a lively round.

Emily plopped down onto one of the long leather couches dotting the perimeter of the big square room. She watched Jefferson use the tip of his cue to gesture to a corner pocket. Tristan shook his head and Jefferson shrugged. Tristan drew out his wallet and plunked a bill down on the side of the pool table. Joe laughed and added his own bill to the pile.

Jefferson took aim and sank the ball, grinning as he pocketed the money.

The soft leather whooshed when Maggie settled her lithe body beside Emily. "You have a nice family," she said.

"I think so, too," Emily agreed, dragging her eyes from watching Jefferson too avidly. She noticed Matthew was following the progress of Jaimie and Sawyer around the floor. "Matthew seems to have eyes for your sister-in-law."

"They do nothing but argue. They started arguing the day they met last year, and they haven't stopped since." She watched the pair dancing. "I haven't danced in ages," she murmured absently.

As if he'd heard, Sawyer stopped before the couch, depositing Jaimie on the arm. "Maggie?" He held out his hand.

Rolling her eyes, Maggie brushed off the offer. "Don't be silly."

"Go on, Mags," Jaimie nudged her shoulder.

Half laughing, Maggie let Sawyer pull her from the depths of the overstuffed couch. Daniel was messing with the music again, switching song to song after just a few measures. Sawyer ordered him to stop messing with it. Tristan hooted over another shot Jefferson managed to sink. And Emily leaned her head back, absorbing the sound of it all.

"Don't you miss this when you're in California?" Jaimie asked.

Emily nodded. "More than I can say."

"Why leave then? Surely they could use your help here."

Emily shook her head. "Not really." She pushed herself more upright. "I'm an accountant," she said. "And Matt doesn't need an accountant. He handles the books very capably. He sends everything to me to handle the taxes, and that's it."

"Isn't there anything else around here you'd be able to do, though? It seems a shame to me that you're not living in the home you obviously love."

"I do love the Double-C," Emily said, nodding. "But it's the people on it that make it what it is." She lifted her hand, indicating the crew of men. "The Clay men. We're just missing Squire to complete the picture, and you're looking at the people that mean the most to me." Emily dropped her arm. "This is the first time in years they've all been in one place."

"They came because of Mr. Clay. How wonderful for support like that." Jaimie looked at her brother, who was taking his turn sinking a ball.

"What about your family? Do you have any other brothers? Sisters?"

"No. Just me and Joe. Our folks...well, my dad had a heart

attack when I was twenty. He didn't make it. Mom followed almost two years to the day later." Her eyes were still on Joe. "I think she just lost the will after Dad was gone."

She blinked and looked back at Emily, the smile back on her face. "Before that, though, they lived in Florida." She leaned over. "They'd bought a condo at one of those retirement places. You know? Golf carts parked in the streets, no kids allowed. That type of place. It was fine for them. It was exactly what they wanted, but personally, the place would have bored me to tears." Her toe was tapping to the beat of the song, and Jaimie finally gave in and stood up. "Come on, Joe, dance with me."

He made a face, but he took her on a lively romp. After a few moments the song changed and he and Sawyer switched partners. Emily noticed the way Matthew was still watching Jaimie dancing with Sawyer, and she got up. "Mind if I cut in?" Emily asked.

"Sure." Jaimie handed over her partner and looked around. Matthew was the only one not occupied with a pool cue. "Well," Emily heard her say as she wandered over to him. "Are you up to the challenge?"

Matthew snorted. But, Emily was pleased to see he didn't turn Jaimie down. Now there were three couples dancing.

"My turn, I believe."

The lilting tune dancing in her head ground to a discordant halt, even though the music played on smoothly. She suddenly found herself standing in front of Jefferson rather than Sawyer.

"Chicken?" He murmured for her ears alone.

Her eyebrow arched. "Hardly." To prove it, she slid her hand into his. "Are you?" she returned.

"I'm over here, aren't I?" He placed his hand on her waist and easily found the beat of the music. "Just dance." he said softly. "We've never done this before."

Emily, ordinarily confident on her feet, found herself awkwardly bumping his boots.

"Relax." He pulled her closer until her cheek rested on his chest and his breath stirred the hair at her temple.

Emily's bones dissolved as she followed his lead. She closed her eyes and savored the first dance of her life with the man she loved. But when he folded their joined hands close to his chest and pressed a kiss to her knuckles, the utterly bittersweet gesture made her want to cry. "I'd better check the lasagna," she said breathlessly and pulled away.

Jefferson watched her race up the stairs. He felt chilled where she'd been pressed so warmly against him. Without thinking, he went after her.

She was standing just inside the kitchen door, her shoulders bowed.

"Emily?"

Her shoulders jerked like a marionette on a string. She grabbed up an oven mitt and opened the oven door.

"It'll be ready in just a few minutes," she said. Without looking at him, she slipped the heavy dish onto a trivet. "I just need to finish up the garlic bread."

"What's wrong?"

She flung the mitt onto the counter. "What's not wrong?" She brushed a strand of hair away from her cheek. "I can't pretend that last night didn't happen, Jefferson. Maybe you can, but I can't. So if you don't like the way I'm acting, then stay away from me."

"I can't forget last night, either," he admitted roughly.

She snapped a piece of foil from the roll and wrapped the bread to toss it into the oven. "Look, Squire's coming home tomorrow, and I'll be leaving soon. Everything will get back to normal. But for now, I'd just like to get through tonight."

"You're going to agree to that stupid job, then."

"What else am I supposed to do? I have bills to pay, for crying out loud."

"Move back here."

"And do what? I wouldn't have to pay for board for Bird, but my car still needs paying off. I'm not going to live off Squire, you know. I do share expenses with Tristan. I have bills, for Pete's sake!"

"Coming home isn't living *off* Squire. He wants you back here."

Emily took a lemon from the bowl of them on the counter and savagely cut it into wedges. "Squire wants all of us back here."

"Not all of us."

She looked at him. "What's that supposed to mean?"

A muscle ticked in Jefferson's jaw. "Squire kicked me off the ranch seven years ago," he said after a long moment.

"What?" She carefully wiped the knife and stuck it back into its slot in the wooden block. "You're not serious. You've been here since—"

"Twice. Two days out of seven years. Both times Squire made it abundantly clear that I wasn't welcome."

"No. Squire would never—" Disbelief clouded her eyes. "Why?"

"It doesn't matter."

"Of course it matters! I was here both times you were—" Her mind whirled. "Oh, my God, it's because of me?" She sank into a chair. "I know the times you've been here, because I was here when you arrived. Why would he do that to you?"

"He was protecting you."

"From what? His own son?" She felt nauseous. "I can't believe this."

"He was right."

"He was wrong," Emily wrapped her arms around her middle. "You're his *son!* How can he treat his own flesh and blood that way?"

"You're the little girl he adored. He knew, sooner or later, that I wouldn't be able to keep my hands off you, and he wanted to make sure it never happened."

"That's why you didn't want to come back to the house last night," she realized aloud. "But I was still in school seven years ago. You hadn't even lived here for years yourself! What good did he think barring you from your home would do?"

"I don't know that Squire was thinking logically at the time," Jefferson murmured with severe understatement. Squire had been beside himself with anger when Jefferson had confided in his father that his feelings for Emily had been more than brotherly. He'd needed his father's advice. But had received his father's wrath. "It really doesn't matter, anymore. This is Squire's house. He has the right to run it how he sees fit."

She bounced to her feet. "That's ludicrous. He had no right. No right, you hear me? And I'm going to tell him so the minute I see him!"

"No."

"*No?* Listen, if I want to tell Squire, I'll tell him! And you ordering me around isn't going to work."

"I'm not trying to order you around. And I also don't need you to fight my fights."

"Your fight? Seems to me I'm the subject of this fi—"

"Shh," he whispered as he dropped a hard kiss on her lips. "You can't bring this up with Squire. He's not supposed to have any undue stress right now."

Emily raked her fingers through her hair. Jefferson was right, as usual. "It just makes no sense."

"Hey, are we going to eat or not?" Tristan skidded into the room. "Whoops. 'Scuse me." He left just as abruptly.

Emily looked at the steaming pan of lasagna. She grabbed the oven mitt and removed the bread from the oven. "We need to eat before it gets cold," she said. "We're celebrating, after all." Her lips twisted. "Isn't that right?"

Jefferson took the bread from her hands before she smashed it in her shaking fingers. "Don't hate him, Emily. It would break the old man's heart."

"What heart?" She swallowed the growing lump in her throat. "A man who tells his own son he's not welcome in his home has no heart."

Jefferson set the bread on the table and closed his hands over her shoulders. "He's the same man who read you bedtime stories and taught you how to hunt and fish. He's the same man who sent you to boarding school, knowing that the education was the best thing for you, even while it broke his heart to send you away, crying. He's got a heart all right."

"How can you defend him?"

"I don't always agree with Squire," Jefferson said. "But I do understand him." With his finger he touched the tear hovering at the corner of her eye. "His kicking me off the ranch was just a gesture, Emily. He knew I'd never allow us to get involved."

That stung. "Really? Then what's he going to say when he learns about last night? What's he going to say if it turns out that what we shared results in a child?"

"We'll deal with that if and when we have to."

"How utterly logical of you, Jefferson," Emily replied caustically. She pushed herself away from him and grabbed up the pan of lasagna, hardly noticing the uncomfortable heat burning her palms. "Get the champagne, would you? After all, we're *celebrating.*"

Emily managed to keep herself in hand through dinner. She smiled and laughed and cleared the dishes and prepared coffee. Inwardly, however, she alternated between seething and wanting to bawl her eyes out.

Maggie and Jaimie insisted on helping with the cleaning up, and Emily even enjoyed their company. But when the Greenes departed for the evening and Matthew had retreated to his office, when Sawyer and Daniel had headed for bed and Tristan was back at his computer, she dropped the front.

She fixed herself a mug of hot chocolate and added a healthy dollop of whipped cream. She'd jog an extra mile, she promised herself. Then she went out the front of the house and sat down on the porch swing. Sandy wandered over and propped her golden head on Emily's knee. "Hey, girl," Emily scratched the dog's silky head. "Why aren't you somewhere dreaming about chasing rabbits, hmm?"

The dog sighed and tilted her head.

Emily took the hint and rubbed behind Sandy's ears. When the dog was finally sated, she turned a few circles and settled herself at Emily's feet. The swing chains gently creaked with a rhythmic, soothing sound.

Emily thought about Tristan's papers sitting in her bedroom.

She thought about Jefferson defending his father, despite what Squire had done.

And she thought about the fact that Jefferson had chosen to share *that* truth with her at all.

Later, her hot chocolate long gone, she stopped the swing's motion and went inside. Except for the thin line of light showing beneath Matthew's office door, the house was still. Apparently even Tristan had called it a night.

She made her way through the shadows to the kitchen and rinsed out her cup. Just about to turn to go upstairs, she noticed a movement outside. Peering out the window, she thought she saw a flash of something near the horse barn.

Leaving the cup to drain dry, she quietly went back outside, carefully preventing the screen door from slamming shut. A single bulb burned in the horse barn, right over the door of the tack room. She looked inside. Jefferson was sitting on a stool, his attention bent over something. A tin of saddle soap was open beside him. "It's a little late to be cleaning saddles, isn't it?"

He jerked in surprise and looked over his shoulder at her. In answer, he held up his boot, which he'd been rubbing the soap over.

"Oh." She recognized the boots he'd worn when she'd pushed him into the swimming hole. "Well, then isn't it a little late to be cleaning boots?"

"Couldn't sleep."

"I know the feeling," she murmured. "So, can you save 'em, doc?" She scooted beside him and saw the other boot, sitting on the floor. She bent over to pick it up. It felt unnaturally stiff.

"Gonna try."

Emily picked up one of the clean rags folded on the shelf beside him. She dabbed it into the tin and started rubbing it into the boot.

"Leave it. I'll get to it," he said, flicking a brooding glance over her.

"Seems only fair," Emily answered softly. "Since I'm the one that pushed you in the water."

His lips quirked. "True." He started to hand her the boot he'd been working on. "Do them both."

Emily tried not to laugh. She loved his unexpected spurts of humor. "Dream on," she said, her tone tart.

He shrugged, casting her another look. "You shouldn't be out here. You'll get cold."

At that, Emily did smile. "Jefferson, we slept outside last night, and I was wearing far less than what I'm wearing now."

Jefferson didn't need the reminder. He'd been having enough problems putting away thoughts of their night together. It was the reason he'd not found any sleep waiting for him in his bed and had sent him, ultimately, out here to try and resurrect these boots.

"It can't ever happen again, you know."

She didn't pretend to misunderstand. "Why?"

"Because I have nothing to offer you," he answered, as if she were dim-witted. "Because nothing good will come of it."

"I disagree," Emily said, staring blindly at the long boot in her hand. "Particularly with the nothing good part."

"I hope you're not referring to a pregnancy."

"I'm going to ignore that," she replied. Her fingernail traced the detailed stitching in the brown leather. "Besides, who said you had to offer me anything?"

"Angelface, you were made for till death do us part."

"I didn't ask you for that, so what're you worried about?" Cranky all of a sudden, she globbed more saddle soap on the rag and rubbed it into the boot with a vengeance.

"Leave some leather," he reached for her hand to slow her movements.

Emily froze when his fingers covered hers.

"Don't look at me like that," he said gruffly.

Her tongue slipped out to moisten her lower lip. "Like what?"

"With your eyes all wide." He took back his hand and picked up his rag once more. "Filled with want."

Cheeks pink, she looked down at her own work. Swallowing, she folded over the rag and continued rubbing the leather. "Then stop looking at me as if you want me," she retorted, her voice husky.

He made a strangled sound.

"What?"

He swore softly and tossed the boot onto the floor. "It'd be easier to ask me to stop breathing," he growled, and reached for her.

She willingly abandoned the boot. His arms circled her waist and pulled her between his thighs. She lowered her head and molded her lips to his. "I love you," she said when the need for air finally broke their kiss.

"Em—"

"I can't keep the words inside, Jefferson. It's no use asking me to try." She ran her fingertips over his forehead, smoothing the frown between his brows. "It'd be easier to ask *me* to stop breathing."

He gently tunneled his fingers through her long hair. "Smart mouth," he murmured.

"I've learned from the best." Her lids felt heavy as she fingered a button on his loose white shirt. It looked like the same shirt he'd worn that first day in San Diego. "Oops, look at that." She looked at the button that was no longer safely through its matching hole. "Somehow your button came loose."

"Imagine that."

"Mmm. Look at that. The problem is spreading. All your buttons are jumping out of their holes."

"Must be a button revolt."

"Must be," she agreed faintly. Her fingers slid beneath the collar of his shirt. His throat was warm and brown. And she felt his pulse throbbing beneath her fingertip. Her lips parted slightly.

His fingers tangled in her hair. His jaw locked and he closed his eyes, calling on a hidden reserve of control.

A tiny sound emerged from deep in Emily's throat. Her palms slid over the hard angle of his shoulders, and the shirt slipped down his back. "I love your chest," she murmured the thought aloud.

He pulled her head toward his. "Not as much as I love yours," he muttered darkly before kissing her senseless.

He set her from him long minutes later and stood.

Emily bit her lip, wanting back in his arms. His arms flexed, muscles moving with coiled strength. But all he did was turn away and pull his shirt back up over his shoulders. "Get yourself to bed," he suggested, his attention fixed on the array of riding gear hanging on the wall.

"Come with me."

He breathed deeply, hands fisted on his hips. "Don't tempt me."

"Are you tempted?"

He snorted. "Beyond reason."

The knowledge brought a curious kind of ease to her. She moved over behind him and set her hands lightly on his clenched hands. She kissed his back through the shirt, right over the spot of that horrible scar. "Does it hurt?"

"It's killing me," he groused.

"The *scar.*"

He shook his head. "Not anymore."

Pressing her forehead against his spine, she felt his fists loosen and her fingers slipped between his. "It hurts me," she told him. "It hurts to think of you injured. Away from your family, God knows where. Away from the people who love you."

She slipped her hands around his waist and hugged herself to his back. Closing her eyes, she rested against him, feeling every breath he took. Feeling the muscles he held so tightly in check gradually relax beneath her touch.

Her arms tightened around him for a moment, then slipped away.

Sensing her presence by the door, he looked over his shoulder.

"Come with me, Jefferson. Come to bed."

"Not in his house."

She seemed very small in her loose clothes. It occurred to him that she looked thinner than she had when he'd arrived in San Diego. Another sin on his conscience.

"Walk me in, at least?" She couldn't bear to think of him sitting out here. Alone.

What harm could that do? He covered the saddle soap and left the boots on the shelf. She snapped off the light, and darkness enshrouded them. He headed for the dim square of moonlight shining in the wide doorway. His feet, in a borrowed pair of Matthew's boots, snagged something and metal clanged. "Dammit, what'd you turn off the light for?"

Emily took his hand in hers. "Follow me," she said. "I won't let you run into anything."

Jefferson felt the suffocating hint of claustrophobia dissipate the moment her fingers slipped between his. A few more yards and they were out of the dark barn, standing beneath the midnight sky. Clouds obscured the moon and stars as they headed for the house. "Smells like rain," he said as he held open the screen door for her.

"Summer's almost over."

Jefferson quietly followed her through the house and up the stairs. His hip ached with a dull, throbbing ache. They stopped in the doorway of her bedroom. He saw the inviting expanse of her bed, warmly illuminated by the dim glow of the small lamp on the nightstand.

She tucked her hair behind her ear. "I won't push you about what happened, Jefferson," she said quietly. "It's your business, just like you said. I won't pry anymore."

She stretched up and sweetly kissed his cheek.

Had she been standing before him wearing nothing but a smile, he couldn't have been more unbearably aroused. There must be a particularly vile place in hell for men like him, he decided. Her hair was a ribbon of silk over the shoulder of her dinky little top. He reached out and ran his fingers through the rain of hair.

The sheen of her dark eyes beckoned.

He stepped into the room, and the door closed behind them with a soft click.

She moved over to the nightstand, reaching for the lamp.

"Leave it on."

"All right," she hovered by the side of the bed.

"Where are your pajamas?" The tip of her pink tongue touched her lower lip momentarily, and he felt the effect clear to his toes in the barely-fitting boots.

"Here," her hand blindly searched under the pillow and she pulled out a froth of white.

He abruptly turned and sat down on the wicker chair in the corner of the room, vaguely surprised when it didn't collapse beneath his weight. "Put it on," he suggested, studying the toes of Matt's boots.

She hesitated a moment and he wondered if he was going to have to endure the sight of her undressing. But she headed for the modest-size bathroom connected to her room.

"You won't leave?" she asked softly.

"I won't leave."

She went into the bathroom and closed the door.

Jefferson sighed hugely and raked his fingers through his hair. After a moment, he heard the water running in the bathroom and reached for a boot. The twinge in his back brought an oath to his lips and he sat back, deciding the boots weren't worth the effort.

The bathroom door opened and Emily stepped into view. He recognized the ruffled nightshirt from that night in Tristan's kitchen. It seemed like a lifetime ago, but could've been counted in days.

The light from the bathroom illuminated the lines of her slender waist through the white fabric. For the brief second when she half turned back to shut off the light he imagined that flat belly swollen with child. Her breasts full. Heavy with milk.

The light snapped off and the momentary illusion was gone. She approached him, a silver-handled brush in her hands. She stopped a few feet away and ran the brush through her hair. "Sleepy?"

He shook his head, visions of Emily, pregnant with his child taunting him. "Here," he held out his hand for the brush. "Sit on the floor."

"You're going to brush my hair?"

"Got a problem with it?"

"No," she said faintly. She handed him the brush and sank down in front of him, tucking her legs beneath her.

Jefferson was glad she couldn't see the way his hand trembled before he lifted the brush to run it through her luxurious hair.

"Ah," she sighed pleasurably. "That feels wonderful."

"I remember this brush," he realized eventually. "It was my mother's."

"Mmm-hmm. Squire gave it to me a few years ago." Her head fell back against his knee. "The bristles have gotten softer, but it's still a beautiful brush." She fell silent as he continued stroking her gleaming hair. After a while she yawned, and he set the brush aside.

She looked back at him, her lids heavy.

"Come on," he said, standing up and pulling her to her feet. "Bed for you." He tossed back the bedclothes and tried not to watch her long legs climb onto the mattress.

He covered her up to her chin and snapped off the light.

"Jefferson? You said you wouldn't leave." Her hand caught his.

There was only one way he'd get through the night, he decided. "Scoot over," he said.

The sheets rustled while she moved and he lowered himself atop the bedding. With the pillows on the other side of her, and his weight pinning the blankets on this side, she was more or less cocooned.

"Jeff—"

"Shh," he whispered. Unerringly, his arm scooped around her waist and, blankets and all, tucked her backside against his front.

"You've still got your boots on," she protested.

He adjusted a pillow underneath his head. "Never mind. Go to sleep."

She shifted a bit. A pillow tumbled softly off the bed and a moment later, her hand slipped about his. She lifted it to her lips and kissed his knuckles. Then tucking their hands close to her heart, she slept.

Chapter Twelve

The dim light of dawn was peeking into her bedroom when Emily awoke. He'd been watching her sleep for quite a while. He'd memorized the cadence of her breathing. He'd known she'd awakened, even before she pushed the hair out of her eyes and peered up at him.

"Didn't you sleep at all?" she asked.

"For a while."

The bed creaked slightly when she turned toward him and propped herself up on her elbow. "Another bad dream?"

Surprisingly, he hadn't had his typical nightmare. He looked at her, sleepily rubbing her face. Perhaps not so surprisingly, after all. "No bad dream."

"I'm glad." She yawned and turned over, snuggling back against him. She yawned again and pulled his arm over her once more. "What's bothering you then?"

Jefferson adjusted the pillow beneath his neck. He closed his eyes and absorbed the sweet warmth of her. It helped that she wasn't looking at him. He was the worst kind of coward, but if he was going to get this out, he didn't think he could do it with her pansy brown eyes looking up at him. Where he would see all that warmth inside her drain away. "I was a hostage in Lebanon for six months."

The only sign that she heard him was the tightening of her fingers over his and the cessation of her soft breathing.

He was glad for her silence. If he tried hard, he could pretend that she was sleeping. Not hearing him at all. He swallowed, lifting his hand to push on the knot of pain between his eyes. "My partner and I were there to arrange the escape of a political prisoner," he continued eventually. "Before Kim and I managed to get back out again, we were caught. Officially, we weren't there, so there could be no official action to get us out."

Emily sank her teeth into her tongue. "You don't have to tell me this."

He was quiet for so long she thought perhaps he'd decided he agreed, after all. "We planned our own escape." He made a rough sound. "Nineteen successful missions in a row, then two miserable failures. We failed going in. We failed coming out."

He'd done this sort of thing *nineteen* times? "But you're here."

"*I'm* here. Kim's not."

She turned over, crying inside at the stark expression in his eyes. How much this *Kim* must have meant to him. "Were you…partners for a long time?"

His chest slowly lifted. "Couple years."

She could take this, she reminded herself roughly. If Jefferson was brave enough to tell her the secrets he was obviously punishing himself for, then she had to be brave enough to listen. "You were close."

"We were friends," he admitted. "He shouldn't have died."

"He?"

He must have read her surprise. "Kim Lee. My partner. He left a young wife and son."

"Oh, Jefferson," she laid her palm on his cheek. "I'm so sorry."

He turned away, swinging his legs off the bed. "If I'd done my job better, it wouldn't have happened."

Emily sat up, too, aching to press herself against his stiff back. "What, um, happened to the person you went there for?"

"He returned to his country and is back in control of the local government. We got him to our contact before everything blew up in our faces."

The whole idea of sneaking in and out of countries was alien to everything Emily knew. She scrubbed her hands over her face, trying to think with some measure of coherence. "Why weren't you able to leave with him?"

"They were right on our butts. We had to get him out of the country, so Kim and I hung behind, stopping them from getting to the pick-up point before our guys had a chance to get off the ground." Jefferson only had to close his eyes to hear the gunfire; the whop-whop of the chopper's blades over their heads as he and Kim fought like fury to give their contact enough time to dart in and back out again, his cargo safely stowed inside.

He pressed the heels of his palms against his closed eyes, blocking out the vivid memory. "Kim should've been on that chopper."

Emily scooted closer to him. "Would you ever have left your partner behind?"

"No."

"Then why expect him to have behaved any differently from you?"

At least a half dozen people had told him that. His own

logic told him that. But between his logic and his emotions, the idea continually short-circuited.

Her light touch drifted over his shoulder. "Is that when you got shot?"

"No." Now that he'd begun telling the sordid tale, he wanted to be finished with it. He wanted it out. Done with. Over. "We were overtaken," he continued. "I swear, they must have had three dozen men out there." At the time it had seemed like a hundred. But even against those odds, they'd fought. Until one of them got close enough to Jefferson to crush his assault rifle into Jefferson's hip. He hadn't been able to walk, but they'd dragged him on the ground back to their unit. Kim had been knocked unconscious and two soldiers had hauled him back by his feet.

He touched the scar on his jaw. "They kept us pretty subdued." He saw no reason to describe the beatings. Or the mental games their captors had delighted in playing. When he'd been conscious enough to do so, he'd tracked the days the best he could by scratching marks on the wall beside his filthy mattress. "Luckily they never resorted to pumping us full of drugs. They kept Kim and me separated for a couple months."

There wasn't a word on earth adequate to describe Emily's horror. She contented herself with threading her fingers through his.

"They were waiting for another team to try and get *us*. Kim and I knew, though, that there wouldn't be any team."

"But why not? Surely they'd try—"

Jefferson shook his head. "Too risky. Sending us in in the first place was as much of a move as they'd make. They wouldn't want to draw the attention that two strikes might've received."

"Our government is supposed to protect its citizens! Why wouldn't they—"

He sighed faintly. "I'm not with the government, Emily.

Hollins-Winword Industries is a private-sector agency. They take on some of the challenges that the government deems too risky, no matter how desirable." He stood up and went to the window. "At a certain level, we have support of the armed services, but basically we're on our own. It's the rules of the game." His words were short. Matter-of-fact.

"Some game," she murmured, her thoughts whirling. "And you've been doing this all along? How on earth did you ever get into this? Does anyone else know? Squire or Sawyer, even?"

Jefferson thought of his surprise at Sawyer's presence at the private medical facility in Connecticut. He snorted. "Sawyer knows, but not because *I* told him." He tugged aside the curtain and looked out at the red glow of the sun just coming over the horizon. "I just sort of fell into it. I had a knack with languages. Knew about agriculture. About weaponry."

He vaguely remembered the way he'd felt when he'd been fresh and green and revoltingly new to the game. "At first, it was an adventure. Exciting. Seeing the world, you know. My specialty was fitting into the local scene." He heard Emily's surprised grunt. "Strange, I know. But—" he shrugged "—I'd go in. Set up the strike. Get out. The pay was good." It wasn't until later that he'd appreciated the work for its small measures of justice in an all-too-unjust world. And not until much later that he'd wondered at the futility of it all.

"All the things I've said I've done, I've done." He wanted her to know that it hadn't all been a lie. "I've worked on bridge crews. I've worked on tankers. I've taught farming techniques to indigenous people in a dozen different countries. But Hollins-Winword has been behind all of it. Placing us strategically with the locals. So we were living among them. Biding our time until it was necessary to do the job we were ultimately sent there to accomplish."

"This is like something out of a fiction novel," Emily stared at him. She slowly ran her hands through her hair. She didn't know what she'd expected to hear, but it certainly hadn't been *this*. She wondered if she was really up to hearing the rest. "So, how did you finally escape?"

He scratched the corner of his eye. "After a while, our guards eased up. They probably figured that no one was coming to get us. It cost manpower to keep Kim and me separated— manpower that they could put to better use elsewhere. So they ended up sticking us in the same cell. It took another several weeks before we had the chance to make a break."

Emily pressed her palm to her pounding heart. "And then?"

"Bad luck. We had the same guard every night. And every night for weeks, this guy would squirrel away an hour or so to visit his woman in the village. It was the only time of the day when they didn't have us under a gun. The cell had a dirt floor. Over the weeks, we dug beneath the wall, hiding the spot under the bare mattress. We just needed to get outside the village. We'd buried an emergency pack before we'd gone inside. Once we got to it, we'd have been able to notify our contact and arrange a pickup.

"The night we crawled out, the guard came back early. That guy, as soon as he saw the empty cell, knew his ass was in a sling. Before Kim knew what hit him, the guard stabbed him. Kim hadn't even finished crawling through the hole under the wall."

Emily didn't even try to stop the tears that sprung to her eyes. "And you?"

"It was him or me, Em. So far, everything had been quiet. I didn't know if Kim was alive or not, and I sure as hell didn't want the guard raising anyone else." He couldn't bear to see the revulsion in her eyes, so he kept looking out the window, his voice neutral as he mechanically relayed the details. "I broke his neck, took his keys and locked him in our cell. I managed to get Kim on my back and hightailed it out of there. I found the pack. Dug it up. It was right where we'd left it. Less than a mile from us the entire time we'd been held. A helicopter arrived within minutes.

"Before it arrived, though, our escape had been noticed. It wasn't hard for the guards to track us. Hell, we'd left a bloody trail leading straight to us. The chopper couldn't even land—just sent down a rope while it hovered. I harnessed Kim and grabbed hold. I was shot before we got twenty feet off the ground."

It was far too easy envisioning Jefferson, dangling from the end of a rope. It was probably a miracle that he'd not fallen when he'd been struck. She pressed her lips together. "And Kim?"

Jefferson was silent for a long, long minute. "He'd lost too much blood. He died before we even got him into the chopper."

Emily held back a fresh spurt of tears. "His poor family." She untangled herself from the sheet and went over to him. "No wonder you have nightmares," she murmured, slipping between his tense body and the window. He wouldn't even look at her. He just kept staring out the window. "What about you? You'd been shot."

"The pilot landed us on a naval carrier. They kept me stabilized. Eventually I ended up in Germany for a few surgeries."

"How few?"

"Hip replacement. Some bones that had to be broken and reset. There's a pin in my knee."

She seriously considered bolting for the bathroom before it was too late. "We could have lost you and never have known why."

His lips twisted. "Pretty revolting tale, eh?"

"It's horrifying. And tragic. But it's over now." She watched the muscle tick in his jaw. "Isn't it? You're not still working for that Hollins-Whateverworth, are you?"

"Winword," he supplied tonelessly. "I'm on disability."

"Do you plan to go back?"

"Nope."

Thank God! "What do you plan to do then?"

"Dunno."

She sucked in an unsteady breath. "As long as it doesn't take you away from me, I don't care what it is. Jefferson," she said as her voice broke. "You *were* all alone, weren't you." Standing on tiptoe, she hugged him to her. If ever there was a man who needed hugging, Jefferson was that man.

Jefferson grabbed her arms and held her from him, giving her a small shake. "Don't you get it? I killed a man. Two, if you count that bastard guard." More, if you counted other casualties from his missions. She still was looking at him with those soft brown eyes. "I was *responsible,*" he growled. "My partner died because of me. His little boy is growing up without his daddy. Because of me."

"Did Kim go on that—that mission unwillingly?"

"No," he growled.

"Then he had to have known the risks involved." She shook her head. "It's terribly sad about his wife and son. No, Jefferson, don't turn away from me!" She scrabbled for his arm. "You didn't kill Kim. The guard who stabbed him did."

"You don't understand."

"I think I do. You take your responsibilities so seriously. It's not a crime to share the burden once in a while. Good heavens, you could have been killed yourself!"

"That's just it. It should have been me. I was the lead man. I should have made sure the mission didn't fail. Kim had every reason to come back alive."

"And you didn't?"

Anger curled through him. Why couldn't she understand? "He had a family."

"So do you."

"He had a son," he bit out.

Her hand touched her stomach. "Perhaps you'll have a son, too."

The words were like a blow. It would be every undeserving wish fulfilled. "You wouldn't want to bring a child into the world with a father like me."

She swiped a tear from her cheek. "You're not going to convince me to blame you for your partner's death. It seems to me that you've cornered the market of laying blame on Jefferson Clay." Her chin tilted defiantly. "And why wouldn't I want a father like you for my children? You're the most decent, honorable man I know."

"I broke a man's neck with my bare hands." He held his hands up. "He wasn't the first," he added stiffly.

She didn't even hesitate. "And you watched your partner die because of the wound that guard inflicted. You're alive, Jefferson. After all you've told me, I consider that a very great blessing."

The back of his eyes burned. "Why?"

"Because I love you," she said simply.

"Even after what I've said?" Was that his voice? Hoarse. Shaking.

"Particularly after what you've said. You didn't have to tell me all this, Jefferson. But you did."

"You weren't supposed to—"

"What? You thought you'd scare me off, perhaps? Jefferson," she said as she shook her head, smiling gently, even while a tear trailed down her cheek, "when are you going to learn? I love you. *You.* Too serious. Too sensitive. And far too handsome for my peace of mind."

He ground his teeth together. His head shook back and forth, denying.

"It's all right," she whispered, gliding to him and pulling his head to her shoulder. Such a strong man. And how he struggled with his emotions. She held his carved face between her hands and kissed his lips. "It's all right now," she soothed. She kissed the scar on his jaw. And when the tear slipped from his shadowed eyes, she kissed that away, too. "Come back to bed."

He let her lead him to the tumbled bed. He let her pull off the snug boots. He even let her unbutton his wrinkled shirt and toss it onto the floor. When her fingers went to the buckle at his waist, however, he stopped her. "This is still Squire's house."

"Yes. It is," she agreed. "But this is Emily's bed," she added. "It was brought from *my* parents' home. And I want to share *my* bed with the man I love. I need to put my arms around him. And hold him. And be held by him in return."

She didn't reach for his buckle again. Just stood before him, waiting quietly for him to decide. And really, what decision was there? To walk away from her was to kill off a portion of himself.

Jefferson stood up, and the buckle jingled faintly as he unfastened it. Watching her closely, he popped loose first one button, then the next. "It'll be morning soon," he murmured.

"A new day."

"Squire is coming home today." He'd had years to accept his father's opinion. For her, she'd had only a few hours. "He won't like this. Are you prepared for that?"

In answer, she took his loose jeans in her hands and pulled them down his hips. "He's gonna have to learn to like it," she said decisively.

He automatically kicked the jeans from his feet and nearly

swallowed his tongue when she whipped the nightshirt over her head and tossed it aside.

"He's been yammering about grandchildren for several years now. Maybe we should give him what he wants," she said.

It was inconceivable that she still felt that way. Even knowing the truth about him. A twinge worried at his conscience. He still hadn't told her about the fragment in his back.

"You are alive. And loved more than you could ever dream." She took his hand in hers and pressed his palm to her abdomen.

He saw the tears gleaming in her eyes. He wanted to give her her every desire. He wanted to give her the world. He'd given her his heart long ago, and she'd never even known it. But could he give her a future? Was it crazy of him to even consider it?

"Give me your child, Jefferson."

"Crazy," he murmured. But he folded her into his arms and gently kissed her lips.

Emily could have cried at the sweetness of his kiss. He couldn't have told her more clearly that he loved her if he'd actually said the words. The ground shifted beneath her feet and she weakly sank down to the mattress.

He followed her down, hauling her in one smooth motion across the full-size bed until she lay diagonally across it. He set about seducing her with gentleness. With unspoken love. In minutes she was arching against him, twining her legs in his, impatient for him.

"Slow down," he soothed, kissing the curve of her neck.

"I need you," she moaned against his shoulder. *"Now."*

"Now?" His fingernails grazed the outside of her thighs. Suddenly he moved, sliding deep inside her. "Like this?"

She whimpered, her hips pressing into his. "Yes."

He lifted his head. Wanting, needing to see her face. Slowly he slid back, almost withdrawing. The sound from her throat was pure yearning.

He drove himself into her. Her eyes popped open, and she gasped. Her breath grew short and choppy. "Like this?"

Her fingernails dug into his hips. "Yes."

He repeated the motion. Again. And again. Until burning color rode her cheekbones and her breath was a near sob. Eyes narrowed, he focused on the woman beneath him. He absorbed her. Her whole body was trembling. And he breathed her.

She struggled to lift her head. To kiss his lips. She did, but the uncontrollable sensations tightening within were overwhelming her. Her eyes flickered and he followed her gaze to that point where they joined. He looked up, just in time to see the tip of her tongue moisten her lip.

It was too much for him.

Her faith in him, undeserved though it was. Her compassion. Her goodness. It washed over him. As surely and insistently as his climax built. His forehead brushed her shoulder and he couldn't hold back a groan.

Suddenly, he felt clumsy. Uncontrolled. She deserved so much more than he could give her. But, amazing at it was, he was the one she wanted. Driven, he arched against her over and over.

"I love you," had she said it again? Or was the knowledge reverberating in his imagination?

Her hand touched his face, and he looked into her beautiful eyes. And for the first time in his life, he cried out as he gave his very soul to the woman he loved.

Jefferson slumped against her, and Emily held him close, tears leaking from the corners of her eyes to roll into her hair. Her breath was still ragged, but it was nothing compared to the harsh sound of Jefferson's. His arms slipped beneath her back, holding her in an achingly tight embrace. And she held him in her arms.

While a slow stream of tears trickled down his cheeks.

Chapter Thirteen

Sawyer and Daniel had driven into town to bring Squire home. Emily was on the front porch, a basket of freshly picked peas from Maggie's garden sitting beside her. She snapped them and dropped the sweet peas into the bowl on her lap. The pile of discarded pods was growing faster than the pile of shelled peas, though, since almost half of them ended up in her mouth rather than the bowl.

As soon as she saw the cloud of dust in the distance, she set aside the peas and went inside. "They're coming," she said.

Tristan set aside the computer printout he was studying and rose.

Jefferson was in the office with Matthew, going over some notes Matthew had been keeping. "They're coming," Emily said, poking her head in the doorway.

Matthew nodded and dropped the papers onto his desk. He smiled at her as he left the office.

Emily looked at Jefferson. He still looked tired. But the

rigid strain around his eyes was almost gone. It would take a long while for him to recover emotionally from what he'd been through. But this morning had been a start. A good start. Her heart did a quiet little dance when the corners of his lips tilted and he held his hand out to her.

"You ready for this?" he asked when she slipped into his arms.

"Mmm-hmm. You?"

He grinned lazily, stealing her heart all over again. "Yup." He kissed her on the nose and headed for the kitchen. "Your fingers are green."

"I've been shelling peas," she said.

"And eating a few, too, if I remember correctly."

"Naturally. What good is it shelling peas, if you can't sample the fruit?"

"They're vegetables, angelface."

"Nah. Nothing that tastes that good could be a vegetable."

He just smiled faintly and pushed open the screen door, then followed her outside and around to the front of the house. Matthew and Tristan were already there, watching the dot in the distance take the form of a car. When the sedan finally pulled to a halt on the gravel drive, Emily's heart was thumping with anticipation. And nervousness.

She didn't want to upset Squire. But she wasn't going to forsake their happiness for his opinions. She and Jefferson had talked about it only long enough to agree that they couldn't shove their relationship in Squire's face. But they weren't going to hide it, either.

Not that she could quite describe yet what their relationship was, exactly. For the moment it was enough to know that he loved her. His touch told her that he did.

Though it would be nice to think that someday he would actually let the words pass his lips.

He caught her eye, and heat streaked through her. It was as simple as that. One look from him, and she was ready to throw herself into his arms. No matter who was standing around to see the sight.

The corner of his lip tilted. He knew what he was doing, darn it all! The car doors were opening, but she kept her attention on Jefferson for a moment, promising retribution.

Sweet retribution.

"Dang it, quit hovering over me." Squire's cantankerous complaint made her smile. A dimple deepened alongside Jefferson's mouth, and he watched his father shove open the car door. "I ain't dead," the man was saying.

"You're loud enough to wake the dead," a female voice retorted.

Jefferson recognized the nurse who'd spoken from the hospital as she rounded the car.

"Git away from me, woman."

The nurse, dressed in tidy tan slacks and a tailored silk blouse, lifted her hands, resigned. "You may call me *Mrs. Day.*"

Squire snorted. Using his big hand on the opened door of the car, he pulled himself upright. Until he towered over the woman. He looked down at her. "Git away from me, *Mrs. Day.*"

Somehow she managed to look down her nose at him. "I cannot believe I agreed to stay on here for a week."

Squire gave a bark of laughter. "I charmed you into it, darlin'. You know you couldn't resist."

Sawyer covered his eyes with his hand, and Daniel was quietly sneaking away from the scene.

"Where you goin', boy?"

Daniel shrugged. He patted his pockets and pulled out a crumpled pack of cigarettes. "Don't want to smoke around you, Squire. Bad for the lungs and all."

"Put them fool things away," Squire said. As if he hadn't

been an avid smoker for a solid twenty years. "Them things'll kill you." He spotted Matthew. "You get that tractor fixed yet?"

Matthew nodded. "Yup."

Squire nodded, his eyes lighting on Emily. "Well, young lady. You got a hug for this old man?"

Emily couldn't resist him. She was still livid over the way he'd treated Jefferson. But livid or not, she loved the rascal. She slipped between Tristan and Mrs. Day. "Welcome home," she whispered, reaching up to hug him.

He kissed her forehead, then cupped her chin in his palm. Lifting her face to his eyes, he studied her. "Well, well. Don't you look mighty fine, Miss Emily. Life at the ranch has brought some color to your cheeks."

She nearly bit off her tongue. Her cheeks pink, she lowered herself back onto her heels.

Squire eyed her speculatively, then lifted his eyes to look at the assembly of his sons. "Damn, Jefferson. You look like a danged woman with that long hair. Get it cut why don't you."

With that, he leaned back into the car and pulled out his small bag.

"You can't carry that." Mrs. Day abruptly pulled it out of his hands.

"Hell, woman, I was carrying my own bag a long time before you came along, and I'll be carrying it a long time after you're gone. Now git out of my way. I want to go sit at my own kitchen table and drink some drinkable coffee."

She stood right in his path, unmoving. "One cup," she said. "Now give me that bag."

Sawyer made a strangled sound and slammed shut the driver's side. He quickly walked around the car. He took the bag out of his father's hand while the man was staring at his nurse. He walked by Tristan and Emily, heading for the back of the house. "They've been at it since we left Casper," he said beneath his breath. "Thought the man wasn't supposed to have any stress."

"What's that, boy?" Squire lifted his silver head. "Never known you to be a mumble mouth."

"Never known you to be rude to a pretty woman," Sawyer retorted.

Squire grunted, but a devilish glint was burning in his eyes. He looked down at his nurse for the next week. "Pretty women ought to be home tending their husbands." He tossed out the chauvinistic comment, testing for reaction.

Emily's eyebrows skyrocketed.

Mrs. Day looked Squire right in the face. And laughed. She laughed so hard her eyes watered. "Oh, please," she gasped breathlessly. "You'll turn my head." Still laughing, she slipped around him and reached for her own small suitcase.

"Tristan, don't stand there like a bump. Take the lady's bag."

He jumped to attention and reached for the suitcase. "It's easier to just go along with him," Tristan told the woman.

She arched an eyebrow and studied the lean length of Squire Clay. "I'll bet," she murmured.

Squire cast her a long look. Emily watched it all with amazement. Squire was attracted to his nurse! Never, in her entire life, had she seen Squire look upon a woman with that particular glint. Oh, she'd known he'd had lady friends. But he'd never brought them back to the Double-C, as far as she knew. And now, the first time a woman was with him, it was because she was his *nurse*. A *Mrs.* nurse.

Squire threw his shoulders back and looked around. "Good to be home," he said at last. He patted Emily lightly on the cheek. "Go and fix some of that coffee, would ya darlin'?" He glanced around and strode around the house. "Yup. Sure is good to be home."

Tristan, Emily and Jefferson just watched his back.

"Wow," Emily finally said.

Jefferson dropped his arm over her shoulder and nodded.

Tristan turned to Mrs. Day. "You," he said admiringly, "are a brave woman. A very brave woman indeed, and I am truly impressed." He extended his arm, indicating that she should precede him. "How do you take your coffee, Mrs. Day? With a shot of whiskey? Or without?"

She straightened the collar of her blouse and smiled serenely as she headed after Squire. "With, of course."

Alone beside the car, Emily leaned into Jefferson. "That was interesting," she said.

"Tell me about it."

"He fancies her, doesn't he."

"Mmm-hmm."

She slipped her fingers into his belt loops. "Do you know that there are now four women staying at the Double-C at one time? That's a first."

"Yup." He halted her wandering fingers with a stern hand. "Stop it."

"What?" Innocently her velvet eyes looked up at him.

"That," he jerked away from her fingertips. "You're tickling me."

"No."

"Dammit," he muttered, trying not to laugh when she poked him. "You'll regret it."

"I doubt it," she pressed herself against his chest, making sure he felt the hard points of her nipples stabbing him through their clothing.

"Witch," he accused gruffly. Then he jerked again when she found that ticklish spot.

She giggled and danced away before he could get a good grip on her. "Maybe you'd better take a trip into town, *boy.*" She darted to the left, then the right, evading his hands. "Git that danged hair cut."

"You're supposed to be in there fixing coffee," he said lazily, letting her romp around him like a frisky pup.

"Obviously Squire's feeling better." Emily twisted and scooted back when his fingers caught the hem of her loose T-shirt. "He was glad you're here. I could tell."

Jefferson shrugged. He wasn't going to think too hard on that, just yet. He allowed the shirt to slip from his fingers. She was quicker than he'd expected, though, and managed to circle behind him, unerringly finding that spot again.

He whirled around. "You're gonna get it."

"I hope so." She widened her eyes laughingly. She dashed across the gravel drive toward the circled lawn beyond. "I *sincerely* hope so."

Her eyes were deep brown, but Jefferson could have sworn he saw the sun shining right out of them. He realized he was smiling like an idiot. She was standing a few yards away, her brow arched in challenge. "Oh, yeah," he promised them both. "You're definitely going to get it."

She was fast. He'd give her that. But he had longer legs. She squeaked and darted for the stand of trees. That was her mistake.

His arms pinned her between three closely growing trees. She was huffing, her chest making the most interesting of diversions beneath her soft shirt. "You have nowhere to go."

"Never say die," she vowed, her eyes sidling this way and that. But there was nowhere to go. Only forward. She reached for his waist and latched on, her fingers tickling for all they were worth.

His laugh was strangled. "Brat," he grabbed her waist and tipped her feet off the ground.

Squire paused before the wide picture window overlooking the front of the house. He watched his middle son. Watched him laugh and playfully wrestle with Emily. Watched them tumble to the soft green summer grass and catch their breath. He saw the moment when they went curiously still, and the way his son smoothed Emily's dark hair away from her ivory face. Before he turned away from the sight, he saw the way their lips met in a kiss. A kiss that was so pure and fulfilling, he practically felt the waves of their emotions rock the house.

Carrying his bag, he headed for his bedroom tucked beneath the staircase. He closed himself in the room, and his boots scraped the wooden floor as he crossed to the bureau standing beneath the window that looked over the side of the house. He picked up the framed picture of a woman and looked at it for a long time. Remembering how he'd felt about the woman who'd given him five fine sons. His thumb moved across the glass, remembering how it had felt to run his fingers through that waist-length blond hair. How her rosy lips had tasted beneath his. "Sarah," he murmured his wife's name. "For a while there, I thought I was finally gonna join you."

After a long moment he carefully set the picture frame back in its spot. "I guess I still got some things to do yet. Or undo, I guess," he said. "But you already know that, don't you." He looked at the black-and-white photo for a long moment. Then he dropped his bag on the bed and headed back to the kitchen.

Emily was there, fixing the coffee he'd asked for. A grass stain marred her otherwise clean pink T-shirt. She was laughing at something Tristan was saying. The rest of the boys were sprawled in chairs surrounding the big table. Squire stood in the doorway, looking at his family, feeling ridiculously grateful and more than a little old.

The refrigerator door closed, and Mrs. Day came into sight. Her thick auburn hair was twisted in a knot at the nape of her neck, and when she leaned over to set the small container of milk in the middle of the table, her slacks tightened over her derriere.

Perhaps not so old, after all, Squire decided.

"Person tends to forget why we built this room so big," he said, walking into the kitchen. Tristan drew up his legs from the middle of the floor, and Squire pulled out his usual chair. "Seeing y'all here reminds my why."

Emily found a plate and arranged a batch of brownies on it. She set it on the table, next to the milk. She added a bowl of grapes and the sugar bowl.

"One cup," Mrs. Day reminded when he reached for the coffeepot Emily set on a hot pad beside his elbow.

"One cup," he mimicked. "I'll drink as much of this as I want."

"Not if you want me to stay the week, you won't," she said pleasantly. "And you made a deal with your cardiologist. You wouldn't want to back down on a deal, would you? If you have to suck coffee down all day, switch to decaffeinated."

His eyebrows lowered. "You've gotta be kidding."

Emily suddenly moved, and a cupboard door slammed closed.

He switched his attention to her. "You git bit by a bug or something?"

She shook her head and slipped into the chair between Jefferson and Tristan. "Nope." Not looking at him, she reached for the grapes and broke off a few.

He snorted. Then busied himself pouring the steaming hot brew into a mug. "Don't hover, woman. Set yourself down."

He looked over at Daniel. "Scoot over son. Give the woman a place to park."

Daniel obliged, pulling up the spare chair that had always sat beneath the telephone hanging on the wall.

Mrs. Day sat in the spot Daniel usually held. Right at Squire's left elbow. He picked up the nearly flat saucer that Emily had placed next to his mug and poured the coffee from the mug. Without spilling a single drop, he lifted the coffee to his lips and sipped at the burning hot liquid. "Ah, Emily, my darlin' girl. You do know how to fix a cup of coffee."

Tristan started to laugh, abruptly cutting off the sound and shooting a glare at Emily.

"Don't be kicking under the table, Emily," Squire said without looking up from the coffee. "Ain't polite."

Matthew laughed and reached for a brownie.

"Now tell me," Squire said as he set the empty saucer down. "What all's been going on the past few weeks?"

Jefferson leaned back in his chair, toying with his mug of coffee as the conversation swirled around the table. He wondered absently whether Mrs. Day was able to follow the multiple discussions crisscrossing the table. It didn't seem to bother her, he decided, watching as she dribbled milk into her cup of coffee and sipped at it, her bright blue eyes drifting across the various faces around the table.

Emily's palm drifted over his thigh, and he caught her fingers in his hand, sending her a warning squeeze. He saw her smile behind the bottle of apple juice she lifted to her lips. He wiggled his toes inside his boot, aware that they were going numb again. Dammit. He shifted on the unreasonably hard wooden chair.

"You okay?" Emily looked at him.

"Stiff," he dismissed. His eyes lifted to see Squire watching him with his piercing eyes. Jefferson just looked back, and after a moment Squire looked down and poured himself another cup of coffee.

"I said one cup." Mrs. Day snatched the brimming drink away before he could pour it into the saucer.

Squire grimaced at her. "Bossy woman."

"Stubborn man."

Squire's lips tilted. "Yes ma'am. You surely got that right." He gave a bark of laughter. He didn't try to have his second cup of coffee. A fact that all of his sons duly noted. "Think I'll go sleep a spell," he announced, pushing his chair back with a scrape. "Want t' be awake for whatever supper Maggie's cooking tonight. Been lookin' forward to decent food for weeks." He gave a nod that encompassed everyone at the table and walked out of the kitchen.

Tristan was the first one to speak. "Impressed," he commented as he nodded across the table to Mrs. Day.

She gave him a bemused smile, her eyes on the doorway that Squire had just passed through. "Your father is an...interesting man."

Sawyer reached for a handful of grapes. "You hear that? Squire's *interesting*." He popped a grape into his mouth and chewed it, reflectively. "Never heard it put quite like that before."

The telephone rang and Daniel scooped it off the hook. He spoke briefly and handed it to Sawyer, who listened for a moment then excused himself. "I'll take it in the office," he said and strode out. Daniel listened at the phone long enough to know when Sawyer had reached the other extension, then hung up. Leaning over, he opened the cupboard door that Emily had so abruptly pushed closed.

He looked at the large new can of coffee sitting on the shelf. Grinning, he pulled out the can. "Old devil never even knew it, did he?" He held up the can, showing the label.

Emily buried her face in her hands. "He'd have strangled me, if he'd have seen that. Put it away, would you?"

Mrs. Day reached for the coffeepot and topped off her cup. "You might try pouring the coffee into a different container," she suggested mildly. "One that doesn't say *decaffeinated* on the label."

Jefferson's back twinged and he grimaced. He pushed back his chair and stood up. "Think I'll go for a walk," he announced.

Emily started to get up, but he stopped her with a light hand on her shoulder. She looked up at him. There was a faint white line around his compressed lips. Before she could voice her concern, though, he leaned down and kissed her full on the lips. Surprise held her in her seat.

"I won't be long," he said.

"Well," Matthew commented after the screen door had slammed shut behind Jefferson, "I guess we know which way the wind blows now."

Even Tristan was looking at her with a measure of surprise in his eyes. "Looks like you kissed and made up."

She flushed, clear to the roots of her hair.

Mrs. Day suddenly scooted her chair back. "Perhaps one of you could show me where I'll be sleeping? I'd like to unpack a few things."

Daniel hopped off the counter. "No problem. To tell the truth, you've got your choice. We have a spare room upstairs, and a spare room down here."

"Where is your father's room? I should stay as close to his room as possible."

"Down here then," he told her, showing her the way through the living room and past the staircase.

Left in the kitchen with only Matthew and Tristan, Emily fiddled with her empty juice bottle. She didn't think that Matthew would disapprove of a relationship between her and Jefferson. But, looking at his sober expression, she wasn't quite so sure anymore.

He must have read the apprehension in her eyes, because he simply poured himself more coffee and smiled faintly. "If you and Jefferson can make each other happy, I'm all for it," he said. "It's about time one of the Clay boys settled down."

Emily flushed all over again. Matthew made it sound as if wedding invitations would be going out in the afternoon mail. And even though she dreamed in her heart of hearts of being Jefferson's wife, the details of that were far, *far* from being worked out. It was ironic, really, considering Jefferson's love-making. And his very definite avoidance of birth control.

Tristan butted her with his elbow. "More Clay boys could settle down if they weren't so all-fired determined to dislike pretty, long-legged redheads."

Daniel returned and slid into Jefferson's empty chair. "What's this about redheads?"

"Nothing," Matt said firmly.

"Ahh," Daniel said, nodding sagely. "I can tell by the look in your eyes, Matt old man. This conversation wouldn't be about Jaimie, now would it?"

"Shut up."

Daniel rocked his chair back on two legs. "Man, you need to lighten up. She's just what—"

"Forget it. Jaimie Greene is a flighty, sassy, little—"

"Whatever she is, she's sure got your shorts in a knot," Daniel delighted in pointing that out. Tristan chuckled beneath his breath.

"We've another redhead at the Double-C," Emily hurriedly said. "Do you think she's got a husband waiting for her at home?"

"Nope," Daniel answered, his eyes still goading Matthew. "She's a widow."

"How do you know that?"

"I asked her."

"You asked her?" Emily blinked. "Lord, Daniel, what business is it—well, I mean— Oh, geez, I hope you didn't offend her."

"Nope. So, Matt, you going to give us all a break and just get it over with Jaimie or not? Or do we have to put up with your bad mood for the next six months?"

"Zip it," Matthew snapped. His chair scraped back as he stood up. His boots rang as he stomped out.

"Geez Louise, Daniel, what was that for?" Emily asked.

"Emily, have you noticed how uptight Matthew is? He's gonna work himself into the grave if he doesn't unbend a little. Seems to me that Jaimie's the perfect one to help him do it. A few hours in bed with her would do wonders for his mood. It sure worked with Jefferson and you."

Emily groaned and scooted back her chair. "I need some air," she announced.

Tristan shook his head. "Dan, old boy, you need to learn some finesse."

Daniel just shrugged. "Maybe. But am I wrong?"

"Probably not," Tristan admitted.

Emily skipped down the back steps, and the smile she'd been suppressing broke free. Daniel was incorrigible. And maybe his methods lacked something, but his heart was in the right place.

She wondered how far Jefferson had gone. His knee had obviously been bothering him when he'd left the kitchen. She really should have found out where he'd thrown away that cane. It was silly of him not to use it, when he obviously still needed the extra support.

She looked inside the tack room, but it was empty. His boots were still sitting on the shelf where he'd left them the night before. She started to walk toward the swimming hole, but abruptly turned back. She slipped a halter over Daisy's head and led the horse out of the stall, then hoisted herself onto Daisy's bare back and clicked her into a trot.

A sense of unease was growing in her, and before they were halfway to the swimming hole, she knew why. She reined in Daisy and hit the ground running.

Jefferson was lying in the grass, his eyes closed. If it hadn't been mown just the other day, she'd have missed him completely.

No, oh no, oh no! Her mind screamed as she skidded to her knees beside him. "Jefferson?"

Sweat dotted his forehead, and he slowly opened his eyes.

Her hands were frantically running over his legs. Automatically feeling for broken bones. "What happened?"

He slowly blinked. "Em?"

"I'm here," she leaned over him, pressing her palm to his forehead, running her fingers over his scalp. "Did you fall? Are you hurt?" It was a needless question. She could see the glaze of pain dulling his dark blue eyes. "What's wrong?"

He grimaced and crushed her hand in his. He closed his eyes, then opened them again, as if gathering his strength. "I can't feel my legs."

Emily's mouth ran dry. She sat back on her heels. "Oh, Lord." She looked at Daisy, only a few feet away. But there was no way she'd be able to get Jefferson up on the horse. If he should even be moved at all. "I have to get help," she said in a rush. "Just…just don't move, oh, geez, that was stupid." She bent over him and kissed his mouth. "Will you be okay for a few more minutes?"

"Yeah." His bruising grip eased up on her hand, and she bounded for the horse. "Em—"

She darted back down beside him. "What?"

His cloudy eyes searched hers.

She frowned. Wiped the fresh sweat from his forehead. "What?"

"Love you," he murmured.

A dart of pure panic pierced her heart. They were the words she'd wanted him to say. But his timing frightened her right out of her mind. Something was wrong here. Something was terribly, terribly wrong. Before she succumbed to the violent fear flooding her, she kissed his lips. Hard enough to bring some sense to her whirling thoughts. "I'll be right back," she vowed.

He closed his eyes. "Yeah."

She lunged for Daisy. Grabbing a handful of mane, she vaulted onto the horse's back and dug her heels into Daisy's flanks. She rode the horse right up to the back steps and jumped off, racing into the house, running smack into Tristan.

"Holy sh—" He grabbed her before she bounced off him into the kitchen cupboards. "What's wrong?"

"Jefferson," she gasped, her hands clutching his shirt. "He's hurt."

"Where?"

"About halfway to the swimming hole."

Tristan was already yelling for Matthew and Daniel. Mrs. Day and Sawyer came running, too. Within seconds they knew the problem and were springing into action. Daniel went for the truck. Sawyer went for the first aid kit, and Mrs. Day gathered up a collection of big towels from the mudroom.

Matthew was on the phone. "What do you mean we can't get the chopper here? No, dammit, I need it— *Yes,* fine. No, we'll get him there ourselves." He slammed the phone onto the counter. "What the hell do we pay taxes for," he growled.

Squire walked into the room. "What on God's green earth is all the fussin' about?"

Suddenly all motion ceased. Mrs. Day recovered first,

pressing the towels into Emily's hands and telling her to go get in the truck. She quickly took Squire by the arm and pushed him in a chair before telling him briefly that one of his sons was apparently injured.

Squire popped up off the chair like a shot. "What the devil we sitting around for, then," he said. "Get the boy home. Is that old stretcher still in the bunkhouse?"

Tristan slammed out the door, already on his way.

Emily swayed in the doorway, her arms full of towels. "Don't go passing out on us, Emily," Squire warned sharply.

Dread numbed her thought processes. She heard Mrs. Day sternly order Squire to stay put, then felt the woman gently push her out toward the truck. Emily climbed up into the cab beside Daniel, sliding over to make room for Mrs. Day. She was absently aware of Sawyer vaulting into the truck bed, the square, white first aid kit in his hand, followed by Matthew.

Tristan trotted around the corner and tossed a stretcher into the truck bed, vaulting in after it.

"Go," he called.

Gravel spewed from beneath the tires as Daniel gunned the engine and set off for the stand of trees. It took mere minutes, with Emily pointing to the spot where she'd left Jefferson. Mrs. Day was out of the cab before the wheels had even come to a complete stop, and Emily was right on her heels. She raced through the grass, falling to her knees alongside Jefferson. He'd lost even more color, but his eyes were open.

She moved toward his head when Matthew and Tristan came up beside him, laying the stretcher on the grass. Mrs. Day had produced a stethoscope and was leaning over his chest, quietly questioning him. All Emily heard was something about his back.

After a moment Mrs. Day sat back, clearly unhappy with the situation. "At least you kept your knees bent," she murmured.

Jefferson grimaced. Simply turning his head seemed a monumental task. He looked straight at Sawyer. "Get me back to the house."

"That's not where you need to go," Sawyer replied.

Tired of watching the unspoken messages passing between the two men, Emily spoke. "What's going on here?" Jefferson's shadowed eyes turned her way, and her stomach dropped even further at the dull pain he couldn't hide. Biting her lip, she gently smoothed his hair away from his forehead.

"On the count of three, okay?"

Daniel and Matthew were at Jefferson's legs, and Tristan and Sawyer were on either side of his waist. "Emily, keep his head steady," Mrs. Day instructed.

"One, two," Emily gently cradled Jefferson's head and when Sawyer counted off three, she moved with the rest as they carefully slid him onto the stretcher. It had only taken a second or two and Jefferson had hardly moved, but fresh beads of sweat rolled off his forehead. She got out of the way as the brothers grabbed the handles of the stretcher and lifted. Jefferson muttered a dark curse, his fingers latching on to her hand like a vise.

"No hospital," he gritted as they slid him onto the truck bed. "Promise me, Em. No hospital."

She climbed up beside him, placing the rolled-up towels beside his head and beneath his knees where Mrs. Day instructed, then carefully moved around so that she could sit near his head. Daniel and Mrs. Day climbed into the cab, leaving the others to follow on foot.

"Jefferson, you need—"

"Promise me," he growled.

Her brows knit together. Using the hem of her T-shirt, she

wiped the perspiration from his face. "All right." For now, she added silently.

Jefferson's eyes closed, relieved. He knew he could count on Emily. She might be small. She might be young. She cried far too easily and looked for the best in people when there was no best to find. But she had a core of strength inside her that would never fail her.

Even though it caused a fresh wave of pain to wash over him, he shifted his head until he could see her. The sun was shining brightly over them, turning her pale pink shirt to white. She looked like an angel. His lips were dry. "I'm sorry."

The soft fabric stopped its daubing. She leaned down and gently kissed his lips. "There's nothing to be sorry for."

The truck rolled to a stop and rocked slightly as Daniel and Mrs. Day climbed out. They waited a few more minutes for the others to catch up, and then Emily moved out of the way while they carefully transported Jefferson into the house.

It wasn't an easy task. The house, though roomy, clearly hadn't been designed to accommodate four large men bearing an equally large man on a stretcher. Squire stood out of the way, uncharacteristically silent, when Jefferson was carried past. There were corners to maneuver around and stairs to climb. But eventually, amid much grumbling and cursing, they lowered Jefferson onto the bed in the room he'd used since childhood.

Mrs. Day supervised the placement of pillows beneath his knees. Her hands quickly wound a tight tube from one of the towels and she carefully slid it beneath Jefferson's neck, while Matthew and Tristan pulled off his boots. Jefferson hissed, covering his eyes with his bent arm.

Sawyer came back in, bearing a wide, flat, cold pack. They managed to gently slide it beneath Jefferson's back. "Damnation," he muttered as the cold penetrated the worn fabric of his shirt. But it wasn't long before he overlooked the cold for the relief it brought.

The brothers seemed to breathe a collective sigh as they hovered around the bed. Jefferson held Emily's fingers tightly, and she sat on the faded, woven rag rug that covered a good portion of the wood-planked floor. She propped her chin on the mattress, careful not to jiggle the bed.

Mrs. Day brushed a strand of hair out of her eyes. "You need more care than we can provide here," she said.

From Emily's angle she could see beneath the arm that Jefferson still had over his eyes and could see his strained expression. "No hospital," he said tiredly.

"You had back problems before?" Daniel asked. "I have. Ever since that last accident I had on the bike. Racked myself up but good. I got the name of a good orthopedic guy in Gillette—"

"No."

Matthew leaned against the tattered wing chair that sat across from the foot of the bed. He crossed his arms. "You should see a doctor. A chiropractor. Something."

"No."

"Dammit, Jefferson, you—"

"*No.*"

Matthew sighed. "You always were a stubborn fool. The older you get, the more like Squire you become."

At that, Jefferson's arm shifted and he glared at his brother. "Bull."

Matthew smiled faintly. "Well, anyway, since you won't go to the mountain of medical help, maybe we should call someone out here." Mrs. Day was nodding in agreement.

Sawyer lifted his hand. "I'll call someone."

Emily frowned at the panic that edged into Jefferson's face.

Her fingers were going numb, and she wiggled them slightly. "Jefferson—"

"I said no," Jefferson grimaced.

She bit the inside of her lip, looking at the other men. Sawyer's narrowed eyes studied Jefferson's prone body. Matthew and Daniel shared an unsurprised look. And Tristan was looking out the window, his expression thoughtful.

"I hope you change your mind," Mrs. Day finally said. She brushed her palms on her slacks. "I'd better see to Squire."

"See if you can change his mind, Em," Matthew said finally.

"I'm not changing my mind," Jefferson said distinctly. "Just let me be."

Daniel shook his head, following Matthew out the door. "More like Squire every day," he agreed.

Jefferson snorted faintly.

Sawyer tugged on his lower lip. "Jefferson, this is really a *bad* idea. A bad idea. You need—"

"I know what I need," Jefferson growled. "To be left the hell alone."

"But you said you couldn't feel your legs," Emily cried out.

Though his face turned a little green, Jefferson's foot moved. Merely a few inches. But it had moved. "It's getting better," he said, inflexibly.

"For how long," Sawyer asked, just as inflexible. He got no reply from Jefferson and, throwing up his hands in disgust, he left the room.

A weary sigh left Jefferson's dry lips. Emily slipped her fingers loose and stood up. "I'll bring you some water."

As soon as he heard Emily's light tread on the staircase, Tristan said, "She knows what you need without you even saying a word."

"Turn the screws a little tighter, why don't you?"

He shrugged and moved closer to the bed, so that Jefferson could see him without having to tilt his head. "Do you know what she needs? Without her telling you?"

"Not now, Tris."

"Then when?" Tristan crossed his arms. "When you're up and about again? That won't work, 'cause you'll probably just head out again."

"I don't have anywhere to head out for," Jefferson said grimly. Nor could he envision leaving Emily again.

"Not even that nice little condo you own down in South Carolina? Oh, that's right. You've signed it over to Kim Lee's wife. Lisa, isn't it? And the boy. What is his name? Oh, yeah. *Jeff.* Appropriately named after his honorary godparent."

Jefferson slowly lowered his arm and eyed his brother. "You've been busy." He waited for some sort of explanation of how his baby brother had come by that information, but none was forthcoming. "You've got one thing wrong, though. Lisa is Kim's *widow,*" he finally said.

Tristan nodded. "True. Sometime we'll have to talk about that, too." He idly scratched his ear. "So, how about going to that little brick farmhouse. You know…the one outside Stockholm?" He didn't give Jefferson a chance to respond. "Or the flat in London? The apartment in D.C.?"

"Enough," Jefferson snapped.

"It's time to finish what you started, Jeff. I know you've sold those places. Over the last six months, you've divested yourself of every piece of real property you've collected around this bloody world. You've closed every account, in every country, under every alias you've used in the past ten years. Except for the bank account you opened in Casper when you were twenty years old, you're strictly cash and carry. The only thing, as far as I know, that you haven't officially done, has been to resign. If they'll even let you."

"They'll let me," Jefferson assured grimly. "They don't have any use for half cripples. And infiltration works better when your nerves don't splinter at the sound of a phone ringing or a dog barking. How'd you get the info? You been doing some hacking of your own?"

Tristan shook his head. "No hacking," he said slowly. "I've got clearance."

Jefferson could have laughed at the absurdity of it all. If just the notion of laughing hadn't caused a zillion darts of pain, he'd have done just that. One of these days, he'd have to have a serious talk with Tristan about the path he was apparently treading.

"The point is," Tristan went on, "that you've been systematically tying up all your loose ends. Like you're preparing for something. The question is, what?"

"Isn't that in your computer files somewhere?" Jefferson asked caustically.

Tristan took no offense. "Oh, I've got it figured out," he said. "It just took me until now to do it. People getting ready to die often put their affairs in order." He uncrossed his arms, hating that Jefferson hadn't corrected him. "I expect Sawyer knows there's a surgical team in Connecticut just waiting for you to say the word. That's who he wants to call, isn't it?"

Jefferson's jaw locked. "I'm not having the surgery."

"You're a damn, stubborn fool," Tristan said, shaking his head. He recognized Emily's light tread as she came upstairs. "A damn, stubborn fool."

"Hand me my bag there."

Tristan looked at the duffel. "Whatcha need?"

"Prescription," Jefferson said, barely managing to keep his eyes open. God he was tired. So tired.

Tristan unzipped the bag and ran his hand inside until he found the little brown bottle. He looked at the label, then twisted off the lid and dropped a tiny pill into Jefferson's hand.

Without water, Jefferson stuck the pill in his mouth and swallowed it just as Emily entered the room. She carried a covered container of water with a bendable straw sticking out of it. She held it to his lips while he drank. He tried to stay awake. He didn't want to frighten her any more than she already was. But the medication worked quicker than his stubborn will. In minutes, his head was swimming and the grinding, awful ache in his back began to dull.

Emily's fingers were laced with his when he closed his eyes, sinking into a painless gray oblivion.

In some corner of his mind, Jefferson knew that he was slipping in and out of consciousness, yet he was unable to do anything about it. Odd, fractured thoughts flitted through his mind.

He remembered his mother. The way she had smelled. The way she'd smiled at her young sons when they'd come tumbling into the house, muddy and disheveled after playing outside. The way her eyes would gleam whenever Squire entered the room.

A vision of Kim swam into his cloudy thoughts. He saw the pride in his partner's eyes when he'd spoken of his young wife. Of their child.

Squire entered the parade through Jefferson's thoughts. Squire, frighteningly silent and stark, watching his wife's casket being lowered into the ground, while in his arms he held a tiny baby tightly wrapped against the blowing snow. Squire, tugging a dark-haired, dark-eyed little waif into the kitchen one night and thrusting her into the midst of them.

Emily, sweetly lovely at sixteen. Innocently alluring at nineteen. He'd felt like a lech, watching her. Wanting her. It didn't matter that he'd always loved her. For the child she'd been. For the friend she'd become. For the mate he'd yearned for. He'd loved her. He'd known he would never hurt her. Could never hurt her.

So he'd stayed away. Until the call of Emily had been too strong and he'd been too weak to deny it, and he'd come back. Just to be near her. Just to look at her beautiful face. And pretend, in the tiny reaches of his mind, that that would be enough.

He knew better now. He knew that his only chance for peace was to keep her in his life. Keep her in his arms and in his heart.

Had he learned the lesson too late?

Chapter Fourteen

"You're a damn, stubborn fool," Sawyer said the next morning when he stopped in the room to check on Jefferson.

Jefferson grimaced at the effort it cost him, but he finished pulling on a clean shirt and turned to face his brother. "So everyone keeps telling me," he muttered. He was standing. Just. But at least he wasn't numb from the waist down. "I'm doing better."

Sawyer grunted. "For now maybe."

Jefferson gave up after fastening just two buttons on the shirt, and leaned his weight against the dresser. "Where's Emily?"

"Still sleeping."

"Good. She needs it."

"She sat up with you most of the night."

"All night," Jefferson corrected. While he'd been fitfully dozing, she'd kept him warm. She'd held water to his lips, and hours later, in the middle of the night, she'd gotten a second dose of medication down him.

The drug had done its job, and he was up on his feet again. More or less.

"Obviously no one can make you change your mind about the surgery. If you're going to throw away the rest of your life, that's your business."

"Give it a rest, would you?" Jefferson raked his fingers through his hair, hating the cloudiness that clung to him because of the medicine. "You think this is easy for me? Christ! I'm sick to death of everybody telling me what a fool I am. How selfish I am. How stubborn. Hell, if it's not Squire riding me not to touch Emily, then it's Tristan digging around in my life or it's you bugging me about that damned surgery! Can't you just leave me be?"

Sawyer's lips thinned. "I'm not going to speak for Squire. Or for Tristan. Or any of the rest of them. But, for myself, I'd like to see you among the living for a good many years to come. And unless you change your mind about the surgery, that likelihood seems pretty slim."

"Come off it, Sawyer. My chances *with* the surgery are pretty damn slim." Moving at a snail's pace, he crossed over to the wing chair. His arms held his weight as he gingerly sank into the chair. "Why don't you go work on Tristan. I guess he's starting to paddle in some pretty deep waters."

"I'd hardly call it starting. He's been on the inside for more than a few years. His, ah, *talents* with the computer keyboard have been useful. And he's not an emotional mess right now."

Jefferson grimaced. Shows how much he knew about what went on in his family.

"What about Emily? Have you thought about her in all of this? What the surgery could mean for her?"

"I've thought about nothing *but* Emily."

"Have you told her? You know she expects a future with you. A *long* future."

"Back off." Jefferson had already made a decision about the surgery. During the long night hours with Emily in his arms, he'd made a few more decisions. But he was sick to death of having his brothers shoving their opinions down his throat.

Sawyer sighed. He raked his fingers through his hair, a man out of patience and out of time. "I wish I could stay here and get you to change your mind. But the fact is, I've gotta get back to D.C. There's a charter picking me up in Gillette in about ninety minutes."

"Guess you'd better get moving then."

"Dammit, woman, I don't care what you say. I'm climbing those stairs and that's final." Squire's roar could have been heard clear to the next county.

"Crazy old man," Sawyer muttered. He moved over to Jefferson and stuck out his hand.

Jefferson reached out and briefly shook his brother's square hand. "Watch your back."

Sawyer's lip twitched. "Always do. Give Emily a kiss for me," he said, heading for the door. "At least it's something I can be sure you'll do."

Squire appeared in the doorway, faintly out of breath from climbing the stairs that Mrs. Day had been determined he was not to climb. "You leaving now?"

Sawyer nodded.

Squire's lips pursed. "Don't wait for me to have another danged heart attack before coming home."

Jefferson saw the absolute and utter surprise in his brother's eyes when Squire reached out and hugged him. Clearly disconcerted, Sawyer stepped back. But he knew he had no time to spare. Lifting his hand in a brief goodbye, he left.

Jefferson and Squire just looked at each other. Finally Squire moved over to the bed. He shoved aside one of the rolled-up towels and sat down, sighing slightly as he did so. "Your brother's done well for himself."

Jefferson nodded slowly.

"Fact is, you've all done well for yourselves," Squire continued, ruminating. "Even little Emily, though I sure wish she'd give up on that danged job and come home where she belongs."

"She likes her work."

Squire grunted. "So, she could work around here. Matt does a fine job on the books, 'course. But truth be told, he hates that sort of thing. Rather be out in the sunshine, he would, but he's too damn stubborn to admit it."

"Seems to be a problem with this family," Jefferson muttered.

"Never did understand why she was so all-fired determined to leave here." Squire shot a look Jefferson's way. "Well—"

Jefferson wished his legs were a little more steady. He'd have walked out of the room right then. "What do you want?"

Squire squinted and tugged at his ear. "Comin' close to death changes a man," he said finally.

"I know."

"S'pose you do, at that." Squire lifted his chin in a typical nonverbal fashion. "Heard you got a problem with that back o' yours." Squire scratched his jaw, rubbing at the stubble he'd yet to shave. "Kinda hard for a man to make a baby when he's dead from the waist down."

Jefferson's eyes narrowed to slits. His hands tightened over the arms of the chair. "What game are you playing, old man?"

Squire shrugged. "Seems a shame to me, that's all."

"*What* is a shame?"

"Em's talked about babies since she was nineteen years old. Didn't want anything more, I'd guess. 'Cept maybe to have her own horse farm. Instead she ended up a bean counter, living way out in Califor-ni-ay." He shrugged. "Women. Go figure."

Jefferson blinked. "Let me get this straight. You're telling me that I'm the one who should give Emily a child?" It didn't matter that that was exactly what he'd already decided to do. "You told me not to set foot on this ranch unless I was sure I could keep my pants zipped around her. And now you're telling me you want me to get her *pregnant?*"

"I ain't saying nothing," Squire snapped. Hell, he'd decided he needed to right a terrible wrong, but that didn't mean it was all that easy for him.

"Bull," Jefferson snorted.

"Don't give me no lip, boy. I don't like it, and I won't take it. Not under my own roof. No sir."

"God, you're impossible," Jefferson growled. "It's a wonder any of us stay sane with your blood running through our veins."

"Don't go insulting your heritage, boy. Good stubborn Clay blood. That's what we got. Kept us going all these years, after your mama passed on, and it's gonna keep us going a whole lotta more years." He pushed himself to his feet. "Well, that's it. I got no more to say. Habits die hard, son. But they do die."

He walked to the doorway, then stopped and turned back, looking over the bedroom. "Good to see you under this roof, boy. It's been too long."

With that, Squire left him. Jefferson realized it was as close to an apology as he would ever get.

Emily wandered into the room. In one hand she was carrying a bunch of paper. "Was that Squire I just heard? I thought Mrs. Day said he wasn't supposed to be climbing any stairs just yet."

"She said that all right," Jefferson murmured. "Come here."

She pushed her tumbled hair out of her still-sleepy eyes. "You're up."

"Yeah." Her tongue dipped over her lip in that movement that never failed to drive him mad. "Come here," he said again.

As soon as she was close enough, he pulled her down onto his knees and carefully absorbed the feel of her warm bottom settling on his lap. He never wanted to forget that sensation. "There's something we need to talk about."

She looped her arms around his neck and laid her head on his shoulder. "I'm not sure I like the way this is starting out," she said softly. "There's something I need to tell you first." She plopped the papers she held onto her thighs. "About this."

He glanced at it, then looked a little more closely. "Where did this come from? Ah, hell, *Tristan.* Am I right? That little punk."

Punk was the most unlikely description she'd ever heard applied to Tristan Clay. But that wasn't the issue. "He gave this to me a few days ago," she said. "The morning after you and I...slept by the swimming hole." She fingered the dog-eared corner of the top page. "I didn't read it."

Had he been presented with an answer sheet to someone's behavior, he wasn't sure he'd have passed it up. "Why not?"

"I didn't think it would be right. I imagine Tristan read it, though. He's nosier than you, even." She shrugged, diffident. "I just thought you should know."

He took the papers, looking at them for a long moment. He sighed faintly and dropped them onto the floor beside the chair. "There was a time," he murmured, sliding her hair behind her shoulder, "when I would have completely blown up over this."

"Yes."

"Coming close to death changes a man," he said softly.

"What?"

But Jefferson just shook his head and lifted her lips to his. When they parted, he could have sworn there were stars shining in her eyes. "I love you, you know," he said.

Definitely stars. "I know."

Yeah, she had. All along. She'd pushed and prodded and slid

beneath his skin, even when he'd been too stupid and too pig-headed to know it was exactly what he'd needed. "I'm sorry it took me so long to say it," he admitted.

"It frightened me," she whispered after a moment. "You said it, lying there in the field, yesterday. It was like you were saying goodbye to me or something."

"I don't ever want to leave you," he said roughly.

"Then don't."

He didn't even have to close his eyes to envision the life they could have together. "I want to marry you," he said at last.

Her eyes grew moist. "You don't have to say that, just to please me."

He knew that. Just as he knew he'd planned to marry her, even before Squire had come in here, babbling about habits dying hard. "I'm saying it to please me. Emily Nichols, I want you to be my wife." He swallowed. "I want you to be the mother of my children. I want to sit across the breakfast table from you, with our son doing his homework at the last minute and our daughter stuffing cereal in her little face, but managing to spread more of it on the floor."

She smiled through her tears, recognizing her own words coming from his lips. "I want that, too," she breathed. "More than anything in this world."

"You're gonna call that Stuart guy this morning and tell him you quit that job?"

A hundred details spun through her mind. Bird. Her clothes. The few pieces of furniture she'd collected. She dashed away a tear and nodded without a qualm.

"I don't know where we'll live," he added. "I think there are too many Clays under this roof right now." Even after Squire's abrupt change. He saw her bite her lip. "I, uh, heard that George Dawson was thinking about selling his spread, now that his wife is gone. He doesn't have any kids to pass it on to. Dan was talking about it the other day. Dawson's got a fair quarter horse program going."

"That would take a lot of money," she murmured, visualizing the bordering ranch. It rivaled the Double-C in prosperity.

He could smile at that. "Angelface, I've got a lot of money." He couldn't resist kissing the O of surprise her lips had formed. "There's just one thing," he said after a long moment had passed. He tucked her head under his chin and held her close.

"What?" Her breath stirred the hair brushing his shoulders.

"I want to make love to you."

He felt her smile. "Sounds good to me."

"Every night."

"Even better."

"Yeah," he agreed, feeling his body stir just to speak of it. "But first, I gotta have a little surgery."

Epilogue

"He said a *little surgery.*" Tearfully, Emily glanced once again at the big round clock hanging on the wall of the waiting room of the hospital in Casper. Between the row of hard, plastic chairs, she paced across the dull gray carpet. "What had he been thinking?"

Tristan reached for her hand when she paced by him for the fourth time. "Sit." He pulled her onto the chair beside him.

"He was thinking of you," Squire said, testy as he usually was around hospitals.

"But this is so dangerous," Emily muttered, rubbing her cold arms through her sweater. To think that she'd gone all that time thinking that he'd just been plagued with knee problems. And he'd let her think it, too, damn the man. She wasn't going to let him forget that in a hurry, she promised herself, stealing another look at the clock. Jefferson had been taken to surgery more than four hours earlier.

"What's taking so long?" She restlessly got to her feet again, and Tristan threw his head back against his seat, giving up on trying to keep her somewhat relaxed.

Gloria Day entered the waiting room, foam coffee cups in her hand. She moved beside Squire and handed him one.

"This ain't that decaffeinated stuff, is it?" He suspiciously lifted the lid. He supposed he could drink the piping hot stuff out of the cup.

"Of course not, darling," she said, patting his leg comfortingly. Squire's big palm covered hers. Her fingers were bare, but it was only a matter of time before Squire put his ring on her finger. Everyone knew it. Except perhaps for Squire himself. The man was exceedingly inflexible about some things.

"You know I can't stand drinking that decaffeinated stuff," he muttered, sipping the coffee. "This ain't bad for hospital coffee," he decided.

"Yes, dear." Without batting a blue eye, she looked at Daniel and Matthew, sitting in the seats opposite. She looked right at them, just daring them to laugh. There was only one way to handle this crew of men. She'd realized that right off the bat.

They shifted in their seats, Matthew turning his attention back to the agricultural magazine in his lap. Daniel absently patted his pockets, looking for the cigarette pack he'd once again abandoned a few weeks ago.

Emily stopped below the round clock and watched the second hand slowly revolve. "This is making me crazy," she complained. "Can't we find out how it's going?" She looked over at Gloria. "Couldn't they at least tell us how it's going?"

Gloria set aside her coffee. She rose, automatically smoothing down the legs of her finely tailored slacks. "I'll go see what I can find out."

"Thank you." Emily was so grateful, she thought she might start bawling again. She seemed to do that an awful lot lately.

Daniel shifted in the hard seat and stuck his legs out. "I can't believe they made Jefferson wait four months before doing this surgery."

Emily pinched the bridge of her nose. She'd thought it ridiculous too, but Jefferson's surgeon had made the final decision. Even though the surgeon had been urging Jefferson to have the surgery immediately, when Jefferson finally agreed, Dr. Beauman had decided to wait, after all. Something to do with wanting the fragment in a more promising position. *A promising position!*

She still couldn't believe that kid could possibly know what he was talking about. But Jefferson had been sure, only insisting that the surgery be done in Wyoming, and that's all that had mattered to Emily.

Gloria returned, smiling faintly, with Sawyer right on her heels. He was a formidable sight in his dark uniform.

Anxiously Emily hurried over to them. "Well?"

Gloria looked up at Sawyer. He dropped his arm over Emily's shoulder and turned her to see Jefferson's surgeon approaching. Emily thought she might faint, while it seemed to take forever for him to walk down the brightly lit hall. She was vaguely aware of Squire coming up to stand behind her, his palm closing over her other shoulder. Matthew and Daniel stood behind her, and Tristan towered over them all.

The surgeon stopped right in front of her, his eyes smiling gently behind his round glasses. "It went well. He's going to be fine."

Emily sagged with relief. She looked up at Tristan, who winked. "Told you," he mouthed.

She turned back to Dr. Beauman. "When can we see him?"

"He's already asking for you," he said.

Emily looked back at her family.

"Git going," Squire said, urging her forward. The rest were nodding, all in agreement.

She quickly kissed Squire's cheek and then followed the surgeon through the swinging doors at the end of the hall. There was a confusing array of curtains and beds, but as soon as she saw a lock of dark gold hair, she headed toward it, forgetting all about Dr. Beauman.

She stepped beyond the curtain partially shielding both sides of the bed. Her eyes raced over his face and the shoulder-length hair that Squire still bugged him about. He was pale, and a tube ran from his wrist to an IV pole beside the bed. But his eyes were open and focused right on her.

"Hi."

Jefferson smiled slightly and held out his hand. "My clothes and stuff," he said, his voice hoarse from the tube that had been in his throat during surgery. "Open the bag up."

"Jefferson, you can't change clothes and walk out of here just yet," Emily said softly. But she retrieved the faded black duffel bag from the rack stretching between the wheels of his bed. One of these days that bag was simply going to disintegrate, right before their eyes. She unzipped it. "What do you want?"

"My ring," he said, eyes heavy. "They made m' take it off."

She looked inside the bag. Sure enough, lying right there on top of his black jeans and white shirt lay a gold band. She took it out and put the duffel bag back on the rack. He held out his hand, and she slipped it on his finger. He smiled faintly and held her hand, his thumb slowly gliding over the matching gold band on her hand.

"I'm not dead," he said after a moment. "Guess it worked."

Emily sucked in a shuddering breath. "Mmm-hmm. Dr. Beauman, boy wonder, said you'd be fine."

The corners of his lips lifted slightly. He was silent for several minutes, while she looked her fill at his wonderful face.

"How you feeling?" he asked eventually.

She smiled, silly tears coming to her eyes again. "Fine."

Again that half smile of his. "Not sick?"

She shook her head. "Not today."

He drew a satisfied breath. "Good." He could feel sleep tugging at him, but he managed to keep his eyes open for a while longer. "Let me see."

She half laughed. "Jefferson—"

"Come…on…angelface," he insisted slowly.

Her cheeks pinkened. "Oh, all right," she finally said. She unwound the scarf at her neck and tossed it onto the foot of his bed. She put her hands on the hem of her blue sweater. "Honestly, I can't believe I'm doing this."

The slash in his cheek deepened. She simply could not resist the man. Every single day it got worse. "Okay." She lifted the hem of the sweater, and after a quick look around, tugged down the waist of the black leggings she wore. Then she moved close enough for him to touch her.

Jefferson's eyes glowed beneath his heavy lashes. He felt woozy even moving, but he reached out and laid his palm on the firm, gently rounded belly she'd revealed. He slept with his hand on that growing belly every night. "Now," he growled, content. "Now…I can…go to sleep."

Emily leaned over, pressing her lips to his. "I love you, Jefferson Clay."

Bending over him, she rested her cheek lightly against his

forehead. The hem of Emily's sweater fell back. Covering the hand that still rested upon their growing child.

He was barely awake. But his words were clear. He told her often now. Several times a day.

They still thrilled her to her very core.

"Love you…too…Emily…Clay."

* * * * *

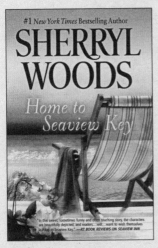

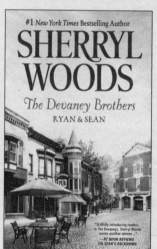

***

"If you didn't meet him on vacation, it must have been a trip
for work," said Brady.

"Remind me not to try and put anything over on you."

Sarcasm was one of his favorite things about her. "So, was it
in Austin? Seattle? Atlanta?"

"I definitely went to those cities. You should know. We were
there together."

She was right about that, but when business hours were
over they'd gone their separate ways. If Olivia had met men,
she'd never said anything to him. Until now.

As crazy as he knew it was, he wanted to know everything.
"Do you have a job lined up in Leonard's neck of the woods?"

"I have an offer."

"I'd be happy to give you a glowing recommendation."

She stood and walked to the doorway of his office. "Any
other questions?"

Why are you leaving me?

Brady didn't say that out loud, even though the idea of it

had preoccupied him way too much since she'd dropped her bombshell. Besides his mother, sister and niece, he had no personal attachments—yet somehow he'd become attached to Olivia. He wouldn't be making that mistake with his next assistant.

She looked over her shoulder on the way out the door. "I'll be lining up more candidates to interview. And if you know what's good for you, you'll approach this process more seriously than you just did."

"I conducted those interviews very seriously."

She ignored that. "You need to ask yourself what's wrong with the two women you saw today."

"I don't need to ask myself anything. I already know what's wrong."

"Care to share?" She put a hand on her hip.

"Neither of them is you."

***

Enjoy this sneak peek from Teresa Southwick's
ONE NIGHT WITH THE BOSS,
the latest installment in her
Harlequin® Special Edition miniseries
THE BACHELORS OF BLACKWATER LAKE,
on sale in April 2014!

⬧ HARLEQUIN®

SPECIAL EDITION

Life, Love and Family

Coming in May 2014

HEALED WITH A KISS
by reader-favorite author
Gina Wilkins

Both burned by love, wedding planner Alexis Mosley
and innkeeper Logan Carmichael aren't looking for
anything serious when they plunge into a passionate
affair. Little by little, though, what starts as a
no-strings-attached fling evolves into something
much deeper. Can they heal their emotional wounds
to start afresh, or will the ghosts of relationships past
haunt them forever?

Don't miss the third edition of the
***Bride Mountain** trilogy!*

Available now from the
Bride Mountain trilogy by Gina Wilkins:

MATCHED BY MOONLIGHT
A PROPOSAL AT THE WEDDING